Redesigning the Mob

The Nina Cocolucci Story

Jodi Ceraldi

by
Jodi Ceraldi

AuthorHouse™
1663 Liberty Drive, Suite 200
Bloomington, IN 47403
www.authorhouse.com
Phone: 1-800-839-8640

© 2008 JODI CERALDI. All rights reserved.

No part of this book may be reproduced, stored in a retrieval system, or transmitted by any means without the written permission of the author.

First published by AuthorHouse 10/31/2008

ISBN: 978-1-4389-0391-0 (sc)
ISBN: 978-1-4389-0392-7 (hc)

Library of Congress Control Number: 2008906630

Printed in the United States of America
Bloomington, Indiana

This book is printed on acid-free paper.

Website: http://www.jodiceraldi.com
E-Mail the author at jodi@jodiceraldi.com

Table of Contents

CHAPTER ONE..1
CHAPTER TWO..11
CHAPTER THREE 27
CHAPTER FOUR 37
CHAPTER FIVE..41
CHAPTER SIX 47
CHAPTER SEVEN 57
CHAPTER EIGHT...59
CHAPTER NINE 67
CHAPTER TEN 77
CHAPTER ELEVEN 85
CHAPTER TWELVE 91
CHAPTER THIRTEEN 101
CHAPTER FOURTEEN 109
CHAPTER FIFTEEN 113
CHAPTER SIXTEEN 123
CHAPTER SEVENTEEN 133
CHAPTER EIGHTEEN 139
CHAPTER NINETEEN 143
CHAPTER TWENTY 149
CHAPTER TWENTY-ONE 157
CHAPTER TWENTY-TWO 167
CHAPTER TWENTY-THREE 173

CHAPTER TWENTY-FOUR	181
CHAPTER TWENTY-FIVE	187
CHAPTER TWENTY-SIX	195
CHAPTER TWENTY-SEVEN	201
CHAPTER TWENTY-EIGHT	207
CHAPTER TWENTY-NINE	217
CHAPTER THIRTY	227
CHAPTER THIRTY-ONE	241
CHAPTER THIRTY-TWO	251
CHAPTER THIRTY-THREE	257
CHAPTER THIRTY-FOUR	263
CHAPTER THIRTY-FIVE	269
CHAPTER THIRTY-SIX	273
CHAPTER THIRTY-SEVEN	285
CHAPTER THIRTY-EIGHT	293
CHAPTER THIRTY-NINE	299
CHAPTER FORTY	309
CHAPTER FORTY-ONE	319
CHAPTER FORTY-TWO	323
CHAPTER FORTY-THREE	331
CHAPTER FORTY-FOUR	335

Acknowledgements

Special thanks to Geri Teran and the Georgia Writers Association who jump started my writing career, and to all of my critique buddies, Connie Bachelor, Gray (Bailey) Bridges, Kathleen Walker, Maria Boiling, and Judith Scruggs for their continuous tutoring and encouragement; to Rosemary Daniell and her entire Zona Rosa group for their interest and support; to my editor Ann Fisher for her corrections and suggestions; and to Gail Kooken, Kay Buhay, Edith Butler, Norma Carver, and Joyce D'Avignon, my friends who were always there to listen.

Dedication

To my children, Cathy, Tony, and Eddie, who without them, the idea and desire to write this story would have never happened.

And to all those people who ever tolerated physical or verbal abuse, for whatever reason, and hopefully found their way out.

The stories we tell ourselves, particulay the silent or barely audible ones. . . become invisible enclosures. Rooms with no air. One must open the window to see further, the door to possibility
—Susan Griffin, *A Chorus of Stone*;

It was one thing to theorize on the detachability of human beings, another to watch them torn apart by the bleeding roots
—Edith Wharton, *Twilight Sleep*
Divorce has become easy, but far from painless.

CHAPTER ONE

Miami/Fort Lauderdale 1970

Nina clutched the divorce papers in her fist as the elevator inched to the ground floor. It should have been her moment to shout: *Look at me! Look! I'm free!* Instead, Vito's voice resounded in her head. *No more Nina, no more Nina.*

Her husband's last words terrified her, but not as much as their children's future. Today, she again vowed never to let Vito drag her sons into the Mafia. A pledge she would keep no matter the consequence.

As the old elevator descended past the third floor, that morning's bedroom scene flashed though her mind. . . .

"Where's the leather bag I put my razor and stuff in?" Vito barked.

"Under the sink," Nina murmured as she continued to dress.

He gathered his razor, comb, and toothbrush and returned to the bedroom for the last of his clothes.

"You know, I can get you fired if I stop by to see Charlie."

I'm sure you can.

"I don't know how you can work for that oversexed pervert."

Like I got a choice.

1

He slammed his suitcase shut and slid a handful of change from the dresser into his pocket. "It'll be a hot day at the North Pole when I pay child support." He stepped in her direction.

She backed against the wall.

He stroked her throat. "Come on, baby, for old time's sake. You know you want it as bad as I do."

"No, Vito. I don't."

He reeked of another woman's perfume and it sickened her.

Forcing her onto the bed, Vito spread her legs with his thighs and pinned her wrists to the mattress. When he tired of her struggle, he used the back of his right hand to smack her across the face—his pinky ring drawing a light red line through the burst of color on her cheek. Then he thrust himself inside her. She lay motionless. After what felt like an hour of pumping his body against hers, he snorted and dropped his full weight onto her small frame.

Nina turned her head and stared at the wall.

He leaned close to her ear and whispered, "You're dead, woman. A door's gonna open and—poof—no more Nina."

The lights blinked again at the second floor, and the elevator slowed as it approached the lobby. It lurched to a halt and the doors slid open.

"Rrrratattattat!"

Nina flung her arms across her face and buried her head.

The machine gun erupted again.

She fell backward against the wall of the elevator and felt the chrome rail pressing into her spine. Nina opened her eyes to get one last glimpse.

A blurred figure hurled into her space—arms raised upward, outward.

"That's it, triggerman! I told you the next time you fired that gun inside, I'd throw it away."

Nina jerked to attention. She pressed her hand against her chest to catch her breath.

A young boy with corn silk hair and Delft blue eyes grinned up at her. "Did I scare ya? Did I?"

"Y-you sure did." Nina scrambled from the elevator and crossed the lobby.

"He's really not a bad boy—I'm so sorry—I'm. . ." The mother's voice faded.

Nina passed through the revolving courthouse doors into the scorching south Florida sun. An Italian beauty, she held her head high. Her long, dark wavy hair bounced each time her platform heels touched the hot pavement.

A twenty-something Latino in tight pants let out a low whistle. "Nice legs."

She quickened her pace toward the parking lot. The sheer number of green sedans overwhelmed her.

"Where's the damn car?"

She thought she had left her battered Pontiac in the third row, or maybe the fourth. Her gaze scanned the endless line until a black Lincoln began to creep closer. The driver stared at her.

Calm down. He's nobody. She stuffed the legal papers into her purse and heard the familiar jingle of keys.

Spotting her car's dented bumper, she broke into a jog. She tossed her suit jacket and pocketbook onto the passenger seat, climbed into the sweltering Bonneville, and locked the door. The Lincoln snaked its way to the exit.

Once the engine started, oven-hot air rushed toward her. Since Vito rarely took care of a vehicle, she was amazed that the air-conditioning still worked. She looked into the rearview mirror and saw black ringlets clinging to her olive complexion. She was not sure if the moisture forming under her Grecian nose came from tropical heat or the Mafia lawyer's bill for two grand.

While Nina waited for the car to cool, she closed her eyes, remembering Vito's first reaction when she told him she was getting a divorce. It had only been two months ago, but it seemed like years. . . .

Nina cornered Vito in their bedroom. "I understand you took Anthony to the U-Tote-M on Mafia business."

"Who told you that?" Vito snarled around the cigar clamped between his teeth.

She put her hands on her hips. "What the hell were you thinking?"

"Watch your fuckin' language." He dropped a marked up racing form on the dresser. "The boy has to learn the business if he's gonna be part of the Family."

"Over my dead body," she snapped.

"That can be arranged." He dropped his jacket across a chair and kicked off his shoes. "He'll be out of school soon, and he needs to know how to make money."

"Anthony's not going to work if I have anything to say about it. I want him to go to college." Nina padded behind Vito into the Florida room.

"Well, you don't have anything to say about it. I run this house." He turned on the TV and flopped into the leather recliner.

"Not for long. I'm leaving you."

"Leave if you want. You're not taking the boys."

"That's what you think."

"Shut up and fix dinner. I've listened to enough of your crap for one night."

"I spoke with your boss." Her heart raced when she spit out the lie. "He told me to make an appointment with Sam Marin."

"What?" Vito stood. "He sent you to *my* attorney?"

"Yes," she whispered.

"You bitch." Vito came toward her. "You talked to Chance behind my back?"

"You touch me, I'll call the police."

He stopped, but his look stung as hard as a slap in the face. Nina had never threatened him before. His fists clenched. The only sound was Vito's heavy breathing. They both knew Chance held the whip hand. She doubted Vito had the nerve to question his boss's instructions.

After that day, dozens of arguments had taken place before Vito apparently realized that fighting for custody was useless; besides, three teenage boys would cramp his style. When they finally met with Sam Marin, Vito told the attorney that he made the decisions in his house, and that it was his idea to get a divorce. He had straightened his tie and huffed from the lawyer's office like a bantam rooster.

Gradually, cool air seeped from the dashboard. Nina shifted the car into reverse,and the old heap crept backward. No cashier or guard at this place—you paid for the whole day when you arrived. Fords, Chevrolets, Chryslers, you-name-its were jammed together.

This was all too easy, Nina thought. Vito was up to something. *I know he'll make my life miserable. Please, God, don't let him kill me.*

She maneuvered to the exit and turned onto the northbound ramp. Cars crawled along at fifteen miles an hour. Time was not important, since she had told her boss, Charlie, that she needed the day off to go to court, but hitting the gas pedal would have been an exhilarating way to celebrate the occasion.

When the heavy traffic came to a complete stop, Nina opened the window and breathed in fresh ocean air. She pulled the divorce papers from her purse and ran her hand across a raised seal on the decree dated March 30, 1970: "Nina DiGregetti, a single woman, is hereby reinstated to her maiden name of Nina Cocolucci."

She relaxed her grip on the steering wheel. The judge had granted her petition and only nodded when Nina requested her maiden name. The DiGregetti part of her life was officially over.

Her lane began to drift forward and a guy in a panel truck behind her laid on his horn. "Move it or park it, lady!" he bellowed.

She resisted the urge to smart-off and concentrated on her own problems. Whatever she did would impact the kids, though the boys were not exactly youngsters. Joey was thirteen, Michael fifteen, and seventeen-year-old Anthony was at the stage when boys become defiant and secretive.

She turned from the highway into a service station and made a call to her bachelor brother. She figured he would still be home, since he only worked evenings at Dania Jai Alai. He gave her a sleepy hello.

"Mickey, come to the Amoco. I need gas and I don't have any money."

"Again?" he grumbled. "When are you gonna do something about that s.o.b.?"

"I already did. I'm on my way home with the papers."

"You went ahead with the divorce? Are you out of your mind?"

Redesigning the Mob

"I'll be okay. Vito agreed to pay a hundred a week for each kid, and the judge said he has to provide for the boys or go to jail."

Mickey whistled. "Why so high? Not that the jerk will ever pay."

"Vito told the attorney to set it up that way. He doesn't want anyone to think he's a piker."

"Humph! You shoulda straightened his ass out, not divorced him." Mickey's voice turned serious. "You'll need to watch your step. Men like him know how to get things done."

"Mickey, please. Bring cash and a little extra for groceries."

Nina parked in the shade of a large ficus tree, rolled down the windows, and let her memory slide back to the day she and Vito met. After graduating from Penn State, she and her college classmates had gone for a picnic at Kennywood Park in Pittsburgh. . . .

A handsome guy standing in front of the shooting gallery took aim three times. All the shots hit their mark, and the vendor set a white teddy bear on the counter. The marksman glanced at Nina, and she smiled. He was not tall, but lean and muscular—like a swimmer, and he looked Italian.

He walked toward her. "What's your name, kiddo?"

The other girls giggled.

"Nina." She paused. "What's yours?"

"Vito." He handed her the bear. "C'mon, let's take a ride on the ferris wheel."

Nina did not usually take up with strangers, but on a Saturday, in plain view of everyone, she agreed. "Don't go away," she called to her friends. "I'll be right back."

She and her new-found beau rode the ferris three times.

The wheel spun high in the air as Nina told him about her future dreams of becoming an advertising executive, and he said he worked with small businesses. When the last ride ended, Vito asked for her telephone number, and she scribbled it on the back of her ticket stub.

Vito called the next night. "I know this guy at Romano's Department Store. He's looking for a window dresser. Ask for Tony. Tell him Vito sent ya."

"Oh, Vito, thank you so much. My parents will be surprised if I get a job right away."

"No trouble, babe. Give the guy a call."

Tony offered Nina a job, and she started working at Romano's the following week.

Her parents were skeptical of a fast-talking man she barely knew, but Nina waited each evening for Vito's call.

He phoned the following Friday, and she thanked him on Saturday by bringing him a cooked meal to his apartment. She used her mother's kitchen to make veal Marsala and gnocchi, since Vito told her that all he had was unmatched dishes, plastic flatware, and no food.

After dinner, he gazed into her eyes. "I like a woman who cooks." He grinned. "In the kitchen and in the bedroom."

"Vi-to!" Nina's hand flew to her mouth. "You're embarrassing me."

Nina looked up just as Mickey's car stopped beside her old Pontiac.

He handed her two twenties. "Hope you're over him for good." He placed his hand on her shoulder. "I don't want to hear you say you're lonely, or that you miss him. Every time you think of him, I want you to remember how he smacked you around, and how many times he gambled your whole paycheck away." He patted her arm. "Call me at work if you need me."

Before she could thank him, he returned to his car and drove off. Nina filled the gas tank and drove to the Winn-Dixie for groceries. On the way home, she tried to think of the best way to tell the boys about the divorce.

Nina turned into the private entrance of the sprawling house on Ambassador Drive in Hallandale, a small town just north of Miami. She stopped at the mailbox, then circled the long driveway and parked in front of the house. She ripped open an envelope from a finance company. They were threatening to repossess the furniture for two months of delinquent payments. She crumpled the notice and went inside.

Nina knew that Mickey could not help forever, and how long would the boys be satisfied with hamburgers and fish sticks when their father bought them filet mignon and lobster any time they asked? Oh, yes, they had to ask. Vito needed his ego stroked. Frustrated, Nina banged the door shut.

The phone on the wall jangled as Nina set the bag of groceries on the large round kitchen table. She lifted the receiver.

"Nina!" Nana Cocolucci's voice reverberated against the kitchen wall.

"Yeah, Ma."

"Well?" her mother crowed.

"Well—I'm not married anymore." Nina laid onions and garlic on the counter and reached for the cutting board.

Her mother let out a long sigh. "So, you're coming home?"

"No," Nina said sternly. "I have a job. The kids are in school. Besides, if I try to take the kids out of state, there's no telling what Vito might do."

"Do you plan to leave the boys alone all summer to kill each other while you work, or do you intend to slowly starve them to death on the money you make?"

Nina took a deep breath.

"Listen to me," her mother snapped.

Nina clutched the receiver. "Living in Bentleyville is out of the question. The kids don't even like to *visit* Pennsylvania. They're warm-weather ducks."

"The boys don't know what decent life is all about," her mother insisted. "They need to be with family."

"We *are* a family." Nina cradled the phone under her chin while she peeled onions. "Mickey visits us on his day off, and Vito has a place nearby."

"Oh, that's wonderful. They can go visit their father and the tramp he spends money on. Already you forget how he took the money you saved for a down payment on a house and loaned it to the mob, just to show he's a big shot. He didn't get it back, and you end up living in someone else's house, feeding your sons Alpo Helper."

"It's Hamburger Helper, and they like it."

"Alpo, hamburger. What's the difference?" Nina's mother huffed.

"They'll be all right. Vito takes them to dinner at nice places."

"Out to eat on stolen Visas? Is that what you want him to teach my grandsons?" Her mother fumed. "You should find yourself a nice husband who goes to Mass like your little brother, Dominic."

"Ma, he's not little anymore. He's a doctor."

"That's right, with a good wife, and four children who come to visit on Sundays."

Nina poured olive oil into a skillet and began to sauté the onions, garlic, and seasonings. "They live two miles from you. Their kids can walk to your house—mine have to fly."

"Always with the excuses," her mother retorted.

Nina turned down the heat and stirred the sizzling mixture.

"So what's Mickey doing? He never thinks to call his mother."

"Mickey's fine. He bought the groceries today, and he asked about you."

"Did you tell him I could use some help on the yard this summer?"

"No, but he plans to come to Pennsylvania at the end of the tourist season." Nina washed her hands and dried them on a tea towel. "I'm hanging up," she said before her mother could start another conversation. "I'm cooking sauce, and I gotta make an important call." Nina breathed a sigh of relief when her mother said good-bye.

Vito and Nina's song, *Inamorata*, played on the Oldies radio station. She jerked the plug from the socket and turned off the gas burner before driving to the convenience store to call Vito's boss in New York.

While Nina waited for Chance to come on the line, she contemplated what to say. Her friend, Ginger, claimed that no one in the Mafia ever got a divorce. She felt certain the Mafia attorney or Ginger's husband, Danny, had already told Chance, but believed the right thing to do was to speak to him directly. When Chance answered, she scraped together the little courage she still had.

"Nina. What a nice surprise."

"How are you?" She didn't expect the truth. He never even admitted the real reason for his bad cough.

"Great." He coughed, as if on cue. "How's the family?"

"We're fine." She took a deep breath while she searched for the right words. "I'm calling because I didn't want you to use our phone to call Vito. I won't be able to get a message to him."

"He out of town?"

"No. He moved." Her throat went dry. "I got my divorce papers today."

"Vito say you upset, but he no mention separation." He was silent for a moment. "What you plan now?"

"I'm still at the tax firm." She pinched the bridge of her nose. "But Vito said he's gonna get me fired."

"He tell you that?"

"Not in those words." Nina found herself blabbering. "I suppose you think I did the wrong thing. I tried not to do this, but I'm concerned about our sons. I'm sure you don't understand, but—"

"I think I see. This no surprise. Vito, he—" Chance coughed again. "I tell you story."

Nina glanced at the few quarters in her hand.

"When I born, my mother name me Chandler, not Antonio like my papa. He no like. So, when I leave streets and go to school, he call me *pappamolle*. He thinks me wimp. Say I disappointment."

"I'm sorry," Nina said.

The operator asked for more money, and Nina dropped the last of her change in the slot.

"Like you, I want new life. Get mail clerk job in bank. Later, I see corporation's got more graft than alleys of market section." He chortled. "I go school, learn English, so when bank give me better position, The Don, Mancuso, take me under his wing. From then on I belong to The Family. I work for corporation, but in my heart, I still Italian."

"It must have been hard for you," Nina said.

"Not good to think about past." He cleared his throat. "You call me if you need job. Every business need clerk—I see what I got open. Maybe I find a little job for you."

"Thanks for the offer." She doubted that he meant it. "Stop when you're in Florida and see the boys. They always enjoy your visits."

"I'll do that."

The conversation ended, and Nina stepped from the phone booth.

No more messages; no more secrets.

Finito. It was over.

CHAPTER TWO

The hearty aroma of meatballs and tomato sauce floated through the house. Nina chopped lettuce, carrots and cucumbers for salad and spread butter and garlic on fresh bakery bread. Thoughts of Vito's violence lingered in the back of her mind as she concentrated on how to tell the boys about the divorce.

The St. Mary's school bus stopped out front, and Joey jumped off. He trudged along the driveway and came in through the back door.

"Smells good." He ripped off a piece of bread and dunked it into the sauce. Like Anthony, his black hair curled up at his neck, but he would not get a haircut.

"Joey, don't do that, you'll drip tomatoes all over the stove."

"Dad does it."

Nina looked out the livingroom picture window. "Where are Anthony and Michael?"

"How should I know? It's not like they ride the bus." He poured a tall glass of milk. "I'm sick of the big yellow banana. Why can't you drive me?"

"Because I work."

"You off today?" He dipped another piece of bread in the sauce.

She put her hand on her hip. "I asked you not to do that."

"I'm hungry. I didn't have lunch."

"Why not? I gave you money."

"For cafeteria garbage." He shoved a chunk of bread in his mouth and walked toward the door that led to the garage. Just inside, he picked up a basketball.

"Don't go away," she called. "We're going to eat as soon as your brothers get here." She heard the rubber bounce along the cement floor before it hit the backboard that hung outside. It was hard to believe that little Joey was already five-foot-nine, an inch taller than his father, and playing first string center for the Catholic Youth basketball team.

At five o'clock, the two older boys still were not home. A worried Nina placed a call to the school. A teacher who was working late answered. She said that all scheduled activities were over, and there were no students at the school. Nina and Joey ate dinner alone, but she barely touched hers. Instead, she paced back and forth from the kitchen through the big house to the glass-enclosed Florida room. Each time she heard a noise, she ran to look out the front door. With the name DiGregetti, you did not call the cops. A half-dozen black and white Plymouth Furys would arrive with sirens blaring and lights blazing. Gung-ho officers would ask questions that had nothing to do with her sons' safety.

At seven o'clock, the red Camaro came to a sliding stop in the gravel. Michael burst through the back door. He was fair, with light brown hair and eyes blue as sapphires, like Nina's Tuscan mother. He was the tallest of the three boys, already six-feet, and built like his uncle, Dominic Cocolucci, who had played college football. However, sports held little interest for Michael, who seemed satisfied to sit on the sidelines. He only competed with Anthony.

"Where've you two been? Joey and I waited on you for dinner."

"You forget Anthony's practice?" Michael pranced backward and tossed an imaginary football in the air. "Oh, and we ah—we saw Dad's new place. Cool."

"It's not your father's. It's Maria's." Nina turned off the TV.

Anthony stumbled into the front entrance and dropped his dirty practice uniform in the foyer.

"Anthony, please pick up your laundry," Nina said on her way to the kitchen.

"Okay." He left the clothes where they fell.

Nina became anxious and went to look for Anthony. His bedroom was halfway down the long, marble hallway that lead to the master bedroom. She found him sprawled on top of his bedspread. "Your dinner's ready."

His eyes were closed, and his strong facial features reminded her of Vito. He was also cursed with his father's Sicilian temper, but so far he had reserved his aggressiveness for football.

"We already ate dinner." Michael called from the kitchen doorway, while he opened a can of Mountain Dew.

"You ate? Where did you eat?" She came back along the hallway and into the kitchen.

"Dad took us out. He told me he called ya." Michael said.

"Your father didn't call me, and it looks like Anthony drank wine again."

"A little." Michael's soda foamed over the top and dripped on the floor.

"If Anthony gets a ticket for drunk driving, you both can ride the school bus." She grabbed a paper towel and swiped at the hardwood floor.

"I knew you'd be mad." Michael stripped off his favorite shirt, an Ocean Pacific his Nana had sent to him.

"I'm not angry. I'm upset because I worry when he drinks. If your father continues to give Anthony alcohol, you won't be allowed to go there."

Joey eased through the back door. "We can't see our dad anymore?"

"I didn't say that. I said—"

"We heard you," Anthony said from the hallway. "You're jealous of his girlfriend."

"That's not true."

"It is so. Dad said *you* divorced him, and now you're mad because he lives with Maria."

"You got a divorce?" Joey squinted at Nina. The basketball fell to the floor.

Nina wished she had gone ahead and told Joey about the breakup, instead of waiting for his brothers to come home. Joey's long arms hung limp at his side, his expression dispatched despair. She reached out to him, but Anthony stepped closer.

"Dad said you're gonna lose your job, and us kids won't have a place to sleep."

Nina spun around to face Anthony who stood propped against the kitchen doorjamb.

"You're old enough to know better than that," she said. "I do a good job at the tax firm."

"Oh, so I'm grown up when I see things your way, but not when I look at 'em from my dad's side." Anthony stomped to his room and slammed the door.

Michael put his arm around Joey's shoulder. "Come on, basketball man. I'll help you with your homework."

They walked toward his and Joey's bedrooms that were in the back of the house next to Nina's flower garden.

The wall clock in the livingroom struck eight and chimed through the quiet house. Nina trudged to the kitchen, put away the leftovers, and turned on the dishwasher. Vito had ruined dinner and her hope of a tranquil talk with her sons.

She watched part of *Welcome Back Kotter* before calling her girlfriend, Ginger. "How about a quick coffee?"

"Sure. Same place?"

"Where else?"

"Can you gimme twenty minutes? I want to see the end of "*M*A*S*H*.""

"Sounds good."

As soon as Nina hung up, the phone rang. It was Frankie, Vito's associate and the owner of the house she and the boys lived in, courtesy of a favor Vito had done for his cohort. He said Vito told him the whole family was moving. She tried to explain that only Vito had moved, but there was no reasoning with the fat, greasy *Calabrian*. He thought he was better than Danny and Vito, and he let everyone know he was their boss.

"I already have a new family that wants the house, and *they're* going to be paying rent. Anyway, I don't want to get involved in your family squabbles."

Before she could plead with him, he hung up.

The phone rang again, and she thought Frankie might have changed his mind.

"Hello," she said as cheerful as possible.

"Nina."

She recognized her boss's voice. "Hi, Charlie."

"I just got a call."

"From who?"

"Your ex. He says he wants to talk with me." Charlie took a deep breath.

"When I asked him about what, he said, 'I'll tell you when I see you,' and hung up."

"It's probably not important. You know how Vito is. Always wants to keep people guessing. I'll talk to you tomorrow."

"You're not holding back something I should know, are you?"

"No, Charlie." She was sorry she had told him about the divorce. He could not keep his hands to himself even knowing she was married. "Vito probably wants to ask you a tax question for one of his corporate accounts. He doesn't tell me his business."

"I can believe that. Vito's asked me questions before, but he's never called ahead to say he was coming. I thought you might know what he wanted."

"I'm sure it's nothing, Charlie."

When he said good-bye, Nina hung up the phone and leaned against the table. *Vito isn't wasting any time. First he has Frankie put me out of the house, and now he's gonna have Charlie fire me.* Visions of late bills and thrift-store clothes passed through her head. *I hope he rots in hell.* But as quick as the words came to her, she was sorry. She refused to let him steal her sanity.

Nina stopped at the door to Anthony's room and raised her hand to knock before she decided it was better to let him sleep. She ran a brush through her hair, added a touch of lipstick, and told Michael and Joey she was going to IHOP.

The traffic light turned red at the intersection where the convience store was located. She thought how easy it would be for Vito to destroy her. He would make sure she got fired wherever she was employed, and if that was not enough, he might blow her away. How the hell could she make a living and at the same time be safe? She glanced at the outside pay phone and pulled into the store's parking lot.

Nina located Chance's direct telephone number in her wallet and checked her watch. He often worked late. She dialed the number.

"Chandler Barozzini." His baritone vibrated in her ear.

"It's Nina," she said. "Today you mentioned that you might find a little office work for me. If you weren't joking—" She caught her breath. "I'm going to need a job."

When he did not answer right away, she felt embarrassed to think she had taken such liberty. Yes, he had always been friendly to her, but he still was part of the mob.

He spoke slow and intentional. "You," he paused, "serious?"

"Yes," she said with no hesitation. "Frankie called and said I have to move, and my boss called and said Vito wants to talk to him. I think he plans to have me fired."

"You no worry, I find you good job," he said. "I catch the red-eye. We can meet at noon—same restaurant as Michael's birthday party."

"Gosh, Chance, you don't have to fly all the way down here. I'll go for an interview anywhere you say."

"Call your boss and tell him you quit."

"Quit? But I—"

"I gotto go," he said. "See you tomorrow."

She heard the phone click and Chance was gone.

Nina leaned against the booth and pondered the conversation. She wondered why he was so eager to help her. It could not be personal. He had always treated her with respect.

"Hi! Over here." Ginger waved from her booth in IHOP. A pear-shaped diamond sparkled as her fingers danced above her head.

Nina slid into the booth. "Did Danny ask where you were going?"

"He ain't home." Ginger's auburn hair was pulled back in a hasty bun. Straggles hung loose, curling along the edge of her round face. "He went to Jersey on business."

"And of course you believe that." Nina knew Danny liked glamorous women. He married Ginger for that very reason. Everyone commented on her great figure and good looks. He expected his wife to remain perfect, but since her fifth child, she had gained twenty-five pounds. She did not seem to care how she dressed anymore, and Danny spent more time away from home.

"Give it a rest, Nina. We're not all ready to start new lives. I can barely get through the one I'm in."

Nina did not want to argue. She knew that like most women in jeopardy, Ginger blocked out the truth.

"I'm not concerned that Danny's in the Mafia. If he gets into trouble, he'll handle it. And when he cheats on me, I look the other way. I accept life as it is."

"And you think I should, too." Nina nodded when Gray, their usual waitress, asked if she wanted coffee. "You think I made a mistake?"

"I don't think you're wrong, but you know Vito. He'll make your life a living hell. Even if you find a smaller place for you and the boys, how you gonna pay for it?"

"For now, I still have my job."

"You can bet that won't last. If he sees you can get along without him, he'll make sure they let you go." Ginger waved to Gray.

She hurried to their table. "Have you decided?"

"Bring us each a hot fudge sundae with lots of whipped cream and chopped pecans." Ginger loosened the drawstring in her sweatpants. "And a couple of clean cups with fresh coffee. This pot's cold."

Steam drifted upward from the spout of the coffee pot, but Gray did not object.

Nina placed a hand above her cup. "Mine's fine."

"Sorry about that." Gray displayed her great smile to Ginger, turned and rolled her eyes at Nina, and carted the pot to the sideboard.

"So, what's got you worried?" Ginger asked. "You said the divorce went like a breeze."

"It's the boys. Vito told Michael and Anthony a bunch of lies, and they believe it." Nina looked away and swallowed hard. "Right before I left the house, Frankie called. He gave me two weeks to move."

"He can't do that even if he's Vito's friend. He has to give you notice, and you can drag your feet for at least six months."

"Here you go." Gray sat a fresh pot of coffee on the table.

"Thanks," Ginger said.

Nina waited until Gray walked away. "We don't pay rent. Vito did a job for Frankie. All we do is live there."

"That's a bummer." Ginger took a sip and fanned her mouth. "Vito never told us about that. Knowing how stingy Frankie is, it must have been a big job. I wonder if Danny knows."

"There's a lot things you don't know. Like how much Vito really drinks when he's not out with the mob and how he comes home and accuses me of cheating on him. He calls me a slut, a cunt, and a bitch. Sometimes that's meaner than him smacking me around. Those words go through my head for weeks."

"I'm sorry, Nina. I had no idea." Ginger looked down at her ice cream. "I guess Danny's not home enough to call me names, but he did tell me I was a fat pig one night, and I was upset for a whole week."

"That's not the worst of it. I found out Vito took Anthony along on a job."

"What did you expect? Anthony will be eighteen soon." Ginger looked away. "Thank God I have all girls."

Gray came bustling across the room, her long blond ponytail bouncing in the air, her tan skirt only an inch below her black apron. Two desserts and large glasses of water balanced on a tray over her shoulder.

"God, I love these." Ginger bit the cherry from the stem. "Eat, Nina. You'll feel better."

Nina took a few small bites, avoiding the whipped cream. She had no intention of adding twenty extra pounds like her friend had.

Ginger did not always like the way Danny treated her, but she seemed to think her marriage was fairly normal. Nina was not convinced.

"Vito gave Anthony wine again."

"We always give our girls a sip with dinner. Wine's good for 'em."

"I think he gave him more than a taste. Anthony came home tipsy after dinner with Vito and the broad." Nina snaked the spoon through the melted cream.

"Her name's Maria."

"I know her name." Nina gritted her teeth.

"It's not her fault Vito runs around. If not her, it'd be somebody else." Ginger reached for the coffee pot.

"I hear she's young." Moisture sprang to Nina's eyes.

"Yeah, she's young, pretty, and dumb, like we were at that age. Don't think about her. He'll be tired of her in a month and move in with a new one."

"Are you hanging around with Maria?"

"No, but Vito brought her to the house." Ginger sputtered on her coffee. "He called her 'Nina' twice."

Nina grinned behind her hand. "What'd she do?"

"Nothing the first time. The second time she walked out, and he ran after her saying, 'Aw, come on, Maria, it's a habit.'"

"Did she come back?"

"Nah, she stayed in the car. They left, and I haven't seen them since." Ginger laughed. "At least now you can have a life of your own."

"Some life," Nina said as Gray walked by checking her tables. "Raising three boys who hate everything I stand for and think their father can do no wrong."

"This is the life you chose." Ginger dug into her sundae.

"I chose Vito, not the mob."

"When you married Vito, you married The Family."

"I thought he worked for a big company in New York. He never told me differently," Nina sniffled.

"And you never asked him what company, or what he did?"

"I was twenty-two, in love, and pregnant. I came from a small town. Vito promised to marry me, but he walked out instead. I didn't know what to do." Nina hung her head.

"How come I never heard about this before?"

"Well, Danny and Vito were close, and I didn't know whether you would say something to Danny or not."

"So, how'd you two get back together?"

"I called his mother, and she gave me a New York telephone number. She said Vito was there. So I dialed the number, found out where the office was, and took a Greyhound to New York City."

"You what?" Ginger leaned forward. "By yourself?"

"Yeah, I thought Vito loved me, and that he was just scared of all the responsibility a baby would bring. I wanted to tell him I'd get a job, and we'd work things out. But when I got there, Chance said Vito had moved to Florida."

"Frankie told us Chance sent Vito to help run the business, but for a long time, Danny and I didn't know anything about *you*."

"Well, to make a long story short, I told Chance how Vito had taken me out all summer, bought me things, told me he loved me, and had even given me a promise ring. Chance told me to go home. He said Vito and I had nothing in common, but you know me, I cried." Nina pulled a tissue from her purse and wiped her eyes. "His friend, Dutch, watched the office while Chance took me out to lunch and bought me a plane ticket to Miami. He even had Vito pick me up at the airport."

"Poor Vito. I'll bet you gave him a piece of your mind." Ginger sipped her coffee.

"No, I was in love with him, I forgave him for everything. And when Anthony was born, Vito was as happy as I was. He went to work every day, and treated me great. I thought we had the perfect marriage."

"So when did you begin to suspect something?"

"Not until after all three boys were in school, and I went to work. Before that, I wondered why Chance always gave me strange messages to give to Vito, but he said that Chance was a worrywart, and for me not to pay any attention to him."

"I thought you told me you went to college." Ginger shoveled in her icecream while she talked. "Didn't they teach you anything?"

"Not about the mob. I think what really made me see the truth was on a day we were coming home from dinner. Vito stopped at an Italian market and told me and the boys to stay in the car. I saw a sign in the window that said 'Fresh homemade Italian cream puffs.' So, I stepped inside the store. An old woman was handing him a stack of money."

"And you wondered what that was all about?"

"Not really. He told me he worked with small businesses and that they paid him for the work he did for them."

Ginger leaned her head back and gave a sardonic laugh.

"It's not funny. The woman tried to give me the pastries and when I insisted on paying, Vito grabbed the money. He made me crazy, and I grabbed it back and gave it to the woman."

"That wasn't very smart of you," Ginger said.

"No it wasn't. When we went outside he said, 'Don't ever embarrass me in front of one of my clients again.' He dropped me and the kids off at home and stayed out all night. After that, he made no pretense of how little he cared for me, and no longer bothered to hide his Mafia dealings. That's when Danny started to stop by, and right after that I met you."

"When Vito first told us about you, he said you were too uppity to hang around with us." Ginger touched her napkin to her lips. "I was surprised when I found out how nice you were. I never dreamed you didn't know anything about us, and you never mentioned it."

"I thought I could live with how he made his living until I saw his plans for our sons. I'm afraid I waited too long to get a divorce." Nina blew her nose and put the tissue in her pocket.

"Don't worry." Ginger said with genuine kindness. "You're a smart girl. You'll do okay. I wish I had your determination and education."

"It's more like blind faith."

"Don't be upset about the boys. They'll grow up fine." Ginger reached across the table and touched Nina's hand. "You'll see."

"I'm afraid they'll end up like Vito. Just the other day he asked Joey, 'What do those stupid nuns think they can teach a smart boy like you?' And you don't think I should be concerned."

"He wants them to be his buddies. He knows you'll raise them the right way."

"I'm not sure he knows what the right way is." Nina glanced over her shoulder. "Did you ever notice how our waitress stands around scribbling all the time?"

"Gray?" Ginger looked over the top of her reading glasses.

"Watch what you say—she might be taking notes. You have no idea who might be paying her for information."

Ginger scooped out the last of her sundae and shrugged. "Being married to someone in the mob is *not* that big of a deal. She's probably just checking the addition on her checks."

Nina shrugged. "I gotta go." She pushed the melted sundae aside. "I don't like to be away from the house too long, and I need to stop and put air in one of the tires."

"Vito didn't get that fixed?" Ginger left Gray five dollars on the tiny tray.

"Are you kidding? He doesn't take care of the car. If anything needs to be fixed, I have to do it, and lately, I haven't had the money."

"Call me. I'll take you to lunch. Danny doesn't ask where I go in the daytime." Ginger waved as she headed toward her car.

"Finish your breakfast, Joey. You have ten minutes before the bus." Nina walked down the hallway. "Get up, Anthony. You'll be late for school."

"I'm not going to school today. I got things to do."

She stopped at his bedroom doorway. "Like what?"

"Dad told *me* to get the oil changed in my car. He gave me money. Said he don't have time to run over here every day to make sure things get done."

"Doesn't," Nina corrected. "You can take care of the car after school. Get up and get dressed." She tapped her foot.

"I can't take orders from two people. You want one thing and he wants another." Anthony covered his head with the sheet.

Nina yanked the sheet back. "We'll straighten this out later. Right now, you're to get up, take a shower, and do it in the next fifteen minutes. I don't want Michael late for class."

"I don't have to do what you say. I can move in with my dad."

"Not today you can't. You're in my custody, and you're going to school. In fact, I'll take you and pick you up." She lifted his keys from the top of the chest of drawers and shoved them in her pocket. "Until you realize who the boss is, that hotrod stays in the driveway."

Anthony pulled the pillow over his head and growled, exactly like his father. Nina turned and left the room.

"It's time for the bus, Joey." Nina handed him a dollar. "Eat in the cafeteria or you won't get any more lunch money."

"You're mad at Anthony, so you yell at me. I go to school every day. I get good grades." Joey's lower lip quivered. "I just can't eat the food."

"Eat in the cafeteria today." Nina hugged his shoulder. "We'll talk tonight."

A loud horn blew and Joey ran to catch the school bus.

Michael slurped the milk from his cereal dish. "Great. You make me ride with Anthony when he's drunk, and now *you're* gonna drive us to school."

Nina sighed. "Tell your friends Anthony's car wouldn't start. Say whatever you like, but his pride and joy stays right where it is."

Anthony swaggered into the kitchen dressed in jeans and loafers. His shirt was tossed over one shoulder. "Mom, give me the keys, please."

She shook her head. "When you come home, maybe you'll have a different attitude. You want breakfast?"

"No." He turned away.

"Get your books." She picked up her purse. "We're leaving."

When she returned from taking the boys to school, the mailman was holding a thick yellow envelope and knocking on the front door.

"It wouldn't fit in your mailbox," he said as he handed her the envelope.

"Thanks." Nina took the package addressed to Vito, tossed it on the table, and went into the bedroom to change her clothes. Curiosity got the best of her, and she opened the envelope. It appeared to be a contract for a loan in the amount of $150,000.00 and indicated that Vito DiGregetti was the lender. Apparently, a construction company owed Vito the money. Attorney, Sam Marin had drawn up the agreement, and obviously his secretary had made a mistake and sent Vito a copy and a $4,000 initial payment to his home address.

How can this be? Vito doesn't have this kind of money.

Nina dropped the papers on the counter and called her boss. While she waited, she pondered working for Chance. She would wait to see what he offered before she quit her job. When Charlie Geller came on the line, she said, "This is Nina. I won't be in today. I have business to take care of."

"You're the second one to call in. Come in early tomorrow."

"Ah, Charlie," she began. "If you don't have anyone in your office, I have a question you might be able to help me with."

"Shoot, kid."

"I got something in the mail today." She explained how she happened to get the package and read Charlie the main part. When she finished, he did not say anything.

"What do you think, Charlie?"

"If you two still have a joint account, you can cash the check."

"Really?"

"But of course if you do that, you'll have to add that money to your income when you file your federal tax return, and by that time, I figure Vito will have found out that you got the papers and the money, and he'll be beating your head in to get it back."

"How do you think he got the funds to do this?"

"I doubt he put up any cash. Say, isn't this the same construction company that Vito's buddy did business with? What's his name?"

"You mean Frankie?"

"Yeah, that's the one. That Frankie guy."

"I think so."

"Word around town says that Frankie's filing bankruptcy. He probably put the loan in Vito's name to keep it out of the Chapter Eleven case. My guess is, Vito cashes the checks and gives Frankie the money. In return, Frankie cuts Vito in for a little slice of the pie."

"But this paper was executed before we were divorced. So maybe I could be held responsible."

"That's right. If you don't report the funds, you could go to jail for income tax evasion."

"Oh, God, what am I going to do?"

"You need to see an attorney. Time's gone by, so you'll be liable for some of the funds, unless you get Frankie to change it to an agency agreement, and backdate it."

"I doubt that will happen." Nina sighed.

"An agency agreement is your only way out. This much I know. Who you get to write it, and how you get Frankie to sign, is up to you."

"Thanks, Charlie. You've been a big help." After hanging up the phone, Nina walked into the bedroom to finish getting ready for her appointment.

Dressed in her best white slacks, a parakeet-green top and casual shoes, Nina sat in the kitchen, drinking coffee. Impatient, she made several trips to her bedroom—once to check her coral lipstick, once to trade her flats for three-inch white heels, and the last time to change her seashell jewelry to the pearl necklace her mother had sent to her for Christmas. As she was leaving the bedroom she touched the silver frame of her wedding photograph, and then picked up the picture and placed it in the bottom drawer.

An hour before she was to meet Chance, Nina stepped into the hot sunshine and took a second look at Anthony's bright red Camaro. She gathered empty paper cups and candy wrappers from inside the sports car, tossed them into the rubbish bin and pulled the seat forward. She drove to the Amoco station for gas and ran the car through the automatic wash.

"Not bad for an old clunker," she said as she turned north and crossed into the fast lane.

CHAPTER THREE

"Please seat me at that small table by the window," Nina said to Merle, the *maitre'd*.

A few minutes later, Chance appeared at the entrance, his steel gray hair glistening in the sunlight. He waved to Nina.

The *maitre d'* rushed to greet him. "Welcome to Fort Lauderdale, Mr. Barozzini," Nina heard Merle say as he shook Chance's hand and moved him in her direction.

Chance looked like a typical high-class tourist in his crisply pressed silk trousers and blue flowered shirt. "You not forget my table," he said, embracing her before sitting with his back to the wall. "You look like angel."

Nina blushed at his compliment, but felt happy with her choice of clothes. After considering a business suit, she was glad she had dressed casual.

The wine steward brought a bottle of Ruffino to the table and Chance detained him with a touch of his hand.

"Let's eat before talk," Chance said to Nina. "I'm starved."

The steward beckoned the waiter and opened the wine.

"In Florida, I order pompano *fra diavola*." Chance smiled at the waiter. "Fish better here than New York."

Nina opened the menu. "I usually get tuna salad."

"Eat. Stay healthy," Chance told her.

"How do you expect a five-foot-four Sicilian girl to eat food that gives her energy and rosy cheeks and still wear a size five?"

"You no worry." He wagged a finger at her. "Soon, no time to eat."

"In that case, I'll have the mahi-mahi stuffed with crab."

"Would you like a salad with your meal?" the waiter asked.

"Just small bowl of your special greens," Chance replied. "The lady and I are watching our waistlines."

Nina laughed.

Chance tasted the dark red wine and nodded. The steward filled each of their glasses and left the table.

"We celebrate demise of wedding rings." Chance reached for his wine glass.

"I thought I'd wear them for awhile. This is a big adjustment for the boys, especially Joey."

"They not *bambinos*. They know. Soon everyone know. Make clean break, or people think Vito influence you."

Nina twirled the rings on her finger and pushed them back in place.

"Gold band don't mean mother, it mean wife," Chance reminded her.

Concealing her left hand with her right, Nina casually slid the matched set from her finger and released the catch on her purse.

He shook his head and handed her an envelope. "Five G's. I know Vito pay less."

Nina laid the rings in Chance's outstretched hand. The diamonds glistened in the sunlight. She hated to part with them, but hell, five-thousand dollars! She needed the money.

"Come." Chance stood up. "Your first big decision." He slid the rings into his pants pocket.

"You knew I'd be wearing the rings?" She followed him to the deck above the sea wall.

Chance waved at the captain of an expensive boat moving leisurely through the slow wake area. "I know you good mother, always do right thing." He turned his head and coughed. "So, yeah, I figured."

He placed the solitaire and the gold band in her palm and closed her hand. "Throw rings in canal."

"I can't." Nina closed her eyes and her fist froze tightly.

Chance put his arm around her shoulder. "Think about it. Marriage over."

For a moment she thought her heart had stopped beating. She tossed the rings into the Intra-coastal Waterway and no one seemed to notice. She might as well have been feeding bread to the sea gulls, but to Nina, it was devastating. She felt like she had just thrown a large chunk of her life away.

When they returned to their table, the salad was waiting for them.

Nina forced herself to sit up straight. She shoved her sunglasses onto the top of her head. "It's hard for me to believe that after all these years I'm single again."

"I remember when you come to New York to find Vito." Chance added more vinegar to his salad.

"I was young and foolish."

"You *donna forte*."

"Not so strong," she said. "Desperate is more like it. I was pregnant and too ashamed to tell my parents."

"I shoulda sent you home."

"It's not your fault." Nina smiled.

After they finished lunch, a snifter of cognac warmed Nina's belly and seemed to ease Chance's cough. Instead of talking about a clerical position, Chance told her about the grocery business and what it would mean to her.

"Mafia now operates inside law. Businesses still pay for protection, but this better deal for them. They buy from our company in Tampa, they prosper, and we both make money." He paused and sipped his brandy.

"We use contracts and offer enticements, just like any other corporation. You understand what I say?"

"Yes," she nodded. "But I don't know anything about security systems or garbage pickup that you say other collectors use as an incentive. I thought you said you would find me a typing or filing job. I don't think I want to do this."

"You no worry." Chance looked around the room before he continued. "I give you list of Vito's accounts. All you do is offer better deal."

"I'm supposed to take Vito's business away from him?" Her voice escalated. "You're joking." Nina's face turned bright pink. "He'll kill me."

Chance put his index finger to his lips. "And lose boys' respect. I no think so. Vito got plan for sons."

"I can't be sure of that." Nina's hands were shaking. "He has a violent temper."

"We no tell him you work for me."

"I don't believe this'll work, even if Vito doesn't know who I work for."

"Customers no like harassment. You offer better arrangements, no more abuse. They no disclose your identity."

"How do you expect me to stop Vito from mistreating them?"

"I handle Vito." Chance patted her hand. "I watch out for you."

Nina's first thought was sure, that's okay for him to say. He'll be hundreds of miles away. *I should tell him to take back his five grand, but I've already thrown my rings away.*

He swirled his after-dinner drink and waited for her answer.

"I haven't quit my job," she said, as though keeping it made any difference. Eventually she would be fired and unable to get another job.

Chance leaned back in his chair. "Don't worry for money. I handle first expenses—make lenient repayment plan."

"This isn't what I expected."

"Boys depend on you," Chance said and shrugged.

Nina was silent.

Chance went on. "Move outta Frankie's house. No make waves. Vito think he's in control. It give you edge." He wiped his mouth with the corner of a linen napkin and laid it on the table.

Nina's chest pounded like a bongo drum. "How will I know what to do?"

He handed her a business card.

"Goldman Food Service? Tampa?" She turned it over. "A company name and telephone number? Nothing else?"

He pressed forward against the table and lowered his hoarse voice. "Last day of April, you call, make appointment. Give name, say you interested in the grocery business. They send salesman. He'll be the contact."

Nina opened her mouth to speak. He raised his hand to stop her questions.

"You give boys good education. They won't seek a life in mob." Chance reached across the table and took the empty glass from her trembling hand. "They be respectable."

"But Vito says—"

"Forget Vito. Heavy hand like seventy-eight record. Still around, but losing money." Chance signed the American Express card receipt. "You can't be Vito's friend. He won't let you."

Nina fidgeted in her chair and twisted the straps of her purse. "I have something to tell you."

"Don't frown. It can't be that bad," Chance said with a warm smile.

"Yes it is." Nina cleared her throat. Then she told Chance about the $150,000 note. "I'm going to take it to an attorney tomorrow."

"Let's not be too quick to see lawyer." His fingers drummed the table, his expression turned dark.

She had never seen Chance so agitated.

"I hear something about this. Let me talk to Frankie. No need to call attorney." Chance's tone was ominous.

Nina shook her head stubbornly. "I know a lot about taxes, and I think I need an attorney. I don't want anything less than a backdated agency agreement, and I want to get a signed copy to protect myself."

Chance got up from the table and spoke close to her ear. "You no tell anyone about papers. I get agency agreement for you. I tell you Mafia is going legit. Now I prove it."

They walked out of the restaurant, and Nina handed the valet her parking ticket.

Chance's eyes narrowed when the red Camaro came to a quick stop.

"It's Anthony's," she said. "Vito gave it to him."

"Does it have a title?"

"I'll have to check on that." She sauntered to the car, her narrow hips swaying in the white pleated slacks, and waved the tips of her fingers as she slid into the driver's seat.

"A title is the least of my problems," she mumbled as she pulled the red car into the afternoon traffic.

Nina turned into the school parking lot. Michael hurried to the Camaro and squeezed into the back seat. She lifted her legs across the console and moved over. Anthony dropped behind the wheel.

"You like driving a sports car?" Anthony said as he shoved the seat backward.

"Not bad. I might get one myself. Would you like to help me pick it out?" Nina smiled at her oldest son.

"You mean that?" Anthony's eyes lit up.

"Sure. I could use some help."

"I mean, you're getting a new Camaro?"

"Well, not new and maybe not a Camaro, but something sporty. A car Michael would like when he turns sixteen and I get a new Jag."

Michael stretched forward between the front seats. "Wow, you're kidding?"

"Yes, Michael, I'm kidding about the Jag, but not about the sports car. We'll see what we can find on Saturday, unless you two have other plans."

"I'm not doing anything," Anthony said.

"Me neither," Michael agreed.

"Did you call your dad today?" Nina asked Anthony.

"No. Why?" He pulled the car into the slow-moving traffic.

"I thought you might be concerned about the oil change."

"I can do it this weekend." He rolled down the window and adjusted the mirror.

"You guys hungry?" Nina asked.

"Yeah," Anthony said.

Nina grinned. "Let's go home and heat up the leftover spaghetti and meatballs."

Nina scowled at the stack of federal income tax returns.

"I put a note on the first two." Charlie advanced toward her desk. "Finish checking them before noon. One's for the chief of police, so call that ex-husband of yours and tell him not to come in today. I don't want the chief to see him hanging around here."

"I don't think he'll come by today."

"Why not—you think a divorce will stop him?"

"Maybe, anyway, I don't know how to get in touch with him." Nina took the first return from the top of the pile.

Charlie ogled her body like fresh meat. "Did you call an attorney?" He sat on the edge of her desk.

"No. I took care of it myself. I'd appreciate it if you didn't mention our conversation to anyone else—especially Vito."

The edges of his lips curved while his gaze lingered on her small cleavage. "You can count on me, Ms. DiGregetti."

"The name's Cocolucci. You need to order me a new nameplate."

"It's nice to have a good-looking single woman in the office, but I can't change your name and let my customers know I hire floozy divorcées, now can I?"

Nina continued to scan the tax return.

"On second thought," Charlie leered, "maybe we could talk about this at dinner tonight." He leaned close, his eyebrows thick as hedges arched over his dreary eyes. "How do you spell your new name?"

Nina printed her last name on a piece of scratch paper and pushed it toward him. "Thanks for the invitation, but I'm cooking dinner for my sons."

"Co-co-lu-che." Charlie smirked. "How about you and me having a drink *after* dinner?"

"Sorry, I'll be busy for a few weeks." Nina got up from her rolling desk chair, walked to the cabinet and dropped in a couple of papers. "I'm moving. There's a lot to do after a breakup."

Charlie followed her. "You don't plan to take time off, do you?"

"No, I'll do my personal stuff in the evenings and on weekends." Nina smiled. She didn't want to make an enemy of him—he knew too much about her.

Charlie crossed the hall to his office and closed the door. The lock snapped shut.

Nina looked up in time to see him close the venetian blinds that covered the large plate glass window that separated his office from hers and the rows of cubicles in the workroom. He did the same thing every day.

Nina's view of the front office was the same as Charlie's. She watched the tax consultants' heads bobbing as they asked their clients questions and filled in blanks. When Charlie closed his blinds, employees without customers made personal phone calls, and today Nina called an apartment rental office.

When Nina arrived home, Anthony was waxing his car. Michael and Joey played one-on-one under the basketball net. Nina carried a stack of returns as she hurried away from the smoking green bomb.

"Are we gonna look for a car?" Michael asked.

Nina shook her head. "Not tonight. We have to find an apartment first." She handed Anthony the newspaper with all the possibilities circled and the prices highlighted.

Michael looked over Anthony's shoulder. "Let's not move until school's out."

"Unfortunately, Frankie called last night." Nina's high heels wobbled on the gravel. "He's rented the house to someone else and we need to move by the end of next week."

Anthony threw the buffing rag on the ground. "Uncle Frankie said we have to move?"

"He's not your uncle. He's a friend of your dad's and apparently no longer one of ours." She shifted the tax returns to her other arm.

Anthony glanced at the ads. "Some of these places are in Forest Hills. We can't live there. I'm not playing football for them. I hate those guys."

"That's because they beat your sorry asses," Michael said with a grin.

Nina frowned. "Michael, don't talk like that."

"Holy cow! That's not a bad word. Third graders use it."

"I'm not changing schools." Anthony snatched the rag from the ground. "Dad said I could live with him if you moved."

Nina's face stiffened. "It was probably your dad's idea to have Frankie put us out."

"I dunno," Anthony answered. "All he said was if you moved, I could stay with him and Maria."

"Take your brothers, too! She can cook and clean for all of you!" Nina turned away, fighting back tears and anger.

"Mom, wait. Dad wouldn't do that."

Nina stifled her feelings.

"Let's go look at these other places." Anthony ran his finger along the ads. "What about those apartments on Azalea Street?"

Michael reached for the listings. "Yeah, we're not hungry. Can we go now?"

Anthony jerked the paper away and handed it to his mother.

"Let me get out of this suit." Nina rubbed her shoulder. "I'll see how late the management office stays open."

"Neato!" Michael banked the ball off the Camaro.

Anthony glared and smacked the dirty rag on Michael's bare legs.

Nina sighed and went into the house. She stopped at the kitchen counter, got a drink of water, and opened the window. The boys were still bickering.

"You're gonna pay for that," Anthony said.

"Like I'm scared." Michael shot a two-pointer from the far edge of the driveway.

Nina shook her head. Without Vito to enforce the rules, the boys were going to be much harder to handle.

CHAPTER FOUR

Chance looked up to see his sidekick, Dutch, walking into the mahogany paneled office on the twenty-first floor of a Manhattan skyscraper.

Dutch settled his thickset body into a calf skin chair. "You're looking chipper this morning."

"I should be dancing." Chance steepled his fingers. "Ya know that problem we got in south Florida?"

"Yeah."

"We gonna edge Vito out."

Dutch chewed on a stub of a burned-out fat cigar. "How you gonna do that?"

"We got a volunteer."

"You're kidding." Dutch leaned forward, his neatly shorn head gleaming under the fluorescent light.

"You ain't gonna believe who it is."

Dutch waited for the answer, but when Chance picked up his phone, Dutch stood.

"I gotta make call." Chance handed him the newspaper. "Get table at Vinny's. We eat breakfast. I tell ya the good news."

Dutch tucked the *New York Times* under his arm and walked toward the door. "I'll tell Vinny to make you fried bread and cut up a little cheese."

"Get some *Fontina Val d'Aosta*. We celebrate with good Italian cheese."

Dutch nodded and left.

Chance punched in the numbers and when the secretary answered, he asked to speak to the attorney.

"Sam Marin," a deep voice said.

"Sammy, is Frankie there?"

"Yes, he's been waiting for your call. A guy named Wendell is with him."

"You got new agency agreement?"

"Sure do." Sam said.

"Get Frankie to sign. Mail copy to Nina today. Put everything in Wendell's name." Chance coughed. "Lemme talk to Frankie."

"It's for you," Marin said to Frankie, who was Chances right-hand man in Miami.

"Yeah?" Frankie said into the receiver.

"You sure this Wendell keep mouth shut?" Chance said.

"He does what I tell him to do."

"That's good," Chance said. "Everything goes well."

"So what do we do about Vito?" Frankie asked.

"We talk about the ex later. You keep eye on him. He fight like mad dog when he start to lose business."

Frankie hung up the phone and motioned Wendell into the office. The secretary carried a stack of legal papers into the room and handed them to the attorney.

"You need to sign here, here, and here." The attorney handed his pen to Wendell.

Wendell put on his rimless glasses, and signed his name. "It says we need a witness." Wendell pointed to the space below his signature.

"My secretary will sign as witness." The lawyer retrieved his pen, took the papers, and went into the next room.

"This will give you a little time to spend at home," Frankie said to Wendell. "You can help Thelma with the housework while she's pregnant."

"I hope she doesn't have another set of twins." Wendell took off his reading glasses and tucked them in his shirt pocket. "Tell me again how I handle this. I don't wanna make a mistake with that much money."

"Go get the car. I'll tell you about it on the way." Frankie made the final arrangements with the attorney and walked outside.

Wendell stopped the Impala in front of the law firm and Frankie climbed into the car.

Wendell pressed the gas pedal and merged the buttercup-colored convertible into the heavy traffic. "I sure appreciate you loaning me the down payment for this car."

"Let's go to the Cheetah for lunch and watch the girls—my treat." Frankie pulled down the sunvisor.

"Wait till Thelma sees these hot wheels." Wendell adjusted the rearview mirror.

"Be sure you make the payments. I told the owner of the used car lot you were good for it."

Heat waves shimmered above the hot pavement. Wendell accelerated and the wind lifted his sun-streaked hair.

Frankie leaned back in the seat. "This builder, John Poplaski, needs bread to construct a small office building on Baker Street. He owns the property, but his cash is tied up in heavy equipment. The bank won't make the note because he's already deep in debt, so I give him the loan."

Wendell seemed to be only half-listening as he maneuvered the car in and out of traffic.

"You watch the job progress and keep me informed."

"Okay." Wendell pulled into the next lane.

"Whew!" Frankie winced as Wendell barely missed hitting a pickup truck. "When he gives you the monthly payment, you cash the check, take five hundred for yourself and give the rest to me."

"That's good, Frankie. I can use the money. Construction's slow right now."

"I'll talk to Poplaski. Get your name on his payroll."

"I thought you wanted me to stay home and help Thelma."

"Don't be a dumb-ass, Wendell. The guy doesn't need another half-assed laborer. Just because I got you that union card that says you're an electrician, doesn't mean you *are* one."

CHAPTER FIVE

The day of Frankie's deadline, Nina and the boys moved into the West Side Apartments on Azalea Street in Hallandale. While their new place was only a couple of miles away, it was on the west side of the railroad tracks and bordered on a deteriorating high drug area. Michael and Joey set up their single beds in the modest master bedroom. Anthony picked his spot, and Nina gazed at the tiny bedroom in the middle of the apartment. She hung her suits on the hook behind the door and immediately confiscated the hall closet for herself.

"Mom," Michael whined. "Joey's dumping his junk on my side."

"Michael, Anthony!" Nina yelled from the hallway. "Get in here and put my bed together. The guys that live downstairs are carrying up the mattress and dresser." She stacked pillows in the corner. "Joey, get that last box from the U-Haul. The truck needs to be returned before five or I'll have to pay for another day."

"Those aren't guys." Anthony rolled his eyes. "I don't want queers touching my stuff."

Nina held her finger to her lips. "Mind your manners." She used a dishtowel to wipe the perspiration from her face. "You want to go down and tell them we don't need any help? And while you're there, bring up the three chests of drawers no one bothered to empty."

Anthony followed Michael into Nina's little bedroom.

She tucked a loose strand of hair behind her ear. "It's a good thing uncle Mickey came by and helped load the truck before he went to work or we'd still be at Frankie's house."

Michael picked up the headboard. "Guess what? I saw my friend Craig. He lives in the next building."

Joey sat in the hallway on an unpacked box. "A boy in my class must be really rich. He lives in that big brick house on the corner."

Loud footsteps tramped up the stairs.

"Where do you want the dresser?" asked a young man with a buzz cut and one earring.

"Will it fit against the wall?" Nina pointed to the only empty spot. "I really appreciate you guys giving us a hand."

"No problem." Buzz Cut squeezed past Anthony. "We'll get the rest of the heavy stuff."

Anthony quickly hooked the metal frame together, and Michael dropped in the slats.

"Mom and I have to take the truck back." Anthony yelled as he ran down the stairs.

"Clear a place on the kitchen table." Nina said to Michael and Joey. "I'll bring Chinese."

The following Monday, Nina went to the Department of Motor Vehicles to change her name and address on her driver's license. When she returned to the office it was after two o'clock.

"Oh, you decided to come back," Charlie sneered. "How nice of you."

"I had business to take care of," Nina said flatly.

"You said you'd do your personal stuff at night or on weekends."

"Some things can only be done during working hours. I'll take tax returns home tonight to make up the time."

"You wouldn't have to do that if you'd be a little nicer." Charlie sidled closer.

"A customer's waiting for this," she lied. Nina picked up a property schedule and clipped along the corridor until she saw Charlie return to his office.

When Nina opened her own checking account, she mailed the first check to pay off her furniture. A couple of days later, a woman who worked with Nina said her son signed up for the Marines and wanted to sell his Mustang. It was five years old and in perfect condition, but he owed almost as much as the car was worth and would be happy just to have the loan paid off.

Up to now, Nina had been unable to find a used car she could afford. So the next day, instead of driving, she rode the bus to work, and the woman's son brought his car to the office.

"It's a beauty." Charlie kicked the tires. "Looks like a good deal to me."

Nina paid off the car loan with part of the money Chance gave her. When she arrived home with the dark blue sports car, Michael jumped into the front seat and blew the horn.

Anthony opened the hood and checked the oil. "It has a lot of miles, but someone took good care of the engine. You did all right, Mom."

Nina had brought home ninety-nine-cent hamburgers and french fries for dinner. After they ate, Anthony left to study with a girl from school, and Michael, Joey, and Craig took the bus to the movies. As Nina set up the ironing board, the phone rang. She picked up the receiver.

"Nina?"

"Vito," she said.

"I haven't seen or heard from the boys. Some kinda of problem over there?"

"Nothing's wrong. Uh—you need something?" She heard the clinking of ice in a glass.

"Nah, tell Anthony to call me. I might be able to get him a part-time job. Boy his age needs a little cash in his pocket."

"I don't want him to get a job while he's in school. Football practice already uses up most of his study time."

"So what's he gonna do when he gets out of high school? You gonna get him a job? You can't get a decent job yourself, even with your high-falutin' college education."

"I'm sure he'll do something constructive when he finishes high school."

"Like maybe sell shoes?" Vito taunted before he asked, "How's the old Pontiac?"

"Not good." She'd been dreading this question. "I bought a Mustang. That way Michael will have a car when he turns sixteen."

"You bought a sports car?"

"I needed something dependable." She hated his third degree.

"You mean flashy," he grumbled.

"It's not new."

"So you don't need my car after all?"

"The judge gave the car to me, and you neglected to sign the title. I'll come by your office on Monday. I need to sell the car before it stops running. You can get the woman in the lawyer's office next to you to notarize your signature."

"I won't be in town, and besides, I don't want that nosey attorney knowing my business. The ink's not even dry on our divorce and already you got a different roof over your head, new wheels and paid off the finance company." He belched into the phone. "What do ya know that I don't know?"

She was glad to be divorced and wondered how he knew about the furniture before she remembered she had told Ginger. "I sold my rings. It was either that or not feed the boys."

"Oh, so I'm still supporting you. I paid big bucks for those rings and you sell them for peanuts so you can drive a fast car. What ya gonna sell when the rent comes due?"

"I'll pay the landlord with my weekly paycheck, the same way I paid the bills when we were together."

"You think your little paycheck paid for everything?" Vito snarled. "The attorney told the judge you needed a way to get to work, and now that's not true."

"Are you going to sign the title?" She drummed her nails on the counter.

"Why should I give the Bonneville to you? I gave you the furniture."

"I *paid* for the furniture." Nina waited. "You're not going to sign the title, are you?"

"Nah, take me back to court. I'm gonna keep my car."

"I'm hanging up." Nina's voice began to waver. "I brought tax returns home and I have to finish before I go to bed."

"You do that, Nina," he snorted. "You charm Charlie, and he'll entertain you. He's as much as told me so."

That does it. "The gas guzzler's parked in front of the apartment. Pick it up by tomorrow morning, or I'll park it on the street facing the wrong direction and let the city tow it away."

"You'd better pray nothing happens to my Pontiac, or you'll never see that Mustang again."

Nina's hands were shaking. She wondered if she had the courage to keep her threat.

CHAPTER SIX

"How do you like your new place?" Ginger stopped to look in the window of a Petite Sophisticate shop as she and Nina walked through the Hollywood Fashion Center.

"The rooms are small, but I don't have to worry about the finance company knocking on my door."

Ginger edged into the store and Nina followed close behind her.

"That's not the best area, but I guess you have to live where you can afford." Ginger said as she headed toward the accessories. "You're lucky Vito didn't pawn your rings before he left."

Nina glanced at her friend's hand. "Oh, Ginger, I'm sorry. I didn't know."

"Danny's pawned the diamond before. Frankie told Danny he'd make a lot of money at the track, but if he does, I don't see any of it."

"I thought Danny sold horse supplies to the trainers."

"He says the trainers don't buy that much, but he has to go every day to make it look good, so they can drug the horses. They bet the trifecta, and they only do it every three or four weeks, so they don't draw attention to the big score they make."

Nina noticed that although Ginger was chatting away her mind seemed to be somewhere else.

"Are you sure you're going to be all right?" Nina put her arm around Ginger's shoulder.

"Don't do that." Ginger shrugged away. "It makes me weepy. Danny'll find a way, he always does." She tilted a green plaid beret on her head and looked in the mirror. "So, what do your boys think about the move?"

"They're okay with it. They still go to the same schools." Nina fingered a cream-colored blouse. The material was scratchy.

"That's a cute top." Ginger looked at the size. "I remember when I wore that size."

"It wasn't that long ago." Nina looked at the price tag and frowned.

"This last baby did me in. I gained more than I ever did before, and now I can't lose it."

"She's only nine months old. Every pregnancy's different. Sometimes you don't get your shape back right away." Nina turned to another rack. "Don't worry. You'll drop the weight."

Ginger raised her eyebrows. "Sure."

"Did you get your tubes tied this time?"

"Danny wouldn't let me. He still wants a boy." Ginger led the way to the food court. "I don't want any more kids, but you know how men are." She lowered her voice. "Danny never uses anything. He says the church is against protection."

"Do you think Danny cares about the church?"

"Now you're talking like a smoker who just quit," Ginger grumbled. "You didn't complain when you were married, but now you think everyone should reshape their lives."

"I didn't complain because I thought I couldn't do anything about it. When my kids were old enough to go to school, I had to go to work. Charlie was the one who told me I was the visible means of support. At first I didn't even know what he meant." Nina hesitated at the hot pretzel rack. "I knew Vito was in the Mafia, but I didn't know what he did. He never got indicted, and back then I believed every word he said. Today, I know better. Ginger, you need to open your eyes."

"Danny's not in the protection racket." Ginger put her hand to her mouth. "Gosh, I forgot." She turned away from the row of fast food counters. "I promised to take my mother grocery shopping this morning."

"I'm sorry," Nina touched her friends arm. "I had no right to say that. I know you love Danny. Look, I'll make it up to you." She smiled. "I'll make one of those amaretto cream cakes that you and Danny like and bring it over tonight."

Ginger continued to walk toward the mall exit. "Uh. . . . about the cake. . . . We won't be home this evening. Maybe uh. . . . some other time."

Nina stopped Ginger before she got to the door. "We're friends, remember? You don't need to make an excuse. This isn't about your mother. It's Danny, isn't it? He doesn't want me at your house. Right?"

"Well, you know." Ginger swallowed hard. "He and Vito go back a long way."

"I understand. Call me if you want to go to IHOP sometime." Nina gave her friend a hug and Ginger disappeared into the parking lot. Nina replayed her friend's last words over and over in her mind as she made her way through the throng of shoppers. She no longer had a husband, and now she was in danger of losing her only friend.

Nina parked in the driveway and noticed the Pontiac was gone. At the top of the steps she found a scribbling from Vito.

"Screw you," it read in large printed letters. "After I talk to your landlord, you'll be sleeping in your sports car."

Nina tore the note into tiny pieces and shoved it deep into the kitchen trashcan. Michael and Joey had left the house before Nina, but Anthony had been asleep when she went to meet Ginger. She checked his room and found a note saying he had gone to a poolside barbecue and would not be home for dinner. She hoped he had not seen Vito's threat.

Unpacked cartons sat everywhere. Several boxes marked "Nina" had been stored in Frankie's garage for at least five years. She cut the tape and turned back ragged lids. Charcoal pencils, brushes, small tubes of paint, and so much more—dreams packed away in three cardboard boxes. Her fingers stroked the paint-stained palette.

She ran her hand across caricatures of the boys, a charcoal sketch of a barn and a canvas of scattered yellow lilies thrown across a white carpet. The canvas was dated the day Vito crushed her prize vase against a wall. They had moved so often, she could not remember where the quarrel took place.

Nina sat down on the kitchen floor and opened a sketchbook. She let her mind flow across the paper. With a charcoal pencil, she drew an outline of *Rosa's Italian Market* where Vito had once taken her. She remembered the old woman and the refrigerated pastry case. According to Chance's list, Rosa's was one of Vito's first accounts. She had paid him protection money for fourteen years, and all she ever got from Vito was grief.

She drew the interior of the store, filling the space with empty display cases, a few cream puffs and sparse staples. The pastries became the focal point. A few strokes later and all the trays were overflowing with bakery goods. Hanging baskets of snapdragons and vases of carnations added a vibrant touch of color.

The sketch pad rested against a box. Nina flexed her fingers and stared at the drawing. She wondered if she really could indeed make a difference in some of the business owner's lives. A few minutes later, she was driving toward town. She parked in front of Rosa's Italian Market. A small bell jingled when she opened the front door.

The store remained half-stocked. Cookies had replaced the pastries and the same stocky woman stood wrapped in a white apron. It was as if Nina had never left, except the woman did not seem to recognize her.

"No cream puffs today?" Nina asked.

The woman shook her head. "The unit, she no cool."

The smell of sweet cookies and freshly baked bread drifted through the store. Nina picked out pinwheels, macaroons and almonds. While she waited for her change, she asked. "How's business these days?"

The woman shrugged. "Is good, but costs to keep store open, so I no fix unit."

"Don't you lose a lot of sales?"

The woman's shaggy eyebrows arched, but she did not answer.

Nina felt a coldness she had not meant to arouse. She accepted her change and turned to look again at the rows of half-filled shelves.

"You could make more money if you offered a bigger variety."

"I suppose." Now the woman's gaze followed Nina more closely, as if she might be a thief.

Nina made a quick exit. While she drove, she opened the bag. The almond cookie melted in her mouth like warm honey. She reached for a macaroon. *I hated Vito's business, and now I'm looking for a way to perpetuate it.* She stopped at an intersection and stared at the street signal. A bizarre notion filtered through her mind. She had an urge to call Chance, but instead she returned home. This decision had to be hers.

Nina took the art boxes to her bedroom and stacked them in the corner. Her right brain had done enough today. Her left brain was only beginning.

Back in her college days, Nina had been employed by a small department store in Bentleyville, Pennsylvania. She had helped create layouts that sparked their ads and boosted sales. Her idea was to use that same strategy to help Rosa's market. The tough part would be to get the market owner to agree to sign a contract.

Uneasy about the whole setup, Nina tried to justify her intentions. *I don't want to take advantage. I just want to make a living that will also help the businesses.*

If she could persuade Rosa to sign a contract, the store would order directly from Goldman's Distribution Center using a code number that Chance said would be assigned to Nina. Nina's code automatically charged the owner of the business two percent more than the wholesale price. One percent would be deposited into the New York bank for the Mafia Family, and the same amount would be deposited in a New York trust account under Nina's name, so she could raise her children. She would explain to Rosa that the two percent covered the amount a store would normally pay for advertising art that Nina would design. The weekly ads and flyers would entice more customers to shop at Rosa's, and that in turn would allow Rosa to once again have a refrigerated pastry case. The cost would be absorbed into the stores inventory and not reported separately to Internal Revenue Service.

This could work. This could really work.

Nina replayed the idea over and over in her head. Chance had sworn to Nina that the mob was changing. "Going legit," he had said.

Redesigning the Mob

Well, then it was up to her to help him keep that promise. Right there and then she made up her mind to not only design the weekly newspaper ads for protection racket businesses, she would redesign how the mob treated their customers. When her customers saw they were getting something of equal or greater value for the extra two percent Goldman's charged them, they would see that she was helping them make a go of their failing businesses that the mob had been raping for a number of years.

On Sunday, the boys again went to the beach and Nina continued to sketch. During the week, she visited other progressive markets for new concepts and stayed awake into the wee hours drafting ads. On the last day of April, she called Goldman's to make an appointment.

Monday morning, Nina entered the kitchen. The boys were eating breakfast.

Nina made herself a cup of coffee and put an English muffin in the toaster as she spoke. "I'll be home a little late tonight. I'm meeting a friend at five o'clock. Maybe you could hang the posters in your rooms and get rid of a few of these big boxes."

"I'll hang them," Anthony volunteered.

"Be careful. The landlord will charge to fix the walls if you knock out any plaster."

Anthony rolled his yes. "I know how to put up posters."

"Will you help Joey and Michael?"

Joey ran out of the apartment to catch the school bus.

Anthony swaggered across the room. "Yeah, I ain't goin' nowhere."

"You aren't going anywhere," she corrected.

"That's what I said." Anthony opened the front door. "Shake it, Michael."

After work, Nina parked behind the library. She went straight to the archive area and entered a small anteroom. A round table gave her a view of the entrance to the larger room. She settled into a comfortable chair, and took her outline and sketches from the briefcase.

Dutch strolled into the main room, looked left and right before he turned toward her. Although curious to see an old acquaintance coming her way, she felt certain his arrival was not a coincidence.

The blue-eyed, fair skinned son of a Holland tailor and an immigrant Italian mother was not much taller than Joey, but built like a diesel engine. Raised in New York City in the early '40s, Dutch's chameleon soul blended into all societies.

"Yo, Nina." He gave a low cackle as he got closer.

She stood and shook his hand. "Don't tell me you're employed by Goldman's?"

He made a so-so motion. "Yes and no. I'm your five-thirty appointment. As of today, I'm on *your* payroll."

"I don't understand. I'm not making any money."

"Not to worry. Chance thinks you need me."

"He does, huh?" Nina grinned. "He still thinks I'm the little mill-town girl who chased Vito to New York."

"I didn't think that marriage would last." Dutch hung his glasses in the V of his shirt.

"Wouldn't *last*?" Nina sat up straight. "We were married for seventeen years."

Ignoring her protest, Dutch closed the door. He sat across from her. "So what's the story?"

"My idea's rather diverse." She stopped talking to gather her thoughts.

"Relax. Give me the scoop."

Nina spread her sketches on the table and told him about Rosa's Market. "I think I can use my past experience and artistic ability to put together a marketing plan and advertising layouts. My ads will bring in more business, which not only means a greater profit, but my customers will be getting something for the protection money they pay."

Dutch leaned forward to look at Nina's sketches. "I think Chance is gonna like this."

"I'm not trying to please Chance. I just don't want my customers to live in fear, and it's only fair that they make a good living.

Dutch sat back in his chair. "I understand you designing advertisements, but you also seem to be re-designing the protection racket.

"Chance said he was working to make the Mafia legitmate. All I'm doing is trying to help. I want to make an honest living, and I want my customers to prosper as well."

"Right," he said rolling his eye balls toward the ceiling. "And how do you plan to do all this art and still run a business?"

"The same way you guys go to the dog track and movies. This is my hobby."

"I didn't know that." Dutch smoothed his stiff mustache. "I never knew no artist before."

He reached into his pocket and handed her an attorney's crumpled business card. "Looks like you need to open an advertising company. You'll need corporate papers. Call this guy. He knows what to do." Dutch rattled off instructions. "His associate will do your taxes, but don't give him any money until you get a business checking account."

Nina smoothed the card. "I understand the operation of the grocery business, but how's Chance going to keep Vito away from my customers?"

"I'm your heavy." Dutch patted his girth. "It's a good thing for us that Vito's greedy. He only has a couple of men. Most of the time, he does his own collecting. He thinks it keeps him close to business."

Nina wondered if Dutch realized what he was up against.

"Here's what I figure. Each store employs me for a short time. I go to work every day." Dutch pointed to his chest. "I know the food business. I'll get the plan implemented, and then move on to your next contracted business."

"Vito will know you the minute he walks in. He said you were a friend of his."

"Nah, I never met him." The chair wobbled under Dutch's weight. "I was in Providence when he skipped Pittsburgh and came to New York. I came back to the city after he left for Florida, then you showed up pregnant. I've heard of him, and maybe he heard about me, but he doesn't know my real name or what I look like. We've never met."

Nina touched Dutch's arm. "I don't want my sons to know about the business."

"No problem." He put on his sunglasses and pushed back his chair. "I go by Egbert van Dermeullen. We'll get together when you get a signed contract." He handed her a briefcase. "Everything you need is in here."

Nina watched him walk away. His heavy thighs were a little thicker than she remembered. His body twisted from side to side, and his pants hiked in the crack of his butt.

She got a sick feeling in her stomach when she thought about Chance's last words. 'You let me worry about that.'

I trusted him and he sends one fat guy to stop Vito and his unsavory associates.

For a split second she was trapped again in the elevator, hearing the rapid fire of the gun, and tasting death. She sat alone in the anteroom until the nausea subsided.

Stopping at Rosa's Market each day to purchase a couple of items and have a friendly chat finally paid off.

"You like Italian coffee?" Rosa held up a demitasse cup.

"Thank you, I'd like that." Nina followed her into the back room.

They sat at a wooden table covered by a hand-stitched linen tablecloth and topped with clear plastic. Rosa's back was bent from years of working in the store, her hands were red and rough from scrubbing the fresh fruits and vegetables that her husband bought from the wholesale produce market each morning. Her smile emphasized the many lines in her face as she twisted a sliver of lemon rind into each tiny cup.

"A little Anisette?" Rosa's husband, Guiseppi, held the bottle over Nina's cup. His arms were thin, but steady as he waited for her answer.

She nodded, delighted to be sharing a beginning with the Santangelos.

He grinned at the pleasure of having a guest and showed the loss of a couple of front teeth.

On Nina's way home, images of a prosperous grocery store filled her mind. She pictured stacks of imported Italian products, a cool mist rising above the pastry unit and outside, *Rosa's Italian Market* in bright red letters on a freshly painted white storefront.

Nina spent hours on a layout for an ad in the local newspaper and sketched flyers featuring trays of decorated wedding cookies and colorful pyramids of fruit. Although satisfied with her results, she realized the Santangelos had no up front cash. Faced with giving up or finding a remedy, Nina searched for a financial solution.

The Small Business Administration might help or, if they did not come through, possibly a minority association. Everything depended on her. She was faced with not only finding a way to keep her children out of the mob, but she could be responsible for the safety of the Santangelos, and over time, the future of many more businesses.

CHAPTER SEVEN

Charlie heard footsteps and looked up from a tax return. He stood when Vito entered his office.

"We need to talk." Vito's words hung in the air like the plague. He kicked the door shut.

"Yeah? What's this all about?" Nina's boss had chastised her for putting up with a lowlife like Vito. Only now did Charlie speculate that Nina might have mentioned this insult to her ex-husband.

Vito hiked his shoulders and the silk suit resettled against his muscular frame. He looked like a Brooks Brothers fashion model. His meanness, often overshadowed by his handsome face and Robert Mitchum half-closed eyelids, caught most people off guard, but Charlie kept one hand close to the phone. He had heard sufficient stories to make him a believer.

"So, how's my wife?" Vito hoisted his polished Florsheim onto the chair.

"Wife? She said you two were divorced."

Vito slowly bounced a cupped hand in front of his chest. "A piece of paper."

The phone rang and Charlie scooped up the receiver. "Hold on a minute." He turned to Vito. "Business, you understand." He waited for Vito to leave.

"Tell 'em you'll call 'em back." Vito ran a white handkerchief over the toe of his shoe. He strode to the raised horizontal blind, lowered the slats and closed off the view to the employees.

"I'll call you back, Marge."

Vito spun around and his jacket flared, revealing a satin lining. "You do business with broads?"

Charlie spread his feet in a military stance.

Undaunted, Vito bristled. "You see, Geller, Nina's taken on more than she can handle. I'm worried about her health. She needs time off, without pay of course."

Charlie frowned. "She was sick last month, but she's better now, and we're behind schedule. You can wait out front if you like and see for yourself. She'll be here soon."

"Is that right?" Vito did not wait for an answer. "What you're saying, is business is more important than my wife's health?"

"It's not that." Sweat beaded on Charlie's upper lip. "It's tax season. It only comes once a year, and right now we're swamped."

"You won't be busy at all if this place should accidentally burn down one night while you're sound asleep." Vito cracked his knuckles before slipping his hands into his pants pockets.

Charlie's knees weakened. He sat in his chair, loosened his tie. "You're right, Vito. I—"

Vito's eyes opened wide. "Vito! You call me Vito?" He shook his fist at Charlie. "Like maybe you think you're my *paesano*?"

Charlie swallowed and spoke quickly. "Mr. DiGregetti. I'm used to Nina saying Vito. She speaks of you often."

"I'll bet she does." Vito leaned over the desk and poked his finger at Charlie's chest. "I want her laid-off, today. *Capisce*?"

Charlie nodded. "I understand."

Vito turned on his heel and strutted from the room. He took a quick look at Nina's dark office, and made his way to the front door. A meter maid stood in front of Vito's white Cadillac. She wrote on a small pad before tearing the page from the tablet. Vito hurried to his car and said something to the young lady. She handed him the ticket and walked away.

"Bitch!" he shouted.

CHAPTER EIGHT

Nina looked at her watch. "Oh my God." She ran to the ringing phone. "Hello."

"Are you sick again?" Charlie asked.

"I didn't feel good, but I'm better now. I'll be there in thirty minutes."

"Don't bother," he said. "The company's got financial problems. You've been laid off."

"Me? You're laying *me* off?"

"I have no choice. You make the most money. I need to keep as many people as I can."

"Charlie, are you angry because I'm late?"

"No, I'm gonna see how busy we are. Give me a couple of weeks. I'm sure I can get you back on the payroll."

"Did Vito come to see you?"

"Ah, no. Na-na-no one came to see me." Charlie always stuttered when he lied.

"You're lying, and I know it," she blurted. "You owe me two week's pay. I'll be in tomorrow to get my check, and don't worry about me, Charlie. I plan to collect unemployment."

"No, Nina, wait." Charlie hollered." You can't do that, I—"

She hung the phone on the wall, sat on the stool in the kitchen and put her head in her hands. *Now what am I gonna do?*

Nina glanced into the bedrooms. She had slept all night in the recliner and had not heard the boys leave for school. She packed her briefcase and drove to Rosa's. The store was empty and no one came to wait on her. She noticed a scattering of cans strewn on the floor.

"Hello, anyone here?" Her voice bounced off the barren walls. "Hello," she called a little louder.

Rosa came from the back room holding her glasses in one hand while she used her apron to wipe her face with the other. Red-rimmed eyes suggested she had been crying.

"What's wrong?" Nina asked.

"We gonna close store."

"Oh, no." Nina set her briefcase on the floor. She went behind the counter and put an arm around the woman's shoulder. "That's why I came today. I can help bring your business back."

"No more help." Guiseppi droned from the kitchen.

Nina gasped when she looked into the room. Blood ran from Guiseppi's nose onto a paper towel, and he held a wet rag against his swollen cheek.

"We no have the money. He broke Guiseppi's nose." Rosa's hands covered her face and she sobbed.

"Who hit him? Did someone rob the store?"

Rosa shook her head.

"Vito." The name slipped from Nina's lips.

The woman's eyebrows rose. "You," she said in a low growl. "You come for the cream puffs. You his woman. Get out!" Rosa picked up a broom. She shook her fist and raved in Italian.

"Wait a minute." Nina knocked over her briefcase as she moved past the canned tomatoes.

Rosa came from behind the counter, and Nina ran into an aisle that had no way out. The fleshy woman bore down on her.

Nina covered her face. "Holy Mary, Mother of God."

The woman stopped and glared at Nina. "You live with man who kills and you pray to the Virgin Mary?"

"No," Nina said. "I don't live with him." She held out her left hand. "Look, no rings."

A young woman and two small children bounced through the front door.

"Morning, Rosa," the woman said. "Do you have eggs today?"

Rosa nodded and set the broom in the corner. She straightened her apron and put on her glasses. Two more people came for homemade bread. Nina located her briefcase and stacked the fallen cans while the customers paid for their purchases and left.

"Please," Nina whispered. "Let me talk to you. After that, if you want me to leave, I'll go and not bother you again."

Guiseppi nodded from the doorway.

A young man stood at a deep sink cleaning vegetables.

"Watch the store." Rosa waved him from the kitchen and motioned for Nina to come in.

"First, let me tell you why I'm here," Nina said.

When she finished, Guiseppi asked, "What kind of woman turns against a husband?"

"An honest one." Nina waited while he thought about her answer. "It's true, you will still be paying protection money, but I won't charge you to design your weekly ads, which will be a savings. Your business will become more profitable, and you'll never be harassed or hurt again. I promise you."

He ignored her while he talked to Rosa in Italian. Nina knew a little of the language, and she thought he wanted to hear more about her proposition. After explaining the offer several times, she promised to go with them to the Small Business Administration to learn how the Santangelos could expand their business.

Nina persuaded them to think about the contract even though Guiseppi told her the man threatened worse pain if he did not have the money next month. She knew the Santangelos would be the ones to suffer if she failed.

The following morning Nina drove Joey to school.

"Be happy," Nina said. "School will be out in a few weeks, and you'll be going on vacation with Uncle Mickey."

Joey tossed his book bag onto the back seat of the car. "I'll be a freshman next year." He paused. "I won't be riding the bus anymore. Hey, will Anthony be an alcoholic by then?"

"No." Nina laughed. "He's only going through a phase."

Joey slouched in the seat.

She tousled his hair. "I'm sorry you're going to Nana's before your birthday. I'll miss seeing you turn fourteen."

"Uncle Mickey says Nana's planning a party with all the relatives. Some I haven't even seen before. Why can't you go with us?"

Nina stopped behind the line of cars dropping off their children at school. "I have to work, but you know I'll be thinking about you."

Joey opened the car door. "I love you," he said.

"Book bag." She pointed to the back seat. "I love you, too."

Nina drove to a small coffee shop. She liked the place. They had good coffee and a private pay phone inside the store. She often wondered what the owner thought when she stopped in a couple of mornings a week to make calls.

"Hi Ziggy. Just coffee today." She took the coffee into the phone booth to drink while she made an appointment for Rosa at the SBA, and then she called Dutch.

"Goldman Distribution Center," a woman's voice said. "How can I help you?"

"This is Nina. May I speak to Egbert?"

"He's not in." The woman offered no assistance, and Nina knew at once that she should not have called.

"Please have him return my call. He has the number."

"Yes, ma'am."

Nina hurried home. The phone was ringing as she came in the front door. She ran through the house and grabbed the receiver. "Hello."

"I'll meet you where we met before, thirty minutes." Dutch hung up.

A half-hour later, Nina hurried into the library. *I haven't even started the job and already I've made a mistake.*

Dutch sat in the anteroom. "I planned to set up a signal, but you called before I could make arrangements. I don't want to talk on your house phone. It might be tapped."

Nina bit her lip. "One of Vito's men hurt Rosa's husband. It was awful."

"You're not quitting, are you?"

Nina studied the pattern on the carpet before she looked at Dutch. "After what happened to Guiseppi? Not on your life."

Dutch nodded. "Good."

She explained the steps she'd already taken. "The owners want to meet you before they sign a contract. They don't believe you can stop Vito."

"I'll go with you. We'll talk to them together," he said.

Dutch followed Nina to Rosa's market. Guiseppi was mopping the floor. He set the mop aside and called Rosa from the back room.

"This is Egbert. He'll handle Vito's collectors if they come back, and he'll help you get ready for the grand opening," Nina said.

"Good." Guiseppi patted the muscle in Dutch's arm.

Even though Nina was against long-term commitments, Chance had insisted that all customers sign a five-year contract. Overruled and under pressure, Nina explained to the Santangelos that the legal agreement with the syndicate would serve them well.

"You don't have a written agreement with Vito, but you still pay him. If I don't provide you with advertising copy, then you're under no obligation to pay."

"Paper don't say you keep Vito away."

"That's true," she said. "But there's a section in the contract that says my advertising company will cover any malicious damage to the property not covered by your insurance."

"Our concern not property damage," Rosa said.

"Egbert will be here when you open and stay until you close. He won't let harm come to either of you. You can trust him," Nina said.

Rosa looked warily at Dutch, but Guiseppi had warmed up to him immediately.

That evening, after Nina had begun sketching an ad for Rosa's, the phone rang. Anthony answered it and turned toward his mother. He clamped his hand over the mouthpiece.

"Dad has a job for me," he whispered. "He said I can help his uncle Louie at one of the game rooms."

Redesigning the Mob

Nina continued to draw, but the hairs on the back of her neck bristled. She wanted to tell him he could not take the job, but she waited to see if Anthony was strong enough to say no.

"I can't," he told his dad. "I'm going on vacation." Anthony paced while his father talked. "Uncle Mickey only lives in Florida during the tourist season. He's going home to see Nana Cocolucci and said we could fly up with him."

"To Bentleyville?" Nina heard Vito's angry words clear across the room. "What the hell you gonna do there?"

"Uncle Mickey goes to see the Pirates play. He gets good seats, and we can drive to Cleveland or Cincinnati and see the Indians and the Reds, too."

Anthony listened while his father spoke.

"My friend John graduated this year. I hardly see him anymore, and football practice doesn't start until the middle of August." Anthony, who'd been excited about the trip to Pennsylvania, now sounded apologetic. "Watching baseball's just something to do this summer." He held the phone toward his mother.

Nina shook her head.

"All three of us are going," Anthony said and turned his back to Nina. The cord stretched tight, and he spoke low. "Working, I guess. She leaves the house every day, like always." He paused. "No, I ain't seen him. Uh, you wanna talk to Joey?" He shifted his weight. "Okay, I'll talk to you when we get back." Anthony said good-bye and hung up.

"Who haven't you seen?" Nina asked.

"Charlie Geller. I don't know why he asked about him."

Nina laid the drawings face down in her lap. "Are you sure you want to go to Bentleyville? The last time you went, you said you were bored."

"There's a lot to do now that Joey's older. We won't be stuck throwing the ball in Nana's backyard and playing cards on the front porch."

Joey came in with his basketball.

Nina thought the ball had permanently attached itself to him.

"Did Anthony tell you we're going to Kennywood Park?" Joey asked.

"I went there when I was young." Nina's smile went out of her voice as she recalled the occasion.

"Uncle Mickey said he'll take me to see Carnegie Tech." Anthony faked a punch at Joey. "That's where John's gonna go to school."

"He's going to college in Pennsylvania?" Nina asked.

"Yeah, and I'm gonna see his school before he does."

Anthony, interested in college? Nina grinned.

"I gotta pick up Michael and Craig at the skating rink." Anthony pulled his keys from his pocket. "You wanna ride along, basketball man?"

"Sure." Joey dropped the ball on the floor beside the sofa. "Bye, Mom." The front door slammed.

Nina tilted the recliner, smiled and returned to her sketchbook.

The following Friday, Nina and Rosa visited the SBA and listened to their suggestions on how to develop a thriving business. They gave Rosa a list of participating banks that offered small business loans. Rosa filled out an application.

Confident that Nina would keep her word, Rosa and Guiseppi signed the contract with Nina's advertising company. Nina's hand shook as she signed her name below theirs. Today, she officially joined the Mafia. No way to change her mind now.

Egbert became a regular employee, and within two weeks he had cleaned, painted, ordered stock from Goldman's, and had the pastry unit repaired, all on the strength of a commitment from the bank to lend Rosa money. Only the advertisement in the newspaper needed to be paid up front. The Santangelos reluctantly paid for the ad with the cash Vito's man would come for any day now.

"Listen to Egbert," Nina told Rosa. "He's your friend and protector, but to anyone else, he's only an employee. It'll be better if Vito doesn't know who's taking his business away." Nina handed Rosa her card. It listed a post office address and a toll free number. "Mail your weekly ad information. If there's not enough time, Margo, my assistant, will send a courier."

"God bless you, child." Rosa hugged her. "We pray for you and your sons."

Redesigning the Mob

Nina's sketch blossomed into a reality. Italian foods spiraled high beneath hanging display signs. The smell of homemade bread filled the air. Bright colors exploded from boxes of Torrone candy, and a refrigerated case, wih trays of cream puffs had customers drooling. The grand opening was not scheduled until the next day, but already customers were patronizing the upgraded market.

Dutch scurried around like a border collie tending sheep. He stocked the deli, added more cans to the shelves, and rang up groceries on one of the two new registers. Nina's gaze caught his eye.

"Time to leave, Nina." He appeared totally confident, as if the National Guard were stationed in front of the store.

She passed through the maze of people. Her mind was on next week's ad for Rosa and a visit to an Irish meat market across town, another struggling customer under Vito's alleged protection.

CHAPTER NINE

A tall man slipped through the front door of Rosa's Market, just as Dutch was about to take off his apron. A feathering of gray filtered through the stranger's black 1940's hairstyle, and his navy blue suit seemed out of place on this hot, muggy night.

"We're closed," Rosa said.

"I didn't come to buy groceries." His thin mustache twitched as he spoke.

Rosa retreated behind the counter.

"I come for the dues. You owe a couple months, and Vito ain't gonna make two trips."

Dutch approached the front of the deli case. His left hand hung slack, the right tucked under a long white apron. "What's these dues you talk about?"

"The obligation she didn't pay last month."

"Oh." Dutch drew out his next word. "The con-tri-bution." He rubbed his raspy throat. "IRS says the donation's not for a worthy cause, not tax deductible."

"Stay out of this." The man pointed his index finger at Dutch. "This is between me and her."

"Nah, you got it all wrong." Dutch's neck sank into his chest like a lion ready to pounce. "This is between me and you."

The man's hand fumbled at the button on his jacket.

"Stop right there, or die regretting you didn't." Dutch tipped his head toward the door. "Lock up, Rosa."

When the metal keys jangled, the man turned and bolted into the street.

Rosa locked the door behind him. "He come back. Next time Vito send two. What you do then?" She took off her apron. "You got one *pistola*, they got two."

"Pistol?" Dutch pulled a wooden mallet from under the apron. "I don't have a gun."

"Get the Bible, Guiseppi." Rosa made the sign of the cross. "Egberg, he crazy. We pray before we die."

Vito sat in the suite next to the ambulance-chasing attorney's office on the top floor of a three-story stucco building. He had waited all day for Paulie.

"What the fuck you mean, you didn't collect the money?" Vito jammed a cigarette butt into the overflowing ashtray. "Rosa's doin' a land office business. I warned you not to fall for that old I-don't-have-the-money routine. I made a mistake givin' her extra time last month. Now she takes advantage."

The phone rang. "Yeah." Vito listened for a minute, then turned to Paulie. "Wait outside, Mustache."

Paulie left the office, closing the door behind him.

Vito sensed a problem. "Hey, *paesan'*. How's New York?"

"What goes on down there?" Chance asked. "You come up short this month."

"Small problem."

"Not so small. At least three places didn't pay."

Vito clenched his teeth. "I'll take care of it." He waited for a favorable response.

"Good. I come down soon. We talk."

"Yeah. Come to Florida, we bet on a little bocci ball."

Vito heard a small click and then dial tone.

He's gonna ride my ass for a few grand.

Vito kicked his desk, and motioned through the window for Paulie to come in. "So tell me about last night. What happened?"

"Like I started to say," Paulie cleared his throat. "I looked in the window—"

The phone rang again and a woman's voice shrilled across the room.

"I'm a little busy. Gonna be awhile." Vito put his index finger to his lips. "C'mon, don't be that way." He held the phone away from his ear, while a woman's voice shouted repeated warnings. "All right, already," Vito barked back and hung up the phone.

"What's up?" Paulie asked.

"You don't wanna know. Maria's a spoiled bitch."

"This'll only take a few minutes." Paulie pulled a chair close to Vito's desk.

Vito shook his head. "I don't got a few minutes. I was late last night and she cut me off. I'm getting me some pussy tonight." Vito grabbed his keys. "Be here early tomorrow," he said to Paulie. "I wanna hear exactly what happened at Rosa's."

The following day Paulie showed up at noon.

"You don't know what early is?" Vito squashed his fourteenth cigarette in the ashtray.

"I stopped for coffee." Paulie set down two steaming to-go cups, and a bag of donuts.

Vito tossed his empty cup in the wastebasket and picked up a fresh one. "What, you only get two creams? That's not even enough for me."

"I'll drink mine black." Paulie took a sip of the hot coffee and swiped his hand across his mustache.

"So, give me the lowdown." Vito said with a mouthful of glazed donut.

"I waited in the car until closing time just like you said. When I looked in the window all I could see was the old lady. She was sweeping the floor, so I slipped inside. I start to talk to her, but this fatso comes from behind the cold cuts. He's armed and has a face like a bulldog." Paulie's hands jutted here and there as he spoke. "You should've seen the size of this guy, and he's not from around here. He's some kind of foreigner."

"And you ran like a cunt." Vito's blood pressure surged. "Sit down, Mustache. Tell me about this bulldog. You say he was big. Bigger than you?"

Paulie's angular jaw dropped, but he recovered and straightened his tie. "Not so tall, but big. Maybe five-ten, and an easy two-hundred and thirty-five pounds, *and* he was packin' heat. My guess is a three-fifty-seven. I could tell by the rise in the apron."

"You're telling me you didn't have a friggin' gun?"

"Yeah, in my shoulder holster. I didn't think I'd need it. I only went in to see the old woman."

"Terrific, you were taken by a cold cuts butcher." Vito rocked in the swivel chair.

Paulie's eyes showed no emotion. "This guy's no deli-cutter."

"Check him out. See where he's from. Talk to the guys at the track, stop at the restaurant and see what the Greek has to say. Be casual. Don't tell nobody why you want to know and don't come back until you find out." Vito's upper lip curled.

Paulie skulked from the office. He passed the attorney's middle-aged secretary on her way back from lunch. He liked her bubble hairdo that smoothed into a short pageboy at the nape of her neck.

"Hi, Paulie." She fluttered her eye lashes. "How are you?"

"I'm fine." Paulie looked back toward the office.

Vito stood in the doorway. He spit a spray of saliva between his teeth as she passed.

The secretary glared at him.

"Up yours." He gave her the finger and closed the door.

After Paulie left, Vito drove to Charlie Geller's office. He figured being laid off had not caused Nina enough grief, or his sons would have complained. *She probably borrowed money from her asshole brother.*

Bright lights shone from Nina's empty office. Geller's door was closed. Vito rattled the handle and found it locked.

"Just a minute," Charlie's voice sang out.

Vito heard a rustle and several drawers slam shut. He waited, then tried to see through the window, but the venetian blinds were closed tight. He banged on the door with his fist.

Several men stood and stared from their cubicles. Vito shot them a bird, and turned his back.

"I'm coming. Hold your horses." Charlie opened the door, face flushed, and trousers rumpled.

"You got a woman in here?" Vito pushed past Charlie. "Maybe Nina?" He opened the closet and found nothing but shelves.

"What makes you think I'd have a woman in here?" Charlie asked.

"Well, for one thing, you missed putting the post of your buckle through the belt." Vito smirked at Charlie's nervousness.

"I got up late and dressed in a hurry." He adjusted the leather strap.

Vito opened the top desk drawer and saw pictures of naked women. "You're one sick bastard." Vito slammed the drawer shut. "I came to see Nina."

"She's not here. I laid her off like you said. She picked up her check and signed up for unemployment."

"Call her up. Find out what she's up to." Vito held the receiver toward Charlie.

"She won't talk. When I call, she says she's busy and hangs up. If I leave a message, she doesn't return my calls." Charlie walked behind his desk.

"Sit down." Vito pushed the phone in front of Charlie. "Try again. And this time make it sound official. Tell her it's important that she return your call."

"I don't see how that will get her to tell me what she's doing or where she working."

"You're the smart one, you and the friggin' IRS. You think of something."

When the answering machine picked up, Charlie left a message.

Vito's handsome features gave way to tight lips and narrowed eyes.

Charlie's heart beat faster. "Ask the boys—they probably know."

"Nina's piss-ugly brother took them to Pennsylvania to see the witch."

"Visiting their Nana." Charlie gave Vito a cocky sneer.

The look faded when Vito's switchblade touched his throat. "You got ways to find out. Call unemployment. Call IRS. I'll be back."

When Vito left, he caught a glimpse of fluffy blond hair in Nina's old office. He stopped. The raised blind gave him a full view of a good-looking woman. *Nice.*

The blonde ran her long painted nails through her hair. Her ripe lips opened into a bow and sooty eyelashes fluttered. He stepped in her direction, and she reached for the calculator.

Don't play hard to get with me, babe. He made a quick U-turn, and smacked into the wall. He touched his forehead to check for blood and sneaked another peek at the blonde.

She grinned.

A low growl escaped his throat. He pushed angrily through the corridor and out to the fire lane where he had parked his car. A tow truck was pulling his white Cadillac down the avenue. He yelled until the car disappeared from sight before waving his arm to catch a passing taxi.

Vito arrived at the race track after the third race. He dropped fifty on the fourth and meandered through the open seating. A few feet from Danny he stopped to study the race form.

Danny was talking with two burly men and did not acknowledge Vito's presence. So, Vito cruised past the bleachers and stopped at the concession stand for a hot dog and a Coke. A few minutes later, Danny sauntered toward the impatient Vito.

"You beefing up the payroll?" Vito asked as he finished his hot dog and tossed the mustard-covered napkin in the trash.

"I don't need muscle to play the ponies." Danny ordered an Italian hot sausage and pepper hoagie. "They work for the crime commission."

"They told you that?" Vito lit one of his skinny brown More cigarettes.

"Nah." Danny paid for his sandwich. "They told me they were on vacation from Cleveland and pretended they couldn't read the scratch sheet."

"You showed 'em?"

"Sure. I bamboozled them, and they think they duped me. You gotta listen if you want to learn something. Can't have your yap open all the time." Danny took a big bite of his sandwich and peppers spilled out. "Now look what you made me do."

Vito stuffed the betting ticket into his pocket and asked the girl in the booth for more napkins.

Danny took the napkins, ate a few more bites and tossed the rest of the hoagie into the garbage. "You come to blow your wad at the track?"

"It's not funny. I got problems."

"Yeah, tough guy. What kind of headaches you got?"

"Knock it off." Vito took a long drag from his cigarette. "This is serious. I'm losing business faster than a dog with diarrhea."

"Not like the old days when you knocked a few heads and things ran smooth." Danny wiped the grease from his hands. "Change the way you operate or come work with me."

"Do I look like the kind of guy who would peddle horse supplies and sneak through stables with crap up to my ankles? And one of these days, someone's gonna figure out that the only reason you're there is to drug horses. Then the shit will really hit the fan."

Danny shrugged.

"Besides, I'm not letting a two-bit, out-of-towner push me around." Vito took a sip of his Coke. "Trouble is—I can't get a line on him."

A loud cheer rose up from the bleachers as the lead horse crossed the finish line. Vito stood on tiptoe to see over the crowd of people that lined the fence to watch the race. "Shit!" He tossed the ticket to the ground as his horse crossed the finish line dead last.

Danny glanced up at the bleachers. "Looks like everyone bet on the winner." He patted Vito on the shoulder and pointed to the tote board. "Horse didn't pay enough to worry about."

"Right," Vito said as he adjusted his sunglasses. "Come to think about it, I'll bet the dike-jumper's behind all the trouble the Donovan brothers are causing."

"What the hell's a dike-jumper?"

"Word around town says the guy that's trying to shove me out is from Holland. Every time I turn around, this guy's in my fuckin' face."

"A dutchman you say. That's interesting. Not that I ever heard of anyone being called a dike-jumper." Danny continued to read the scratch sheet.

The wind picked up and blew Vito's hair. "Let's go inside. I don't like the heat, and I hate the wind."

Danny started toward the clubhouse. "If you don't like the weather, why live in Florida?" He turned the corner, and the wind caught his straw Panama.

Vito sputtered as the hat smacked him in the face. Danny turned and grabbed for his hat, knocking Vito's Coke down the front of his pale blue seersucker suit.

Vito dabbed at his jacket with a handkerchief. "Damn! Look at my suit." His jacket, white batiste shirt, and even the top of his pants were stained a muddy brown.

"The suit'll clean," Danny said waving his hand. "You expect me to lose my favorite hundred dollar hat?" He roared with laughter at the seething Vito. "Don't be such a grouch. Let's get a table, and I'll buy ya a drink."

Vito disappeared into the men's room. When he came out, the stain was almost gone, but the suit still looked wet.

Danny sat inside a large glass enclosure. He had placed a bet on Midnight Dream, a horse that was running in the fifth. The bell rang and the horses were off. The cheers of the crowd mixed with the pounding horse's hooves. He and Vito watched the race and a few minutes later the ticket runner picked up Danny's stub. When the runner returned, he counted out a stack of hundred-dollar bills and Danny tipped him fifty bucks.

"Thank you, sir." the young man beamed and stuffed the bill into his pocket.

Danny handed the runner another bill. "Bring us another drink." Danny turned back to Vito. "How are Nina and the boys getting along without you?"

"Who knows? She sent them to her mother's in Pennsylvania, quit her job, and now I can't find out what she's up to."

"Call and ask her. She'll tell ya. She always treats you good."

"And let her think I care?" Vito smoothed back his hair.

"So, I guess you and Maria are getting it on pretty good?" Danny winked.

"You mean the mouth? She complains from the time I come in until the time I leave. Now she's talking about a wedding. Soon as I clear up this mess, I'm outta there."

"You miss Nina?"

"What I miss is a decent home-cooked meal, clean clothes and no one telling me what to do."

"You can't have everything. Take my Ginger. She puts on a little weight, but she's a good cook, don't ask no questions, and keeps a clean house."

"Yeah, but does she give you what you need?"

"*Menz-a-menz*. When I want more, I go out, but not like you. I don't flaunt my impropriety."

Vito raised his shades. "Your impro-what?"

"My sleeping around."

The race went off and Danny watched through binoculars while Vito fanned his damp jacket.

"Will you look at that?" Danny fingered the ticket. "Another winner."

"Lady Luck's with you today, but what about tomorrow?" Vito asked.

"Tomorrow I sell horse supplies. And if you're smart, you'll do the same thing." Danny stood and touched the brim of his hat. "See ya around," he said as he left the clubhouse.

Vito leaned back into the chair and sipped the last of the third drink that Danny had bought him. *I'll do things my way, and it won't be traipsin' through horse shit.*

CHAPTER TEN

Nina had stopped by Donovan's Meat Market, where the brothers, Patrick and Sean, told her they were making their own stand against Vito.

"We threw Vito's crummy collector off the property, and we don't intend to pay anyone protection money," Sean told Nina.

She wished them well, and left her *Elite Advertising* business card.

The next store on her list was the Come & Go, a convenience store with very little parking space. It was operated by a Pakistani family, who did a small volume of business, but stayed open 24-7.

She found the owner out behind the store refurbishing secondhand shelving. Mr. Mohammed Khan did not seem to understand English, but when she mentioned Vito, he spoke in a staccato voice.

"I pay. I give once a month. Go way, go way." He signaled toward the street.

"I didn't come to collect money. I only want to talk." Nina kept her voice low and moved closer.

The thin brown man backed away. "I do not talk." He waved his hands. "I want no trouble."

"Please, Mr. Khan," Nina said. "I want to help."

He laid down the brush and wiped his hands on the bottom of his long tunic. "I am listening for five minutes."

"Thank you." Nina bowed her head slightly.

Mr. Khan, an astute man, said her advertising plan interested him, but claimed he could not sign the contract. "City owns adjoining property. Without parking, I do not make good living."

"I'll help you fill out an application to lease the city property for parking, if you agree to consider the contract." Nina held out the agreement.

He reached for the paper, tentatively. "I will read."

The next morning, Nina finished her coffee, rinsed the cup and placed it in the drain rack before telephoning her parents. She talked to each of her boys. Anthony said after going to a Pirate's game, he had joined a sandlot baseball team. The girl who lived next door had taken a shine to Michael and he was spending most of his time with her. Nina chuckled when Joey told her he talked his Nana into buying him all new regulation basketball equipment. All three boys said they missed her, but she noticed they were not eager to come home, and none of them asked about their dad.

Nina sighed. It was fine for now. She didn't want them to know how much time she spent away from the house.

She went outside and picked up the morning paper, eager to see Rosa's full-page ad. She gasped. Her fingers tightened on the *Fort Lauderdale News*. A spectacular photo of Donovan's Meat Market splashed across the front page. The headline read: GUARD DOGS TRAPPED IN FIRE. She scanned the article: Two guard dogs deliberately trapped in fire after arsonist gains entry through window. . . Firemen find wrappings from beef roast purchased from nearby Winn- Dixie Supermarket. . . Investigators say the blaze generated black smoke from strategically placed metal buckets filled with oil soaked rags. . . Fire Chief Guadagno declares structural damage to be minimal. The distraught owners were quoted as saying, "I don't know who could've done such a terrible thing. . . ." Organized Crime Commission, present at the investigation, claim the fire has the markings of an underworld job, and is possibly connected to a small-time hood in the protection racket.

Nina could not believe what she just read. When she had spoken to Patrick and Sean Donovan the day before, they seemed satisfied that

Jodi Ceraldi

Vito would not bother them again. She shivered. *What if the Donovans think I had something to do with the fire?*

Nina clipped the article from the newspaper and placed it in her briefcase. She left the house and drove to a pay phone to call Margo for her messages.

"Only one," Margo said. "A Mr. Donovan. He left a number."

"Did he say anything else?"

"Only that he wanted to talk to you right away."

Nina glanced at the article again. *If they're going to accuse me, why didn't they tell the police?* Regardless of the outcome, she felt obliged to make the call. Her hand was skaking as she dialed the number.

"Tam O'Shanter Moose Club, Quinn speaking."

Nina held the phone for a moment without saying anything.

"Moose Club," he said again.

"I must have the wrong number," she murmured.

"And who you be callin'?" the man asked.

"I received a message to call a Mr. Donovan."

"Sure an' you have the right number. Give me your name."

Nina hesitated. "Elite Advertising."

"You be comin' to the club's back door, lass. Eight tonight." The man hung up.

Nina, left standing on the busy street corner with the receiver in her hand, had no idea where the Moose Club was located. She reached for the ragged phone directory and found the address. She ripped the page from the telephone book and ran into Henry's Lunch Shop. She bought a ham sandwich to eat on the way to the meeting with Mr. Khan. She did not think he approved of people being late, and his contract was important to her.

There was a long line of people waiting for answers to various questions that the city commissioners had made rulings on. And Nina was surprised when Mr. Khan's case was called first. To her amazmnet the secretary presented a typed paper to Mr. Khan for his signature.

"You read," Mr. Khan said to Nina.

Nina quickly read the one page document along with her client. Mr. Khan pointed to the annual cost and smiled. It was lower than he had expected. Nina handed him her pen. While the secretary made a copy of the agreement for Mr. Khan, Nina pulled her clients folder from her briefcase, and Mr. Khan signed the Elite Advertising contract. Nina was elated. Everything had gone smoothly and they were out of the building in thirty minutes.

The asphalt lot in front of the Moose Club was crowded with cars. Neon lights advertising various alcoholic beverages flickered from every window. The sun was setting when Nina parked behind the club. A small roof covered a closed-in stoop and shadowed the back entrance. A Dumpster surrounded by stacks of whiskey boxes sat in a far off corner of the lot. Nina got out of the car and walked cautiously toward the building. As she reached the entrance, a husky man with red hair pushed the door open.

"Sure an it's her," he said to someone inside. "Come right this way," he said to Nina.

"Please, sit down." Patrick pulled out a chair. "Would you like something to drink?" he asked Nina.

Nina shook her head and sat on the edge of the chair.

Sean Donovan motioned to the husky man. "Quinn," he said. "Bring Pat and me a pint of Guinness."

"I guess you heard about the fire," Sean's brother Patrick said to Nina.

"Yes, and I'm sorry about the dogs." Nina sat back in the chair. "It'll be hard to replace trained guard dogs."

"They weren't guard dogs." Sean's eyes were moist. "They were pets—wouldn't step on a bug. Friendly as they could be, they was."

"We want to know more about your offer." Patrick pulled his chair closer.

"Why are we meeting here?" Nina stared at the cartoons of liquor piled against the walls.

"Because we don't want anyone to see the Mafia hanging around our place. It's bad for business."

Nina frowned. "I own an advertising company."

"Right." Sean rocked in his chair. "Like an ad in the newspaper will keep Vito away."

"Well, first you need to sign a—"

"We'll sign the contract." Patrick held up his hand. "We know it was Vito who set fire to our place."

Nina shook her head. "Why didn't you tell the police or the fire inspectors that you thought Vito set the fire?"

"What good would that do?" Patrick retorted. "He warned me he would do it, but I can't prove it. A guy like him has connections." His fist hit the table and the glasses shook. "The police won't do anything, and the next time it might not be dogs."

"How soon do you think you can be back in business?" Nina asked.

Sean looked at his brother.

Patrick thought for a moment. "Couple of weeks. There wasn't as much damage as we thought. Most of the equipment can be cleaned."

"We already got an electrician to repair the wiring," Sean added and took a gulp of beer. "A lot of the damage came from smoke. That's what killed the dogs."

Patrick pulled his chair closer to Nina. "I want to know how you plan to keep Vito away before we order the meat."

"You can count on the syndicate for that. They're just as much against Vito's violence as you are."

Patrick rubbed the stubble on his chin.

"I'll meet you here in two days," Nina said. "I'll bring the contract and the man who will handle Vito. After you talk to him, you can decide what you want to do."

"Deal." Patrick pushed back his chair. "Same time?"

"Eight o'clock is fine." Nina got up to leave.

Sean walked with her to the door and stood on the stoop until she drove from the parking lot.

The next time they met, Quinn, who seemed quite taken with Nina, convinced her to have a look at the newly added screened-in deck. Nina was anxious to have the contract signed and politely walked through the bar and dance hall to the deck. By the time they got back, Dutch had the contract signed. Once again, Nina had not found out how he convinced the client that he alone could stop Vito's harassment. And like always, on the ride home, Dutch would joke about the subject, but he would never tell her how he managed to cajole them into believing he could stop Vito and his men.

A few weeks later, Nina took an afternoon out of her schedule and donned a pair of peacock blue shorts and a white halter. She met Dutch at a Tiki bar on the beach. Most of the patrons were in wet bathing suits.

"You look more like a Playboy bunny in those short shorts than an executive."

"I'll bet you say that to all the women."

"Who me? Who'd want a fat pig like me?" Dutch ordered Mai Tai's. They came decorated with little pink umbrellas stuck in a slice of orange. "After I lost Polly to cancer, I never gave women another thought. Besides, Chance keeps me moving around so much, I don't have time to settle down."

"I'm sorry, Dutch. I didn't mean to bring up old memories."

"That's okay. It was a long time ago."

Nina sipped her drink. "The city gave Mr. Khan a lease on the parking lot and he signed a contract."

"That's good," Dutch chugged half of his drink. "I knew you'd be able to convince the commissioners."

Nina rolled her eyes. "I can't believe Vito hasn't showed up to collect from the Donovans."

"A couple of days after the Donovans signed the contract I stopped by the meat market to see how things were going. I was standing behind the counter when Vito, and the same guy that came to Rosa's, stopped in." Dutch tossed an orange slice to a small wren pecking at the sand. "They looked around the place, had a little conversation together and left. I think he's beginning to get the picture."

"How come you didn't tell me?"

"Cause you got enough to worry about."

I'm beginning to think there are a lot of things you don't tell me.

Nina rubbed suntan oil on her legs while Dutch visited the buffet. He returned with paper plates filled with chicken wings, cheese, chips, grapes, and Hawaiian dip.

She filled Dutch in on several new contracts she was working on while he scarfed down the free food.

"Food makes me think clearer." He licked his fingers. "You sure you don't want some?"

Nina pushed her plate in front of him.

"How do you do it, Dutch? Vito's guys aren't scared of anyone."

"I giv 'em an offer they can't refuse." He laughed at the pun.

Nina figured she should have known better than to ask.

"I look for the Crime Commission to charge Vito with the Donovan fire." He shoved the food aside. "They'll grab The Squirrel. He'll squeal to get amnesty and Vito will find himself in court."

"The Squirrel?" Nina's forehead wrinkled.

"He's one of Vito's boys. His name's Stanley, but everyone calls him 'The Squirrel,' because he's a little nuts."

"You think Vito started the fire?"

"Maybe." Dutch wiped his chin.

Nina pushed her sunglasses on top of her head. "If he did, it's because I pressured him into it." Nina folded her arms and stared at the ocean.

"Stop with the guilt thing. These Irish brothers didn't even know you when they started their fight against Vito. You just happened along at the same time. But it's true, Vito's being crowded out, and sooner or later, he's gonna learn you're the one doing it." Dutch touched Nina's hand. "He's gonna fight, and he'll play to win. You have to be ready."

"Chance promised me he'd see that Vito got a different job that didn't involve violence." Nina said with confidence.

"He will, when Vito gets off his high horse and asks. In the meantime, he might take out his frustrations on you." Dutch finished his fourth Mai Tai and asked the waitress, "What's in these things, lemonade?"

Nina laughed and took the last sip of her drink.

"Call your brother." Dutch said. "See if Mickey can stay in Pennsylvania until it's time for school to start. It'll be better if the boys aren't around right now."

"I miss them." Nina sighed. "But you're right."

"Don't worry. This won't last forever." Dutch walked with her to the parking lot.

"I can't maintain this pace," Nina said, anxiety in her voice. "I didn't expect the business to mushroom so fast."

"You can't let up," Dutch warned. "Now that the groundwork's laid, we hit the rest of the stores before Vito knows what's happening."

Nina massaged her temples. "What will I do when the boys come home?"

"That's another reason to work hard while they're not here."

"I'll catch up on the advertising, but after that, I'm going to sleep." Nina felt a headache coming on. It seemed as if she bought a bottle of Aspirin every week. "I don't think I can keep tomorrow's appointment at Freddie's Fish Market."

"I'll cover for you. I'm workin' at Rizzo's. Freddie's is right on my way home." Dutch opened her car door. "I'll stop for some catfish and see if I can close the deal. If not, I'll tell him you'll call him next week."

When Nina and Dutch left the parking lot, they went in different directions. Nina noticed a white sedan that pulled out behind her. When she stopped for a red light, the white car stayed several car lengths back. When she turned onto the highway the car followed. Nina drove in the slow lane and the car tracked behind her. It was broad daylight and there were a lot of cars on the road, but still she worried.

She turned off the highway and so did the white car. The first traffic light she came to turned yellow. She slowed almost to a stop and at the last minute she sped up and drove through the intersection. The white car ran the red light. Now it loomed closer and she could see two men in the front seat. There was a large spot light, next to the side mirror, and a tall whip antenna shot up from the back of the car. She turned into the Publix Super Market, and the tag-along picked up speed and drove past the entrance. In a few moments, it was out of sight.

Nina was shaking. She sat for a few moments, until another car pulled in behind her and blew the horn. Nina pulled into a parking space. Naturally, her first thoughts were of Vito, but the men in the white car did not look like Vito's type. By the looks of the shoulder on the one man she could see, he appeared to have on a dress jacket and he looked clean shaven with short hair.

A plain white sedan, with a spot light and big antenna. "Hm." *Maybe a couple of detectives.* She was not sure, but she felt better thinking it might have even been the FBI or someone from the Organized Crime Cimmission.

CHAPTER ELEVEN

Vito drove into the quiet development where Paulie's girlfriend rented a house. The street was lined with palm trees and all the houses had fake brick fronts. He pulled into the driveway and blew the horn.

Paulie was pulling a pair of shorts over his swim suit as he came out of the house. "Whad ya' come here for? You want my girlfriend to start asking questions?" He opened the passenger door and got into the Cadillac.

Vito drove down the street until he came to a 7-Eleven. He parked behind the store, cut the engine and pushed his seat back. "Whad ya find out about the bulldog?"

Paulie was silent as he looked down at the floor mat.

"Talk to me, Mustache," Vito barked. "Where's he from?"

"I don't know. I didn't find out anything."

Vito rolled down the window and lit one of his skinny brown cigarettes.

"How come you killed the dogs?" Paulie asked.

"What dogs?"

"You know what dogs. It's all over the TV."

Vito took a long drag from his cigarette before he answered. "I don't kill dogs. I love dogs."

"So who set the fire for you? Was it The Squirrel?" Paulie shook his head. "Don't you know Stanley's half crazy? If they catch him, he'll rat on you as fast as he killed those mutts."

Vito tapped his fingers on the steering wheel. "I didn't have no fire set."

"Come off it. You asked me to do the job."

"I was joking. I didn't start the fire, and I didn't have the dogs killed." He tossed the butt out the window. "You can see what a pain in the ass these Irish are. They probably stiffed someone else, and they did it."

Paulie opened the car door.

"Listen to me, Mustache." Vito pointed his finger at Paulie. "I want you to stay on top of this. Go talk to the bulldog and see what he's up to."

"Like hell. He threatened to blow me away and you expect me to walk up and have a conversation with him?"

"You don't like making a lot of money while you sit around your girlfriend's pool? Maybe you want a job with a road crew directing traffic in the hot sun for a few nickels a day."

Paulie clasped his hands.

Vito started the engine. "Close the door, I'll take you home."

"I'll walk." Paulie got out of the car.

"C'mon, get back in." Vito stretched across the seat. "I didn't mean it."

"Nah, it's all right, I need cigarettes." Paulie stepped away from the car.

The minute the sandwich shop opened, Paulie slithered through the front door. Rizzo always paid, but talk on the street said the store might have fallen to the Chicago mob. Paulie stepped toward the counter. He placed a hand across his waist and lightly fingered the Beretta.

Dutch appeared from the back room. "What can I get for you?"

Paulie tensed. He tried to smile, but only managed to show his teeth.

Dutch placed both of his hands flat on the counter.

"Small coffee to go." Paulie's shoulders tightened.

"Coming right up." Dutch grinned from ear to ear.

Paulie wanted to turn and leave, but he didn't know if someone else might be lurking around the corner and drawing a bead on him. He wasn't ready to get shot in the back. He watched while Dutch poured.

"Cream and sugar?"

"Black." Paulie was sick and tired of being screamed at by Vito, and this job was not getting any easier. He could not think of a single word to say to the Dutchman.

"It's good to see you again, Paulie." Dutch topped the steaming container with a lid.

Paulie backed up a couple of steps.

"What took you so long to pay us a visit?" Dutch took a rag and wiped a drop of coffee from the counter.

"I don't drink much coffee." Paulie glanced at the to-go cup and then at the exit.

"Smart fellow like you might be looking for a job," Dutch said. "I might be able to find a spot for the right guy, and the people who work for me get paid on time."

The two men stared at each other.

"Well?" Dutch waited.

Paulie relaxed his arms. "Say what you gotta say."

"Hey, *paesano*," Dutch shouted as Chance emerged from the crowd that had just disembarked from the plane that flew nonstop from New York to Miami.

Chance slapped Dutch on the shoulder. "You fat bastid, I miss ya." He handed Dutch his overnight bag. "Hold this for a minute."

"I miss New York." Dutch hefted the small duffelbag. "This all you brought?"

"It's enough." Chance searched the signs along the corridor. "How's Nina?"

"She's holding up, but I don't know for how long."

"You shoulda called sooner." Chance swung into the first men's room he came to.

Dutch set the bag on the floor and lit the stub of an old cigar. While he waited outside the restroom, he scanned the concourse for familiar faces, but saw no one that concerned him.

Chance came out and picked up his bag. His long strides propelled him swiftly through the terminal.

"I'm parked across the street," Dutch said as he jogged every couple of steps to keep up with Chance. "I'll take you to a hotel."

"Not good to be seen together. I catch cab." Chance slid his plane ticket into the bag's side pocket. "I want to see Vito alone. Bring Nina to The Willows tomorrow, around noon."

The next morning, as Vito crossed the street to his office in North Miami, he noticed a cab idling in front of the building. *Probably waiting for the ambulance chaser.*

The offices stood in darkness behind frosted glass doors, except for Vito's. He did not remember leaving the lamp lit, but a small glow radiated from his suite. He unlocked the door, gave it a shove and peeked inside. Chance sat behind Vito's desk.

Vito tried to hide his surprise. "You shoulda called. I'd a bought breakfast." He stepped inside and set a cup of coffee on the edge of the desk. "How'd you get in?"

"The Super."

Vito knew that no superintendent hung around this building. He offered the coffee to Chance.

Chance shook his head. "I go by Frankie's old place. New people live there. Why you no tell me you and Nina move?"

"I musta forgot."

"You forget a lot. Like money you owe. What's happenin' to business?"

"Nothing I can't take care of." Vito lifted the lid from the coffee container. "I've been busy. Couple of my men got probation problems."

"So where these guys at?" Chance rocked in Vito's chair.

"In jail. Petty shit." Vito stood beside the only other chair in the room.

"You don't go their bond? You leave 'em in jail to run their mouths?"

"Like I said, I've been tied up. I'll go tomorrow." Vito took a sip of coffee and burned his tongue.

Chance tapped his chest. "Don't give me angina. You go today."

"Don't worry. I'll handle the situation."

Pointing to the straight back chair, Chance said, "Have a seat. Tell me why people no pay."

Vito saw no reason to play Chance's game, since his boss always knew the answer before he asked the question, but Vito had no choice.

"There's this guy. He comes into town a few months ago. He must be from Chicago. He thinks he can take over my business. He's got men packing heat. Maybe you know him?" Vito looked for a sign that Chance would help, but got no response. "You get me a lead and I'll get rid of him. Right now, he's like the wind—blows in, knocks things around and disappears."

"So you say customers no pay?" Chance's tight lips strained along the edges.

Vito shifted his body on the hard chair. "They pay all right. They pay the bulldog. He beats the hell out of my guys right in front of the storeowners, and nobody talks. This son-of-a-bitch is shaking down my customers, and for some friggin' reason, they like him."

"Shoulda listened to me."

Vito stood up. "Okay, okay. I'll do it your way, but you gotta help me get rid of the poacher first."

"He ain't my problem." Chance got up from the chair and walked across the room. "You're behind thirty-two grand. Needs to be in New York in thirty days."

"Wait!" Vito called as Chance shut the door behind him. Vito went to the window and watched his boss strut to the elevator. *Miserable bastard. Did he think I would beg?*

Offices occupied three sides of the U-shaped building, and the lobby was enclosed by three floors of plate glass. It allowed Vito to watch Chance as he got out of the elevator and left the building. When Chance climbed into the waiting taxi, Vito seethed with vengeance, but he knew any act of reprisal would be the same as signing his own death warrant. He returned to his office and shoved a small snub nose revolver into the back of his waistband. *I'll exterminate the bulldog myself.*

CHAPTER TWELVE

Nina had been sound asleep when the phone rang. "Hello?" She said into the wrong end of the receiver before turning it around.

"It's Ginger. I'm coming over."

"What time is it?" Nina rubbed her eyes and tried to focus on the clock.

"Ten o'clock. I'll be there in fifteen minutes."

Nina pushed back the covers and yawned. "I'll make the coffee."

When Ginger arrived Nina was already dressed. "Would you like breakfast?"

Ginger's face was red and puffy. She shook her head.

Nina set the carton of eggs on the counter and pulled out a chair for her friend. "What's wrong?" She filled Ginger's cup.

"I haven't slept in three days." Tears ran down Ginger's cheeks.

"Why are you crying?" Nina asked. "Are the girls okay?"

"Haven't you heard? It's been in all the papers." Ginger was on the verge of hysteria as she handed Nina the Fort Lauderdale News.

"The only thing I looked at this week was next week's ads, but I ran into that girl Eunice—the one that lives with Frankie. She said they made a ton of money. I didn't know they put stuff like that in the newspaper."

"No, Nina. They didn't put that in the newspaper. Danny, Frankie and two other guys were indicted for fixing a horse race." Ginger sniffled. "The article said Danny's going to jail when they find him."

"But Danny's been out of town for ages. Why are they after him?"

"It happened a while ago, when Danny was selling horse supplies at the track. The paper said it took a long time for the FBI to get all the witnesses and build a case."

Nina's heart catapulted. She knew if Danny got locked up, Ginger would face serious financial problems.

"It'll be all right," Nina said. "When the cops arrest Danny, you can take some of the money Danny made at the track and pay a bail bondsman to get him out."

"You think I got cash? Danny didn't get any of the winnings. All he ever got was the commission he made selling horse supplies." Ginger wiped her face with a tissue and blew her nose. "He wasn't making any money at the track—that's why he went out of town. He's doing some bingo thing in Atlanta."

Nina put her arm around Ginger. "Who's taking care of the girls?"

"My mother."

"Did you call Vito? Maybe he can help."

"He doesn't answer his phone." Ginger's hands trembled.

Nina pulled her chair closer. "Did you check with Maria? Maybe he's with her."

"She said he moved out two weeks ago. I've been going crazy ever since this happened."

"C'mon," Nina said as she led Ginger to the bedroom. "Vito left some Doriden. It's in the medicine cabinet. Take one, get in my bed, and go to sleep. I'll see what I can find out."

Nina drove to the Stop n' Go. She called Vito and reached his answering machine. She looked up the other indicted men's names in the newspaper and called their homes. The telephone numbers were disconnected. She hung up and dialed Frankie. His girlfriend answered.

"Eunice, is Frankie home?"

"Who's this?"

"It's me, Nina, Vito's ex. Do you know where Frankie is?"

"Why you wanna know?"

"This is important. Is Frankie in jail?"

"I dunno."

Nina hung up. *Why do I always end up in the middle of their problems?* As a last resort, she called Chance, but he was out of town. When she returned home, she found Ginger asleep.

A few minutes later, Nina received a pre-arranged telephone signal from Dutch. She checked her watch, wrote a note to Ginger, and drove to the parking lot behind her dentist's office. Dutch was waiting.

"Chance wants to see you," he said when Nina pulled into the space next to him.

"Is he in town to bail Frankie out of jail?"

"Sam Marin got him out two days ago. Chance didn't arrive until last night." Dutch put his car in gear. "Follow me."

Dutch parked in the rear of a large Italian restaurant on Biscayne Boulevard. The place did not open until four, so they entered through the kitchen. An old man with a mop stopped scrubbing when they came through the door. In the dining room, waiters and busboys were setting tables.

Chance sat alone in a dark corner of the bar. He stood and pulled out a chair for Nina. "I call my office. Deanie say you phone."

"Something terrible has happened." Nina started to talk about Danny and Ginger.

Chance touched his forefinger to his lips, and Dutch got up to play the jukebox.

Nina finished her story in motions and whispers. "I don't know what to do about it."

"Nothing *to* do." Chance assured her. "Danny turn himself in. Marin got him out. The guys spend a little time together—get story straight. Danny, he go home."

"But Ginger says they're broke. She can't even buy groceries. I know Danny pawned her engagement ring. How's she going to feed her family?"

"I not play nursemaid to every Italian in South Florida. I got Danny job. He gambled his pay."

Nina sighed and slouched in the chair.

Chance handed her a glass of room temperature Chianti wine. "Drink," he said. "Not to worry. This case take months, maybe years. I talk with Danny."

Nina relaxed her shoulders and sipped the red wine.

"Dutch say you do good job, but now time to move."

"What do you mean, move? The boys will be home soon." Nina looked distraught. Chance put a hand on her arm.

"Arrest of Frankie and Danny, Vito suspect in arson, nosey reporters, over-zealous crime commissioners, and now Calder Racetrack brings in FBI." He raised his hands. "Apartment vulnerable. I worry for you." Chance poured more wine into Nina's glass. "I have nice place, close to downtown Fort Lauderdale, right on New River. You be safe there."

Nina shook her head as she spoke. "The boys would need to change schools."

"Holy Trinity better school. I call the good father."

Nina frowned and shook her head. "The boys don't want to go to a parochial school. Besides, Anthony's counting on a football scholarship." Nina sipped her wine.

Chance gave her a paternal look. "I tell you job difficult. You agreed."

"I didn't agree to move."

Dutch came back from the bar carrying a glass of beer. He pulled out a chair and sat down.

"You must do what's best," Chance said, patting Nina's hand.

Nina looked at Dutch for support.

He shrugged.

"You forget why you took job?" Chance whispered.

Nina sighed, remembering the day the white car followed her. "I know you're right, but what am I supposed to do? The boys are going to put up a fuss."

"Make move now."

"What about my appointments?"

"Change them."

"I don't know how I'll get all that furniture moved. My brother's in Pennsylvania and I don't know anyone else who can help me."

Chance turned to Dutch. "Call that Move Anytime place. Send bill to me."

Dutch nodded. "That okay with you, Nina?"

"I guess if I have to move."

Chance smiled. "It be nice change for boys."

Nina rolled her eyes.

Nina went home and woke Ginger. "Danny's home."

"Those pills are really strong," Ginger said drowsily, stretched and rubbed her eyes.

"I hope you only took one."

"Maybe two." Ginger got out of bed. "I'll pick up the girls at my mom's after dinner. I want to see Danny. We need some time alone."

"See, things turned out all right. Danny will handle everything." Nina wanted to tell her friend about moving, but thought Ginger might say something to her husband. Then everyone would know.

The first thing Nina did after Ginger left was to phone her mother in Pennsylvania.

"Hi, Ma. Do you feel better today?"

"The same. Your father sits in his chair, doing nothing. I don't know his problem. He hardly ever works in the yard anymore."

"Maybe he's tired from working all these years. Let him rest a little."

"Rest? That's all he does."

"Look, I called to give you my new address. We're moving into a nice house. It's next to a river and has a boat dock."

"You're gonna buy a boat?"

"No, but it'll be nice to just sit on the dock and watch the boats go by."

"I got a pencil," her mother said.

Nina gave her the address. "I'll call you again when I get the new telephone number."

They said good-bye, and Nina thought a little more about her father. He was getting older, but not that old that he could not go out in the yard. *I need to go to Bentleyville.*

Nina called the apartment complex office to see if she could break her lease.

"I understand, Mrs. DiGregetti," the manager said, without any argument.

"You're paid through the end of the month. As long as you're out by then, there won't be any further charge."

At first she was stunned, but she thanked him and hung up. She was positive that the name on her lease clearly read Nina Cocolucci. *At least the name DiGregetti is good for something.*

Nina registered all three boys at Holy Trinity Catholic High School, and two weeks later she moved into the house Chance had picked out for them. The movers packed and marked most of the boxes, then deposited them in the proper rooms at the new place. They also set up the beds and placed the furniture.

After emptying the boxes marked "kitchen," Nina made a cup of Lipton tea. She looked around the big house, satisfied and even happy to be out of the small apartment. She took her tea and strolled down to the dock.

Nina watched the boats speed up and down the river until she remembered she had to go to the pharmacy before it closed. With peaceful thoughts still in her head, she drove to the drugstore. She picked up her prescription for a bladder infection that the doctor had found when she went in for her annual checkup. When she cleaned out her medicine chest, she had thrown most of the stuff away, so she picked up bandaids, q-tips, hydrogen peroxide, tape, a bottle of aspirin, and vasoline. Everything would be fresh and clean for the new and much bigger bathroom.

She was almost ready to leave when she saw Vito walk in the front door. Her heart surged as he walked toward her. She looked at the items in her cart and remembered how Vito had always been able to patch up the boys cuts and scratches, kiss the hurt away, and have them laughing in no time at all. But as soon as he opened his mouth, she knew he was not the Vito who had also kissed her tears away.

"Well, will look who's here. Miss Businesswoman herself. You moved," he said.

"Yes."

"Where to?"

Nina stalled. "To Fort Lauderdale."

"Got an address?"

"Yes."

"Well?"

"Well, I guess I'd better be going," she said.

He stepped in front of her. "If you expect me to send child support, you need to gimme an address."

"Support? Is that something new you've been thinking about?"

"What? I had financial problems. I got cash now." Vito glared at Nina.

"Sure," she finally said with resignation and handed him a business card.

"Elite Advertising? What the fuck is this?" He flicked his finger against the card.

"It's where I work. You can send the child support there."

"I'm not sending any money to a post office box. You think I'm stupid?"

She stifled a laugh. "It's the only address I give out."

"Well I'm not one of your customers. I happen to be the boys' father, and I'm entitled to know where they live. With all your education, you should know you can't get away with moving and not telling me." Vito's loud voice was causing a scene.

Nina paid for her purchases and started for the door.

"I'll call my attorney. You'll see which one of us is right and which one is wrong." Vito shouted.

Nina didn't look back.

"You just wait and see," His voice faded as the door to the pharmacy swung shut.

The summer whizzed by. Nina was very busy with work and so was Ginger, but they talked on the phone. Vito, true to his promise, did not send money. Still, Nina was happy. Mickey was bringing the boys home that day.

She drove to the airport early, excited to have her family back again. She sat waiting at the gate for her sons to arrive. Joey and Michael came through the door first. They both ran to her and gave her a hug and a kiss.

Redesigning the Mob

Mickey came huffing and puffing behind them. "Slow down," he said to the boys, before giving Nina a hug.

Anthony was a few steps behind. "I'm going to live with my dad." Anthony announced as soon as he got to his mother. "And I'm not changing schools."

"Have you talked to your father?"

"Not yet, but I will." Anthony walked ahead to baggage claim.

"Your dad moved out of Maria's apartment." Nina said, following her son. "I think he might be sleeping on the cot in the room behind his office." Nina hurried to keep up with Anthony's long strides. "Take a look at the new place before you make up your mind."

Anthony nodded as his mother spoke, but he stared straight ahead.

Nina glanced at Michael and Joey who were walking along beside her. She hoped they felt differently about the move than Anthony.

At home, Nina showed the newspaper to Anthony as he sat on his bed.

"I want you to read about the men who got indicted for fixing a horse race."

Even though he did not acknowledge her presence, Nina said, "And your dad might be drawn into court over the meat market fire. "It may be difficult for Michael and Joey to face the other kids. Changing schools might help."

Anthony remained tightlipped.

Nina shut her eyes for a moment to gather some strength. "You can visit your dad anytime you want, but he can't come to our house." Her voice held firm. "And I don't want you to give him our telephone number or this address."

Anthony tossed the paper aside, went to the window and stared at the river.

"Will you at least think about it?" Nina said walking to the doorway. "Please." She left him alone.

Nina was relieved to see that Michael and Joey were not upset about the move. They even accepted going to a Catholic high school. But Anthony moped around the house. He never brought any books home and did not talk about school, *until* he met Catherine. He was surprised to find out that she lived in the house next to his, but since each house along the river was built on three acres and sat behind heavy foliage, he had not seen her.

After a couple of months, Nina happily noticed that Anthony was spending more time on his homework, and she often found him reading.

Anthony came home late from school after football practice one day and tossed his geometry test onto the kitchen table. A big "B+" branded the top of the page.

Joey walked in without any books. He dribbled the basketball on the kitchen floor.

"Joey," Nina raised her eyebrows. "No homework tonight?"

Joey caught the ball in mid air. "I did it while I was waiting on Anthony to get done with practice."

"Nina picked up Anthony's paper, smiled and nodded. "See, the change has been good for you."

"Catherine helps me sometimes." Anthony dropped several books on the counter.

"Catherine and half a dozen other girls he lies to." Michael said coming into the kitchen and opening the refrigerator. He pulled out a can of Mountain Dew, opened it and took a swig.

"You're not cheating on your tests, are you?" Nina asked Anthony.

Anthony gave his mother an incredulous look. "In Catholic School? Those nuns walk up and down the aisles using a ruler like a medieval axe. If I even glance up while I'm taking a test, they raise the ruler."

Michael laughed. "The only reason he pays attention to Catherine is so she'll help him with his homework."

"I passed the test myself, and my grades are getting better every day," Anthony boasted. "*You* need to get a smarter girlfriend."

"I like Jennifer, even in that plaid uniform. I don't use her like you do Catherine, and I still made the honor roll," Michael snapped back.

Anthony glared defiantly at his brother. "By the time I get done with football practice there's not much time left to study. So what's wrong with combining my personal life with homework?"

Michael dropped his books on the kitchen table. "The only reason you're such a hotshot on the team is because Catholic schools don't play triple-A teams like public school."

"You're just jealous because girls like jocks."

Joey watched with amusement as his brothers insulted one another.

"Right, like I wish I smelled like a sweathog all day and got a kick out of pushing smaller guys around." Michael retorted.

Nina sighed and rubbed her forehead, "That's enough, guys."

"I get straight A's, and made first string center on the freshmen team, and I don't even like girls," Joey said proudly. "They always want you to carry their books."

"You're not old enough for girls." Anthony cuffed Joey on the arm.

Nina opened the refrigerator to see what she could make for dinner, and Michael and Anthony took off together with their tennis rackets.

Joey poured himself a glass of milk and turned to his mother. "If Dad was here, Michael and Anthony wouldn't get away with talking like that."

Nina gave Joey a hug. "You're probably right."

CHAPTER THIRTEEN

Wendell, who had been conned into signing on a mob owned construction loan, and Frankie drove to Miami to meet with Attorney Sam Marin. They waited in the reception area until Marin finished a phone call.

"Come in, Frankie, Wendell," Sam said from his office doorway. "I got your message. The papers are ready." Sam sat behind his desk and motioned to two chairs.

"The building's only eighty percent completed, and the Polack's already three months behind on his payments," Frankie told the attorney. "The note says if he gets over three months behind, the whole loan is due in full, or I own the place."

"True," Sam said, "but are you sure you want to foreclose? You're making a lot of interest on this loan."

"Damn right I do. I want the job shut down and the equipment locked up. I can lease that equipment for a ton of money, and I got men who can finish the job."

"Wendell has to sign the papers. You know that's prime property—the judge will be looking at this real close."

"It's all legit, ain't it?" Frankie said with a smirk.

"Yes, everything is legal, but it might raise some eyebrows about where Wendell got the cash to finance the deal in the first place."

"That's my business." Frankie snapped. "No judge is going to tell me how to spend my dough." Frankie lit a cigarette. "Anyway, it's your job to find a judge who knows how to play ball."

"You understand, Wendell, that if we encounter any problems, you will be the person the court will want to talk to."

"You don't need to worry about Wendell. I'll take care of everything," Frankie told Marin.

"This isn't a traffic violation," Marin said with obvious irritation.

"So, money buys favors."

"There are costs involved, including my fee. If you end up in court, it could cost you a bundle, even if you win."

"It's okay," Wendell said. "I'll do what I have to do."

"Be quiet, Wendell," Frankie said as he stepped between Wendell and Sam. "File the papers," Frankie told Sam, as he took a drag on his cigarette and exhaled the smoke in Sam's direction. "I'll see that ya get paid."

It didn't take long for Vito to worm Nina's new address and telephone number out of Joey, but it didn't help. The day that he tried to get through the security gate, he found that Nina had left strict orders not to let him in. Vito was furious and frustrated as he drove back to the office. Nothing seemed be going right. In fact, nothing had gone right since he left Nina.

Two days later, Chance sent a New York wiseguy to collect Vito's debt.

"I don't know why you're here. Barozzini knows I'm good for it." Vito said, his teeth clenched.

"Chance says you should talk to Frankie," the New Yorker said, leaving Vito's desk. "Run some credit cards. Get into something you can handle." He dropped his cigarette on the office floor and ground it out with the toe of his shiny shoe. "I'll be in touch."

Vito spent the next week ducking the wiseguy. It was only a matter of time before the collector would make his move again. Vito knew that the next time it might not be to give him a suggestion.

A desperate Vito decided to make a last-ditch effort. He met Frankie at a social club he had not frequented for some time.

Frankie came in the door and walked to the table where Vito sat waiting.

"Hey, goombah," Ernie the bartender called out to Frankie.

Frankie held up two fingers and Ernie brought double shots of Crown Royal, with ice and water on the side. The bartender stared at Vito.

Vito glared back. "What?"

"Pay the man," Frankie instructed as he lifted the shot glass and drank half of it. He followed it with a small amount of water.

"Pay? I didn't order this," Vito retorted.

"You ask *me* to meet, and you don't pay?" Frankie's remark sounded more like a threat than a question.

Vito reached into his almost empty pocket and found some money. "How in the hell do ya drink that stuff straight?" He poured his shot over the glass of ice and added a little water.

When the bartender went back behind the bar, Frankie said, "So how do you plan to pay for the plastic?"

"I'll get the money." Vito shifted in his chair.

Frankie laid the front section of the morning paper on the table. "Fixing horse races didn't make the front page today. We're not popular anymore." He laughed and the scar on his cheek danced. "It'll cost you fifteen hundred apiece."

"For what? We help each other out." Vito opened and closed a pack of matches with one hand, leaving a fresh match sticking on the outside. "I want two."

"You got three large?" Frankie's barrel chest pressed against the table as he turned to the sport pages of the *Miami Herald*.

"Three grand? We had a deal. I took care of your problem, and now you got your house rented to someone else."

Frankie shrugged. "It was your idea to put Nina and the kids out."

Vito narrowed his eyes. "How'd you like Chance to know you got drunk and let the redhead know his business?" Vito knew Frankie was Chance's snitch, and Vito hated Frankie's holier-than-thou *Calabrese* attitude. They had pulled a few jobs together, and Frankie was as cutthroat as any *Sicilian*, but now he, Vito had the upper hand. He sipped the whiskey and waited for Frankie to squirm.

Redesigning the Mob

Frankie shrugged, faking no reaction.

"You did a sloppy job," Vito sneered. "Who else could you trust to get rid of the mess?"

Frankie's expression still did not change. "I can let you have them for—"

Vito's thumb slid the match across the phosphorus and a bright flame burst. Frankie scrambled from the table. "You're gonna set the whole damn place on fire," he said nervously.

"Cost, that's all I pay." Vito grinned and lit his cigarette.

Frankie sat back down. He folded the paper and swirled the rest of the liquor into the melting ice cubes.

Vito had used stolen plastic before, but only for personal use and in places he knew cooperated with the mob. He hated peddling stolen property. "I wouldn't do this if I knew another way. Too many people involved. Too easy to get caught."

"You can make a lot of money, fast, if you do it right," Frankie said downing the last of his drink, and getting up to leave. "Cost," he said without any emotion. "Let me know when you get the cash."

"Sure." Vito smirked, but his stomach sent a wave of nausea to his throat. He pushed the rest of his drink aside and hastily left the Italian social club.

Vito realized he should never drink on an empty stomach. He drove to the IHOP that he and Nina used to go to before the divorce..

Gray, Nina and Ginger's usual waitress, was on duty. "Good to see you again, Mr. DiGregetti," she said as she poured his coffee.

He nodded. "I'll have the breakfast special, over easy, with crisp bacon."

As Gray picked up the menu and went off to the kitchen, Vito glanced around the restaurant with a faraway look in his eyes. It reminded him of the late nights he had spent here with Nina. He pictured her smile, and the way she gave him all her attention. His eyes misted.

Gray came by to warm his coffee and his memories vanished. When she returned to the counter, his gaze followed her legs. He had often thought about making a pass at her, but she never stayed around his table long enough for him to talk to her.

As the weeks went by, Vito lost more of his customers and money got even tighter.

"Mustache, come in here a minute," Vito called from the back room of his office on a swelteringly hot and humid afternoon. Paulie entered his boss's office with a questioning look.

A city map spread across a six-foot table. "These red crosses are the stores still under our protection," Vito said. Each mark was accompanied by a collection date.

Paulie leaned over the map. "Yep, looks about right."

"It don't *look* about right. It *is* right. I worked on it all night," Vito barked.

Paulie shifted the toothpick between his teeth.

"The bulldog seems more interested in the grocery stores, so I've changed the schedule." Vito pointed to several of the red marks. "We'll hit the food stores two weeks early. The Morello brothers will take Speedo Grocery on Monday morning." He traced his finger along the map. "Gonzalez can make a run on the North Miami Jew Market. He can catch old man Stein when he's ready to skip out to the bank before two o'clock."

"Sounds like a plan." Paulie continued to survey the map.

"You can ride with me. We'll park a couple of blocks away. The brothers pass the cash to us and we move on to meet The Spic."

"What about Julio's Cigar Store?" Paulie asked. "Julio's don't have any red mark, and it's time to make their pickup."

"Yeah, you go see Julio. Barozzini don't know about him. That's pocket money." Vito folded the map and locked it in his file cabinet. "I'll meet you back here late Monday afternoon. If all goes well for a few weeks, we'll be back in Fat City."

Times were not so good for Dutch. Vito had hired new men, and they began to drop in on the accounts he had lost. Nina received three anxious messages from customers before Chance sent two new guys from Providence, Rhode Island, to give Dutch a hand. One was tall and one was short, so Dutch dubbed them Mutt and Jeff, but Paulie, Dutch's newest recruit, remained his best weapon.

On a Monday morning, the guys from Providence waited in a service station behind Speedo's. Dutch went inside to talk to Ronald Walker, the owner of the store. A few minutes later, the Morello brothers eased inside the delivery entrance of the grocery store.

Dutch came out of a dark corner. "Customers are supposed to use the front door," he said from behind the intruders.

Gus, the older Morello, turned his attention away from Walker. "What the fuck—?" Gus reached in his belt.

Dutch grabbed Gus's wrist with his left hand and busted him in the jaw with his right fist, then slammed the arm across an iron railing. Bone cracked and Gus screamed. A gun spun across the floor. Dutch let the limp arm fall, and drove his fist into the man's lower ribs. Morello dropped to his knees.

The shaking store owner picked up the gun and pointed it at the open mouthed younger brother who reached for the piece holstered to his ankle. Ron Walker fired, barely missing Mutt and Jeff coming in the back door. The kid flinched and Dutch slammed him against the wall.

"Get up and get outta here," Dutch said as he kicked the older Morello in the ass. "Take this kid with you and don't come back."

The kid looked toward the handgun still strapped to his leg.

"Choose the door or suffer the consequences," Mutt yelled as he motioned toward the exit with his revolver.

Vito's gunman left with the help of his kid brother.

Walker dropped the gun on a table and shooed his employees away from the office door. "Show's over. Go back to work."

Vito lowered the window of his Cadillac and saw blood on Gus Morello's face. "What the hell happened?"

"You sent us into a trap. We ran into the fat guy you told us about. He was waiting for us. We didn't have a chance," Gus said as the blood seeped from his swollen mouth.

"They couldn't have known. I changed the schedule."

"Two shooters came in right behind us," the younger brother said. "We know an ambush when we see one."

Gus winced and held his arm. "I don't need this kind of action. I'm going to the emergency room."

Vito shot him a panicky look. "Are you outta your mind? The feds will be all over you. Go see Doc Fields. He'll set your arm with no questions."

The kid got out of the car. "What about our money?"

"After you get fixed up, come see me at the office." Vito put his car in gear.

"What's wrong with right now?" the young man said as he hurried toward Vito's slow-moving car. The window was already rolled up. The Cadillac swung onto the highway and headed south. Vito wanted to put as much distance between himself and the Morello brothers as he could. He needed to get to Gonzalez before the mouthy brothers started spreading the bad news.

Vito found Gonzalez leaning against a newsstand drinking Cuban coffee. Vito stopped his car at the curb and motioned for the Cuban to get in. Gonzalez drained his cup and studied the crowd before he stepped off the sidewalk and into the Cadillac. Vito immediately pulled into traffic.

"I figured you'd get here early," Vito said as he closed the dark tinted window. "I told you before; it's not good to hang around before or after a pickup."

"I check things out. I don't walk in blind," Gonzalez said defensively.

"He's an old man." Vito stopped for a red light.

"How'd the Morello brothers do today?" Gonzalez asked.

"They were in and out in five minutes. It's a one-man job. I only keep the kid around because I knew his old man."

Gonzalez looked sideways at Vito. "Word on the street says the Chicago mob's on its way in."

Vito glared at the Cuban. "Guess you don't need the money. If you're chicken shit, I'll handle it myself."

"I'll do the job," Gonzalez said.

"Where's your car?"

"I left it across the park. I take my dress shirt off when I leave and wear my undershirt. That way I look like a jogger."

Vito laughed sarcastically. "So you're a jogger in black dress shoes? No wonder the Chicago mob thinks they can take over. I got myself a bunch of pansy-ass queers." Vito stopped around the corner from Gonzalez's car. "Stay out of sight until one o'clock. I'll call you tomorrow and let you know where to meet me."

Gonzalez got out of the car without saying a word. Vito knew the Cuban would not listen to him. He thought maybe he was getting soft, letting people off too easy. In the old days, he was mean, and everyone did as they were told. He had to set the record straight if he wanted to stay in business.

CHAPTER FOURTEEN

Nina decided she was tired of her car and very tired of shifting gears. She opted for a used MonteCarlo with an automatic transmission and blue interior—a low mileage sports coupe unexposed to cigarette smoke. It was nice to have a car without a clutch. She never realized how many plain white cars there were until she came out of the drugstore a day after she bought the car and could not remember where she parked.

Michael, who was not yet sixteen, but had his learner's permit, begged his mother every day to let him practice. It would not be long before he would be driving the Mustang full time, he told her. Nina was not crazy about the idea, but Jennifer already had her driver's license, and when Michael pled, Nina let them take the Mustang to the roller skating rink.

On the second Saturday in October, the backyard of Nina's river house was festooned with balloons and crepe paper streamers. Anthony had turned eighteen on Thursday, and tonight he and his friends were celebrating his birthday with a catered luau and a three-piece band.

Nina said no alcohol, but one girl hid a half-pint of vodka in her purse. Mickey spotted it right off, but he ignored the situation since twenty kids were attempting to share it. He kept an eye out to make sure no more booze surfaced.

Lush trees grew along the river's edge, and no one seemed to miss the few couples who went for a walk and did not return for a while.

Nina was grateful that Anthony had not been one of them. He showed off by placing leis around the girls' necks and giving each of them a kiss. He also let the Hawaiian dancer put a sarong around his hips while she attempted to teach him the hula. All the girls applauded. The boys rolled their eyes and went off to toss a football.

Occasionally, Anthony left the group saying he had to check on the food, or the band, or whatever. It was an excuse he used to make the rounds, talking to each girl separately. "I'm sorry I can't spend more time with you," he would tell them. "We'll talk next week."

Part of the football team resented Anthony showing up at Holy Trinity for his senior year and his ability to make the first string, so only a few of his teammates come to the party. A shortage of boys put fourteen-year-old Joey in demand, and he appeared to be enjoying it. Michael, who stood taller than most of the seniors, attracted a bevy of girls all night.

Nina paced every time Mickey came inside the house to watch television.

"You think anything's going on out there?" she asked.

Mickey propped his feet up on a hassock. "You worry too much."

"Why don't you check on the food? That way, they'll think twice."

"About what?" Mickey turned on the eleven o'clock news.

"You know." Nina went to the kitchen and put on a fresh pot of coffee. She did not want to fall asleep until every kid had gone home.

Mickey eased his tired body from the chair and slid his feet into flip-flops. He walked outside to the smoldering fire and see if he could find some left over chicken *hekka* or shrimp *ono nui*.

Two Hawaiian women in sarongs and the Polynesian fire-eater were packing everything in their van. "They ate all the food," one of the women said. "We're ready to leave."

The fire-eater doused the last of the hot embers.

Mickey handed him Nina's check. "Need any help?"

"Nah," he answered. "Here's the bucket we borrowed."

Mickey carried the empty bucket and sauntered toward the band, which played to an empty backyard. "It's time to go home," he shouted into the bass player's ear. "They're getting a little too cozy down there on the dock. You guys can cut out."

The musician nodded to the leader, and they swung into a short version of *Goodnight, Sweetheart.*

Mickey turned the five-gallon bucket upside down in the middle of the yard and sat on it. Soon everyone left. Anthony walked Catherine home, and Michael and Joey went to bed. Mickey came inside again and plopped down on the couch. The TV was still on, tuned to the Johnny Carson Show. Nina brought him a beer and sat on the couch.

"So how's the business coming along?" Mickey asked.

"Elite Advertising has made a name for itself." Nina lowered the volume on the TV.

"Is that good or bad?"

"Really, I've done better than I expected. In addition to Vito's customers, I do business with companies outside the protection racket. I've had to hire two full-time girls to help Margo in customer service and three art students from the university are working part time."

"That's good. When the Mafia contracts end, you should think about getting out of the protection racket and only dealing with legitimate contracts."

"All my contracts are legal."

"You know what I mean. Get away from the mob, before you end up like Vito." Mickey tilted the bottle and took a long drink. "I can't believe you haven't heard from him. It would take an idiot to not know what's going on." He burped.

"Mickey, no wonder you don't have a steady."

"I can get a girlfriend. I just don't want one."

"I think Vito's involved with someone new—he hardly ever calls."

"Is that right?" Mickey got up from the couch as if he was ready to leave.

"Maybe he knows I'm the one taking over his business and he doesn't care. Letting me have the business could be his way of paying child support."

"Now who's the idiot?" Mickey picked up his beer bottle and drained the last swallow. "He's the same scaly snake he's always been. When the time's right, he'll strike."

Nina shrugged. "I don't know if he will or not."

"Don't let your guard down. I don't trust him."

"I don't think the boys think so much of him anymore," Nina said as she walked Mickey to the door. "They know their dad isn't sending support, and they've stopped asking, 'Did Dad call?'"

Mickey gave her a hug.

"Thanks for always being here," Nina said and kissed him on the cheek.

CHAPTER FIFTEEN

Vito mulled over the loss of his business. *If Chance lost this much cash flow to the Chicago mob, there'd be blood in the streets, and I'd have gotten more than a slap on the hand.*

"Something stinks," he muttered to himself, then entered the IHOP where Frankie was waiting for him.

"You talk to Chance?" Vito's lips curled into a crooked sneer as he slid into the booth across from Frankie.

Frankie shook his head. "I haven't seen him." He fiddled with the salt shaker.

"That's a buncha crap. Like you didn't know he came to see me last week."

"How would I know? I mind my own business."

"You bring the cards?" Vito motioned to Gray for coffee.

"You think I drove over here for coffee?" Frankie grumbled. "You got cash?"

"I got the bread." Vito stirred two heaping teaspoons of sugar into his mug of coffee.

Frankie handed Vito a small booklet of credit card numbers. "This is a new printout. It comes out every two weeks. Cards are good for at least a week, sometimes two."

"I done this long before you came along." Vito brushed away Frankie's information with a flick of his hand. "Get on with it."

"Yeah, well, don't drive your own car when you use them. Never know when something might happen. Use a rental car in case you have to ditch it." Frankie reached inside his jacket and pulled out a small white envelope. It held two MasterCards and blank New York driver's licenses. "Use alcohol to take the signatures off the cards and re-sign them."

"What for? I can copy anyone's writing. I'm good at it."

Frankie pulled the envelope back. "You get caught using a stolen card, that's one charge. You get caught for forgery, that's something else."

"Yeah, yeah." Vito reached for the envelope.

"Gimme the money first."

"You don't trust me?" He slipped Frankie the folded bills.

"Get yourself a honey to work the cards. You go along as pickup man."

Vito stood. *They think they shoved me out, but this plastic is only temporary. I'll get back what I lost plus a whole lot more.* He left the building muttering, "I'm a DiGregetti. My old man has connections. If Chance gave my territory to someone else that someone's gonna see where the alligators live."

A man and woman stared at him as he passed them.

He glared back. "What?" He shoved his hands in his pocket and felt the credit cards. *All I need is the money to make it happen. No one pushes me out. Not even Barozzini.*

Frostiness hovered around Maria when Vito stopped by her apartment and tried to ingratiate himself with her. She pushed him away when he tried to kiss her.

"C'mon, get dressed," Vito said as he changed the TV channel and flopped on the sofa. "I'll wait. We'll go someplace nice. Anywhere you want."

"People have been calling here for you."

"So what?"

"So, you make me look like a fool."

"C'mere."

Maria stood with her hands on her hips.

He smiled, his eyelids half closed, his head tilted to one side. He ran his tongue along his upper lip.

Maria slipped onto the sofa beside him.

He wrapped his arm around her and nuzzled her ear. "I missed you, baby." He cradled her chin in his hand and turned her head until her lips met his. He surprised her with a soft kiss, but he cringed when she fluttered her eyelashes against his cheek. "Put on that black, low-cut dress. We'll hit the town."

In the morning, Vito dressed in blue linen slacks and a white short-sleeved shirt. He drove to the beach where a few women he knew hung out on Sundays while their kids played in the sand.

He unbuttoned his shirt, put on dark glasses, and strolled along the boardwalk. He spotted Alice, a girl he used to party with when he and Nina were still married.

Vito sat next to her at a sidewalk table and motioned to the bikini-clad waitress. He scooted his chair under the small circle of shade made by a big umbrella. "Bring us a couple of drafts and get something for the kid."

It was easy for him to make a deal with Alice. Frankie had mentioned she was not working and did not get child support. With Christmas not far off, the young divorcée was easy to convince.

"I'll meet you Tuesday morning." He stood and patted Alice's little girl on the head. She poured lemonade on his sandals. He clenched his teeth and gave her an Archie Bunker smile.

Vito stopped at a pay phone and called Gonzalez. His father, Romero, answered the phone.

"Where's the *Chico*?" Vito asked.

"He's in the bed. He work airport last night."

"Get him up. Tell him I'll meet him at the Greek's in an hour."

Vito drove to the Mediterranean Café and tapped on the open office door. "Hey."

Vito could hardly see Thesy, the owner of the Greek restaurant. He sat behind a desk piled high with paper and had a phone in each hand.

"C'mon in." Thesy used one of the phones to point at a chair stacked with magazines. "Shove 'em on the floor," he told Vito.

Thesy spoke into the other phone. "So what's the book?" He took a pencil from behind his ear and scratched on a large pad. "I'll call ya back." He hung up and spoke into the other phone. "It's five to one and bring cash." He looked at Vito. "These guys, they think I'm a branch of the First National Bank." He hung up the phone. "What *do you* need?"

"The loan of your office to make a few calls. I moved out of downtown, and my new place ain't set up yet."

"Sure, I gotta check the kitchen anyway," Thesy said. "Don't make any long distance, or I'll be on your ass like a wasp on flypaper."

Vito tried to reach the Morello brothers but their phone was disconnected. *Good riddance. Why pay someone to do something I can do better myself?*

Charlie answered *his* phone, so Vito said, "You know who this is?" Charlie said he did, and Vito asked, "You got information for me?"

Charlie stammered "She—she works for Elite Advertising."

"Tell me something I don't know."

"That's all I could find out," Charlie said.

"You kikes are useless."

Vito made his next call to Maria. He needed someone to make his day better, but she whined when he said he could not take her out to dinner. To shut her up, he told her he would come by her place in an hour.

Gonzalez stuck his head in the doorway. "Busy?"

Vito motioned him inside. "So, what's the story?" The look on Gonzalez's face told Vito the Cuban had not collected any money.

"I stayed out of sight, like you told me to. Found me a window seat in Havana Canteen across the street from the market. I'm eatin' a bean burrito and watchin' the place."

"I don't give a damn what you ate." Vito snapped and opened yesterday's newspaper to the crossword puzzle. He pulled out a pen from his pocket. "Tell me what happened."

"Around noon I see this Pontiac pull in. Three guys get out. They look up and down the street." Gonzalez's turns his head back and forth. "Two go in the front and one goes in the back."

"The old man has lots of friends." Vito filled in a couple of empty spaces of the brain teaser.

"I wait two hours. Nobody takes that long to shop. Pretty soon all three come from the back of the store and get in the car—one fat dude, well over two-hundred pounds, and two guys wearing oversize jackets in the middle of a ninety-five degree day."

Vito began to pay attention. "You got jumpy because they used the backdoor, and wore jackets? It could have been anyone." He pretended to fill in the spaces of the puzzle. "I should have made the collection myself."

Gonzalez leaned forward. "Unless I miss my guess, you woulda walked into a nest of rattlesnakes. They left in the rented GrandAm. So I go to a phone and call the place. I asked for the owner. The girl says he's off sick today."

"Hm." Vito pushed his scribbling aside. *I might of missed my chance to blow that asshole Dutchman away.*

"I got more bad news." Gonzalez looked at the floor. "They found Stanley. He was shot." The Cuban pointed to his forehead. "Right in the middle. A guy in an airboat found him in the Everglades. I hear he had a dog collar around his neck. You didn't have Stanley kill the Donovan's dogs, did you?"

Vito turned gray as cement. "Nah, I liked the kid. You know I wouldn't do that. Besides, you couldn't trust him, he was half nuts." Vito opened a new pack of cigarettes. "Who told you about Stanley?"

"The barmaid at Shorty's, but it's already on TV."

When Gonzalez left, Vito drove to his office in Miami. He had promised to pay the rent today. He waited in the coffee shop across the street until he saw the landlord leave. He spent the rest of the afternoon emptying out his office. He tossed most of the junk in the Dumpster and packed the Cadillac with his briefcase, a box of toiletries he kept in the bathroom, a few office supplies, and pictures of the boys. He heaved his small safe onto the seat of the rolling chair, and pushed it to the elevator, and out to his car. The chair didn't belong to him, but once he got it outside, he decided to put it in the trunk with the rest of his stuff.

He called the landlord. When his answering service picked up the call, he told the woman, "This here's your boss's lucky day. Tell 'em Vito

DiGregetti called, and my office is available for a new tenant." Vito was three months behind on the rent. He did not bother to have his phone shut off. The notice he had received in the mail said the telephone company was disconnecting it tomorrow anyway.

Vito drove to Maria's, but he left his clothes and office supplies in the car.

Maria was happy to see him. "I made your favorite for dinner," she said as she poured the wine at the glass- topped table in the dining area.

"Looks good." He kissed her on the cheek and pulled out her chair. "I've been thinking about us. You're right, we belong together."

"I'm glad you came back."

"I gave up the office and put a deposit on an apartment, but I'd rather live here." he said. "I want to be close to you."

Maria's eyes glowed in the candlelight.

"This here's a nice apartment, but if we're going to live together we need a bigger place. I need a room to use for an office."

"Live together?" Maria's voice rose.

"I mean until we can make it permanent." Vito set his half-eaten salad aside.

She smiled and passed the veal *piccata*.

"I'll be out of town for a few days. I got a business deal in Orlando. While I'm gone, you look for a nice out-of-the-way house. When I get back, we'll move and get an unpublished number so nobody bothers us."

She stood to refill his wine glass. "How's the veal?"

"Fan-tastic, just the way I like it." He blew her a kiss.

Vito waited inside his friend's two-car garage. When his friend, Benny, saw Alice's car turn the corner and head down the tree-lined driveway, he pressed the button on the garage door opener. She drove inside. Alice removed the price tags and store names from the hot merchandise and Vito packed the items in his trunk. When all the swag was transferred to Vito's Cadillac, he gave Alice and Benny their cut.

"Same place, same time, tomorrow," Vito said and backed his car out of the garage.

On the way home, he stopped at an Italian meat market. A red and green beret sat on top of the butcher's dark hair. He rang a little bell and several men in white aprons appeared from the back room.

"Cut me a couple of two-inch tenderloins," Vito said.

The meat cutter wrapped them in white paper and placed them on the counter. The men watched every move Vito made.

"What?" Vito glared at the butchers. "You think because I lose a little no-nothing business like this, I wouldn't still buy my meat here? Unlike some dagos, I'm a loyal Sicilian customer. I believe in honor." He picked up the steaks. "Gimme a thin slice of *prosciutto*. I need a snack for the ride home."

Vito waited impatiently in line for his turn to pay at the checkout. He reached to the far side of the counter to get a box of chocolate covered cherries for Maria and blinked. An Elite Advertising business card was taped to the side of the cash register. He ripped it off and put it in his pocket.

Vito left the market and drove past a few of the places that used to be under his protection. By the look of the crowded parking lots, they were all busier than usual. Storefronts were newly painted and similar colored signs offering specials were mounted on the plate glass windows. Even the parking lot of the lousy Bar-B-Q takeout was filled.

They said they didn't make enough to pay me, but now they pay the bulldog, and have money left over to fix up the place. I treated them good, and they lied to me. Being nice never pays.

Vito arrived at Maria's apartment before she got home from work. He went into the bedroom and searched his jacket until he found Nina's card. The exact same card he took from the meat market. He stared at the print, checked his watch, and dialed the 800 number.

"Elite Advertising. May I help you?" Margo said.

"I wanna talk to Nina Cocolucci."

"I'm sorry, she doesn't work in this office," the woman answered. "May I give her a message?"

"Gimme a number where I can reach her."

"We don't give out that information, but if you leave your name and number, she'll return your call."

"What's your address?" he asked.

"You can reach us at post office box—"

"Tell me how to get to the place."

"We don't give out our location—all business is transacted by phone or mail. If you give me your name or account number, maybe I can help you."

"I doubt it." Vito slammed down the receiver, leaned back in the chair, and waited another ten minutes for Maria. She parked her black Lincoln in her parking space and hurried into the apartment.

"In here, sweetie," Vito called.

She came into the kitchen, plopped on his lap, and gave him a juicy kiss. He turned his head and wiped his mouth with the back of his hand.

"Were you able to find a little out-of-the-way place we can rent?" He pulled her close.

She nodded. "You're going to love it," she whispered. "It's west of the city, in a quiet area."

"Sounds good already." He began to nuzzle her neck.

She pushed him away. "Wait until I tell you about the house. It's a quaint two-bedroom bungalow with a high redwood fence that goes all the way around the property. It's not fancy, but it has two old ficus trees in the front yard, so the house is almost invisible from the road."

"You did good, babe. When can we move in?"

"Two weeks. I've already made arrangements to take off work."

He held her close, but instead of making love, he said, "I want you to do me a favor." He kissed the tip of her nose. "Call this business number and pretend you're Nina. I'll tell you what to say."

Maria hopped off his lap. "You haven't heard a word I said."

"Yes, I have. Don't get all upset." He grabbed at her, then caught himself and eased her into his arms. "Lemme explain." He kissed her long and hard. "This is business information I need, so that we can get a good start together. Okay?"

She nodded and squeezed him tight.

He picked one of the more vulnerable businesses. "I want you to keep your voice low and soft. Talk nice like you do at work."

She stuck out her tongue when Vito picked up the livingroom extension to listen to her conversation.

"Golden Dragon, Hung speaking."

"This is Nina Cocolucci, Mr. Nguyen. Did you receive the advertising layouts I sent to you?" Maria asked.

"Yes, ma'am, you do good job. I tell you yesterday. I by myself, have many customers. I must go now."

Maria hung up. "Are you satisfied?"

"Wait a minute." Vito dialed two more telephone numbers of businesses he had lost. When Maria spoke to them, they both knew Nina quite well.

"I knew she was working for an advertising company, but I didn't know about the connection to my business." He shook his head. "So, Nina works for the bulldog." He made a mental note to get his detective friend, Slimy Sam, to put a tail on Nina.

Maria turned sarcastic. "If you're so interested in what your darling Nina's doing, why don't you call *her*?"

"This is business."

Maria threw the wastebasket at him. "Take your shit and leave."

"You're upset over nothing." Vito seethed inside, but he needed a place to sleep. "I brought you something." He held up the box of chocolates.

She grinned and reached for it.

He ran his hand under her short skirt and up her thigh. "You're some hot woman."

She pushed her leg against him. Red silk panties fluttered to the floor.

CHAPTER SIXTEEN

Nina arrived at her Elite Advertising office late in the day. Each time she went there she took a different route and checked her rearview mirror to see if anyone had followed her. She had begun to see how much her life now resembled Vito's, but with all the new business not connected to the protection racket, she had to make even more trips into town to oversee designs.

Margo followed Nina into her office. She closed the door and whispered. "I got a strange call today."

Nina was used to Margo's dramatics. "Who was it this time?"

"The man didn't give his name. He said he wanted to talk to you. He slammed the phone in my ear when I refused to give him the actual office address."

"Maybe one of our customers has a problem."

Margo frowned. "I'd have recognized a *client's* voice."

"He could've been a referral," Nina said. "People like to know who they're doing business with. Maybe he'll call back." She swallowed hard, thinking it could have been Vito, but kept her composure. She did not want to frighten Margo.

Nina checked the ads and designs, and left. She had always parked her car in a large garage a block away and cut through two other office buildings to get to her office. Inside the second building, she stopped to use the pay phone to signal Dutch. They met an hour later at a coffee shop.

"So, what do you think?" Nina asked after telling Dutch about the mysterious call. "I don't wanna jump to a conclusion, but Vito's man didn't show up to make a collection at the Jewish market. He could be getting wise." Dutch did not want to tell her how they found The Squirrel, but figured she would see it later on the news anyway.

"You think Vito killed that guy they found in the Everglades, don't you?"

"He had a motive." Dutch shuffled his feet.

"The Donovan brothers had a motive. Maybe they did it," Nina said.

"Or someone made it look like the Donovan brothers."

"I know you don't like Vito. I was blind to stay with him for as long as I did, but I still can't see him killing men or dogs."

Dutch grunted. "Frankie says Vito's got a girl running credit cards for him, and he treats her rough. Frankie warned him to be careful, but he's too busy being a hotshot." Dutch got up to leave.

Nina picked up her purse and joined him. "Treating someone rough and killing is two different things. Besides, maybe Vito doesn't have time to harass me now that he's making so much money. He talks nice if I answer the phone when he calls the boys. Don't you think if he knew something, he'd come after me, or at least scream at me?"

"Who knows what that man thinks? Watch your step." Dutch held the door open for Nina. "Get in touch with me if anything happens. Ralph is always at the apartment, and he knows your signal and I make sure he knows where to reach me."

"What would he do without you?" Nina smiled.

"He might be in a wheelchair, but he gets around the house with no trouble. Actually, I don't know what I would do without him."

When Nina arrived at the gate to the river house, the guard came out. He was a quiet man, dressed in a sharply pressed blue uniform, and all business.

"A nice looking man around forty-five or fifty came here today. When I asked his name, he told me James Wilson." The guard held out his clipboard. "He had identification, but Wilson's not on your list."

"Did he have black hair and drive a white Cadillac?" Nina asked.

"Black hair, but he drove a black Lincoln."

Maria's. "That's his girlfriend's car." She pulled a picture of Vito from her wallet. Is this the man?" she asked.

The guard nodded. "I believe so."

"He's my ex. I don't make appointments at my house. Please don't let anyone in under any condition, especially my ex-husband."

"We'll do our best. Would you like to leave the picture so I can show it to the men who work security?"

"Sure. I appreciate your help."

He tipped his hat and Nina drove past the black iron gate.

A month had passed since the mysterious phone call, and Nina had managed to forget about it. She drove to her office, parked her car on the third floor of the parking garage and walked toward the elevator. Vito stepped out from behind a square column. He cupped his hand over her mouth and pulled her behind the pillar. Her purse and briefcase fell to the cement floor.

"You fuckin' bitch. You think I'd let you make a fool outta me?"

She struggled, but her arm was bent behind her, and his hip pinned her against the post.

"I'm taking my hand away. Scream if you want. I'd like nothing better than an excuse to knock your teeth out." Vito took his hand from her mouth and lessened his grip.

She turned toward the man she had once loved and cried over.

Vito sneered at her. "You call Chance and complain about your big bad husband?" His nails dug into her arm. "Whose bed you sleeping in now?"

Nina stifled a gasp, knowing from the past that even the slightest sound, whether defiant or submissive, could cause instant rage and a possible beating. Tires squealed as a car looped up the circular ramp from the lower deck.

Vito released his grip and gave her briefcase a swift kick. Sketches scattered across the garage floor. He picked one up and flung it at her. "Quit this friggin' job and go back to Bentleyville before the boys end up without a mother."

Without another word, he disappeared between the parked cars. Nina stooped down to gather up her designs. As a car passed by she smiled as if she had simply dropped the briefcase, but her hands were shaking, and she could barely pick up the papers.

For two weeks, Nina tried to put the encounter with Vito behind her, but this time she could not. She had bad dreams, woke up at night in a cold sweat, and was frantic with fear each time she left her house. She met Dutch at the coffee shop and told him about Vito's threat.

"I knew this was going to happen. I just didn't know when." Dutch shook his head. "If I make a point of threatening him, I'll blow your cover, besides if he really wanted to hurt you, I think he'd of done it right then. You need to pay more attention to your surroundings—and watch where you're going."

Nina sat her coffee mug down hard. "What do you want me to do, carry a gun?"

"Wouldn't be a bad idea."

"Great." Nina could barely control herself. "He smacks me, I shoot him and go to jail. Then who takes care of my children?"

"You want to file a harassment charge against him?"

"Oh, you are funny. I guess I should go make my funeral arrangements first." Anger made Nina's face flush.

Dutch shrugged.

"You think I should call Chance?" she asked.

"That might just set him off. Remember how furious he got when you told him Chance told you to talk to Sam Marin."

Nina gaped "You knew about that?"

Dutch laughed. "Bad news travels fast in the mob."

Nina sipped her coffee. "Short of moving to Bentleyville, there's nothing I can do. I guess I've always known that. Maybe that's why I stayed married so long."

For more than a month, Nina kept her terror bottled up inside. Then right after Thanksgiving, she tried to reach Ginger. She needed to talk to someone. She had been leaving messages, but Ginger had not returned her calls.

This time her friend's mother, Josephine, answered the phone. "She's not home. I'm watching the kids."

"Did she get my messages?"

"Yes, but Ginger has a job at Jordon Marsh and most of the time she's not here."

"Isn't Danny working?" Nina asked.

"He doesn't come around anymore," Josephine hissed. "I think she's too embarrassed to call you, since she stayed friends with Vito after you got a divorce."

"She didn't have a choice," Nina said. "Danny and Vito are old friends."

"Ginger always pretended Danny didn't fool around with other women like your husband. I don't know where that girl's brain is." Josephine sighed. "Even when he stopped coming home at night, she still made excuses for him. I thought I raised her better than that."

"She loves him, and the girls love their father. What else could she do?"

Josephine grunted. "I don't know why they all love him so much. He never does a damn thing for them."

"Taking care of five is a big job," Nina said. "You must be tired by the end of the day."

"I don't mind taking care of *my* grandchildren, but Ginger let this woman, Thelma, move in. She has three kids, and she shares the bedroom with Ginger. They put the crib for Thelma's new baby in the room with them."

Josephine must have put her hand over the receiver, but Nina still heard the muffled yell.

"Stop running through the house." Ginger's mother never missed a beat. "Thelma's twins share a room with two of Ginger's girls. They have two sets of bunk beds in one room."

"Thelma's a nice person," Nina said. "Her husband Wendell is an electrician."

"Humph! I didn't know she had a husband."

"What time does Ginger get home?" Nina checked her watch. "I'll call back."

"She won't come to the phone."

Nina thought for a moment. "What time do you expect her home?"

"A little after five, if she gets out on time."

"Don't tell her I called. I'll just show up. I won't tell her we talked."

"Thanks, Nina. She misses you."

When Nina arrived, all the kids sat in an assortment of odd chairs at the kitchen table.

"Pull up a chair and have some escarole soup," Josephine said as she fussed over the table, placing spoons and pouring milk. "Thelma left for work and Ginger's not home yet."

"You go ahead and eat. I'll wait here." Nina set her purse on the couch.

"No, no." Josephine scooted another chair up to the big table and filled another bowl. "There's plenty."

"It smells delicious," Nina said.

The girls complained about each other until Josephine took a fly swatter and hit the counter.

"You kids be quiet before you wake Thelma's baby, or one of you is going to have to stop eating and rock her back to sleep." Josephine eyed the oldest girls.

Nina grinned. Ginger's oldest, Dana, hunched down and ate her soup. Ginger's youngest banged the spoon on the tray of her highchair and shrilled one long note like an opera singer.

Nina pulled the baby's highchair close to her. "I'll feed her."

Josephine handed Nina a towel. "You better put this around you, or she'll have more on you than in her mouth."

After dinner, Ginger's youngest fell asleep in the playpen, and the rest of the kids went outside. Josephine and Nina were drinking Italian coffee when Ginger came in the front door.

"I see you got a new car," Ginger said and went straight to Nina to give her a hug. "I haven't heard from you in awhile."

"I'll go check on the girls." Josephine made a hasty exit to the backyard.

"Your little one is adorable," Nina said. "She's the spitting image of Danny."

Ginger poured a cup of coffee for herself and warmed Nina's. "Another dark head of curls."

"With dimples." Nina added.

They both laughed.

"I hear you're working at Jordon Marsh."

"I only work part time. Danny's away on a new job." Tears filled Ginger's eyes and she reached for a napkin. "Oh, Nina, what am I going to do? I can't take much more of this."

"What do you want to do?"

"I want Danny to come home, but he won't. He's doing some sort of bingo thing in Atlanta." She sniffled. "The judge still hasn't set a court date for the horse fixing indictment. If this thing goes to trial, Danny may end up in jail for a long time."

"You're not going to change him if that's what you're thinking," Nina said, pulling a folded tissue from her pocket and handing it to Ginger.

"My mother's my biggest problem. She wants me to get a divorce and move in with her. I can't do that, but I can't afford a full-time babysitter either."

"Doesn't Thelma help out?"

"She hardly makes enough to feed her own family."

"Where's Wendell? Why doesn't he help?"

"Wendell signed as lender on a loan Frankie made to a contractor. When the guy got behind on his payments, Frankie foreclosed. They had a lot of money for a few months." Ginger took a sip of her coffee. "Then the builder talked to the FBI. The state charged Wendell with doing business without a licence, assault, and extortion. They wanted Wendell to rat on Frankie, but he refused."

"So what happened?" Nina remembered her conversation with Charlie and thought he might have been right. She wondered if Vito appreciated her saving his ass.

"It was in all the newspapers."

Nina rested her elbows on the table and leaned forward. "I didn't see the story."

"The judge was outraged, and made Frankie return the builder's equipment and hand over a clear deed to the structure that Frankie had finished with his own money." Ginger shook her head. "Dumb

Wendell, he's so stupid. Frankie talked him into pleading guilty for extortion in exchange for the State dropping the assault and loan sharking charges. He promised Wendell he'd send money to Thelma while he served his time."

"What did they do to Frankie? They must have known Wendell didn't have that kind of money."

Ginger's two oldest girls came in and clamored for Kool-Aid.

"I'll make it," Nina said. "You girls go play. I'll bring it out when it's ready." Nina shooed the children out of the room.

"They knew all right, but they couldn't prove anything," Ginger said. "Wendell went to jail, Frankie didn't help, and Thelma came to stay with me." Ginger shrugged. "What could I do? She has three kids and no money."

"Where's Wendell now?"

"Tallahassee. Thelma's leaving next week. She's going to get a job there so she can visit him."

"How long will he be there?"

"Probably two or three years. I'm not sure. It could've been worse. If he'd gone to court, they might've thrown the book at him."

"I'll help pay for a babysitter, and your mother won't need to come every day."

"There are too many kids to get a sitter. When Thelma leaves, I'll make better arrangements."

"Talk to Frankie. He'll help *you*."

"Are you kidding? He doesn't even return my calls." Ginger opened a cabinet and took out seven plastic glasses and filled them with icecubes. "I'm not sure Eunice gives him the messages. She's either on drugs, or she's an idiot."

Nina took the cold drinks outside and handed them to the girls.

When she returned to the kitchen, she put her arm around Ginger. "I know this is difficult for you. Heaven knows I've been down this road myself, but right now I have an even bigger problem."

Ginger, who rarely seemed concerned with Nina's welfare, reached across the table and touched Nina's hand.

"Is there something I can do?" Ginger asked.

Nina sighed. "No, I think I just want someone to know, in case something happens to me.

Ginger frowned. "What are you talking about?"

Nina breathed deeply, and told Ginger how Vito had again threatened to kill her.

"He said he would kill you?" Ginger asked.

"Well, not exactly, but that's what he meant."

"I don't think he'd ever kill you. And you have to admit, no matter what his reputation, he's sort of a chicken. Most of the time he gets someone else to do his dirty work.

Nina could see that Ginger did not truly share her concern. *It's not that she doesn't care, she just doesn't understand.*

"You're probably right," Nina said and pulled two hundred dollars in twenties from her purse and laid it on the table.

Ginger shook her head. "Keep the money. You have your own family to worry about."

"Remember when I used to sketch and paint in the wee hours of the night, and you thought I was crazy for working all day and staying up all night for the company I worked for?"

"Yeah."

"Well, the truth is, I own the advertising company. It's sort of what I wanted to do when I graduated from college."

"Wow, that's wonderful." Ginger pushed the money toward Nina. "I'm happy for you, but I still can't take the money."

"Business is good." Nina left the money on the table.

Ginger gave Nina a hug and surprised her by saying, "Be careful; Vito's still jealous of everything you do."

"I will. Don't worry about me, you have enough problems." Nina glanced at her watch. "I'm taking Mickey and the boys to Pennsylvania for the holidays. Before I go, I'll see that you have money for Christmas. Your little ones still believe in Santa."

They said their good-byes and Nina left.

CHAPTER SEVENTEEN

The next day Nina left work early, hoping to finish her Christmas shopping that evening. She hurried through the parking garage.

"Nina," Dutch called out when she reached her car.

She unlocked the MonteCarlo and waited.

"I'm glad I caught you." Dutch said. "Chance wants you to call him."

"What about?"

"I don't know. He said it was important." Dutch hurried off without another word.

She watched as he got into his car and pulled away. It was not like him to leave abruptly without talking for awhile.

On the way home, Nina stopped at a public phone. "Merry Christmas," she said when Chance answered.

He wished her the same. "Dutch tell me you go home for holiday."

She would have liked to ask Dutch and Chance to come to her parents' place for Christmas dinner, but that would not work. They were well known in the northeast and her father disapproved of both men, the same as he did Vito. After the divorce, Mr. Cocolucci told his friends about his daughter's new advertising company. She did not dare think about what would happen if her father found out who she really worked for.

"Dutch said you wanted to talk to me. Is anything wrong?" she asked.

"You got meeting on twenty-fourth."

"That's Christmas Eve, Chance." She tried to keep her voice steady. "We're leaving the twenty-third. My parents already arranged to have some of my old friends over to the house while I'm there." "Leave next day. Catch afternoon flight. You miss one day." He coughed. "Inconvenient, I know, but—it's with big advertising agents."

At first Nina resisted, but soon realized Chance was not about to take no for an answer.

Before they boarded the plane, Nina gave each of her sons a hug. "The soonest I could change my ticket was for Christmas morning, but I think I can fly standby tomorrow afternoon. I'll call you," she told Mickey.

She waved until they were out of sight before trudging along the terminal concourse. With nowhere to go, she stopped at Dobbs House for a club sandwich then left the airport to go home to an empty house.

The next morning it was dark, dreary and raining. The house was damp. Local news expected the high to be sixty-five degrees; not cold enough for a jacket, but Nina pulled a sage green sweater from the drawer and put it on over her cream long-sleeved blouse and beige skirt.

Dutch arrived at eleven. He parked his car in front of the garage and came inside.

"You're early," she said.

"I didn't know what traffic would be like. Did Mickey and the kids leave yesterday?" Rain from Dutch's fedora dripped onto the kitchen floor.

"Yeah, they were all excited. Are we taking your car or mine?"

"My rental," Dutch said. "I don't want your car anywhere around there. Could be a leak and the cops might come sneaking around writing down license plate numbers."

"License plate numbers? I thought we were meeting advertising people."

Dutch grinned. "Advertisers are kinda touchy."

Nina picked up her umbrella and gave him a look, but she did not question him further.

Again the meeting was at The Willows. The rain stopped and Dutch parked at a strip mall. They walked a block to the side door of the restaurant and entered through the kitchen. Dutch led her to an area at the rear of the dining room where private parties were held. Several men in casual clothes sat at a large round table drinking wine. Chance made the introductions, using first names only.

"You wonder why this meeting?" Chance said to Nina.

"Yes." She looked from one man to the other. Gold watches, heavy gold chains, and diamond pinky rings seemed to be the dress code.

"You have many new customers." Chance swirled a small amount of wine in his glass.

"Yes."

"They buy layouts you sell cheaper than other agencies?"

"I don't know what other advertising companies charge," Nina said rubbing her hands together.

The room grew quiet. Chance did not display his good-humored face, and the rest of the men were just as solemn. Even Dutch seemed to have deserted her.

"What's this all about?" she asked. "Was I supposed to ask permission before I took on any new business?"

"You remember our agreement?" Chance asked.

"Yes. Every name on your list was interviewed, signed up, and called into Goldman's, exactly as you requested." Nina sat a little straighter.

"You no tell me about *new* business."

"These contracts are different. They have no connection to Goldman's. Most of the companies are service related."

"They still buy advertising."

Nina took a good look at the men. These were not advertising executives. They were part of the syndicate.

"It's same as stealing," Chance said.

"I didn't go to these people. They wrote to me and solicited my services. That's not stealing."

Chance finished his wine and set the glass down hard. "It is when you undercut price and don't pay association."

"Then I'll stop. I can't handle any more accounts anyway."

"Association protects advertising agencies," Chance said.

All eyes were on her.

"You must pay for the good life you live," one of the men added.

The picture was now clear. The mob was telling her how to run her business, and she had to pay their so-called protection if she wanted to survive.

Dutch came around the table and sat beside Nina. "This is new to her. She needs time to think about it. We can work this out." He nudged Nina's knee. "Ain't that right?"

She wanted to slap Dutch, scream at Chance, and tell them all to go to hell. Nina stood up, and they all rose.

"I'm spending the holidays with my family. Dutch will make arrangements for us to meet when I get back." When she left the room, she passed the bartender coming into work. "Could you please let me out the front entrance?"

Dutch caught up with her at the door. "Wait," he said. "We need to talk."

"Now you want to talk? I trusted you with my life. You knew about the new business, knew this would happen, and you let me find out this way. What could you possibly tell me now that I don't already know?"

Dutch reached out to her, but she moved away.

"When we started, I didn't know how much you knew about Vito's business." For once, Dutch looked serious. "I was concerned, but you fit right in. You convinced the storeowners to sign the contracts. So, I figured you knew more than you let on. You weren't afraid of Vito or his men, and you hustled every day."

"You got it all wrong. I'm scared to death of Vito, but I'm more concerned about my children. I wanted a job he couldn't touch. I needed money to raise my sons." Her hand tightened on the door handle. "I convinced my clients to sign because I thought they would do better with me than Vito. It seemed like a mutual agreement. They helped me, and I helped them."

Dutch took another step toward her.

Nina cracked open the door. "I was against five-year contracts, but Chance wouldn't have it any other way. I felt that at least in five years my clients would be free to run their own businesses. Now I see the crime commission and the FBI are cracking down on protection racketeering. If I had stayed out of the mob, these people would soon be free to buy from whomever they pleased. All I've done is add another few years of misery to their lives." Tears welled, but she held her chin high and did not cry.

"It might've taken years for the authorities to break Vito's protection racket." Dutch retorted. "Most of your customers would've been out of business, physically hurt, if not killed, by then. Get off the guilt trip. You have a major problem of your own."

Nina shook her head and scowed. "Not today I don't. I'll make a decision next week."

"They won't wait another week," Dutch warned.

"They waited until I built up a hefty business so they could get a big fat cut. They can damn well wait a week for me to make up my mind. Whether I pay for protection, or cancel the contracts and get myself killed is none of your damn business." Nina grimaced. "Either way, it's my decision."

She walked across the street to the Holiday Inn and hailed a cab.

Nina arrived home and went straight to the phone to call the airline. The ticket agent said they were unable to find an earlier flight, so she was still booked for Christmas day.

"What time is the next flight to Pittsburgh scheduled to depart?" Nina asked. "I'll come to the airport and fly standby," she told the ticket agent.

"You can if you like, but we're way overbooked," the ticket agent said apologetically. "We have twenty people waiting. I don't think you have a chance, and besides the flight would cost you three times as much as the ticket you now have."

Nina would have to spend the night alone. She called Mickey with the bad news, then took an Orange Crush and walked barefoot to the dock. The river showed signs of the holiday as more boats skimmed along. She enjoyed a few moments before thoughts of the day took over. *I should've kept my job with Charlie. There has to be a way out of this.*

Redesigning the Mob

She thought about the legal documents the new service related customers had signed. Most of the contracts were only for two years, and the better part of a year had gone by. After Chance was satisfied that Nina always wrote five year contracts, he had never come back to check on the new accounts. She guessed the Mafia Family was making so much money off of her that no one suspected she would be smart enough to write short term contracts for the new service related companies.

Nina dangled her feet in the water and sipped her cold soda. *There's no way I can get out of giving the mob their cut on these new accounts, but I think I can protect the customers.* She walked back to the house, turned off the dock lights and checked the alarm. Everything was secure. Having made her decision, she took a shower and hung her travel clothes on the closet door. She went to bed early, but lay awake listening to the sound of the motors as the boats roared up and down the river.

Right now she was glad the boys were in Pennsylvania, and she was glad they had moved, but she no longer felt safe. Today she had stepped over the line.

CHAPTER EIGHTEEN

Vito arrived at IHOP late in the afternoon and pushed past the hostess. He held up two fingers as he made his way to a table. Gray carried a pot of coffee and two cups to the corner booth. She complained about working on Christmas Eve, but he paid no attention. A few minutes later, a dark complexioned man came in and joined Vito. The Cuban poured his coffee, added a large amount of sugar and stirred slowly.

Vito slammed his fist on the table. "You want I should sit here until you finish your coffee, or are you going to tell me about the flight?"

Gonzalez was used to Vito's brash conduct. The Cuban peered over the rim of the cup and took his time. "I parked outside the complex and followed your ex, her brother, and your three boys to the airport. Nice lookin' kids you got. Look like their mother."

"You don't get paid for your opinion," Vito snarled.

"She and the boys got out of the car and went in the terminal. I watched as her brother entered long-term parking. I waited until he came walking back and entered the airport through the same door that your family had gone in. The plane left at two o'clock, and no one came back out. So, at half past two, I left. I had to give the airport security guard ten bucks to let me wait in the drop-off lane."

"You'll get your ten. You should've gone inside and made sure they all boarded."

"Security wouldn't let me leave the car at curbside. If I'da looked for a parking place, I coulda missed someone comin' out."

"Anthony told me they were all leaving on the twenty-third. I wanted to make sure they went. They won't be back until after New Year's." Vito lit a cigarette and blew the smoke across the table. "Nina's working for the Bulldog. All we gotta do is get into her house. I know her. She's like the IRS, keeps records of everything. She's bound to have some names and telephone numbers. We'll find out who this guy is, where he's from, and where he lives."

"Then we whack him, right?" Gonzalez rubbed his hands together.

"Don't put words in my mouth," Vito grumbled.

"When I left the airport, I went to the Greek's restaurant. I like the belly dancers." Gonzalez held his arms out and shook the upper part of his body.

Vito glared. "Don't be dancing on my time."

"I asked Thesy about the Chicago mob. Said he ain't heard nothin' bout Windy City boys bein' in town. He said if they were here, they woulda stopped at his place to eat." Gonzalez sipped his coffee. "Thesy said it was a bad thing about Stanley getting shot. He said, whoever killed The Squirrel just brought on more heat and he didn't like the idea of a bunch of detectives snooping around askin' questions."

"Why would Thesy talk to you about a guy that just happened to get shot?" Vito fidgeted.

"Don't know, but Thesy got a phone call and told me to leave. I left, but I didn't close the door tight. I stood outside and listened."

"Did you get a tip on the ponies?"

"I got a tip, but not on a horse. He was talking to Chance and said he'd meet him at The Willows this morning. I think it had something to do with Stanley."

"You telling me Chance come to town because The Squirrel got iced? Barozzini's a prick. He wouldn't care if it was his grandmother."

Gonzalez added more sugar to his coffee.

"You should've told me about the meeting." Vito's mouth turned down. "I would've staked it out. Seen who showed."

"I couldn't get holda ya, so I hid behind the Dumpster across the alley. I could see the whole parking lot. They all came in rental cars and went inside for about two hours."

"Did you make anyone?"

"Only three, Salami Sam, Barrozzini, and Thesy. There was one other guy that I didn't see go in, but he came out with the rest of them. He was the same stocky guy, with light hair, and stiff mustache that came to the Jew market. This time I got a better look at him. He ain't Italian."

"That's him," Vito whispered. "He's the one they call the Bulldog. What kind of car did he drive?"

"He got in a rental with Chance."

"I knew it! Chance sent the Bulldog. That's how Nina got a job working for him." Vito slipped Gonzalez a hundred dollar bill. "Take a hike, and meet me back here at dark. We got plans for tonight."

CHAPTER NINETEEN

The security alarm went off and Nina bolted from the bed. In seconds, the alarm stopped its piercing cadence and she heard whispering. She reached for her robe in the darkness, but couldn't find it. Dressed in nothing but a cut-off top and bikini panties, she tiptoed into her bathroom and felt for the lock on the sliding glass door. Normally, an alarm would resonate when she pushed back the lock and opened the door, but tonight all was quiet. *Someone must have cut the wires.*

Her breath came is short gasps as she pulled the slick metal silently along the groove, closing the burglars inside. She ran to a large tree and climbed as high as she could go. The limbs scratched her arms and legs and bugs swarmed. She prayed there were no snakes.

A few inside lights came on and she could see Vito and what appeared to be a Latino man outside the Florida room door.

"Open the damn door!" Vito yelled. The door slid open. "What the hell happened, Shank? Why'd the fuckin' alarm go off?"

"Moe missed one of the wires."

Several more lights came on.

"I thought you said you were professionals. Did you search the house?"

Another man stepped outside. He held his gun out in front of him. "I checked. Nobody's home."

"Aim that Saturday night special someplace else." Vito pushed Moe's arm away. The gun now pointed at the one Vito called Shank.

"Put that cheap piece of crap away," Shank said. "Ain't nobody here."

"Wait by the boat," Vito instructed Shank. "And Moe, you watch the front." Vito pulled something from his pocket. "Put these rubber gloves on," he said to the Latino, "and look in the kitchen. She keeps a lot of stuff in drawers."

Nina watched as the men dispersed to their positions. Vito and the skinny Latino pulled on a pair of bright yellow gloves and tromped inside the house.

All was quiet. Nina figured the only reason Vito would come here was to kill her. She couldn't imagine why they were searching the house. Vito knew she had sold her rings.

A minute later, Vito and the Latino ran out of the house.

"Gonzalez, go out front and get Moe," Vito said. "Shank, get back here. She's hiding in the house. We gotta find her."

Nina climbed higher in the tree. The small limbs bent under her weight. All the men were inside now, and every light in the house was on. Two of the men came outside and searched the bushes. She was grateful that the outside lights were dim.

"Those sirens are getting closer," Shank said. "They might be headed this way."

She prayed the sirens belonged to police cars that were coming to help her.

Vito burst from the house. "I can't find her. If she didn't catch the plane, she must have gone out somewhere tonight." He spat on the ground. "Barozzini's in town, she's probably with him."

"There's a car in the garage, and two more in the driveway," Moe said.

"Nothing in the drawers," Gonzalez said as he came outside.

The four of them left the lights on and hurried to the dock. Nina strained to see the boat, and almost fell out of the tree.

"Who's got the keys?" Vito's shoes pounded the hard packed path as he ran back toward the house.

Nina's hands were shaking, and she felt like she was losing her grip.

"Vito," a hoarse voice filtered through the night. "I found the keys."

Blue lights shimmered between the trees as patrol cars screamed along the quiet road.

Vito huffed his way back to the boat. The motor cranked, but nothing happened.

"Get out of the way!" Vito's voice echoed through the night.

The engine started, and the motor roared. The bow of the boat lifted high in the air, and in seconds was out of sight.

Nina sat frozen on the limb. The house lights seemed brighter than usual. The outside lights sent a subtle glow across the yard and along the deck. Dew glistened on the lawn. Two squad cars skidded to a stop in her driveway. She watched as two policemen, with guns drawn, started toward the house. Dampness coated her face and hair.

When a blond officer moved in her direction, she gasped. "Wait! Please don't come any closer."

He stopped. "Who's up there?"

"Nina Cocolucci. I live here." She hugged her body.

"Do you need help to get down?"

"No, but I'm not dressed. Could you get my robe from the house and throw it under the tree? It's somewhere in the bedroom."

Once the cop brought Nina her robe, she climbed down and wrapped it around her near-naked body. She was adjusting the sash when she noticed the blond cop lurking in the shadows.

"Did you get an eyeful?" she snapped.

The officer disappeared inside the house.

When Nina came in the back door, a thin officer with dark hair pulled out a chair from the kitchen table. "Please sit down," he said. "I'm Detective Schmidt. It appears the perps came by boat and left the same way. Try not to touch anything tonight. As soon as it's daylight, I'll have an investigation crew check for footprints outside and fingerprint the house." He sat down and took a pen from his pocket. "If the perpetrators were professionals looking for something of value, we might get a break if we can match the prints."

Redesigning the Mob

Nina pulled the robe tighter.

"You say you think there were four men?" Schmidt asked.

"Yes," Nina answered.

"Did you get a good look at any of them?"

"No."

"Did you recognize any of their voices?"

"No."

"Do you have any idea why they did this?" he asked.

"No."

"Do you know if anything's missing?"

"There's nothing to take."

"No jewelry, no money?"

"Not enough for someone to break in."

"Would you like us to station a man here tonight, in case they come back?"

"No."

"Do you have a gun?"

"No."

"Maybe you should get one."

"Would it help to keep Peeping Toms away?" She scowled at the blond officer who stood across the room.

His hair was cut fairly short, but a few strands fell carelessly over his forehead. He didn't act cocky or seem ashamed. His cool green eyes were part of an easy smile. When his gaze caught her stare, Nina thought of the vivid emerald paint in her art supplies.

She looked away.

"We'll keep a car in the area in case you need us." Schmidt stood up and turned the clipboard toward her. "Sign here."

"What am I signing? I don't want this incident to appear in the morning papers."

"I have no control over what happens to my paperwork."

"I guess they'll have to take your word that you were here, because I'm not signing anything."

"Oh. I forgot. You're Vito DiGregetti's ex."

"Thank you for responding to the alarm." She pointed toward the door. "I think it's time you left."

Detective Schmidt walked outside without saying a word.

"I'll bury the report," Green Eyes whispered. "But I don't think it's a good idea for you to stay here tonight, even if we watch the house."

After the patrol cars left, Nina locked the door and turned on all the outside lights. She drove Anthony's car to the Holiday Inn and checked into a room. She climbed into bed but could not sleep. The blond cop's green eyes danced in her memory. She wondered why he was so helpful, and if he liked what he saw before she put on her robe. At daybreak, she returned to her home. The blond cop's image still lingered in her mind. *For heaven's sake girl, get a grip. He's a cop.*

The investigation crew arrived at seven. A man with a stack of papers gave instructions to the rest of the team.

They took pictures and dusted for fingerprints while Nina finished packing. She called First Defense Alarm Company and asked for Billy, the technician who had installed her alarm system, but he was out of the office. She arranged for them to repair the damaged wiring. "I'll drop off a spare key for Billy."

The crew chief waited for her to finish her conversation.

"Yes, the police were here right away. I think the sirens scared the intruders off." Nina held the phone with her shoulder while she put on her gold hoop earrings. "Ask Billy if he can put some kind of motion detector by the dock. Tell him to install whatever is necessary. I don't want this to happen again."

By the time she hung up, the men had completed their inspection.

"Doesn't appear like they found whatever they were looking for," the photographer said.

Nina's organized papers were now a mess, but she assured the investigators nothing was missing.

"We'll call you next week if we make a match," the man in charge said.

As soon as they left, Nina locked the house. She needed to hurry if she wanted to drop off the key and still catch her flight. She eyed her MonteCarlo suspiciously then opened the trunk of the Camaro and placed her luggage inside.

Nina worried about what would have happened if Vito had invaded the house when the boys were home. *Probably one of the boys told him we were going to Pennsylvania. He seemed shocked when he thought I was in the house.* She mulled the thoughts over in her head. *He might not have come to kill me, but if he'd found me here, I think he would've.*

CHAPTER TWENTY

1971

Christmas turned out better than Nina had expected. As soon as her mother found out that her daughter was going to be detained for an extra day, she had rearranged the holiday schedule. Nina was amazed at how many of her old friends showed up at the Cocolucci home to help celebrate Christmas.

Her college friends, most of whom had married and still lived in Bentleyville, did not work. They wanted to hear all about her advertising business, and praised her for having the perseverance to follow her college dream. Nina smiled, allowing the deceptiveness to thrive in her friend's minds and hearts.

Before Nina and her family returned from Pennsylvania, she called the alarm company and had Billy check her car for any signs of sabotage.

They arrived home Friday, New Year's day. The sun felt good after a week of snow and freezing rain, and the boys were happy to get back to their friends and the beach before school resumed on Monday.

As Nina unpacked, her mind wandered back to the December meeting. She felt betrayed by Chance and let down by Dutch. Maybe she would quit, turn her business over to the mob—or could she? Maybe she knew too much. They might not let her walk away. She had to talk to Chance alone, without all the other men who had been at the meeting.

On the way to the grocery store to restock her refrigerator, Nina stopped to use the pay phone. She dialed Chance's number and waited anxiously for him to come on the line.

When he finally did, she said, "I'd like to see you alone. We need to talk about the money you say I owe the association. I can't make a decision when I don't know where all this is leading."

"Sure," he said. "Come to New York. I show you the city. You work too much. You need to have fun."

"Not paying attention to business is what put me in this position. I can't see how a night on the town will change my predicament."

He chortled. "We work this out. I promise."

The call ended, and Nina had not even mentioned Vito breaking into her home. She decided she would tell Chance when she got to New York.

She walked out of the grocery store to see a squad car parked next to her MonteCarlo. As Nina wheeled her cart to her sedan, the green-eyed officer walked up behind her car.

"I noticed your Chevy and wanted to apologize for my behavior last week." He held out his hand. "My name's Larry Macklin."

Nina ignored his gesture and eyed him suspiciously. "You spied my car in a crowded lot after seeing it only once in my garage?"

"Well, not exactly. I was looking for it." He pulled a handkerchief from his pocket and wiped his brow. "When you first moved on my beat, we were told to keep an eye on your house. I got used to watching you come and go, but nothing happened, so we were told to no longer stake out your place."

"That's wonderful. Cops were watching my every move without my permission. You must feel like the KGB."

"The chief meant no harm. It was a safety precaution. They thought your husband might bring an unwanted element into the neighborhood."

"I beg your pardon. I have no husband."

"Yes, ma'am, I know." He stared at his shoes. The bill of his cap covered most of his face. "That was a rude thing I did last week." He paused. "I don't know what came over me. I don't do that sort of thing." He hesitated again. "I wanted you to know that you were only a shadow."

Nina stared at him.

He cleared his throat. "Even though we weren't supposed to watch your residence, I was puzzled by the way your lights stayed on long after midnight, and I continued to drive by. I wondered how you went to bed late, got up early, and still looked bright and cheery in the morning?"

The officer's compliment had been a first for Nina in a long time, but she thought he might be up to something, so she reached into her pocket for her keys.

"I'm on the graveyard shift," he explained. "I start at eleven and finish at eight a.m." His emerald eyes sparkled in the afternoon sun.

Nina opened the trunk of her car and started lifting her groceries out of the cart.

"Here, let me help you with those," the officer said.

"You don't have to—

He interrupted with, "I know you don't want any publicity, but if you need anything—I'm only a cop forty hours a week. The rest of the time I'm a pretty nice guy." He handed Nina a card, grinned then turned and left.

Nina stared after him as he walked to his cruiser. *Nice ass.* Once she got into her car Nina came to her senses. The last thing she needed was a cop hanging around her place.

She called Mickey as soon as she got home, and he agreed to stay with the boys while she went to New York.

There was not much for Mickey to do. She had taught the boys to take care of themselves. Besides, Bertha, a buxom woman whose gray hair faded into a brownish knot at the back of her head, came in to clean once a week. She only lived a few houses away, and if Nina worked late, Bertha would often cook for the boys.

Nina felt it was important to straighten out her business problem with Chance, but feared that if she had to pay a big cut to the mob for the money she made on her new clients, she would have to tighten her belt. That meant she would no longer be able to help Ginger, and she might have to give up Bertha. Both were depressing thoughts for Nina.

Chance met Nina at LaGuardia Airport. He took her small carry-on bag, hailed a cab, and whisked her off to a restaurant where he had made reservations. Nina was glad he planned to spend the evening with her. They had a lot to talk about.

"This is a great place," he said as he ushered her through the doors of La Flambé. A crowd of people jockeyed for space in the entranceway. Loud cheers and clapping erupted from the dining room.

Chance handed Nina's coat and small suitcase to the hat check girl behind the counter who was dressed in a black body suit, tuxedo jacket and a top hat. He gave her a large advance tip. "Place valise with lady's coat and keep eye on it."

"Yes, Mr. Barozzini," she said with a smile.

Chance pushed his way toward the blond hostess, who recognized him at once.

"Right this way." The willowy hostess pivoted and slithered through the packed room.

"After you." Chance bowed to Nina.

Nina followed the slinky hostess between the wedged-in chairs to a table occupied by a group of rowdy customers. When Nina started to speak, Chance pulled out a chair for her next to a handsome dark-haired man.

"Well, hel-lo, sweetie." The stranger, a Vic Damone look-a-like, winked at her.

Nina's mouth quivered into a forced smile. She turned to Chance, who was busy greeting the other men and women at the table.

"This here's Nina." He introduced her to the man next to her. "Meet Storm Landon."

"My pleasure." The sexy hunk raked her with his eyes.

Her face flushed. "It's nice to meet you." She leaned toward Chance and whispered, "I thought we were going to have a quiet dinner and talk?"

He patted her shoulder. "Relax. Enjoy tonight. What you drink?"

Nina reluctantly sat down. "Just a Coke or better yet, make it iced tea."

"Double Dewars on the rocks," Chance said to the waiter. "And iced tea for the lady."

Odd dishes of chili peppers, chips with garlic dip, and hot wings were scattered on the table. "Try some." Chance placed a couple of the small platters close enough for Nina to reach.

"No, thank you," she managed to say.

"C'mon." Storm Landon picked up one of the dainty forks and offered her a wing.

Nina shook her head.

"Please," he said. "It'll spark your appetite." He displayed a star-quality smile.

Nina relented. She liked chicken, and who knew what kind of food they might serve here. She took a big bite and began to chew. The wing was good, but suddenly her mouth was on fire.

The waiter returned with an assortment of cocktails for the whole table. Her beverage stood high above the other glasses.

Nina waved her hand in front of her mouth, and the waiter set the frosted refreshment in front of her. She took a big swig. It tasted different from most iced tea, but then this was New York, and her mouth and throat were burnt. She did not hear anyone order, but soon crostini with white truffle oil and olive paste appeared on the table, followed by oysters casino.

"You're not eating?" Nina asked when Storm pushed his plate aside.

"I don't eat before a performance." He ordered another drink for himself and a fresh one for Nina.

He did not offer any further explanation about entertainment, and she did not ask for fear he might be leading up to something risqué.

The diners continued their boisterous eating and drinking. It reminded Nina of the dinner parties with the mob in Florida, but a lot louder, and there were no children running between the tables. Nina's mouth still burned fiercely, and she gulped more tea to cool her tongue and throat.

Two waiters wheeled a cart close to their table. There was a surge of fire, and soon after, everyone had a hot dish of veal flambé placed in front of them. Again, Storm Landon pushed his plate aside.

Redesigning the Mob

During dinner, Chance included Nina in his conversations with the men, but she noticed he said little to the other women. However, it did not prevent their flirting with him and Landon by batting their eyelashes and leaning forward in their seats to reveal ample cleavage.

Nina became engrossed in a conversation with another friend of Chance's, and Storm Landon slipped away without saying good-bye. The dinner plates were cleared and soon coffee and bananas flambé were served.

A few minutes later, the big band sound of the forties burst upon the room. Surprised, Nina turned to look behind her. Chance rearranged their chairs to face a raised platform, and handed Nina another iced tea.

"Thank you," she said. "My mouth feels much better now."

The platform's curtains opened and Storm Landon strolled onto the stage. He arrived at the microphone at the exact moment for him to belt out *Love is a Many-Splendored Thing*.

"He good," Chance said.

Nina nodded, keeping her eyes on Storm.

When the song finished, there was a round of applause, and the handsome singer swung into *That's Amore*. The patrons cheered and sang along. Nina thought that most of them were drunk. As a matter of fact, she felt a little woozy herself.

She was about to turn the chair and face the table to finish her coffee when the singer came down a short flight of stairs. He was singing *When I Fall in Love,* and walking straight toward her.

"Everyone's staring at us," she whispered to Chance. "I don't want him to do this."

He grinned. "Enjoy. It's part of show."

Storm Landon stopped in front of Nina while he continued to sing. Aware that all eyes were on them, she blushed and felt warm all over. The room spun. *This is ridiculous. I can't be swooning.*

Nina woke up in her hotel room. A queasy stomach and a headache prompted her to move slowly. Glancing at the clock, she saw a note from Chance. "I'm in room 1010. Call me when you get up."

Leaning against the pillow, Nina thought about the night before. All she remembered was Storm Landon singing. *What happened after that?*

Her fingers tentatively dialed 1010.

"Ready for breakfast?" Chance asked.

"Did I do anything last night?" She swung her legs over the side of the bed and winced at the pain in her head.

"You had good time."

"How did I get to the hotel?"

"We left when show close. I call taxi."

"I mean, was I acting odd?"

"You sing in elevator. Maybe Long Island Iced Teas do this. I hear liquor very strong."

"I didn't order liquor," Nina snapped. "I don't even remember going to bed."

He laughed. "I think you high. You take off shoes—walk in stockings. I leave note and go to my room."

Nina was quiet as she tried to remember.

"Something wrong?" he asked.

"No." She pressed her hand against her forehead. "Are we going to have time to talk today?"

"Sure. I show you city."

"Chance, please. My plane leaves at five. I won't even have time for dinner."

"We see sights, eat lunch, and talk."

Nina sighed with relief. "It'll only take me thirty minutes to get ready."

"Good, I check us out. Bring your valise. I hire driver for day."

"You gonna love Harry's Café," Chance said. "Food good, but most people come to see pictures."

Amusing caricatures of well known personalities hung randomly on the walls of the quaint '50s café. Nina wondered if Chance had picked this particular eating place to switch her mind from the present money problem to her love of art.

They placed their order and Nina again tried to talk to Chance.

"You make too much of this," he said. "If you artist, and me gallery owner, I get piece of profit. You think fair?"

"Yes, but this is different. I could quit an artist job and go to work somewhere else."

"Not if you sign contract."

"But this is *my* company."

"Think like this. Price go up for one, price go up for all. Syndicate protect you, must protect other ad agencies. Chance pushed his plate away and lit a cigarette.

"What if I walk away from everything? Do something different."

"Like what?" Chance asked. He seemed to be genuinely curious.

Nina fanned the smoke away with her hand.

Chance crushed his cigarette in the ashtray. "Ya wanna work for Charlie?"

"I have experience. I could get a good job with an advertising agency."

"Maybe two-bit company in Idaho," Chance scoffed. "Big advertisers know what goes on, they no hire you."

Nina leaned back in her chair. She thought about the boys, their education, and wondered how she would manage.

Chance looked at Nina sympathetically. "This not my decision. I can do nothing." He touched the napkin to his lips. "You must pay percentage to Family."

She nodded. *Why tell him about Vito breaking into the house? It won't change anything.*

"You decide to move to Idaho. We talk again." Chance stood up and helped Nina put on her coat. "We ride through Times Square on way to airport."

CHAPTER TWENTY-ONE

Ginger hadn't been home when Nina dropped off the money for Christmas presents. Then, with the tourist season in full swing, they both worked long hours, and it was February before they finally met at IHOP.

"Hi, Mrs. DiGregetti," Gray said.

Nina snickered. "I'm not Mrs. DiGregetti anymore. My name's Nina—Nina Cocolucci."

"Wow, that's a mouthful," Gray said as she handed them menus.

"Then just call me Nina."

"Nina and Ginger," Gray said. "I haven't seen either of you for awhile. You must have come in when I was working days."

"We've been too busy to come in. We both have jobs now." Nina turned to the sandwich page of the menu. "I'll have a grilled cheese on whole wheat and iced tea. No, make that lemonade."

"Me, too." Ginger handed Gray the menu. "They come with pickles?"

"Dill pickles and chips."

"Great." Ginger licked her lips.

"You're not pregnant again, are you?" Gray whispered. "After you lost all that weight—I mean you look terrific—not that you didn't before, but—"

Ginger burst out laughing. "No, I'm not pregnant, but thanks for noticing. We women have to stick together. Bring on the pickles and chips. We're celebrating."

Gray hurried toward the kitchen.

"You do look good," Nina said. "Getting out of the house agrees with you."

"I've lost twenty-five pounds." Ginger patted her stomach. "Size five."

"I'll bet Danny likes that. He used to brag about your tiny waist."

"Nina, he hasn't seen me since the day he turned himself in for that trouble at the track. When the judge let him out on his own recognizance, he came to the house, picked up some clothes, and left for Atlanta, or who knows where. I thought for sure he'd come home for Christmas."

"Are you telling me he hasn't even come home to see the kids?"

"He called a couple of times when I was at work and talked to them."

"Does he send you any money?"

"No. One time Dana told him she needed school clothes, and he promised to send something the next week, but he didn't. She was so disappointed."

"Did you ever get in touch with Frankie?"

"He doesn't return my calls, but I ran into him one day. He said he had his own problems."

Gray set their lemonades on the table and went back to the kitchen.

"Frankie didn't help Thelma, and she couldn't get a job in Tallahassee, so she's living on welfare. Wendell's doing better than she is. He's getting three squares a day and goes to rehabilitation school."

"Maybe he'll get out early if he doesn't make any trouble," Nina said.

"Thelma says he acts as if he likes it there. He plays cards, works out in the gym, and has a little business making leather belts." Ginger took a long drink of lemonade. "He sells them to the visitors."

Nina's mouth fell open. "Does the penitentiary know what he's doing?"

"They encourage it. I guess it shows he's attempting to fend for himself. The last time Thelma saw him, he had men working for him making the belts. He said he couldn't keep up with the demand. He has money for cigarettes, candy, and magazines while his kids go without milk."

Gray served their sandwiches, refilled their glasses and went on to her next customer.

Ginger reached for a pickle. "Wendell told her he needs the cash to make more money, so when he gets out he'll have a stake to get started again."

"He wasn't like that before," Nina said. "He did everything for her, even helped dress the kids."

"Frankie told him the mob was taking good care of Thelma, so he probably thinks she's blowing the cash they give her. Frankie hasn't even called to see how she is."

"Does Wendell put the money he makes in some kind of savings account?" Nina picked up her sandwich and bit into the delicious metlting cheese.

"Ha!" Ginger uttered. "He uses it to run a loan shark racket."

"In prison?" Nina's eyes opened wide. "I guess the authorities don't know about that."

"Maybe they do." Ginger hadn't touched her sandwich. "Who knows what goes on inside?"

Gray was standing by the sideboard scribbling in her notebook when Nina motioned for her.

"Can I get you anything?" Gray asked.

"No, I just wondered what you're always writing in that little notebook. I've seen you do this every time we're here."

Gray blushed. "I keep a journal."

"You're a writer?"

"Sort of. I'm taking a college course in journalism. We're learning about why, what, where, when, and how."

"I hope I'm not in your notebook," Nina said.

Gray lowered her voice. "I haven't written anything about the two of you. I was just writing a description of that homeless woman in the corner booth. She comes in once a week for soup. I give her extra crackers and a cup of coffee." Gray lowered her voice. "She talks crazy to herself and sometimes it's pretty funny, so I write it down."

Nina knew that Gray often waited on Vito. She had to ask. "Do you write about my ex?"

Gray shook her head. "That man has a reputation. I stay as far away from him as I can. I did write a description of a man that came in with him one night." Gray reached into her pocket and flipped through her small pad.

Nina looked at the description, but it didn't fit anyone she knew. She handed it to Ginger.

"Oh, that's gotta be Gonzalez. He's a Cuban from Miami. He works for Vito."

Nina looked at the pad again. She read "12/24/70" scrawled at the bottom of the page and looked up at Gray. "What's this date mean?"

"That's the day I was working. It doesn't mean anything. It's a habit I have of keeping track of the days I spend here."

Nina recalled the break-in at her house on Christmas Eve. She thought the Cuban might have been the dark skinny man Vito brought with him. She returned the notepad to Gray.

"I know you and Ginger have problems," Gray said.

Ginger and Nina looked at each other.

"Do you listen to our conversations?" Nina asked.

"No, but I can't help overhearing some things. My ex isn't as scary as yours, but he doesn't support my kids, either."

"Did you ever overhear anything my ex said?" Nina asked.

"I don't repeat anything I hear, and I would never cause you two any problems, but—" Gray hesitated. "If it helps, he comes in every other Thursday to meet a guy named Frankie. Ginger's husband hasn't been in for a long time."

"This is not a conversation you should repeat," Nina warned Gray.

"I won't tell anyone." Gray looked over her shoulder. "I have to wait on my other customers." She moved to the next booth.

"What do you think of that?" Ginger asked.

"I don't know what to think."

"Should we call Frankie and tell him to be careful about what he says in here?" Ginger whispered.

"No!" Nina said loudly.

The next table of customers turned and looked at her.

"Let's forget this conversation ever took place," Nina whispered. "Besides, I believe Gray. Anything we say might land her in big trouble. I don't want that on my conscience. I've got enough to contend with."

Ginger frowned. "What's your problem? You have a great job, no husband to worry about, and no cops knocking on your door. Sometimes I think about getting a divorce myself."

"That's all the more reason to forget what's been said." Nina finished her sandwich, dropped her napkin on her plate, and unlike the old days, was able to leave a nice tip.

As they walked outside to their cars, Nina stuffed a few bills in Ginger's purse.

"I didn't come here for that," Ginger protested.

Nina smiled. "I know you didn't. Think of it as a gift to the girls for all the times I didn't have any money to buy them a present on their birthdays." Nina's smile faded. "Anyway, this might be the last time. Business has been a little slow, so I'll probably not be able to help you out for a while."

When Nina pulled up to her house on the river, two squad cars were parked in front and both officers were talking to Anthony.

"What's the problem?" Nina asked her heart pounding as she got out of her car.

"These guys think I was speeding," Anthony said.

"Were you?" she asked her son.

"I was doing about forty. Nobody drives thirty-five on this road."

Nina looked at the cops. One was Larry Macklin, and she had seen the other one sitting in his car by the guard shack.

"Hello, again," Larry said. "This is Officer Ingram. He clocked your son at fifty and gave him a warning, but Anthony doesn't have the owner's registration. He said you had it. We can clear this up right now, and then you can talk to him. He needs to drive slower in a residential area."

"I'm not sure where the registration is." Nina stumbled through the words. "I'll have to look for it. Can I bring it to the station later?"

"What do you think, Ingram? Can his mother bring it in?" Larry asked.

Nina waited. *Please God, give me some time to take care of this.*

"It's his first offense," Officer Macklin said to the arresting officer. "I'll follow it up myself. I'll see that we get the information."

Ingram grunted a questionable agreement and left.

"Go inside," Nina said to Anthony. "I want to talk to the officer."

Anthony put his hands on his hips. "I don't know why you—"

"Inside." Nina glared at him.

Anthony moseyed around the house and went down to the dock.

Nina looked at Macklin. "I don't know what got into Anthony today. He's usually not like this. He's a good kid."

"I understand. I have a son, too. When I was young, my dad used to call it growing pains."

"I didn't think you were married."

"I'm not anymore. My son goes to the same school your boys do. I try to see my kid on weekends. We went to the football game on Friday. Anthony's a good player. He plays smart and gives a hundred percent right up to the last whistle. It's a shame they lost." Macklin grinned. "I've seen *you* there a couple of times."

"Well, I still have your card, Officer Macklin." "Larry," he said. "No need to be formal. Call me when you get the registration. I'll stop by the house for it. You won't have to come into the station."

Nina thanked him and watched as he pulled from the driveway. *He sure is cute, but why is he being so helpful?* Years of living with Vito taught her not to trust anyone's motives, even a cop.

"Anthony!" she yelled. "Get in the house. I want to talk to you right now."

When Anthony came in, all his frustrations with the cops seemed spent. "I'm sorry, Mom."

"You're lucky you didn't get a ticket."

"I think the guy with dark hair planned to give me one until his backup came. The cop that stopped me stood by the car writing while the big blond guy called in and checked my license." Anthony shuffled his feet. "They talked before the blond guy came over and said I was getting a warning, but I had to come up with the registration. I didn't know what to do, so I told them you had it."

"You need to get in touch with your dad."

"How? I don't have his new number, and I don't know where he lives anymore."

"Great," Nina mumbled.

"It's not my fault I don't know where my dad is."

Nina swallowed hard. She knew he was right. *It's not my fault either, or maybe it is.*

"I'm going next door to see Catherine." Anthony picked up his trigonometry book.

"You spend too much time with her. Do her parents get home this early in the day?"

"They get home at five-thirty."

"Then you need to wait until they come home."

"Mom, you're acting crazy again. All we do is study. Her parents don't say anything. They trust *their* kid."

"I trust you, but I know how easy it is for things to happen."

"Yeah, I know. You didn't get married until after you were pregnant with me."

"Who told you that?" Nina asked in shock.

"No one. I saw the date on the back of your wedding pictures when I was at Nana's."

Nina cringed. "I think it took us awhile to get those pictures developed."

"There was a wedding announcement, too."

"Oh," Nina sighed. "Did you tell your brothers?" She blinked to chase away the tears.

"No, it's not important." He turned and walked toward the door. "I'll be back in time for dinner."

After Anthony left, Nina stood in front of the refrigerator with the door open. Nothing she saw appealed to her, and she was in no mood to cook. She picked up her keys and drove around for a half-hour before stopping at a service station to call Chance. When she tried to talk, her voice broke.

"What's wrong?" he asked.

"Do you remember asking me about the title for Anthony's car?"

"Yeah. What Vito say?"

"Nothing. I forgot all about it until today. Anthony got a warning for speeding, but he didn't have the registration." Nina closed the booth's folding door. "He told the police I had it, but I don't, and I don't know how to get in touch with Vito."

"I handle this," Chance said. "You call back. I need make, model, ID, and mileage."

Nina thought Chance was a hard man to understand, but he came to her aid without asking questions, and she was thankful for that.

When she returned, a black Chrysler blocked her garage, and two strapping men were lolling around her front door. They did not seem to notice her at first. One looked like he was trying to peer into the house.

They turned toward the street, eyes squinting into the sun. She thought about putting the car in gear and leaving, but she did not know where the boys were. She sat staring at the men. The shorter of the two looked to be in his late twenties. He had on gray slacks and a bright orange pullover. The older, taller man was dressed totally in black.

She got out of the car and walked a few cautious steps toward the men.

"You live here?" the younger man said.

She nodded.

"You Nina Cocolucci?" he asked.

She stopped. A dozen thoughts raced through her mind, most of which included Vito. She thought of the Donovan fire, the death of The Squirrel, and the break-in at her house. "Who are you?" she asked, thinking surely nothing could happen to her so close to the street in broad daylight.

The man in black reached inside his pocket and Nina's knees shook. He pulled out a business card. "We want to talk to you about your son, Anthony."

Nina edged forward. "What about Anthony? Where is he? What's happened to him?"

"Nothing, I hope." He handed Nina a card. "We represent Florida State University. We'd like to talk to him about a football scholarship."

For an instant, Nina did not comprehend his words. "How did you get past the guard gate? I don't allow unannounced guests."

"We came to see Don Graham. He plays for St. Thomas Aquinis. We didn't notice that you lived in the same development until we were ready to leave his house," the tall man said. "We planned on calling and making an appointment for later, but figured we'd stop by and see if you were available."

"Oh." Nina was thinking that Vito could do the same thing.

"You all right, ma'am?"

Nina composed herself and smiled. "Yes. Please come in." She unlocked the door and disabled the alarm.

By the time they got settled in the living room, Anthony had came home from Catherine's.

The tall man said to Anthony, "Put'er there," and extended his hand.

Anthony stepped back and looked at his mother. "What's goin' on?"

"They're here to talk to *you*," Nina replied. "About a scholarship."

"Yeah?" Anthony's mouth dropped open.

"That's right. We caught your Friday night game. We're with FSU," the young man in the orange shirt said. "We actually came to get a look at a running back on the other team. You got amazin' moves, kid, and you left nothin' on the field."

"We lost," Anthony said.

"We didn't come to see the score. We came to see the players.'

Michael and Joey came in the back door carrying their tennis rackets. When they saw visitors, they went quietly to their bedrooms.

"Don't get too excited," the tall man said to Anthony. "We don't know how you'll do against a big line. Best we can offer right now is a two-year scholarship. If things work out, you might get an extension."

"I haven't even graduated yet," Anthony blurted.

"Listen to him," the tall man said to his partner. "He's gonna wait for a better deal."

"No, I didn't mean that." Anthony pushed his hair from his face. "I just didn't expect this."

The man in black handed Nina a piece of paper. "This is a preliminary notice of what the scholarship will cover. Your son has time to think about it. I want him to be sure before he makes a decision.

Of course, his grade point average will be a consideration." He shook Anthony's hand. "We'll be in touch."

The two men left the house. When the front door closed, Anthony let out a whoop and his brothers came out of their room to see what was going on.

"I guess we should celebrate." Nina hugged Anthony. "It's not every day you get a scholarship."

Anthony looked at the floor. "Maybe they'll change their mind. Do you know how big college jocks are?"

"You're not small. You're five-eleven."

"And skinny as a rail," Michael jeered from the hallway.

"And slow to boot," Joey added.

Anthony glared at his brothers. "Laugh all you want, but the scouts came to see *me*. I was the one who got offered the scholarship." Anthony's chin jutted out with pride.

"You could go to the gym and bulk up this summer," Nina suggested.

"Do you know how much that costs?" Anthony asked.

"You're worth every penny."

"More like every dollar," Anthony said. "Can we have pizza tonight?"

"You bet." Nina was never more proud of her son.

CHAPTER TWENTY-TWO

A week later, Anthony came home from school and dropped his books on the kitchen table. Nina handed him two documents.

"What's all this?" Anthony said before even looking at them.

"It's the title for your car and a bill of sale," Nina said as she washed a handful of dishes in the kitchen sink. "I have to show them to Officer Macklin.

Anthony shrugged and picked up his math book. "I'm going to Catherine's to study."

She didn't show Anthony the attached note that read: "Camaro on stolen property list. If law check, they will impound car, but papers show car purchased in good faith. Anthony no responsible. Car in Vito's name. Let me know outcome." The note was signed with the letter "C."

Nina took the papers and went into her bedroom. She called the home telephone number that Larry Macklin had written on the back of his card. When he answered, she said, "This is Nina Cocolucci. I have the title for the Camaro."

"Great, I'm not working tonight. I'll stop by and pick it up."

"I'd rather meet you someplace. My younger sons look up to Anthony. I don't want them to know he was speeding. How does the recreational building sound?"

"I understand, but since I'm not on duty, I don't want my partner to wonder why I'm sitting in the park."

"This is getting awfully complicated. You'd think we were espionage agents."

"Or part of the Mafia," he added.

Nina gulped, grateful he could not see the look on her face.

"I have a better idea," Larry said. "Why don't we meet in town? There's a little coffee shop on the corner of Broad and Main."

"I know the place." Visions of his broad shoulders blurred her mind. "Seven o'clock?"

"Seven's good. I'll see you there."

I think he likes me.

When Nina arrived, the coffee shop was packed, and Larry sat at the counter in washed-out jeans, a plaid shirt, and cowboy boots.

He walked toward her. "It's a little crowded—would you like to try another place?"

Nina nodded.

In the parking lot, Larry steered her toward a blue, four-wheel drive and loaded with chrome. He opened the door, and Nina looked at the high step. Without any hesitation, he picked her up and sat her inside.

"I'll have a running board installed for the next time," he said as he closed the door.

Next time? Nina watched him walk around the pickup.

"Have you had dinner?" he asked as he climbed in the driver's seat.

"No, but I'm not hungry. Anywhere for coffee or tea is fine with me."

Larry pulled out of the parking lot and drove along Main Street. Nina leaned into the soft leather seats. She felt strange and yet somehow safe inside a big truck with an officer of the law.

"If I had my choice, I'd go to the movies." Larry slowed the truck as he approached the local movie house. "Have you seen *The Sting*?"

"No, but I told the boys I'd be right back."

"Call them. I hear it's a helluva movie. You like popcorn?"

"I really should go home. I'll just give you the title."

Larry pulled into the theater parking lot. "Last chance to change your mind." He winked.

"It's been ages since I've been to the movies."

"So?" He waited for her answer.

Nina hesitated. "You're right. Why not?"

Larry shut off the engine, came around to the passenger side, and helped her to the pavement.

Her short skirt slid up and Nina blushed.

"Come on." He took her hand. "The previews start in ten minutes."

While Larry went to the concession stand, Nina telephoned home. The old, ornate theater brought back happy memories of the times she and Vito brought the boys to Saturday matinees. Soon she was eating popcorn, drinking an orange soda, and laughing like she had not done in a long time. Halfway through the movie, Larry straightened his legs and stretched, leaving his arm on the back of her seat and his hand resting lightly on her shoulder. Occasionally, he squeezed her upper arm when something funny happened. Twice she thought he touched her hair, but it was so brief and delicate she was not sure.

When the movie was over, he asked, "Would you like to go somewhere for a drink?"

"I don't think so," Nina said, remembering the Long Island Iced Teas. "But pie and coffee sounds good."

"You talked me into it." He took her hand and started through the parking lot. It felt like a first date. He drove back to the small café.

After they ordered apple pie á la mode, Nina reached into her purse and handed Larry the title to the Camaro.

He scanned the information with his eyebrows drawn together. "Is Anthony's real name Vito?"

"No. The car belongs to his father."

"Why didn't his father transfer the plates to Anthony?"

"I don't know," Nina said. "I thought he took care of it. He gave me the bill of sale from when he bought the car." She pulled the second paper from her purse. "It's probably my fault, I should've asked him to apply a long time ago, but I forgot all about it, and I guess he did, too."

"Do you know more about this than you're telling me?" Larry asked.

Nina shook her head, but kept her eyes averted.

Larry looked over the papers. "Your son's driving a stolen car."

Nina sat up straight. "Officer Ingram didn't say anything about the car being stolen."

"He didn't know. I checked it out myself."

"You must be mistaken. You can see his father bought the car from a man in north Florida."

"I'd bet a week's pay the title's a forgery. This paper's fresh off the press." He turned the papers upside down. "I kept hoping all week that there was some kind of mistake."

Nina looked out the window into the darkness. Neither one spoke. The pie and coffee sat untouched.

Larry reached across the table and lightly placed his hand on hers. "I'm gonna take these papers and make copies to put in the file before I destroy the originals. I'll make a note that the car belongs to Vito DiGregetti, and that a new plate has been applied for. I can't get rid of the records right now, but I can close the file and see that it's misplaced. Maybe, in time, the whole folder will disappear."

Not knowing what else to do, she nodded and he withdrew his hand.

"I want you to give the car back to your ex. Let this be his problem. Don't let Anthony drive the car again. Not even once."

"Okay." Nina could barely talk. "I appreciate what you're doing for me."

"I'm not doing it for you. Anthony's a good kid. I can't believe a father would jeopardize his son's whole future for the price of a used car. The best advice I can give is to make sure your son understands legal registration." Then unexpectedly, Larry grinned and picked up his fork. "Eat your pie before the ice cream melts."

When Nina came home, she called Frankie, and he agreed to come get the Camaro.

Nina got up early and went to Anthony's room. She tapped on the door.

"I'm awake," he called out.

"Can I come in?" she asked. "I need to talk to you."

"Door's not locked."

Nina came in and closed the door behind her.

"Is something wrong?" Anthony rubbed his eyes and looked at the clock.

Nina stood at the foot of the bed. "We have a problem." She paused, not quite sure how he would take the news. "The Camaro your father gave you is a stolen car."

Anthony sat up and pushed the hair out of his eyes. "Who told you that?"

"The title Chance sent us was a forgery. Officer Macklin said for you not to drive the car anymore, and I promised to give it back to your father. You've been driving on illegal plates."

"Dad wouldn't do that. The cop made a mistake."

Nina looked directly into her son's sleepy eyes and shook her head. "There's no mistake. Frankie's sending a guy to pick up the car this morning."

"So, what do I do now? How do you expect me to get to school?"

"You can drive the Mustang until I can get you another car."

"When will that be?"

"Probably this month. Maybe this weekend," she said. "Michael needs at least a month to get used to driving his car before he takes his test on his birthday."

"Did you tell Michael and Joey my car was stolen?"

"No."

"Don't tell them. A couple of guys at school said things about Dad, and Michael's already been in a fistfight. He has a hard time dealing with gossip."

"Why didn't you tell me about this? I could've gone to school and gotten Father Mendezino to intercede."

"That's why we didn't tell you. We agreed to handle it ourselves. We don't want you to do anything."

Nina sat down on the end of Anthony's bed. "But I want to help. You boys aren't responsible for what your father's mixed up in."

"It's not our fault what you're mixed up in, either." Anthony yawned.

"I'm not mixed up in anything," Nina said, her tone defensive.

"A kid from school has an uncle named Sean Donovan. He said his uncle pays you money to keep the Mafia from setting fire to his store again."

"Do you believe that?" Nina asked, afraid to hear the answer.

"Yes, but I told Sean Donovan's nephew he was full of shit, right before I gave him a bloody nose."

Nina's hand flew to her mouth, her voice cracked. "I had no idea you boys were going through all of this."

"Michael and Joey don't know anything except what a couple of creeps said about Dad. I shut them up in a hurry, but *I* figured out what was going on a long time ago."

"Why didn't you tell me?"

"What good would that do?"

"Listen," Nina whispered "It's okay if you want to stay home from school today. We can decide what we need to do about all of this."

"I'm going to school. I plan to get a scholarship just like my friend John did."

"You'll graduate soon, but Joey and Michael have to keep going. I have to do something."

"It was bad for awhile, but since the papers stopped writing about the fire and drugging the horses, things have quieted down. That kid ain't gonna tell anyone else about you. Not if he wants to live."

Nina gave her son a terrified look. "Please, Anthony, don't talk like that. Whatever I've done was to keep you boys out of this kind of life, not bring you into it."

"I'll tell Michael and Joey the Camaro's not running good, so I'm getting a different car. That's all they need to know."

Nina was amazed how much Anthony knew, and that he handled it so well. In fact, he seemed a little too cool for an eighteen-year old, and it worried her. *What else don't I know about my son?*

CHAPTER TWENTY-THREE

Shortly after the boys left for school, a tow truck arrived and hauled the Camaro away. It was a rainy, dreary day so Nina decided to stay at home to sketch a new ad.

Nina worked for several hours at the kitchen table. She was coloring in a green four-leaf clover for next month's St. Patrick's Day sale-a-thon at Donovan's Meat Market when she heard a car door slam shut. She looked out the window and saw a yellow cab in the driveway. Her pulse quickened. She had not called a taxi.

A long buzz sounded from the doorbell.

The sunroom projected from the house next to the front door, but the draperies were closed and Nina could not see out the window. She went to the door and looked through the peephole. She saw no one.

"Taxi!" a man's muffled voice bellowed.

She touched the doorknob, but something was not right.

It could be Vito disguising his voice, or some other guy Vito sent.

Nina crept along the hallway to the sunroom. The windows ran from floor to ceiling, but if she tried to look between the panels, the man would surely see her. Even if she could see who it was, she might not recognize him.

She placed a hassock on a chair and climbed on top. Still not high enough, she reached toward the grandfather clock. If she peeked through the top of the drapes the person would need to be looking straight up to notice her.

Whoever stood outside was getting impatient, because he struck five resounding blows on the door.

Vito could've borrowed the cab. He's done it before, but why didn't the guard call?

With one hand on the clock and the other opening the heavy material, Nina stood on tiptoe. The footstool flew out from under her, the chair turned on its side and crashed into a floor lamp, leaving Nina sprawled on the floor. Unable to move, the wind gone from her chest, she watched the room fade into darkness.

Nina vaguely remembered being scooped up, carried, and dropped on a bed. She blinked and focused on Vito. When she tried to move, the pain in her shoulder ricocheted down her arm. She grimaced, her eyelids fluttered and closed again.

She felt a cold washcloth being applied to her forehead and Vito's presence beside her on the bed. Her body tensed as she realized she was alone in the house with him. She hurt all over, but did not want to move until she found out why he was there. She opened her eyes and surveyed the room.

Vito let out a half laugh. "I came here to knock the shit out of you, but it looks like you managed that all by yourself. What the hell was you doin'?"

"Trying to, to see who, ah, was at the door," she whispered. "The guard." She paused. "He didn't call."

"That's because he's not too bright. It was like sneaking past a baby. Besides would you have opened the door if you knew it was me?"

"No."

"There you go." He smirked. "I heard a crash and called your name, but you didn't answer."

Nina's eyes opened a little wider. "How did you get in?"

"When you didn't answer, I went to get a tire iron from the cab to break a window, but on my way back I saw the garage door wasn't all the way down. I opened it, came in, and found you on the floor."

Her words came out slowly. "You have no business coming—"

"I have no business, all right." He leaned close to her face. "That's why I'm here."

She made an attempt to sit up and her face contorted.

He shoved her back against the pillow. "I'm not through with you yet."

The thump-thump of Joey's basketball echoed on the front steps.

Vito stepped out of the bedroom, closing the door just as all three boys came down the hallway.

"Who came in a taxi?" Joey asked.

"I did," Nina heard Vito say.

"Where's Mom?" Michael asked.

"She's in bed resting." Vito chuckled as if this was a common occurrence. "C'mon, I'll help you kids start dinner."

"What's the matter with her?" Anthony asked.

"She called me. Said she didn't feel good and wanted me to come over."

"So why'd you come in a cab?" Anthony's voice grew louder.

Vito said something about his car being on the blink and he had to take it to the dealership. "I was worried about your mother, so I borrowed Jimmy's taxi and came straight here. You remember Jimmy. He bought you that red bike when you were ten."

"No, I *don't* remember."

Vito moved the boys toward the kitchen.

Anthony balked. "Did you call Doctor Andrews?"

"Nah, when I got here, she said she felt better. You boys leave her alone. She doesn't want to be bothered."

The boys went into the kitchen, and Vito came into Nina's bedroom with a cup of tea.

"How did you get by the guard?" she asked again.

"I borrowed Jimmy's cab and waited outside the gate until a taxi came out. As soon as it passed, I came in and told the guard we forgot something. He didn't even look in the back seat to see if I had a passenger."

"He didn't question you?" Nina lifted her head to sip the tea. She relaxed and let the tea sooth her aching body.

"Nah. That's what you get for living in a classy neighborhood. Lots of cabs run in and out of here."

He came around to the side of the bed and thrust his hand toward her. She jerked away when he touched her hair.

He laughed at her reaction. "Ya musta cracked your noggin. You got a lump up there, and it looks like you're gonna have a bad bruise on your thigh."

The room seemed to waver. Nina rubbed her upper arm and moaned.

"You don't need to put on an act for me. I could care less how you feel."

"Would you hand me that yellow blanket from the top of the closet?"

"You think I came here to play nursemaid?" He took the thin blanket from the shelf and tossed it onto the bed.

"I'm cold."

"Well, I'm not Florence Nightingale." He walked to the foot of the bed and stared at Nina. "I know who took over my business."

Nina dropped the cup, spilling tea onto the bedding.

"Damn. Whad ya' do that for?"

Her hands shook as she tried to gather the fleece blanket together.

Vito set the cup on the dresser and threw the blanket on the floor. "Take a nap. I'm helping the boys cook. After dinner, we're gonna settle this." He took the empty cup and left the room, closing the door behind him.

She cringed and sank lower in the bed. Pots and pans rattled in the kitchen, and as much as she tried not to, she fell asleep.

The next time Nina woke, she heard loud voices. She strained to hear the conversation.

"That's a bunch of bull crap," Anthony shouted.

"Keep it down," Vito grunted. "Your mother needs to sleep."

Nina was now wide-awake and felt like she could get up, but she stayed in bed and listened.

A few minutes later, Joey peeked into her bedroom. "Are you all right?" he whispered.

"Yeah." She held out her hand to him.

He hurried to the bed. "I was really worried about you." He leaned close. "Dad's here," he whispered.

"I know. It's okay."

Vito carried a bowl of chicken soup into the room. "Brought you something."

Joey pulled her vanity stool close to the bed and Vito set the tray on it. Michael and Anthony hovered in the doorway. Nina eyes filled with tears. *Anyone looking in the window would think we were a normal family.*

"You boys take a walk." Vito hiked his thumb for them to leave. "Your mom and me gotta settle some things."

Joey and Michael left the room, but Anthony refused to leave

Instead, he walked to the side of Nina's bed. "Maybe she doesn't feel good enough to talk right now." Anthony stood three inches taller than Vito, and although he was thin, he had developed strong muscles playing football. "I'm not gonna let you push her into anything she doesn't want to do."

Vito gave his son an ironic look, "Oh, the boy thinks he's become the man of the house?"

"Vito, don't start anything. He's just concerned about me." Nina pushed the sheet aside.

"Don't get up," Anthony said as he placed his hand on his mother's shoulder. "You two can talk when *she's* ready."

"I don't need permission from a kid to talk to my wife. Now get the hell out of here, like I told you." Vito gave Anthony a shove toward the doorway.

Anthony pushed back, but Vito, more experienced, saw it coming. He wrapped his arms around his son and held him in a locked position.

"I don't want to hurt you." Vito's vice-like grip burrowed deep into his son's upper arms.

"Stop it!" Nina screamed, forcing herself to sit up on the edge of the bed.

One firm elbow rammed his father's gut, and Anthony burst out of Vito's arms. "You wanna talk—talk! There's nothing you have to say I don't already know."

Joey and Michael had come back in and were standing in the doorway.

"What's going on?" Michael looked at his father suspiciously.

"Anthony's getting a little too smart for his own damn good." Vito assumed a boxer's stance. "Come on, show your old man how tough you are," he challenged.

Nina got up from the bed and stood in front of Anthony. "Leave, Vito. Leave now, or I'll call the police."

"You make a fool out of me in front of my sons? You treat them like babies. They'll never amount to anything." Vito stormed from the room. "This ain't over." He left by the front door and slammed it behind him.

Nina slumped on the bed, shaking.

"Are you going to be okay?" Joey asked with tears in his eyes.

She nodded.

Michael sat on the edge of his mother's bed, his hand touching her arm, while Joey went to the kitchen for paper towels to wipe up the soup that had somehow been knocked to the floor.

"Michael," Nina whispered. "Take care of Joey. He doesn't understand how things are."

After Vito pulled the taxi out of the driveway, she heard Anthony walk toward the back door. She knew he was headed for the dock. She decided to give him some time to sort things out before she spoke with him.

After a while, Nina went into the bathroom, washed her face, and straightened her clothes. Joey and Michael were in their bedroom doing their homework. Nina made herself a cup of tea and carried it to the dock.

"I don't understand," Anthony said. "Why did you call Dad to help you?"

"I didn't call him." Nina sipped her tea and slowly told Anthony how she ended up in bed.

"Are you gonna do anything about him coming here?" Anthony asked.

"No. It wouldn't accomplish anything." She took another sip of tea. "And physically fighting with your dad won't do any good either."

"He lied to me." Anthony kept his eyes on the river. "I asked him if he knew the car was stolen, and he told me a stupid story."

Nina sat down on the dock beside her son.

"He acted like I was a five-year-old with no brains. I should've hit him before he came back into your room, but I thought he'd leave and let you sleep."

"I really think he only wanted to talk," she said.

"Sure, that's the way he always starts. Then, when you don't give him the answers he wants, he's through talking. Why'd you let him smack you around all those years?"

Nina had always sent the boys to their rooms when Vito started to boil, and she had no idea how much Anthony may have seen or heard. "Because he's your father, and you love him, and he loves you. I didn't want to ruin all of that."

"I didn't love him then, and I don't love him now. I tried to *please* him. I kept trying until I realized that nothing I did would ever satisfy him."

"I guess that's what I did, too." Nina put her arm around her son. It was the first time she had seen tears in his eyes since he entered first grade.

CHAPTER TWENTY-FOUR

Two weeks later, Nina spotted Larry Macklin's squad car backed into the parking lot by the subdivion's tennis courts.

She pulled her car beside his and lowered her window. "I gave the Camaro back to Vito."

"I thought so," Larry said. "I saw Anthony driving a Firebird. Tell him to watch out for Ingram. He's hell on sport cars, even old ones."

Nina shifted her car into reverse. "I'll tell him."

"Wait a minute."

She hit the brake.

Larry drifted forward until their windows were again side by side. "I'd like to see you again."

"I don't have much time. I work a lot of hours."

"We could go to another movie, or maybe dinner?" He waited for her answer.

Nina hesitated, knowing it was not the smartest thing to do, but deep down she really wanted to be with him. "Dinner on Friday sounds good."

"I'll pick you up."

"No," Nina insisted. "I'll meet you in the theater parking lot. I'm not ready to tell the boys I'm going out with anyone. They're going through a lot right now."

Redesigning the Mob

He nodded.

Nina drove out of the parking lot. She looked in the rearview mirror to check her makeup. *It feels good to be wanted.*

Since Vito's stormy visit, neither Nina nor the boys had heard from him. The family settled back into their regular routine, and Nina pushed the unwanted encounter to the back of her mind. It was time for final exams, and the boys were looking forward to summer vacation.

Catherine, now Anthony's steady, often came to the house. Her two older brothers were students at the University of Florida, but her parents felt she should attend the local community college. They wanted her to live at home for the next two years, but Catherine was determined to go to Florida State University with Anthony.

Friday evening at seven, Nina started getting ready for her date with Larry. Two statements that came in the mail that day lay open on her dressing table. She had charged presents for the boys, given Ginger money, and purchased two cars before knowing how big of a percentage the mob would demand as their cut of her new business. She wished she had not used the credit card.

"You got a date tonight?" Anthony asked.

Nina laughed. "Actually, I do."

"You do?" he said. "I was just joking."

"I'm meeting him at the theater." Nina snapped the catch on a gold bracelet.

"Why doesn't he pick you up?"

"Well, to tell you the truth, I didn't know what you boys would think about me going out." Nina blushed. "His name's Larry Macklin. He's a police officer. I could ask him to dinner, so you can all meet him."

"We know Larry, the cop," Anthony said. "He plays basketball with us."

"His son, Brian, is in my class." Joey said as he walked in on the end of the conversation. "Once in a while, Mr. Macklin comes by the school and takes us to lunch."

"Oh he does, does he?" Nina fastened an earring.

"Hurry up, Joey, before all the courts are filled," Michael said from the doorway.

"How come you're not taking Jennifer out any more?" Nina asked Michael.

"We broke up. She's dating some guy with a pad of his own on the beach. He takes her to bars."

"She's not old enough to drink," Nina said hoping Michael would tell her more, but all he did was shrug and walk out the door with Joey.

After the Mustang left, Anthony asked his mother, "How much does this cop know about your advertising business?"

"I don't know. The subject hasn't come up." Nina began brushing her hair.

Anthony sat on the velvet covered stool in front of Nina's dressing table. "You're asking for trouble," he warned.

"I plan on getting out of the business," Nina said. But right now, I don't know how."

Anthony picked up the bill for $2,000 from attorney Sam Marin. "What's this for?"

"Sam handled the divorce. Your father said he paid it, but as you can see, he didn't."

Anthony turned over the MasterCard bill for over five grand. "Wow! Who does this belong to?"

"It's mine. I took contracts to do advertising that had nothing to do with the mobs protection racket, so I didn't think I had to give them a cut of my profit. I was making plenty of money when I made the purchases." Nina put on a final dab of lipstick. "I found out later that I have to pay the organization an even higher percentage for my private accounts. By the time I pay the business bills and the mob, there's not much left."

"Why didn't you say something?" Anthony ran his finger down the list of charges. "You didn't have to buy all this stuff for us. I'm gonna get a job and help pay this off."

"No, you're not. Finals are next week. You need to get good marks if you want that scholarship." Nina picked up her purse and keys. "Don't worry about the bills. You have a nice girlfriend and you're going away to college. These should be happy days for you."

Anthony laid the monthly statement back on the table. "I wish you'd let me help."

Nina took one last look in the mirror. "I'll find a way."

Royal palms lined the bank of the intra-coastal canal behind Mariana's Restaurant. Thick gray trunks rose thirty feet into the air, where large green shoots sprang out in all directions. Nina and Larry chose an outside table so they could watch the water rush by and listen to the gentle rustle of the swaying fronds. They sipped vodka gimlets while they waited for their clams' oreganata appetizer.

"I understand you made a point of getting to know my sons," Nina said with a smile.

Larry picked at a mini complimentary shrimp cocktail that had been delivered to the table with the drinks. "I've played basketball at the park ever since I started working in this area. I didn't seek your boys out, but they spend a lot of time on the court and so do I. Eventually we met." He motioned toward the shrimp. "Would you like one?"

She nodded.

"I have to admit I knew who they were and welcomed the chance to be their friend," Larry said.

"And school?" Nina opened her mouth when he extended a tiny shrimp on a toothpick.

"You can't blame that on me." He dipped another shrimp into the sauce. "Joey and my son are in the same homeroom and have identical schedules. When the two of them became friends, I was pleased to see that Brian was taking an interest in basketball."

"Joey's in his glory when he's on the court." She shook her head when he offered a second shrimp.

"Taking the boys to lunch means I get to spend a little more time with my son. I like Joey. He's a smart kid. Brian's learned a lot from him."

"So, you not only spoil your son, you indulge mine," Nina teased.

"A little extra attention can't hurt. They're good kids. Brian plans to go to community college. They have a good course in criminal justice. He's got his heart set on being a detective." Larry laughed. "He watches every cop show on television."

"Joey hasn't decided what he wants to do." Nina rolled her eyes. "Other than play basketball."

"Sports'll wear off. His sights are set much higher."

"On what?"

"He said he gets good grades in math and science, and his teacher suggested something in the chemistry field, but that's not what Joey wants. He says he's going to be a lawyer."

"I haven't heard anything about this."

"I think he misses his dad, so he talks to me sometimes." Larry moved his drink aside when the waiter set the clams and small plates with cocktail forks and lemon wedges on the table.

"Did Joey say he missed his dad?" Nina picked up a tiny fork.

"No, that was my thought." Larry squeezed lemon on a stuffed clam. "All he ever said to me was, 'My dad's busy, so I haven't seen him in a while.'"

A small combo played inside, and speakers carried the music to the patio. Dusk settled in, and an array of colored lights sparkled around the edge of the open area. A busboy lit the flaming torches that provided outside lighting. When the waiter served their rack of lamb, Larry ordered a split of red wine. Nina relaxed. She was becoming quite fond of Larry and hoped he felt the same way.

After dinner, a water taxi docked and the driver asked if anyone wanted a ride. A young couple came out of the restaurant, giggling, and climbed into the boat.

"Last call," the driver shouted from the dock.

"Wanna go?" Larry asked Nina.

"How will we get back?"

"He'll bring us. If not, we'll catch a cab." He reached across the table and touched her hand. "C'mon."

Nina smiled and agreed.

Larry hailed the water taxi, paid the dinner tab, and a few minutes later Nina's hair was blowing in the breeze. They turned left into a smaller canal and stopped in front of Harry's Riptide Bar. Upbeat chords blared from the open structure. They disembarked and climbed the wooden steps into a throng of barefoot dancers.

When the conga line passed, a young man grabbed Nina by the waist and put her between him and a friend. Larry jumped in between the next two girls and off they went. They drank and danced, and by midnight Larry was holding Nina close, and she loved every minute of it.

Nina looked at her watch. "I've got to go home," she said, her tone saying she wished she didn't.

The water taxi had come and gone several times and was ready to leave again.

"Hold on!" Larry shouted to the driver as he tossed bills to the bartender.

Nina grabbed her sandals, carried them to the boat, and climbed into the hull. She settled on the back seat and took a deep breath.

Larry jumped in, causing the craft to dip and water to splash. The boat became packed with people on their way back to wherever they were picked up. Nina found herself squashed between a sailor and Larry.

"I can't breathe," she said.

He picked her up and put her on his lap. Everyone on board applauded. After each stop, the speedy taxi took off fast, and Nina was thrown against Larry. She finally quit saying, "I'm sorry," since he obviously was enjoying it.

The last time they collided he held her close and kissed her. After the long, deep kiss, Nina kept her arms around Larry's neck. She swallowed hard and took a deep breath. For a fleeting moment Nina felt secure pressed against Larry's two hundred pounds of muscle. In reality, Nina knew no man could give her freedom from the mob, or safety from Vito. Not even a cop.

"Want some more?" he teased.

"Not right now." Nina gently took her arms away.

CHAPTER TWENTY-FIVE

Vito was still fuming over Nina's calling Chance about the stupid Camaro title when he ran into a grifter at the racetrack.

"I've been lookin' all over for you," the guy said.

"Yeah, how come you're lookin' for me?"

"I got a message from Danny. He said to give you this number." He handed Vito a scrunched up piece of paper. "He's there on Fridays between one and five."

The telephone number had a 404 area code and was scratched on the back of a K-Mart receipt. Vito shoved it in his pocket and handed the guy a twenty-dollar bill.

On Friday, Vito called Danny from a Miami coin phone.

"Pilgrim's Print Shop," a man answered.

"Let me talk to Danny," Vito said.

"Danny," the man called out. "You got a call on line two."

"Yeah," Danny said into the receiver.

"You wanna talk?" Vito asked.

"Hey, big shot, I hear you're outta work." Danny sounded as cheerful as ever.

"Who told you that?"

"It's no secret that you're getting pushed out. Frankie tells me you're running plastic. I thought you might like bingo better. Wanna come to Atlanta?"

"I ain't living in red clay or getting chummy with redneck Bible thumpers."

"It's not like that. This city's growing fast."

"Like the *melanzanas* found a place to call home," Vito scoffed.

Danny snorted. "At least the blacks speak English."

"If that's what you call that jive talk."

"I heard Nina's doing great." Danny taunted. "Ginger said she's got her own advertising company."

"Nina's got her own business?" Vito repeated.

"That's what she said. My oldest girl, Dana, knows what's going on, and she says Nina gives Ginger cash to buy presents for her and the girls. She's blowing your support money while you're hustling your ass trying to get by."

Vito didn't mention he had never honored his obligation to support the boys. "She's back drawing pictures again, but she don't own the business. Remember when I thought the Chicago mob was taking over my territory? Well, I found out it's a wiseguy Chance sent here, and Nina's working for him. He's a stocky guy with fair skin, about 200 pounds, with a thick brush mustache."

"That sounds like Egbert Van der-something. He's a New York triggerman. They call him Dutch. I thought you told me you worked with Dutch when you were in New York."

"Yeah, I uh, now that you mention it, I do remember him," Vito stuttered as he remembered lying to Danny. "We shouldn't be talking about this stuff on the phone."

"It's all right. This here's a straight business. The guy's not connected, at least not yet."

When Danny hung up, Vito beat the receiver on the tempered glass spreading a spiderweb of cracks across the window. The mouthpiece of the telephone broke off and flew into Vito's face. Pedestrians glanced nervously as they walked by, but did not dare come closer.

I'm gonna kill that broad.

Vito got into his car, and at the first available entrance, he turned onto the interstate. Traveling at ninety miles an hour, he screamed his threats. "I'll break every bone in her friggin' body!"

How could she do this to me? She's turning my kids against me after all I did for her.

His mind wandered to his nights with other women and the hurt look on Nina's face when he came home. *No big deal; every man does that.*

He swerved the Cadillac into the outer lane, passing every car in sight.

So, I smacked her around every once in a while; she asked for it.

He saw the flashing light in his rearview mirror, slowed down and moved over two lanes.

Shit, a stupid cop.

Vito got off at the next exit just as an ambulance whizzed by in the fast lane.

He stopped at the first bar he came to and ordered a double shot of vodka and grapefruit juice. It went down like a soft drink.

After his fourth double, he accused the bartender of stealing his money and threatened to bust the place up.

A dark-haired woman, a good six inches taller than Vito, left the pool table and walked toward him. "I'd say it was time for you to leave."

Vito blinked. "You talking to me?"

"Yeah, I'm talking to you. I own this place, and I'm telling you to get out."

"No fucking bitch is going to tell me what to do."

"You calling me a bitch?" The bar owner maintained her composure.

"All you women are alike. You get yourself a little business, and you think you grew balls."

"You can walk out of here, or be thrown out. Take your choice." Her voice was calm but adamant.

"You act like a man, you get treated like one." Vito spun off the bar stool and swung his fist at the woman's jaw.

She ducked, and when he lost his balance from the force of his swing, she slammed the pool stick across his back. There was a loud crack. Vito hit the floor with the wind knocked out of him. He tried to get up and slipped on the scattered peanut shells.

The woman was back shooting pool when two bouncers tossed Vito out the door. It was all he could do to get to his car. He crawled in and drove a couple of blocks to a cheap motel. He did not want anyone to know what had happened to him.

He woke up the next afternoon, his rage dissipated, but his back throbbing. He could not stand the thought of facing Maria, and he needed 'the hair of the dog' to feel better.

Not wanting to run into any of his friends, he stopped at a neighborhood tavern called Bo's Bar. The room was small and dark. Most of the men had a pitcher of beer in front of them—the usual construction crew that quit work between two and three in the afternoon. Vito had his eye on an appealing young woman with Marilyn Monroe hair who came in right after he arrived. She did not seem to be interested in anyone, but when she looked his way, he decided he did not need another bellyaching broad and turned his head.

She came over and sat beside him. "Hi, my name's Dahlia." She was quiet, gave yes and no answers, and did not ask for anything, not even a cocktail. The conversation started out innocently enough, but Vito was lonely and began to spill his guts about the raw deal he was getting from Maria. After his fourth drink, he realized he was talking to much and once again drinking like a lush.

"Let me see if I got this straight," the blonde said. "Are you telling me that this chick you live with pays all the bills, and you crash there when you don't have anywhere else to go?"

"Nah, she ain't no chick, she's a lady. I like her, but she needs a guy that works nine to five and doesn't have the kinda needs I have."

"What kind of needs?"

"Aw, you know."

Her voluptuous lips parted. "I understand. I have a few yearnings of my own."

"A pretty girl like you?" Vito's snug trousers got tighter.

"You think I'm pretty?" Dahlia asked.

He leaned forward to order another Dewar's, exposing a bulge where an automatic was stuck in the waistband in the back of his pants. "Yeah, I think you're pretty. How 'bout I buy you a drink?"

"I think I made a mistake." She slid off the stool and walked out the door into the sunlight.

"Wait up," Vito called, as he tossed a few bills on the bar and followed her. "What the hell's wrong with you? I offer to buy you a drink and you think I'm making a pass."

"No, I don't think you hit on me; I think you're stupid."

"C'mon, slow down. I wanna talk."

"Why, so you can pull out your badge and arrest me?"

Vito stopped. "You're a prostitute? Didn't you know you were in a fuckin' construction bar? Those guys drink more than they make."

"I don't wanna talk about this. Especially on the street with a guy in a suit I ain't ever seen before."

He stopped in the middle of the sidewalk. "Take a good look at the suit, lady." He turned all the way around. "It ain't J. C. Penny. How many cops do you see in imported Italian threads?"

She rolled her eyes.

"Get in your car and follow me." Vito motioned toward his Cadillac.

"I don't know," she said.

"Listen. We'll go to a nice restaurant with a lot of people, and I'll buy you dinner. If you need money, I'll give you some. We'll sign a paper that you owe me. You can't go to jail for a loan. No hanky panky."

By the end of the evening, Dahlia agreed to get a few more girls, and Vito had himself a lucrative new business.

"I know somebody who'll cut us a deal, "Vito said with confidence. "He already has a bevy of girls working for him. He'll tell us what clubs to work and which hotels to use." He squeezed one of her breasts. "We'll give him a little cut."

She wet her lips and sealed the arrangement with a kiss.

"Don't do that." Vito wiped his mouth with the back of his hand. "I was just checking to see if they were real." He touched his glass to hers. "You and the girls get protection from the law, and fifty percent of what you make."

"Sixty," Dahlia said.

"You're getting a damn good deal. If you worked for a lowlife pimp, he'd take ninety."

"That's why I picked you. I knew you'd treat me good. I could tell it the minute I walked in the bar."

"Aw, go on. You're putting me on."

Dahlia got into her car. "I'll wait for your call."

Vito spent two weeks convincing Frankie to put Dahlia and her friends to work. Finally, Vito and Frankie had a meeting at a patio bar beside a saltwater pool on the beach. They were both dressed in Bermuda shorts and open Hawaiian shirts. Frankie wore black socks with his brown sandals.

Vito looked at Frankie's feet. "You look like a senior citizen from South Beach."

"I wouldn't talk if I were you. Men who get pedicures shouldn't wear flip-flops."

"It ain't polish, dumbfuck. I have'em buffed. Fancy women like the look."

"Keep your mind on business." Frankie picked up his glass. "You keep ten percent, I take my cut, and the rest goes to Chance. And don't abuse your privileges." Frankie swirled his bicarbonate of soda, then polished it off. "No rough stuff. You don't damage a showroom Cadillac."

"Wait a minute," Vito protested. "I get twenty. I'm the one providing the girls."

Frankie snickered. "Well, New York provides the setup, and you shoulda thought about that before you told Dahlia that the girls could keep so much. Did you make that promise while you were getting laid?"

Vito swallowed his pride. He wanted the deal. "Look." He put his hand up to calm Frankie. "Let's keep this between you and me. New York doesn't need to know about my girls. We can split Chance's cut. It'll be good for both of us. Whad'ya say?"

"Wise up, Vito. You're lucky to still be around." Frankie tapped his fingers on the bar.

Vito pointed to four gorgeous women lounging on the other side of the pool Beads of moisture shimmered on their deeply tanned bodies. Dahlia, her skin glistening in the noonday sun, sidled up to the bar next to him.

Vito lightly smacked her on the rear. "This is Dahlia," he said. Then pointed to Frankie, "This here's the man."

"Have them take a stroll around the pool," Frankie said to Dahlia

Dahlia fluttered her fingers and the women casually stood and made their way to a small snack stand a few feet past the bar.

"They're all divorcées, a couple of them have kids, and one has a day job." Dahlia said shifting her supple frame and leaning forward. The tips of her nipples strained against the low-cut fabric. "They don't wanna work the streets, and they're afraid to go into the better places and get picked up by the cops."

"Any of them ever have a run in with the city authorities, for any reason?" Frankie asked.

Dahlia shook her head

"Tell me now," he said. "Because if I find out later, getting caught by the law will look like a walk in the park."

Frankie winked at Vito as a tall brunette sauntered by.

"I did my part." Dahlia said. "They're young, beautiful, and well built. We're all ready to make you money, and don't forget my bonus," she quipped.

Frankie rubbed his hairy chest as the indigestion began to fade. "I have access to the most fashionable hotels in the city and the hottest clubs on the beach. I set the price and the girls get twenty-five percent."

Dahlia frowned. "Vito promised fifty and that's what I told the girls. They might not want to work for less."

Frankie glared at her. "Do me a favor, Dahlia. March your ass over there and tell them the fuckin' price has changed before I walk out of here, and they can all go to hell. Don't waste my friggin' time."

"I'll tell 'em. It'll be okay." Dahlia glanced over at the women.

Frankie punched his chest and burped. "Once in a while, you do us a favor. Everyone works on the honor system, which means nobody lies about money. No one gets hurt, and no one goes to jail. Break the code, and I'll know before you have your morning coffee." Frankie tucked Dahlia's bonus into her bikini top.

"I'll make sure they understand," she said.

"Good." Frankie stood up to leave.

Vito eyed the large bill. It was double what he had promised Dahlia.

Frankie grinned at Vito. "Don't worry. I'll take it out of your cut."

Vito was clearly tired of being pushed around, but he shrugged the remark off. "I'll be in touch," Vito told Dahlia. He knew Maria was waiting for him, and he did not want to listen to her mouth if he was late.

Vito turned on the radio and drove along A1A. Alice, the girl Vito had hired to run his stolen credit cards, had lured a couple of her relatives to help her and in turn the swag payoff tripled. With money no longer an issue, Vito put his problems with Nina on the back burner. He needed time to calculate the deal with Frankie.

Control is what he wanted, and control is what he would have. He hummed along to the music on the radio.

Dahlia, I like the sound of that name. I got me one sweet flower, and she's mine anytime I—he snapped his fingers.

CHAPTER TWENTY-SIX

Excitement ran high at the end of May. Anthony and Catherine graduated from high school and were busily making plans for college. Florida State University again contacted Anthony. Although he had graduated with average grades, they were adequate to qualify him for a two-year scholasrship and a place on the football team.

Nina threw a party for Anthony and told Joey and Michael they could each invite a close friend. Bertha cleaned the house the day before and arrived on the afternoon of the party to do the cooking.

"What time you want me to set out the food?" Bertha asked Nina.

"Anytime after the first guests arrive. It'll be mostly kids."

Nina had planned to tell Bertha she could no longer afford to have her clean or help out with the cooking. However, working extra hours to compensate for the decrease in her profit had left her exhausted. Besides, she wanted the boys to see her as a successful businesswoman. They had suffered enough from the bad publicity caused by their father, so Nina decided she would have to tighten her belt when it came to her personal expenditures.

"When you gonna have a real dinner party so I can show off what I can really do?" Bertha asked Nina on her way to the kitchen.

"I don't know many people. I guess we moved too often to accumulate friends."

"I'll bet Larry knows lots of people," Bertha said with a wink. "You could invite his friends."

Anthony walked into the kitchen and snitched a large prawn from Bertha's tray.

"You need to start having fun instead of working so much." Bertha told Nina.

"Yeah." Anthony agreed. "That's what I told her."

Nina ignored their remarks and stepped inside the pantry to make sure the boys had covered the drinks in the big cooler with ice.

Anthony slipped in behind her. "Hey," he whispered. "I got a job."

"That's great." Nina closed the lid on the cooler.

He hesitated. "I'll be working for Uncle Louie in one of his game rooms."

Her dark eyes opened wide. "Is your dad behind this?"

"No. I don't think he even knows about it."

"And why are you calling him 'Uncle Louie'? He's not your uncle. He's your dad's uncle."

"Louie likes it when I call him that. I phoned him myself and told him I could start as soon as school got out. I'm going to Hialeah to see him tomorrow."

Nina's face grew red hot with anger. "No, you're not."

"It's not what you think." Anthony argued.

"Oh, yes it is."

"I know it's a place they launder money, but all I gotta do is make change." Anthony shifted his weight from one foot to the other. "Other guys work for him, and they're not even Italian. Just kids working part time."

"You can find another place to work," Nina insisted.

"No one else is going to pay me as much, or give me as many hours as I want to work. I'll have working experience when I go for a job in Tallahassee. He said he'd give me a good reference."

"You'll get experience all right, but it'll be the wrong kind." Nina's voice escalated.

"I won't get mixed up in what he does. All I want is money to go away to college. The scholarship doesn't pay for everything. I'll be playing football, and that doesn't leave much time to study. I won't be able to hold down a decent paying job during the school year."

Bertha opened the pantry door. "Need any help in here?"

"No, everything's done," Nina said. "Get Michael to help you carry the cooler to the patio," she told Anthony. "We'll talk later."

Larry and Brian came early to help set up the volleyball net and put white lime on the grass to mark the boundaries. When the other kids arrived, Larry and Mickey went to the family room to watch TV. Bertha and Nina set out the food, and when Ginger arrived dressed in short yellow shorts and a white midriff top, Nina took her to meet Larry.

"Ginger, this is Larry." Nina touched Larry's arm as he stood up. "Larry, meet my best friend, Ginger."

He said hello and shook her hand. Nina noticed that he tried to appear as though he had not taken a full look at her petite body.

"You look familiar. Have we met before?" Ginger asked.

"I don't believe so," Larry said. "Hey Mickey, isn't it time for the game to start?"

"Just about."

Larry turned on the television.

Teasing Ginger, Mickey said, "I see you dropped a few pounds and dress sexy now that Danny's out of town. I guess you couldn't do that when he was here or you'd have three more kids by now."

"When's *your* baby due?" Ginger punched Mickey in the gut. "If you get any bigger, they'll have to do a caesarian."

Mickey hugged his belly. "Careful, I'm in training for a 5K road race."

"Believe that and he'll tell you a bigger story," Nina said.

"All kidding aside, you look terrific," he told Ginger. "Maybe I'll slip over and keep you company one evening." Mickey waggled his eyebrows and sat down to watch TV.

"See what I mean?" Nina laughed.

Ginger giggled. "My mother would beat him with the broom handle."

Mickey did not appear to hear Ginger's remark. He was already listening to the pregame baseball commentators.

The adults gathered around the TV watching baseball and making small talk while the kids played volleyball and cruised the patio snacking on Bertha's special party dishes. When Anthony's friends tired of volleyball, Mickey came out to fire up the grill.

Ginger said she had to leave and Nina walked outside with her.

"You got yourself a real hunk." Ginger said, a tinge of envy in her voice.

Nina waved the idea away. "We're only friends, and we live in two different worlds."

"Ain't that the truth?" Ginger took a small box from her purse and took off the square lid. "I got this for Anthony. I wanted to give it to him when we were alone, but he's been busy with the kids." She showed Nina a gold cross with Anthony's initials engraved on the back. "Tell Anthony I said it's to keep him out of trouble."

"I will." Nina took the gift with tears in her eyes and gave Ginger a hug. "Thanks for coming."

"Ya know," Ginger said as she tilted her head, "the more I think about it, the more I feel I've met Larry before."

"Maybe you did. He's a police officer for the city. His son Brian goes to school with Joey. They're best friends. Larry used to work for the county, but he changed jobs so he could spend more time with Brian."

"That works out good for you," Ginger teased.

"Don't be silly. I told you we're just friends."

"That's what everybody says right before they walk down the aisle," Ginger chuckled.

Nina looked down at the driveway.

"Look," Ginger sighed. "We've been through a lot together. If you can't tell me, who can you tell?"

"Well," Nina started.

"You're in love. I knew it. I could tell by the way you two looked at each other." Ginger put her arms around Nina. "Is he good in bed?"

"You gotta know everything." Nina said as happy tears slid down her cheeks.

Ginger grinned. "That's what friends are for."

"I've been to Larry's place a few times when Brian spent the weekend with his mother, but I don't want anyone to know. I think it would bother the boys."

"I think you're crazy," Ginger said. "Those boys know more than you do."

"Maybe so," Nina said as she looked into Ginger's eyes, "but I don't want you to tell them or anyone else. Okay?"

"I promise," Ginger said. She climbed into her car and waved as she backed out of the driveway.

Nina stood for a long moment, thinking about what her friend had said about walking down the aisle, and the impossibility of it all. *Maybe I should put a stop to this relationship with Larry before it goes any further.*

CHAPTER TWENTY-SEVEN

The Monday after Anthony's graduation party, he sat alone in the living room watching TV. He had the whole summer to enjoy before starting college. With Catherine's help he had done well in high school, but he worried about how he would make it through college without her.

The phone rang and Anthony let it ring four times before he answered. It was Catherine wanting him to come over to her house.

"Nah, I can't today," Anthony said curtly.

"Then I'll come there," she said. "There's something I want to talk about."

"Not today, I have things to do."

"All of a sudden you don't want to see me anymore. Why are you treating me this way?" Catherine whined.

"I'm not treating you any different. I have something I need to do. I'll see you tomorrow," Anthony's words were gruff.

"Call me later. Please," she begged.

Reluctantly, he agreed. "Okay."

After they hung up, Anthony went into his room and picked up a legal pad. Catherine had spent hours writing pages of notes for him to study for his finals. He knew that had it not been for her, he would never have gotten decent grades, and would probably not find another girl as good as Catherine.

He ripped out the page from the legal tablet where he had written a number and reached for the telephone.

"Uncle Louie, this is Anthony. Can I come to see you today?"

"If you wanted a job, you shoulda gotten off your ass and been here already," Louie scolded.

"I can come over right now."

"That's okay if you can be here in the next hour."

A couple of well-dressed men were sitting in Louie's messy office when Anthony arrived.

"This is Vito's son," he said by way of introduction to the two men.

Anthony nodded toward them.

"Speak up," Louie said. "I can't hear what's rattling around in that head of yours."

"Yes, sir, I'm Vito's oldest son."

Louie smiled proudly. "I'll be right back," he said to the men. "This'll only take a minute."

He put his arm around Anthony's shoulder. "Come with me."

He walked to the back of the game room. There was a counter with a cash register and a TV. A young boy sat in a chair drinking a can of Coke.

"This here's Skylar," Louie said. "He's gonna go to work over at my new place. He knows the whole set-up. You watch him today, and tomorrow you do what he does." Louie walked back toward his office.

Skylar, a sixteen-year-old redhead with acne, had a filthy mouth. He stared at the TV with his feet propped on a box and made each player wait for change until he felt like getting up. Anthony stood in front of the counter observing Skylar.

"Sit the fuck down," Skylar told Anthony. "You're blocking my view of the door."

Anthony tried to talk with his arrogant young boss, but Skylar could not be bothered. He appeared unable to distinguish Anthony from the empty chair; Later Skylar opened the register and handed Anthony a roll of quarters.

"Go play SeaWolf." Skylar said and shuffled out the back door.

Anthony dropped two of the coins painted with bright red nail polish into the slot and scored fifty thousand points. When he got bored, he looked for Skylar. Two young Cubans stood by the counter waiting for change, and Anthony handed them the last of the red quarters.

"Use these," Anthony said. "I'll go find the boss."

Skylar and another kid with long black dreadlocks were standing just outside the back door. As Anthony approached, he noticed they were passing a joint between them and taking deep drags.

"What's wrong with those games in the backroom?" Anthony asked.

"They're broke." Skylar took a long draw, held it, and passed the reefer to his friend.

"I can see that. What's wrong with them?"

"How the shit should I know? Ask Sal when he comes to fix them. He'll be around sometime today."

Black dreadlocks offered the marijuana to Anthony. He shook his head.

"You don't do grass?" Skylar's friend grinned.

"Not today. I got other things to do."

"Suit yourself," the friend said.

"Two guys inside need change." Anthony motioned toward the Cubans.

Skylar glanced through the open back door. "Let 'em wait." He took one more toke before ambling inside.

Skylar's friend cupped the lit cigarette in his palm. "Stick around. My girl gets off work soon," he said to Anthony. "Sometimes she brings a friend."

Anthony went inside, crossed the mini mall, and bought a frankfurter special at one of the fast food counters. He took his lunch and sat outside on the busstop bench. Anthony ate the hotdog and scarfed up the French fries as he watched people go in and out of the small plaza. Time dragged for Anthony. He did not know if he wanted to do this or not, and hated the fact that he felt he had no other choices.

In the afternoon, Anthony watched Sal, the repairman who had come to fix the broken machines. Sal opened a black briefcase that held an array of tools. There were even tiny screwdrivers so small you could barely see the tips. Each instrument had a particular purpose and fitted into a special place in the satchel.

Anthony stooped beside the man. "What's wrong with this machine?"

Sal's hands were small and deft. "Leave me alone, kid. I got work to do."

"Can I watch?"

Sal did not answer.

Anthony stayed by the repairman's side for two hours. First, he worked on Space Invaders, then he moved to Pong. Most of the games had the same problem, so after the third, Anthony started to catch on. One of the Space Invader machines was really screwed up, and Sal said he would buy a new part and come back the next day.

It was nearing five o'clock when Louie shuffled in through the front door and walked straight to his office.

Anthony followed him. "You know, that Skylar didn't do a damn thing all day."

"I know, but he's not smart enough to steal much," Louie replied as he searched under the piles of paper until he found a pen.

Anthony leaned over Louie's desk. "I can do this job, and I can learn to fix those machines."

Louie's white hair hung past his collar, and a chunk of it hung across his face. "Your mother sure didn't teach you anything, did she?"

Anthony grinned. "I know enough. I don't steal, I don't do drugs, and I can run this business. But I won't take the job unless you get me a set of those tools and have Sal teach me how to do the repairs."

"Well, I'll be damned. You're as bossy as your old man," Louie said with a smile.

When Nina came home from work that night, Anthony was waiting for her. He immediately came into the kitchen and helped her put away the few groceries she had picked up at the Publix supermarket.

"I worked for Uncle Louie today," Anthony announced.

The can of minestone soup in Nina's hand fell and hit the counter with a loud bang.

"Before you say anything, let me tell you about the job." Anthony picked up the can and placed it in the cupboard.

"I'm not changing my mind," Nina said and sat down at the table.

"It's only for two and half months. No other place will hire me if they know I'm gonna leave soon," Anthony reasoned.

Nina's eyes narrowed. "I see signs all over town for summer help."

"Two or three months, that's all I ask." He made her a cup of tea while he talked. "I can work overtime and that means more money. Besides, there's a guy that comes in to fix the games and he's going to teach me. Uncle Louie's gonna buy me my own tools."

"Is that what you want to do for the rest of your life? Work in a rundown mini-mall in a bad part of town?"

"Not work in a mall, Mom, repair digital processors. Every game is a computer. I know I can learn."

Her nails tapped the table.

"Please, give me a chance. If I get the hang of it, I'm gonna change biology to a computer class. Biology is a waste of my time."

Nina thought living on the edge had attracted her son, but still Anthony had never taken a real interest in school. This was the first time she had seen even a spark of enthusiasm. She thought about her own love of art boxed away and put on hold for so many years.

"Okay," she relented. "Two and a half months, then you're off to college. No ifs, ands, or buts." Nina glared at her son.

"You got my word." He gave his mother a hug.

"Oh," Nina said, "I almost forgot. . . ." She got up from the table and took a small box from a corner shelf and held it out to Anthony. "It's from Ginger. She wanted to give it to you herself at the party, but you were busy, and she had to leave." He opened the box and took out the gold cross.

His dark eyes shined. "It's great." He held it up to his neck and looked along the edge of a small mirror that Nina used to reflect a vase of silk violets. "Look, my initials are on the back."

"Here, let me." Nina took the cross and fastened it around her son's neck. "You need to call Ginger and thank her. She said if you wore the cross, it might keep you out of trouble."

"*Me*! Get into trouble?" Anthony laughed, but Nina gave him a worried look.

CHAPTER TWENTY-EIGHT

During summer vacation from school, Mickey took Michael and Joey to Bentleyville to spend a couple of weeks with Nina's mother, Nana Cocolucci.

The house seemed quiet with Michael and Joey gone and Anthony working late. Nina no longer had a reason to hurry home, so her first Saturday alone she stopped at the mall to shop. When she came home, Catherine was sitting outside on the front steps.

"Anthony's working," Nina called as she got out of the car. "He won't be home until late."

"I know. I wanted to talk to you." Catherine said, her tone somber.

"Come on in." Nina was puzzled, but not worried.

She made a pot of hot green tea and sat at the kitchen table with Catherine. "So, your parents still won't let you go away to college?"

"It's not that." Catherine twisted the edge of her T-shirt. "I didn't get my period this month," she blurted out.

"Are you sure of the date?"

Catherine nodded. "I'm not real late, but I'm afraid."

"Did you tell Anthony?"

Catherine nodded again. "He said to wait a few days and see what happens."

Like that's a solution. "Does your mother know?" Nina asked.

"Gosh, no, my parents would kill me. I can't tell them."

Nina rolled her eyes. "If you have a child, they'll eventually get used to the idea."

"No they won't." Tears began to stream down Catherine's face. "They'll throw me out of the house. They've told me that ever since I was fourteen." Her lips quivered. "They believe one bad apple spoils the whole barrel. They said if I got pregnant, I'd never see my sisters again."

Nina thought she should have been prepared for this, but she was not. She had believed Anthony when he told her that he and Catherine were just friends. *How dumb could I be?* "Do you want to go to a doctor and make sure?"

Catherine nodded once more.

"I'll make an appointment and take you myself. We won't go around here. No sense taking a chance of someone seeing you in a doctor's office with me." Nina's shoulders sagged, but she kept her voice steady. "I told Anthony this was going to happen." She saw the look of dread on Catherine's face. It was the same way she had felt when her own mother chastised her all those years ago. Nina wanted to take the remark back, but it was too late. She pulled out the city phone book and copied the numbers of several doctors. "I'll call for an appointment in the morning."

Three days after Catherine's visit, the doctor's office telephoned with the test results.

"Yes, this is Nina Cocolucci." She glanced toward Anthony, who was sitting next to Catherine at the kitchen table. There was a long silence as Nina listened to the voice on the other end of the phone. "I'll have her call for an appointment." Nina hung up the phone and turned to Anthony and his girlfriend. "It's definite. Catherine's going to have a child."

Anthony slumped in his chair. "They know for sure?"

"Yes." Nina joined Anthony and Catherine at the kitchen table.

"Well, there's no reason to look so gloomy," Catherine bubbled. "Anthony and I are going to have a baby. We should be happy."

Nina glanced across the table. Catherine radiated as if the pregnancy had been a life-long ambition. *What had happened to the frightened young girl?*

"Anthony said if I was pregnant, we'd get married. So all we have to do is decide when and where."

"Ah, yeah, Mom, we talked about it."

"And, what do you plan to do?" Nina asked.

"We're gonna get married and keep the baby," Anthony said as he put his arm around Catherine.

"What about your parents?" Nina asked Catherine.

"I can't tell Mama."

"You can't lie to your mother," Nina said. "And sooner, rather than later she's going to *know*."

Catherine shook her head. "You don't know my parents." Catherine got up from the table and paced the kitchen floor. "I'll go to Tallahassee with Anthony. I'll have the baby. We'll wait three months after the baby's born before we tell her."

"How will that help?" Nina's brow knitted.

"We'll make an excuse not to come home until the baby's older. By then she won't know when the baby was born."

Nina could see the lie was growing faster than the pregnancy, and she thought Catherine was making it up as she went along. "No, Catherine, you can't get away with this. It won't work out like you think."

Catherine stood firm. "After she gets used to the idea, I'll tell her. It'll be easier for her to accept then."

Nina shook her head.

Anthony laid his hand on his mother's. "We're not asking you to lie for us. Just keep our secret."

Nina knew she was making a terrible mistake. "Oh, God. I wish you hadn't told me."

"How could we not tell the one person who loves us?" Catherine hugged her.

Nina melted. What was there to say after that?

The next day, Nina called Chance.

"Ah, Nina, good to hear from you," he said. "I see business grow, receipts bigger."

"*Your* receipts are bigger. Mine aren't nearly as large. Can't you do something about this, at least until these service related contracts run out?" She searched for the words to convince him. "When the customers' contracts mature, I can charge a higher rate to renew them. It'll be better for both of us."

"No promise," he said. "But I look into it."

"Thanks." *Why am I thanking him? He caused this problem for me.*

"I hear Anthony work for Louie."

"News travels fast," she said. "That's not the worst of it."

"Don't blame boy, Louie he tough to work for."

"Anthony gets along fine with Louie. The problem is. . ." she paused . . .Anthony's girlfriend, Catherine, is pregnant, and her parents will cause a major problem when they find out."

"A bambino, that'sa nice. Maybe they run away and get married."

"No, her parents expect each of their children to have a big church wedding, and Anthony can't even afford to buy her a plain gold band."

"No problem."

"Not for you," she shot back.

"Not for you, either. I still got rings."

"What rings?" Nina felt sure he was not listening to her.

"Your wedding rings."

She wanted to throw the phone at him. "Don't you remember? I threw my rings in the canal."

"No, you threw fake set away." He laughed. "You think I let you throw five grand in canal?"

Nina's breathing became labored as she tried to make sense out of the conversation.

"They not even good copies, but you no bother to look," Chance said with a chuckle.

"I don't believe this." Nina leaned against the pay phone. "Why did you do that to me?"

"So you be strong. If you wear rings, Vito control you."

"Stop making decisions for me."

"I no do because of authority. I want for you a better life."

"I'm not so sure this is a better life," Nina shot back.

He chuckled again in his usual good-humored way. "You plan wedding. I send rings. Tell Anthony save his money. He need good job to raise family."

For a moment, Nina felt Anthony slipping away from her. "Anthony's going to college," she declared. "I don't know how, but he's going to Florida State, and nothing anyone says or does will change that. Nothing!"

"Is good to see you still strong woman," Chance said.

Nina opened the courier package delivered to her business office and found the rings that Chance had sent. She noticed the scratch on the side of the solitaire. It was made the day she had used Charlie's car and caught her engagement ring in the electric window. She had never had it repaired, but today she decided to take it to a jeweler to see if he could fix the scratch and clean and polish both rings.

Anthony and Catherine were watching TV when Nina came home. She handed the box of rings to Anthony. He turned them around slowly. "These are the rings Dad gave to you. Are you sure you want to give them to Catherine?"

"I'm giving them to you. It's up to you if you want Catherine to have them."

He held out the engagement ring. "Try it on," he said to Catherine.

"They'll fit," Nina said. "Catherine tried on my emerald ring a couple of nights ago."

Catherine gasped when she saw the diamond. "Oh, Nina, it's beautiful."

"When do you plan on telling your parents?" Nina asked.

"I already told them Anthony was giving me a ring." Catherine slid the diamond back and forth on her finger. "They thought it was okay to be engaged, but they want us to wait until after college before we get married."

"I see," was all Nina said. *So, they're not against diamonds, just marriage and pregnancy.*

"Can we go show my mother?" Catherine asked Anthony.

"Right now?" Anthony barked and slouched deeper into the couch.

Catherine tugged at his arm. "Maybe it'll make Mama feel differently about us getting married."

"Showing her the ring will just give *your Mama* another chance to put me down."

"Come on," Catherine coaxed. "Please."

Catherine hugged Anthony as they left to go see her mother.

Michael and Joey had only been home from Bentleyville for two days, and Michael had taken Joey and Brian to the beach. Nina figured that today was as good as any to tell them about the wedding. She thought it would be best not to mention Catherine's pregnancy just yet.

A few minutes after Anthony and Catherine left, the Mustang pulled into the driveway. Michael and Joey bounced in the front door.

Nina called to them from the living room. "I want to talk to both of you."

Michael sat down in the chair across from his mother. "It's my fault, the boys wanted to go for pizza, and I figured you'd be tired after working all day, so I took them. I guess I shoulda called first."

Joey stood in the doorway, his shoulders sagging. "It's not Michael's fault, I coaxed."

Nina laughed out loud. "What I have to say is not all that serious."

Joey grinned as he came into the room.

"I only wanted to be the first to tell you that Anthony and Catherine have decided to get married."

"Why's he gonna do that?" Joey asked.

"Because he's horny," Michael answered.

"No shit!" Joey blurted out.

Nina's eyes popped open wide.

"Oops, I meant, No. . . kiddin'," Joey said, "I thought you were mad beause I broke your favorite glass."

Nina was amazed that the boys took the news in stride. Maybe they expected it. "Anthony and Catherine are making plans for the wedding and of course they expect you both to be in the wedding party. This is just a heads up so you can be prepared. It'll be an important day in Anthony's life, so no joking around."

The boys agreed and carried their wet clothes to the laundry room.

"Can I go with Brian to the roller skating rink tonight?" Joey asked. "Michael said he'd drive us."

"You just got home." Nina got up from the couch.

"But we only have a few nights before school starts again," Joey begged.

"How much is this gonna cost me?" Nina asked.

"Nothing." Michael answered. "We still have some of the money Nana gave us."

"All right," Nina said, "but straight home after skating." At least the house would be quiet while she worked on the books tonight. She had to be ready for her meeting with the mob's accountant tomorrow.

Nina had finished balancing the books when Anthony and Catherine returned.

"So, how'd it go?" Nina made tea and placed oatmeal cookies on a dish.

"Not good." Anthony headed into the living room, turned on the TV, and flopped on the sofa.

Catherine sat at the table with Nina.

"First, they said we couldn't get married right away, so I told Mama how almost everyone who's going to be in the wedding party has to go back to college by the middle of August." Catherine grinned. "I told her if she made us wait, it would be impossible to get them together during the school year, and my brothers might not get to be in the wedding."

"Did she go for that?"

"She still didn't give in." Catherine rolled her eyes. "She wanted us to wait until *next* summer. So, I did what I had to do."

"Which was?"

"I lied."

Nina was sorry she had asked. "Oh, Catherine, you didn't?"

Catherine put her hand over her mouth and giggled. "What else could I do? I agreed to stay home and go to the community college if she let us get married right away. After the wedding, I'm going to Tallahassee with Anthony. I'll be a married woman, and she can't stop me."

Nina shook her head. "This charade is *not* going to work."

"Mama says we don't have enough time, but Aunt Victoria promised to help. She's going to make the bridesmaids' dresses." Catherine moved closer to Nina and whispered, "Auntie Victoria thinks Mama's an old fuddy-duddy. It's hard to believe they're sisters."

Nina felt sure it was something Catherine had heard whispered before, probably by her Aunt Victoria.

Catherine came from a big family, and she told Nina that most of her relatives planned to attend. Nina's mother and dad, her brother Mickey, and her younger brother, Dominic and his wife Ruth were all coming to the wedding. When Nina's mother called to ask why Nina's aunts, uncles and cousins were not invited, Catherine's mother agreed to mail the additional invitations immediately. The wedding was mushrooming, and no one but Nina seemed to be concerned.

"There are close to 250 people coming." Nina told Larry over dinner at the local Steak and Ale.

"I didn't get an invitation," he said.

"I wasn't sure you wanted one. I planned to ask you before I returned my RSVP. There will be a lot of, ah, Italians. You might feel uncomfortable." Nina pushed her empty plate aside, and the waitress brought coffee.

"I earn my living in the middle of every nationality." Larry reminded her.

Nina laughed. "I'll need you that day. It's not going to be easy with the whole family there. They're having the reception at the Sons of Italy hall. The women's organization is preparing the food. I'm glad I'm not responsible for that menu."

"I thought the bride's family was responsible for the wedding."

"True, but it's not as simple as that. Both sides have obligations, and I certainly didn't expect my son to get married so young."

"You'll do fine," he said. "What does Anthony have to say about getting married?"

"Not much." She touched the napkin to her lips. "His friend, John, is home from Carnegie Tech. He's the best man. They've been spending a lot of time together."

Larry signed the credit card receipt, tucked it inside the restaurant's leather folder and handed it to their waitress.

Nina could see Larry was not interested in the wedding details, but he continued to be polite and she needed to talk.

"I don't know why you're worried," he said. "Things sound like they're under control."

"I'm concerned about Catherine's mother. The guys are getting dressed at John's house, and Catherine wants to come to my place to dress. She's so flighty. I'm not sure whether it's her idea or her mother's. I just don't want to be in the middle of a family squabble."

"This isn't your problem, Nina. Let the kids work it out for themselves."

He reached across the table and held her hand. "It's better this way. If they don't get hitched now, she might end up pregnant. Look at the mess you'd have then."

Nina almost choked. "For heaven's sake, Larry, she *is* pregnant. I thought you knew."

"No I didn't, but it doesn't matter. Some unwed girl gets pregnant every minute."

When Nina and Larry came back from dinner, the phone rang as they were walking through Nina's front door. She hurried to answer it.

"So, how are you taking the wedding news?" Vito asked.

"I'm fine with it." Nina held the phone away from her ear and rolled her eyes.

Larry walked outside to the patio.

Vito was quiet for a moment. "I called to tell you I was bringing Maria. I don't want you to pitch a fit when you see her."

"We're divorced, Vito. I thought you knew. I don't care who you sleep with. Just be careful how you flaunt her in front of my father if you don't want to pick yourself up off the floor."

"You better think about the way you treat me at the wedding, because I ain't forgotten how you double-crossed me. You made a big mistake stirring up trouble at the Irish Meat Market."

"What did you say?" Nina's hands were shaking.

"I said I haven't forgotten the way you stabbed me in the back. I built the fuckin' business, and I want a cut of the profit."

"We've been through this before. I didn't take *anything* from you. I own my own advertising company. It has nothing to do with you and your mob."

"My mob? You got some big *cogliones*, but that's only because Chance is watching your back."

Nina's heart beat faster. "You're blaming me because your customers were fed up with you shaking them down? Sean and Patrick Donovan rebelled against you long before our divorce. The other businesses followed their example."

"Next thing you'll tell me is that you and Dutch don't work for Barozzini."

"Dutch? I haven't seen him since before we were married."

"You telling me you're blind?" He lowered his voice. "If it wasn't for our sons, you'd be six feet under."

"Vito, are you ready?" Nina heard a woman's voice sing out in the background.

"You won't have Chance's protection forever, so don't get careless." Vito hissed. "Accidents happen." The line went dead.

Nina steadied herself by holding onto the desk. There was no way out of the mob even if they would let her. She needed the income, and she needed their protection. She patted her face with a tissue and went to the patio. Larry opened his arms, and she welcomed the comfort.

"You look tired," he said.

She wondered how much he had heard, but he did not say anything else, and she did not want to discuss the subject. Deep down, she knew eventually it would come out, just like Catherine's pregnancy, but until then, she wanted to pretend something in her life was normal.

CHAPTER TWENTY-NINE

At St. Mary's Church, Vito and Maria sat in the second row, next to the aisle. Vito's mother and father sat in front of them. The DiGregetti family took up the entire first two pews.

The church was almost filled when Larry walked Nina to her seat. She looked radiant in her electric blue gown that flowed along her curves. Delicate silver and rhinestone earrings twinkled through her shoulder length hair.

Vito appeared surprised when he noticed Larry escorting Nina down the center aisle. For a moment, Vito looked like he intended to speak to Larry, but at the last minute Vito turned his head in the other direction.

"Hey, Rudy," Vito called out to his brother. He waved his hand around the church. "Nice, 'eh?" he acted as if he had orchestrated the entire event himself.

Nina and Larry sat directly behind Vito in the two places Nana Cocolucci had saved for her daughter.

"Who's this man with you?" her mother whispered.

"His name's Larry. I introduced you to him last night, Ma."

"I know, but what country does he come from?"

"He comes from America. Can we talk about this later?" Nina could feel Larry shaking with repressed laughter.

Redesigning the Mob

"Does he go to Mass?" her mother continued.

"No, Ma, and neither do I." Nina rolled her eyes at her brother, Dominic who sat behind them. "Shush, the music's starting," Nina said.

Dominic leaned forward between Nina and Larry. "Pay no attention to her," he whispered. "It's your life, not hers."

The DiGregetti-Cocolucci side of the church was a sea of black tuxedos and thick black hair, sitting next to over-dressed women with heavily teased hair and unruly children. Across the aisle, Catherine's relatives were all well dressed, and had a folksy style about them. Little groups of Irish-Italian families huddled together in peaceful kindred whispers. Nina could not help but notice how the children sat quietly with their hands folded.

When everyone was seated, the ushers approached the altar from a side entrance. They stood in a line like mannequins. Their bodies only partially faced the front—leaving them ample view to watch for the girls who attended the bride. When the music began, the bridesmaids, dressed in an array of pastel colored gowns, glided down the walkway, which was covered with a white sateen runner sprinkled with rose petals.

Larry held Nina's hand. "You're doing great," he whispered.

Vito turned around when the first bridesmaid passed and looked straight into Nina's eyes. He mouthed the words, "You look nice."

Maria sat stiff and straight. Her blond hair was pulled up on one side, and flipped out on the other. A small rhinestone tiara nestled into her crown of curls. She tugged at the hem of Vito's suit jacket, and he turned back to her. Nina glanced at Larry.

He squeezed her hand and winked. "You don't look nice," he whispered. "You look spectacular."

When Catherine's father walked her down the aisle, everyone stood. Her wedding dress had a wide scoop neckline with the tinest of cap sleeves, showing off her smooth summer tan. The bodice was a high sheen, embroidered taffeta with a curved basque waist. Layers of pleated tulle fell from the waistline.

Some of the guests smiled, some nodded approvingly, and some cried. Nina did a little of each. Despite how lovely Catherine looked,

Nina felt badly for her new daughter-in-law and hoped she would not pass out from the tight corset before the ceremony ended.

The Sons of Italy parking lot was fenced in, and two handpicked Mafioso's checked the register before permitting the guests to enter the gate.

Music played while attendees piled wedding gifts on top of a decorated table. A platter of homemade Italian cookies adorned each of the large round tables. Families made themselves comfortable in little groups, and children ran wild around the big room. Heavy-set women, who belonged to the club, wore long white aprons and hustled about filling the buffet table with lasagna, sausage and peppers, veal parmigiano, eggplant, zucchini, and a host of other homemade Italian dishes.

The bridal party arrived after their pictures were taken and stood in a line to greet all the guests.

When Nina hugged Catherine and Anthony, she whispered. "Larry will drive you to the port. Your bags are on board, and the ship sails at ten." She tucked the reservations into Anthony's vest pocket.

After that, the day and evening became one big blur. Nina danced with her son and then a few steps with Vito while everyone applauded, until Larry cut in and spun her away. She and Larry watched from the sidelines while the bridal party danced, then joined them with the rest of the guests that filled the dance floor.

At one point, Nina picked at a plate of food, but she did not recall the cutting of the cake or the throwing of the bouquet, even though Larry insisted they had watched both events and had even eaten the cake.

The one thing Nina vividly recalled was the dance with her father. Her mother said he did not dance anymore, but he had whirled her around the room that night. "You will always be my beautiful little girl," he had said. It was a dance to remember.

Nina watched Catherine play her part. She hugged, kissed and smiled while dancing in her stocking feet with all the uncles, cousins, brothers, and friends. Catherine's parents had given her a lavish wedding, and friends and family had filled her wedding purse with the *aboost*. She had held hundred-dollar bills between her fingers that encircled the neck of whomever she was dancing with at the time, to show off both of the families' and friends' generosity.

After a dance, Larry was leading Nina away from the dance floor. Just as they passed Chance's table, Nina heard Vito say, "I'd like you to meet Maria."

Chance stood as he acknowledged the meeting. Then he reached out for Nina's hand. "You have good daughter-in-law," he said as he waltzed Nina onto the dance floor.

Larry turned around to see what happened, and Nina shrugged.

"Yes, I like her." Nina leaned close to Chance's ear. "I know you plan to return to New York tomorrow, so I need to tell you something now."

"Nothing so important, it can't wait." He twirled her under his arm.

"You don't understand." Nina caught her breath. "Vito called and threatened me again. He wants a share of the business profit. I'm frightened," she said louder. "He said I'd be dead already if it wasn't for your protection."

"Not to worry. I talk to him." Chance danced her across the room where Larry had been left standing.

Nina was furious with Chance's answer, but she had no choice at the moment. She introduced Chance and Larry to each other, and they shook hands.

"Larry's with the *police* department," Nina said.

Before Nina could say anything else, Catherine came over to them and whispered to Nina, "I need help," she said. "I have to get out of these clothes. Anthony said we're leaving."

Nina excused herself and was tugged through the dancers by Catherine. They made their way to the back of the kitchen and into the employees' bathroom. A small bag with Catherine's things was sitting in the corner. Nina helped her slip out of the wedding dress and into a pink Jones of New York suit that Nina had bought for her. Catherine brushed her hair while Nina hung the wedding dress in the plastic bag.

Catherine handed the corset to Nina. "Can you ditch this someplace?"

Nina nodded and shoved the merry-widow into an empty bag.

"Thanks." Catherine gave Nina a long hug. "I couldn't have gotten through any of this without you."

Nina wiped her eyes with a tissue. "Larry will drive you to the port, and he and I will pick you up on Friday. The islands are beautiful. Have a good time."

Minutes later, rice was flying, and the couple left for a week-long honeymoon cruise in the Caribbean. Soon, most of the family members left the reception, but the newlyweds' young friends partied into the wee hours of the morning.

When Larry returned from the port, Nina saw him talking to Chance in the bar. She wondered what the two of them could possibly have in common. She thought about joining them, but she was too tired. When all the guests had finally departed, Larry and Nina drove home.

"You looked wonderful tonight," he said as he helped her from the car.

"And you were as handsome as ever." She snuggled into his arms, and he kissed her. "Thanks for taking such good care of me." She paused. "Are you staying tonight?"

"Not while your family's here. No need to ruin your impeccable reputation." He grinned and strolled back to his truck.

Nina waved from the porch as he backed out of the driveway.

The day the newlyweds returned from the islands, Nina had to work late, so Larry went to meet them at the ship's dock. He helped carry their luggage to the truck and then dropped them off at Nina's house.

When Nina came home from work, Anthony was lying in bed staring at the ceiling.

"Hi. How was the trip?"

Anthony barely grunted.

"What's wrong?" she asked, her heart skipping a beat.

"I don't want to talk about it." He turned his back.

"How come you're all alone?" she asked. "Where's Catherine and where are your brothers?"

"Joey had a game and Michael took him."

Nina narrowed her eyes. "Is something wrong with Catherine?"

"She's okay. She's over at her mother's. We told her parents that she's going with me to Tallahassee and that we're renting an apartment close to the college, but they're making a big deal out of it."

"Did you think they'd miraculously change their minds while you were on your weeklong honeymoon? Catherine made a promise and broke it." Nina put her hand on his shoulder. "I feel bad for both of you, but I feel sorry for her mother, too."

Anthony turned to look at his mother, but he showed no emotion. "I called the school. They're gonna give me a small credit toward the rent since I'm not gonna stay in the dorm."

"That's good. When do you plan to leave?"

"Right away. School starts soon, and we have to find an apartment."

"Hi," Catherine said as she came into the room holding her arms open to Nina.

"Did you have a good time?" Nina hugged her.

"It was great," Catherine said. "We wouldn't have had a honeymoon if it weren't for you."

"How are your parents?"

"My mother isn't talking to me." Catherine shrugged. "I packed my clothes. I really don't have much else, except a box of pictures and a few knick-knacks. If you don't mind, I'd like to leave them here until we get settled."

Nina wondered if Catherine's Italian mother was second-guessing the quick wedding.

"We'll take your junk with us," Anthony said. "I'm not running back and forth every time you decide you want something."

"All right," Catherine said so softly that Nina could barely hear her.

"When are we gonna get your clothes?" Anthony grumbled.

"We can get them now if you want. Pop took my sisters to the mall and Mama's in her bedroom. She won't let me in, and she won't come out."

Anthony stood up. "C'mon."

Catherine wiggled her fingers and Nina gave her a little wave back. She followed the newlyweds to the door and watched them leave.

Anthony swaggered through the yard much the same way Vito did when he was young. Nina wondered why she had not noticed it before. She did not like his being so abrupt with Catherine and planned to talk to him about it. *I hope he doesn't turn into another Vito.* Nina shivered at the thought.

The front door banged and Anthony set a large box in the foyer. "I carried the heavy boxes," he said to Catherine. "I'm not going back to your parents."

"Why? There are only a few more things."

"Your dad might come home, and I've had enough of him. Get the rest of the crap yourself." Anthony turned on the TV and plopped down on the couch.

Catherine left without saying a word.

Nina walked to the Florida room. "What's going on?" she asked Anthony.

"Nothing. Why?"

"For one thing, you don't sound like the happy married couple who left here five days ago."

Anthony looked sullen. "Ever since we started home, she's been a pain in the ass. It's 'Anthony do this, and Anthony do that.'"

"Welcome to married life." Nina said with a laugh.

"It's not funny. I can't sit down for one minute."

"I'm not telling you to jump for her, but I think you can talk a little nicer. You sound like your father."

"It's better than sounding like mushy, I'll-take-care-of-that, Larry."

Nina bristled. "You mean the *mushy Larry* who took you to the ship and picked you up, or do you mean *I'll take care of that Larry,* who worked for two weeks helping to get everything ready for your wedding?" Nina's voice was calm, but her face was taut.

"Are you going to throw him in my face for the rest of my life?" Anthony snapped back.

"What's gotten into you?" Nina stood with her hands on her hips.

Anthony's chest rose and fell. "I don't know. It's like my life is over. I can't enjoy college. I have to get a job, study, play great football or lose my scholarship, and pretty soon, I'll have to take care of a kid. I didn't want this."

"Do you think Catherine's any more thrilled about the situation than you are?" Nina asked angrily.

"Then why are we doing it?" Anthony went over to the window and looked outside.

Nina followed him. "You both chose to have sex, and the two of you said you wanted to get married and keep the baby. I can help you with the apartment, but you both have to work at least part-time to get along." Nina thought for a while. "If it'll help, Catherine can stay with me."

"No, I can't," Catherine said, lugging in several more small suit cases. "At least not until after the baby's born."

Anthony did not make any move to help his new wife.

"Your mother's going to guess what happened when the baby comes in seven months." Nina helped Catherine stack the bags in the corner of the room.

"Not if you come to Tallahassee when the baby's born and tell her it was premature."

"Your mother can tell a newborn when she sees one." Nina rubbed her forehead, hoping her headache would not start again.

"My mom's not going to see the baby when it's born. She won't drive that far. So, I'll wait awhile before I come home. After the baby is around her for a few days, she'll accept the birth date."

"And what am I to do in the meantime?" Nina asked.

"Just don't say anything," Anthony growled.

"I'm tired. Let's talk about this tomorrow." Nina wanted no part of the deception. She turned to Anthony. "What time did Joey and Michael say they'd be home?"

"Late." Anthony turned up the TV.

Catherine followed Nina to her bedroom. "Would you mind if we left our wedding gifts with you? Pop said we don't deserve them, and there's no telling what he'll do with them."

"That's fine," Nina said as she went into her bathroom, opened the medicine cabinet and took out a bottle of aspirin.

Catherine stood at the foot of Nina's bed, smiling in her typical pleasant mood.

"Get Anthony to help you put them in the closet in my office. There's plenty of room."

"Thanks, Mom. I can do it." Catherine said. "He's watching a movie and I want to get them moved before Pop comes home from the mall."

Nina wanted to say something, but decided it was none of her business. She swallowed the aspirin with a gulp of water and snuggled into a pair of soft pajamas. Just as she was about to lie down in bed, the phone rang.

"I guess you're happy the newlyweds are back safe and sound," Larry said with a chuckle.

"I'm not sure."

"What do you mean? I figured you'd be busy planning a baby shower."

"There's not going to be a baby shower. I told you Catherine's parents didn't know about the baby, and the bride and groom already sound like The Bickersons."

"You should let them handle their own problems."

"You sound like Catherine's parents. I'm sorry I told you about the baby." Nina rubbed the pain that was still moving across her forehead.

"Why jump all over me because your life isn't going smooth?"

"I'm sorry." Her tone was clipped. "Maybe it's me, but between work, the wedding and college expenses, I've had it. I'm going to bed."

"Fine," Larry said and hung up.

Nina watched as Anthony spent the next morning packing the car. They had their wedding money and Nina had promised to pay their rent.

"I'm going to get a full-time job and work as long as I can," Catherine said. "I'll start college next year." She beamed.

Anthony gave Joey a bear hug and cuffed Michael on the arm.

He turned to Nina. "I'm sorry, Mom. I didn't mean all that stuff I said last night." They hugged and kissed before he slipped from her arms and climbed in the car beside Catherine.

Nina watched them drive off. Tears stung her eyes.

CHAPTER THIRTY

"Can I have Anthony's bedroom?" Michael asked as soon as Anthony's car disappeared from sight. Nina shook her head. "They'll be back in the summer."

"Why are they coming back?" Joey asked. As he held the front door open for his mother.

Nina went straight to the kitchen. "It takes four years to get through college," she explained. "It's hard to go to school and raise a child. They'll be back a lot. You'll see when you get older."

"Not me," Michael said, leaning against the refrigerator. "I'm not getting married and raising kids when I'm eighteen."

Nina gave Michael a grateful smile. "I'm glad you learned something," she said. "Remember boys, none of this is to be discussed outside of this house."

"Larry knows," Joey argued.

"That's true, but what I said still goes." Nina turned on the Mr. Coffee machine.

"Brian's staying with his dad this weekend." Joey put out a clean cup for his mother and got the container of half and half from the refrigerator. "Larry said I could sleep over if I wanted to."

Nina laughed to herself at Joey's not-so-subtle gestures. She started to object, but she yearned for some peace and quiet, and Michael would hole up in his room with books if Joey was not around.

"Please," Joey coaxed. "He's got a pool and a regulation basketball hoop."

"Sure." Nina grinned. "That sounds like a good idea."

Several weeks later, Nina got a call from Ginger, and for the first time in a long while, she had some good news.

"Guess what?" she said. "I got a promotion. I'm now a department manager at Jordon Marsh, and that means more money."

"That's great news. I'm so happy for you," Nina said. "Hey, I saw you dancing with Danny at the wedding. Are you two getting back together?"

"It was all a big show."

"Why do you say that?" Nina asked. "Danny told everyone what a great job you did taking care of the kids and the house until he could get a start in Atlanta."

"He didn't mean it," Ginger said, her tone cynical and certain. "Danny came to the house acting like a big shot and gave each of the girls a twenty-dollar bill." She sighed. "Nothing's changed. The girls were tired when we got home and ran straight into the house. I thought he was coming inside, but when I got out of the rental car, he left. He didn't even say good-bye to his kids."

"I'm sorry," Nina said.

"It's the girls I feel bad for. I keep making up excuses for him, telling them he's too busy to come home or call, and we all know that's not true." Ginger paused. "He's got a new life, and it doesn't include me *or* the girls."

"You don't know that for sure," Nina said.

"Nina, he won't need me until he ends up in jail. Then he'll want me to come see him and bring him stuff."

"Maybe he won't go to jail." Nina glanced at the calendar on her desk. "They've put off the hearing for a long time. I read in the paper that one guy died of cancer and another one's in a mental hospital. They don't seem to be trying very hard to convict them."

"I think the only one the FBI wants is Frankie. He controls everything down here. Eunice told me the prosecuting attorney tried to get Danny to testify against Frankie, but I don't think he'd ever do that."

"No, I don't think so either."

"My boss is coming down the hall, I have to hang up."

"Okay. Congratulatons again on the promotion," Nina said, but Ginger had hung up before Nina finished her sentence.

Summer ended, Anthony started college, and Michael and Joey were back in high school. Nina now worked six days a week and many evenings to cover her growing expenses. It seemed as if every week something happened to one of the cars and Nina had a perpetual mechanics tab.

Even though Anthony had a scholarship, Nina continued to help with his family's living expenses. She called Tallahassee as often as she could, but most of the time Anthony was not at home. So one evening she called around ten o'clock. Catherine answered the phone. "Hi, Mom," she yawned.

"Did I wake you?"

"I worked a double shift, so I went to bed as soon as I got home."

"Double shift! You shouldn't do that when you're pregnant. It's not good for you or the baby."

"Anthony lost his job, so I've been working a few extra hours."

Nina tensed at the news. "How come he lost his job?"

"The boss caught him studying one night, and the second time his boss walked in, he found Anthony sleeping."

"What's he going to do without a job?"

"I don't know. Part-time jobs are hard to find during the school year."

"Where's Anthony now?" Nina could feel that sick headache coming on again.

"He might be at the library or maybe football practice. I can't keep up with his schedule."

"Go back to sleep," Nina said. "I'll call you another time."

Nina called back several more evenings but Anthony was not at home. If he was there, Catherine would always say he was sleeping. Nina did not know whether he was avoiding her or had just taken on too much in school. She told Catherine to have him call her, but a whole month went by and he had not phoned.

The Thanksgiving and Christmas holidays were on the way and Nina had special ads to get ready for her clients. She had not seen much of Larry, but not because she did not want to. He seemed to always be busy working extra shifts or was tied up at some kind of meeting. She noticed that he still had time to stop in at the school and take Brian and Joey out to lunch, but his phone calls to her were becoming fewer and far between. She thought he might be seeing another woman.

The only good thing that had happened was that she had not heard from Vito, except when he called and asked the boys to meet him so they could to go Christmas shopping together. Michael and Joey came home with bags of clothes from all the fancy department stores, and dumped them out on the kitchen table.

"Look." Michael said and held up three new pair of jeans and several pullover shirts.

"What's in that big box?" Nina asked as she opened a package of frozen mixed vegetables and dumped them in a pot of boiling water.

"Stuff Dad had in the car. He said we could have it."

Nina went over to the table and opened the box. A mini camcorder, two thirty-five millimeter cameras, a stereo with head-sets, and a couple of electronic games were piled inside.

"I don't know about this stuff," she said.

"Dad said you'd probably say they were stolen, but he said he bought them to give to us and didn't get around to wrapping them."

Nina did not know what to say. She could not prove they were stolen, and maybe they were not, but she had her doubts.

"We're gonna send the stereo and one of the cameras to Anthony," Joey said hoping to appease his mother.

Nina did not respond except to ask the boys to help her set the table for dinner.

Nina mailed Christmas presents to Catherine and Anthony, then on Christmas Eve, she telephoned them. Catherine was sick with a cold. She told Nina that Anthony had gone out with some of his friends.

"It won't be long now," Nina said. "You'll feel better after the baby's born."

"I know," Catherine blew her nose. "I can't wait to come home."

"I can't wait to see you. You be sure to call me when you go to the hospital." Nina felt sorry for Catherine, but there was not much she could do. "Tell Anthony I hope he likes his Christmas presents, and you take care of yourself."

"I'll be fine," Catherine said. "Love you, Mom."

"Love you, too."

Christmas morning was as depressing as Christmas Eve. Nina called her mother only to listen to her complain about her father.

"He just sits in front of the TV watching football," her mother said.

"Let me talk to him," Nina said, but he would not come to the phone.

Mickey came to Nina's house for Christmas dinner and their brother Dominic called to wish them all a Merry Christmas.

All in all, it was the worst Christmas Nina had ever had—maybe even worse than when she was living with Vito.

After the holidays, Nina met Ginger at IHOP one evening for dinner. Ginger was late and when she slid into the booth, she apologized and then said, "I had one problem after another at work. My mother says I spend more time at the department store than I do at home."

Nina nodded. "I thought I worked a lot of hours for Charlie, but now that I'm single, I work almost twice as many for myself." Nina sipped her coffee. "How are the girls?"

"They're growing like weeds." Ginger poured her coffee from the hot decanter. "I'm glad my mother's there to help. She sold her house and moved in with me permanently." Ginger paused. "So, how's your love life?"

"I don't see much of Larry anymore. I've been too busy worrying about Anthony and Catherine." Nina leaned forward and spoke low. "I don't know if this marriage will last." She shrugged. "I call, but they don't say much. Anthony lost his job. I knew it'd be hard for him to go to school and keep even a part-time job. I don't think he gives Catherine enough credit for all the hours she puts in."

"A lot of kids go to college and work. They'll figure it out." Ginger stirred sugar into her coffee. "Did you go out New Year's Eve?"

"No, Larry and I spent a quiet night at home. I was worried about Anthony and didn't want to leave the house. The next day, Larry left for a two-week training course."

Ginger reached across the table and touched Nina's hand. "I think you're the one with the problem. What's the real reason you're not seeing much of Larry?"

"I work days and he works nights." Nina sighed. "I'm not even sure if he's what I want."

There was a long silence. Then Ginger said, "Come on, tell me what's really wrong."

"I need to get out of the advertising business."

"Why? You're earning a good living, and if you hadn't told me, I'd have never guessed you owned a mob business. You sure kept that a secret. I really thought all you did was work for an advertising company." Ginger poured more coffee for both of them.

"Owning your own business isn't as easy as you think." Nina sipped the fresh coffee.

Gray came bouncing over. "Man, is this place crowded. I'm sorry I took so long. Strip steaks are on special and everything comes with it." She pointed to a flyer stapled to the menu.

"I'll have the special." Ginger said. "Medium."

"Me too. Make mine medium-rare." Nina handed the menus to Gray.

When the waitress left, Nina continued. "Sometimes I think I made a mistake quitting Charlie, or maybe I should've taken the boys and moved back to Pennsylvania."

"How can you say that? Besides, Charlie would've fired you anyway."

"I don't practice what I preach. I'm afraid my boys will grow up thinking what I do is right."

"It doesn't matter what you do. Kids do as they please, anyway."

Nina rolled her eyes. "You can't stop what a child does, but you need to set a good example if you want them to have a chance of making the right choice."

They sat quietly for a while. Nina knew this was a moot issue they would never agree on.

Gray delivered their dinners.

"There's nothing like a good steak to make you forget your problems." Ginger picked up her knife and fork and began eating with gusto.

As Catherine's delivery date came closer, Nina began to call them more often. One night, Anthony answered the phone.

"You don't have to call all the time," he said. "We'll call you when the time comes."

He sounded like he had been drinking. Nina felt helpless and frustrated.

"Okay, but you make sure you call me."

A week later, at 4:00 a.m., when Nina was sound asleep, the phone rang.

"Nina?" an unfamiliar voice asked.

"Yes, who's calling?" Nina looked at the illuminated dial on her clock and rubbed her eyes.

"Victoria, Catherine's aunt. Remember? I spend morning at your house on wedding day."

"Is something wrong?" Nina asked.

"No, no," Victoria said. "Anthony tell me to call you."

"Where are you?" Nina sat up.

"We bring Catherine to hospital. The baby is coming, and Catherine, she so skinny. The doctor, he worry." Victoria sniffled. "Catherine say, no tell her mother. You *capisce?*"

"I understand. Tell Anthony not to worry. I'm on my way."

Nina called Delta Airlines, but did not have much success with the schedule or the price. Not wanting to waste any more time, she showered, dressed, and packed. Driving seemed to be the cheapest and maybe the quickest way to get to Tallahassee. As she got ready, Nina's mind raced with worrisome thoughts. Would the baby be all right? What if something happened to Catherine?

She wrote notes on the layouts to give to Margo and sealed the contents in a large brown envelope. When Michael and Joey got up, Nina gave them the news.

"Why can't we all go?" Joey asked.

"Because you're in school, and what would you do after you saw the baby?"

"We could visit Anthony's college." Joey's mouth parted into a pout; a ploy he often used when he wanted his way.

"Not this time. Hurry, Joey. You'll be late for school. Michael's already in the car."

After the boys left, Nina called Margo at home. "I'm going to be out of town for a few days. I'll drop off the work to be distributed." She had not used a housekeeper lately and decided the boys could fend for themselves for a few days.

She did not call Mickey for fear he would say something to her mother and Nina was not ready to be chastised again for her own youthful mistake.

Larry was still at work when she called his house and left a message. It bothered her that he was not there just at a time when she felt a need to lean on him for support.

Nina opened the door to leave, and heard the phone signal from Dutch to meet him as soon as possible. While she agonized over what to do about Dutch's request, the phone rang again.

"Mom, what are you doing at home?" Anthony asked. "I was calling Michael."

"I had things to take care of, and Michael's gone to school."

"What kind of things?" His voice wavered. "You promised to come when Catherine went into labor."

"Don't worry. She'll be fine." Nina looked at her watch. "I'll be there as soon as I can."

"You don't understand. Catherine's been in labor since four o'clock this morning. The doctor says they might have to take the baby caesarean. Please, come now, Mom. I need you."

"I'm driving, but it won't take me long. I just have to drop off next week's ads at the office." Nina hung up before Anthony could protest again.

Dutch and Nina's covert meeting place was a mile from the house, and in less than ten minutes, she spotted Dutch's car backed into a parking space. She pulled in beside him and rolled down the window.

"I hope I didn't wake you," he said.

"No. I got up early."

"I have good news. I got a message from Chance. The Don Lobianco is in town. The godfather has requested that you meet him for lunch. This is a rare occasion that you don't want to miss."

Nina did not share Dutch's awe. "I can't. Catherine's in labor. I only stopped to met you, because it was on my way."

"You don't understand. The word request is only a politeness. It is not something you say yeah or nay to." Dutch waited for his words to sink-in. "Postpone the trip."

Jolted by Dutch's frankness, Nina said, "Maybe you could go to the meeting and tell him about the baby."

"Not me," Dutch said. "The Don doesn't even see Chance unless it's a special request. And I'm not calling Chance with your excuse, either. It's just for a couple of hours. Go to Tallahassee after lunch or call and make your own apologies."

"Where and what time?" Nina snapped.

She scratched the information on the back of a piece of mail, and drove off.

These people think they own me. She took a deep breath, remembering how many times she had heard Vito say the same thing.

She stopped at a pay phone and dialed the hospital telephone number. The switchboard operator connected Nina to the nurse's station, and the aide called Anthony to the phone.

"Something's come up," Nina said. "I need to meet with some people at noon. I'll leave as soon as it's over."

"Is that how you feel about us? Business came ahead of Christmas, and now business comes before the birth of your grandchild. You're no better than Dad."

"Please, try to understand," Nina pleaded. "I can't get out of this."

"But it's okay to get out of helping your family." Anthony hung up.

The appointment was four hours away. Nina dropped off Margo's instructions and went home to change her clothes. She could not meet the godfather in jeans and a T-shirt.

At noon, Nina walked into Alfonso's Italian Restaurant. The owner ushered her into a private banquet room that other times served as an Italian social club. Some family, she thought. There was no wife, no daughters, and no grandchildren. It appeared to be almost the same deal as when she met with the advertisers, except these men were loosely related, and a few vaguely resembled each other.

They ordered lunch, including hers, which she resented. They proceeded to tell her what a good job she was doing. The Don looked older than she had expected. His back was bent, and when he went to the restroom she noticed he walked with a slight limp. Although he was dressed in expensive clothing, his hair was tousled, and he looked like he had a three-day growth of beard. He kept his distance from her while the others conveyed their appreciation for her excellent business skills. Any other day, she would have been amused at their attention and recognition, but today she was clearly preoccupied.

"Isn't that right?" The Don's oldest son, who appeared to be the spokesman, said.

When she glanced up from her plate, they were all staring at her. "Uh, yes, I agree." Nina smiled, not knowing what she had consented to.

"You're quite unique," the spokesman with a thick growth of salt and pepper hair, said. "An attractive woman with the intelligence of a man."

Nina wanted to reach over and snap his red suspenders. "I beg your pardon." She looked deep into the darkness of his wide-set eyes.

"And feisty," he added.

A stir of muffled laughter came from the rest of the group. The old man wrapped his hand around the neck of the empty bottle of Ruffino, encased in a straw basket. He tapped it on the table. The laughter stopped. All eyes looked toward the Don.

"The meal is over. Get the car," he said to his youngest son.

Nina was happy to end the meeting and immediately got up from the table.

The Don took her hand in his to thank her. "*Grazie.*" He kissed her on both cheeks and for a moment, Nina froze.

The spokesman said, "I understand you have another appointment. Do you need transportation?"

"No, thank you." All Nina wanted to do was get away. *I'm missing the birth of my grandchild for this.* Hatred for their self-centered egos warred with her own self-loathing. *All this fuss about a meeting, and they didn't even want anything. They just happened to be in town and wanted to meet me.*

She hurried outside and drove to the nearest public phone to call the hospital. The switchboard transferred her to Catherine's room.

"We have a beautiful girl," Anthony said. "Her name's Krysta Leigh."

"Wow!" Nina tucked the phone under her chin while she searched her purse for a pen. "Where's Catherine?"

"Right here, but she's asleep. They didn't have to take the baby cesarean after all. You should've seen Catherine," Anthony said excitedly. "It hurt something awful, but she didn't complain. I stayed with her the whole time."

"How's the baby?" Nina asked cautiously.

"She weighs less than five pounds, and the doctor said she might lose a couple of ounces before she starts to gain. He wants to keep her at the hospital until he's sure her lungs are strong." Anthony's voice broke. "I told Catherine she should eat more. She took her vitamins, but she barely ate during the last months. She only gained ten pounds the whole time she was pregnant. All because she's afraid of her mother."

Nina didn't remember Anthony saying this much at one time since he won the history debate in junior high. "Are you all right?"

"I'm doing great. I love the baby, and I love Catherine."

Visions of the day she delivered Anthony went through Nina's mind. She remembered Vito murmuring how much he loved her and the baby. At least Anthony did not appear to be angry with her now that his wife and daughter were out of danger. For that, Nina was truly grateful.

"Catherine's aunt only gave me the name and telephone number of the hospital. Do you know the address?"

"Yeah, I have it, but I'm glad you called. I tried to reach you at the house."

Happy now that all had gone well, Nina was anxious to be on her way. "The meeting's over and I'm ready to leave."

"That's what I wanted to talk to you about." He paused and then spoke tentatively to his mother. "Catherine hadn't been feeling well the last few weeks, so we called her Aunt Victoria. She flew in from New York. She knows how narrow-minded Catherine's parents are."

"They'll feel differently by the time you bring the baby home," Nina said. "As soon as I get there and see the baby, I'll call Catherine's mother."

"You don't need to come now," Anthony blurted. "Her aunt said she'd stay until Catherine and the baby can manage on their own, and we'll be coming home as soon as school's out."

"Oh." Nina's eyes filled with tears. She tried to sound chipper. "But since I'm all packed, I'll come anyway. We can both help out for a while."

"We really don't have much room at the apartment." Anthony hesitated. "Catherine thinks her mother would be more likely to believe the baby was premature if Aunt Victoria told her, rather than an outsider."

"I'm not an outsider," Nina balked.

"Not to us, but think how Catherine's mother will feel if you're here and she's not. She might even decide she has to come, too." Anthony paused. "If you come, it could ruin everything. Catherine's worked hard to keep the baby's birthday a secret from her mother. It'll be better if you stay home."

Nina sighed. "I understand." But she did not. Apparently, Anthony had not forgiven her for not coming as soon as he called.

"We plan to stay with you this summer, if that's okay? I'm going to work for uncle Louie again, and Catherine can spend time with Krysta before she goes back to work in the fall."

"Did she change her mind about going to college?"

"We, uh, haven't decided yet," Anthony stuttered. "She sends her love, and said she'll call you when she gets home from the hospital."

I'll bide my time. Nina believed Anthony would get over his anger. *Maybe he'll want me to come down next week.* "It'll be nice to have you home for the summer," she said, fighting to keep her voice calm and optimistic.

"I have to go now," he said.

Nina replaced the phone and walked to her car. She sank into the seat and lowered her head. Tears poured over her face.

When the sobbing subsided, she drove home. Later she shoved the unpacked suitcase into the closet and called Ginger to tell her Catherine had a baby girl.

"I'm not going after all."

"Is anything wrong?" Ginger asked.

"No, everything's fine. I may go next week. I'll let you know."

Since it was still early in the day, Nina decided to go to her office and distract herself with work. Right now she was even too embarrassed to let Larry know that Anthony had asked her not to come to Tallahassee.

Nina parked her car behind Elite Advertising. Now that Vito knew where she lived and the location of the business, she no longer walked through the dark parking garages. Even though she had not heard from him in a while, she never knew when or what he might do.

Nina continued to call Anthony over the next few weeks, but by the end of the month she realized she had lost her chance to be close to him. All he talked about was how much Catherine's Aunt Victoria was doing for them.

CHAPTER THIRTY-ONE

During the winter, Vito flaunted his cash. Gonzalez had an in with a fellow Cuban in air cargo operations, and Vito's Cuban crew hijacked trucks on a regular basis from the Miami International Airport. Most of the time, they only ripped off a few boxes, which made it look like a shipping loss, but sometimes they made off with an entire truckload.

Alice handled Vito's credit card business, which had grown into a six-man team that floated from one apartment to another, always operating a few short steps ahead of the law. "Middling" was a get-rich quick proposition, if you did not get caught.

In one of his weaker moments, Vito told Danny, who told Eunice, who told Frankie that Dahlia was his personal piece. He also said Maria knew too much for him to dump her. All this news found its way to Chance.

Vito's visit to Dahlia's one night was not what he had expected. He had big plans for the evening, and Dahlia was in a bad mood.

"Did you make up your mind?" She asked, looking from the TV as Vito entered her apartment.

"About what?"

"Are you gonna live here or with Maria?"

"It'll work out better if she throws me out." He took off his shoes, and wiggled his toes. "It's gonna take a few days."

"That's a lot of bull crap." Dahlia went to the sink where a decanter of bourbon sat. She poured a double shot and topped it with a splash of water.

"Don't be giving me any shit." Vito lit a cigarette. "I pulled you out of a construction bar, and I could put you back on the street tomorrow. What would you do then?"

"I'd go to work for Frankie. He doesn't force his girls to take care of his needs."

"Oh! So *now*, I force you? Not so long ago, you thought me and you were a good thing."

"I've changed my mind. I don't need anyone threatening me." She downed the liquor, sat the glass in the sink and started toward the bedroom.

Vito's hand shot out and caught Dahlia on the side of her face. It stung, and her whole body swiveled. She pressed her fingers against her cheek.

Vito glared at her. "That wasn't a threat, it was a promise. Now get cleaned up. We're going uptown tonight. I have three friends in from Atlanta, and I promised them you'd show them a good time—on the house."

She held her cheek and backed away from him. "I'm not doing three of your friends for nothing."

"You'll do what I tell you." Vito started toward her.

Dahlia dodged out of his reach. "Okay," she said cringing. "Don't hit me again."

"That's better." Vito snatched a bottle of merlot from the wine rack and went to the kitchen for a corkscrew.

After that night, Dahlia avoided Vito for almost a week. She was sick and tired of him dividing his time between her and Maria. It stroked his big fat ego to have two women. Plus, hardly a week went by that he did not force her to turn several free tricks for him. If Vito cared about her, he would not want to share her with other men, and he would not slap her around. Nothing had worked out the way he had said it would.

Friday night, he showed up unannounced at her front door. "Come on," he snapped his fingers. "We're going out to dinner.

The Seahorse Restaurant was a rustic, yet elegant place. They ate on the veranda. Dahlia watched large waves break on the shore, and the twinkle of a steamer's lights as it passed by far out on the horizon. She wished she was on the ship sailing far away from Vito. She glanced at him, and he acted as if they were the perfect couple, smiling at other patrons, and treating her cordially in front of the waiter.

She pushed the food around her plate.

"You're not hungry?" Vito reached across the table and stabbed her Florida lobster tail. "There ain't any sense in letting this baby go to waste." He cut off a piece and motioned to the waiter. "More melted butter."

Dahlia moved her plate aside and wiped her mouth with the linen napkin.

Vito smiled at her. "I told a friend to meet me at that ten-story hotel you like so much. He's staying at a place on the beach, but we don't do business there." Vito ripped opened a small packet of hand sanitizer and wiped the butter from his fingers. "I'll hang out in the bar until he's ready to leave. This is a freebie. It won't take long. He wants a quick and easy before he goes to a high stakes poker game."

"If he's got that much money, why doesn't he pay?" Dahlia kept her voice low.

"Because I say so. This guy has bucks, and I got a stake in the game."

"Then why don't you do him?" she mumbled as she lit a mentholated cigarette.

Vito shot her a bird, but didn't say anything.

Dahlia wanted to end the affair, but before she could say anything, the waiter approached and Vito handed him his credit card.

"Take care of the bill. I'll be right back," he told the waiter, then went down the steps toward the men's room.

Dahlia considered leaving, but she would have to call a cab, and if he didn't catch up with her right then, well, hell, it wasn't like he didn't know where she lived. A few minutes later, he came up the steps and met the waiter at the bar. She watched as Vito signed the tab and tucked the credit card into his wallet.

Dahlia's hips wiggled as she strolled up to the now familiar hotel desk clerk. He made a pretense of checking her into the room Vito had reserved. She tilted her head and took the key between her long painted nails. It was a nice room, but not like the suites she booked for entertaining.

Fifteen minutes went by. She stared at the door, wishing she could stand up to Vito. There was a light knock. She stepped into her three-inch-heels and opened the door.

"Dahlia?" the man asked

"Come in." She moved aside and thought what an idiot she had been to get involved intimately with Vito. The whole night would be shot, and she would go home without a dime.

The man walked in, slipped off his jacket, and hung it over a chair. "I don't have long." He looked at the floor and shifted from one foot to the other. "I have an appointment."

Dahlia rolled her eyes. "So I heard." She took his hand and led him toward the bed.

When the bashful john was ready to leave, Dahlia helped him put on his suit jacket.

He laid seventy-five dollars on the pillow. "I won't mention this. I know how Vito likes to be in charge."

As soon as he left, Dahlia tucked the money into her purse. She suddenly realized that she was more frightened of Vito than she had previously thought. She needed the money, but she could not be sure the john would not tell. Vito might even have set her up, just to see if he could trust her. Frightened, she ran down the steps and turned into an alcove that held a bank of public phones. She moved to the last one, dialed a number and stepped as far around the corner as the metal cord would reach.

"Please," she whined softly. "Please be there."

The bartender answered, and she asked for Frankie. She shivered as she waited for him to come to the phone. When he said hello, she blurted out the whole story of all the freebies Vito gave away and how he threatened her and slapped her around.

"They're paying all right," Frankie said. "Only you and me aren't getting our cut." He paused. "Where you at?"

She gave him the name of the hotel. "Vito's with me. He's at the bar, but he won't be long. I gotta get back."

"What's the room number?"

"Five twenty."

"You think you'll be okay tonight?" Frankie asked.

"If he doesn't catch me on the phone."

"I'll take care of him."

Dahlia took the steps two at a time. When she reached the fifth floor, Vito was standing in the hallway.

"How come you're out here?" "Vito asked with obvious suspicion.

"I went for a cigarette. I thought you were driving that guy somewhere, so I got some fresh air."

"What's wrong with the balcony?"

Dahlia's gut clenched. "I didn't know there was one."

"Don't give me that crap. You spend more time here than you do at home."

She tried to put her arm around him, but he shoved her into the room. She started for the bathroom to fix her makeup and get the rest of her things.

"Get down on the floor." Vito locked the door and fastened the chain.

Dahlia stopped in the middle of the room. "I'm tired. I wanna go home," she pleaded.

Vito forced her to the carpet. "Now stay there until I tell you to get up." He ripped through her purse. "Well, would you look at this?" He shook the bills in the air. "This is some tip."

"It's not a tip. I saved it from last week. I need the money to pay the rent."

"Is that what you told my friend? You needed cash to pay your rent?" Vito growled.

"He gave me twenty bucks. The rest is mine."

Vito shook the bills. "Crawl over here."

Dahlia sat—afraid to breathe.

"You're not gonna get the money until you come over here and beg."

He waved the bills again. "This is your last chance to dance, baby."

Dahlia crept across the floor. She stopped in front of him and cringed like a whipped puppy.

He unzipped his pants. "Earn it, sweetheart."

She turned her head, but not in time. His fist hit her jaw. She heard the crack and felt the pain.

"You whores are all alike. You love to be treated rough. You're not happy until you get me so riled I have to smack the shit out of you."

Blood ran from her mouth.

Vito took her hand and rubbed it across his crotch. "See what you done? Go clean your face, then come back and take care of me." He shoved the seventy-five bucks into his pocket.

Anxious to get away, she pulled herself from the floor and went into the bathroom. Her face was red, the pain unbearable.

In the mirror, she saw Vito light a cigarette and saunter toward the balcony.

The phone rang. Dahlia's friend at the desk wanted to know how long she would be.

"Call Frankie at the club." She rattled off the number. "Tell him I'm *not* all right."

Vito came back into the room as she hung up the phone.

"Who was that?"

"The front desk. They wanted to know how long we'd be."

Vito grunted.

"I told him that I'd call him when we were ready to leave."

"Good girl. I'll finish my cigarette while you shower."

Dahlia hurried into the bathroom. She leaned against the closed door and wondered if her friend would call Frankie. *Even if he does, will Frankie do anything?* She stayed in the bathroom holding a cold washcloth against her cheek.

Vito banged on the door that stood between them.

"What's going on in there? I'm ready to go." He rattled the handle.

She was glad she had turned the lock.

"Aw, c'mon, I'm not mad anymore. Let's go downstairs and get a drink."

She looked in the mirror at her swollen face. One eye had started to close. When she did not answer, she heard the volume on the TV rise. She sat for a long time, determined not to open the door. Thirty minutes passed. She wondered if he had fallen asleep watching TV, like he usually did, or maybe he had left without telling her.

Dahlia heard a knock and thought it might be Frankie. She pressed her ear against the bathroom door and listened. The TV went silent.

"Vito DiGregetti!" a man's voice boomed. "Police, open the door!"

Dahlia's heart skipped a beat. *Great! Now I'll go to jail.*

An eerie quiet came over the place and several minutes passed. All at once, she heard a commotion in the bedroom and men laughing. Someone rapped on the bathroom door.

"Is there anyone in there?" a man's voice inquired.

She did not answer.

"Dahlia, are you okay?"

Even though she knew it was not Vito, she just stood there. Common sense told her the cops would break down the door and add more charges like resisting arrest, so she cracked the door and peered out. One, a tall good-looking blond man with green eyes, and the other, a light skinned black man with a beard, stood in front of the bathroom door. They were both dressed in black pants and shirts.

"Good Lord," the black man said. "What happened to you?"

"I think my jaw's broken," she said through clenched teeth.

The blond man gently opened the door and touched her chin. "Open your mouth and close it again."

She did.

"I don't think it's broken, but it probably needs to be checked," he said.

"Who are you?" she asked.

"Police," they both said at the same time.

"Undercover, ma'am," the blond said.

"I don't have my car." She looked from one to the other.

"We'll take you to a clinic," the blond cop said.

"You gonna bust me?"

"We don't arrest people for getting beat up."

"I don't have any money."

"Don't worry." The bearded man picked up her purse from the bathroom and handed it to her. "We'll see that you get home."

Redesigning the Mob

"What happened to the man who was here with me?" she asked.

"I don't know," the bearded man said. "When we entered, the balcony door was open. I guess he took the fire escape."

Dahlia looked a little perplexed. "Thank you for handling everything quietly."

The guys shot each other a look. Dahlia held a washcloth against her cheek and followed the officers down the back stairs to an unmarked car.

Just before the cops came into room five twenty, Vito had bolted onto the balcony and climbed down the fire escape to the next floor. He found the room below unlocked and empty so he fled through the room, into the hallway and down the back stairs. After driving a few blocks from the hotel, he looked in his rearview mirror. No one had followed.

As soon as he was away from the beach, he parked his rental car behind an abandoned mall. He walked almost a mile to a heavy traffic area and flagged a cab. When he figured he was far enough away from the hotel, he got out of the cab and called Benny.

"Pick me up," Vito said. "I need a place to lay low until I find out what's goin' down."

"I can put you up for a couple of days, that's all. I don't want any trouble at my house."

"That's all I need." Vito hung up the phone. *Couple of days. Sure.*

"You did what?" Chance pressed the phone to his ear.

"We fixed the fire escape so he could get away. He took it like God himself put it there." Frankie howled.

"The girl? She all right? She gonna talk?"

"Nah, she's cool."

"I figure he cheat, but again the violence." Chance sighed. "If anyone talks, Feds clamp down. Give girls few days off. Let this pass."

"Then what?" Frankie asked.

"He psychopath. He call for help. When he does, you take him in. I think on this."

"So, what do I do while you're thinking?"

"Treat him like your *goombah*," Chance said. "When I get the word, I call you. You break an egg."

Frankie convinced Dahlia to meet with attorney Sam Marin.

"As soon as you sign the papers, you can leave for New York," Frankie said and showed her the plane ticket.

"It's not a strong case." Marin laid the paper in front of Dahlia. "You'll have to come back for the trial, if it goes that far. In the meantime, he won't know where you are."

Dahlia kept her hands folded in her lap. The sheer black scarf tied around her head partially concealed her bruised face. "It's hard to tell who your friends are around here."

"He's no friend of mine," Marin said. "Hell, he still owes me for his divorce."

"If he gets a jail sentence, you can leave New York and come home." Frankie said. He nervously twirled a pen between his fingers. "The complaint says you two had been dating for a month and had agreed to spend a night at the hotel. An argument ensued and he assaulted you."

She took the pen from Frankie's outstretched hand and scrawled her name.

Marin handed the signed statement to his secretary to witness.

Frankie gave Dahlia an envelope filled with cash. "For expenses," He said with a shrug. "Chance will find you a place to stay. When the bruises are gone, he'll get you a job."

"What if Vito doesn't get convicted? Or if he does and he's only in jail for a short time, then what'll I do?" She tucked the plane ticket and the money into her purse.

"We'll worry about that when the time comes." Frankie got up to leave.

"You got what you wanted," Dahlia whined. "I'll never hear from you again."

Frankie pulled out a pack of cigarettes and offered her one. "Vito's going away for a long time. I can promise you that much. You'll be back working for me in no time."

Dahlia's hand shook as she stuck the cigarette between her lips and dug through her purse for a match.

Frankie snapped open a Zippo and held it close to the trembling cigarette.

"Will those two cops be at the trial?" she asked.

"I don't know who you're talking about," Frankie replied." He held the door open for her.

"The officers who broke into the hotel room after Vito beat it down the fire escape," Dahlia said.

"I don't know anything about cops, and the hotel didn't complain about any broken door. When I called your friend at the desk, he said a couple of your friends came in and he gave them the room number."

"They took me to an apartment building. A nurse cleaned up my face and gave me antibiotics so the cut in my mouth wouldn't get infected. After that they took me home."

"What apartment building?" Frankie waited to see if she had an answer.

"I don't know. It was late, and dark. I didn't pay attention. When I left the apartment, I had a compress over my eye and most of my face was covered with a scarf."

"Well, now we know it must have been friends. Cops wouldn't take you to an apartment."

"They weren't my friends," Dahlia insisted. "They said they were police officers. I thought you called them."

"Me, call a cop. Are you kidding? I didn't call anyone. You said you'd be okay. I left the club right after I talked to you."

"You didn't get my message?" Dahlia stood with her mouth open.

"Not until the next day." Frankie put his arm around her. "Tell me about the cops. What did their uniforms look like? I'll see if I can track them down."

"They were dressed in black street clothes and said they were undercover cops." Her voice grew louder and frightened.

"Calm down, Dahlia. I'll take you to your girlfriend's house. We can talk on the way. If you saw cops, we'll find them." Frankie ushered her into the elevator away from the prying eyes and eavesdropping reporters who hung-out around the court house, and the commercial office building next door, where Sam Marin had his office.

CHAPTER THIRTY-TWO

Visions of Nina's two-month-old granddaughter played across Nina's mind as she stopped for gas one day. Anthony's first year of college would soon be completed, and he, Catherine, and baby Krysta would be coming home. Nina searched through her purse for money and tucked the bills and her keys into her jacket pocket. When she got out of the car, Vito stepped from behind another vehicle.

"Oh!" she gasped. "Get away from me."

"I'll do this." He took the hose and began to fill her gas tank.

The numbers began to roll, and so did Nina's stomach.

Several cars pulled into the service station and her self-assurance returned. "Why are you bothering me?"

"I saw you turn in and thought I'd come over and say hello." Vito shrugged. "You seen Catherine since Anthony left for college?"

Nina stared at him, not sure what he was trying to accomplish.

"That's a silly question," he said grinning. "Of course you see her all the time. She lives right next door to you. Well, not right next door, but the next house on the street."

"Do you and Anthony talk on the phone?" Nina asked.

"Yeah, he calls me at least once a week. He's a smart kid. I'm driving up to see him, and I've misplaced his address." He pulled a pen and a small card from his vest pocket. "What is it again?"

"I don't know."

"Don't tell me you don't know. You probably rented it for him." When the tank was filled the pump shut off, and Vito hung up the nozzle.

Nina screwed on the gas cap and locked the car door.

He grabbed her wrist. She glanced around at the crowded Amoco station, and he pulled his hand away.

"Wait a minute." Vito touched her arm. "I need a place to stay. I think the cops are after me."

Nina shook her head. "So that's why you wanted Anthony's address. You want to involve him in the mess you made of your life."

"It's not that, I just wanted to see him."

"Sure, so why is the law looking for you?"

"I don't know. A friend of mine who knows a cop mentioned it." He leaned close to her.

Nina stiffened. "Well, it could be for any number of things."

"If I get picked up, I could tell them what you're doing."

Nina backed up and glared. "What do you suppose Chance would do if he heard you were threatening to talk?"

"Aw, you know I didn't mean that. Let me lay out at your place until I can straighten this out." Vito paused. "I'd be surprised if they'd even consider looking for me there."

"You're right. Even I can't imagine you living in my house."

"Then I can stay for a couple of weeks?"

"No." Nina went inside the station and paid for the gas.

The tires on Vito's car screeched as he pulled from the station.

Although Nina and Larry still talked on the phone, they both were busy, and he rarely came over. Later, after running into Vito, she returned home and was surprised to see Larry's truck parked in front of her house.

He stood next to the grill on the back patio, turning fish. "Hi." He waved a spatula in the air. "I made potato salad, and the boys sliced tomatoes," he said through the screen door.

Nina went outside to give him a hug.

Joey and Brian raced around the corner of the house on their ten speeds and slid to a stop.

"Hi, Nina," Brian said as he picked up the basketball.

Joey dropped his bike. "Did you see all the fish we caught?"

Nina laughed. "Larry said this is the one you reeled in." She pointed to the smallest one.

"Like the devil. Brian and I caught 'em all. Larry just sat in the shade and watched. He never even put his line in the water."

"Is that true?" Nina gave Larry a playful punch.

"They caught the fish, but I'm cooking."

After dinner, the boys went to the tennis courts, and Nina and Larry watched a rerun of *Football Follies*. Larry roared with laughter, but Nina's thoughts were far away.

When a commercial came on, Larry went into the kitchen and brought back a bowl of popcorn and two root beers. "You worried about something?"

"No." She took a sip of the cool drink. "But I saw Vito today."

Larry sat across from her. "Where?"

"He was at the Amoco station when I stopped for gas." She reached for a handful of popcorn.

"Did he see you?" Larry leaned forward.

"Yeah, he pumped my gas."

Larry's brow furrowed. "He must want something."

"No, he just asked how the boys were. He hasn't seen them in a while."

"Where's he living now?"

Larry seemed more interested in Vito than Nina had ever noticed before.

"I have no idea."

"You need to be careful," he said.

"We were in a busy station. He wouldn't blow me away in front of twenty people. Anyway, he's not as mean as he used to be. I think he's more talk than anything else."

"Don't be too sure."

A few days later, The Fort Lauderdale News and The Miami Herald carried the story of Vito's arrest for the assault and battery of his girlfriend, Dahlia. The papers also noted he was the ex-husband of Elite Advertising executive, Nina Cocolucci.

Nina threw the paper in the garbage.

"Mom?" Joey called from the doorway.

"Hi," she said as if nothing was the matter.

"Did you hear the news?" he asked.

Michael came in behind Joey. "Where's the newspaper? Dad's in jail."

"You don't need to read all the trash they print."

Michael spied the paper and rolled his eyes. "You can't keep stuff from us, anymore than Father Mendezino can stop the school kids from talking."

Nina felt helpless. "It's probably not as bad as the article makes it sound."

Michael grabbed the newspaper, and both of the boys went out on the patio.

That night the ringing phone woke Nina from a sound sleep. She switched on the lamp and looked at the clock. It was close to midnight. She grabbed the receiver and heard Anthony's voice. "Is something wrong?" Nina asked.

"I was studying. When I finished, I turned on the TV to hear the news. There was a picture of Dad being arrested. I couldn't believe it was on the local Tallahassee station." Anthony's voice was hoarse. "He must have hurt that woman bad."

"I don't know," Nina said.

"What if they keep him in jail?"

"Don't worry about him. He'll be out on bond by morning."

"I think I should come home."

"Frankie will take care of everything. By the time anything happens, you'll be out of school on summer vacation."

"Are you sure?"

"You know how these things go. Remember when Danny got arrested? The attorney is still finding ways to keep it from going to trial, and then one of these days it'll just get dropped." Nina pulled the covers around her. "I want you to keep your mind on your finals and take care of your family. I'll let you know if anything happens."

"I think you should've called the cops when he first started hitting you, and maybe he wouldn't have gotten this bad." Anthony said.

Nina bit her tongue. *So now it's my fault his father has a violent temper.* "Go to bed. Nothing will happen tonight."

"If you hear anything, you'll call me, right?"

"I promise." Nina took a deep breath. "How are Catherine and the baby?"

Aunt Victoria finally went home, and Catherine and Krysta are doing great. It's good to have our privacy again," Anthony said. "Wait'll you see your granddaughter. You're gonna fall in love with her."

"I already have." Nina admitted. "It's all I can do to keep from driving up there regardless of how Catherine's mother feels about it."

"She's still a tiny baby. She's going to be petite like Catherine. Her mother will never guess that Krysta's two months older than we say. As soon as she gives us her blessing, Krysta will be yours for the summer. Catherine's already told her mother we're staying with you when we come home."

The thought of having the baby at the house was reason enough for Nina to be excited, but Anthony's happiness about coming home, heightened her spirits even more. She looked forward to summer and was thrilled with the idea of having her family back together.

CHAPTER THIRTY-THREE

Chance and Dutch arrived in South Florida the day after Vito's arrest. Frankie sent Paulie to meet them at the airport at 6:00 p.m. Paulie was told to bring Chance straight to the meeting place, but Chance was in no hurry. He had thought of a harsh punishment for Vito to keep others from skimming, but that would not solve the problem. Sooner or later Vito's violence would attract the attention of the law, and this was somethimg he had to prevent.

"Let Frankie wait," he said. "Stop at that Italian restaurant across from the racetrack."

While they ate dinner, Chance talked to Paulie. "So, how long Frankie know about this thing between Vito and the prostitute?"

"I dunno."

"You think this Dahlia's the only one?"

Paulie hunched his shoulders. "Maybe yes, maybe no."

"You no keep in touch with Vito?"

"Not since Vito started to question me about how Dutch knew when Vito was going to make a collection. That was when Frankie told Vito you needed me in Tampa." Paulie's cheek twitched. "After that I was on Dutch's payroll." Paulie had never spoken to an out-of-town Mafia boss before and moisture glistened on Paulie's mustache. "Frankie said you wanted me to lay low for a while."

"You okay. I like you, but no more maybe answers." Chance jabbed a finger at Paulie's chest. "You keep eyes open. No sleep on job."

Paulie sat up straight.

"Listen to Frankie, but when we spring Vito, you act like you unhappy with Frankie. I want for you to stick close to Vito—like shoe polish."

Paulie nodded.

Chance leaned close to Paulie "Vito *avere un carattere violento.*"

"Ah, I see his temper many times," Paulie said.

"You no tell Frankie or Vito we have this little talk. *Capisce?*"

Paulie nodded again.

"You see problem—you no go to Frankie—you call me." Chance tucked a hundred dollar bill into Paulie's shirt pocket. "A little C-note for your trouble." Chance tapped the flap of Paulie's pocket. "Get the car."

When Paulie left, Chance ordered another drink. Dutch took care of the tab and then went to the restroom. When he came back, Chance motioned for him to sit.

"We take our time," he said to Dutch. "Give The Mustache time to think."

They came out the back door and found Paulie in the car with the engine running. He drove them to The Horseshoe Bar, a little hole-in-the-wall on Hollywood Beach. Frankie sat at a small table in the back room waiting for them.

Chance made the usual small talk while he listened to Frankie's side of the story.

"Make sure Vito feel . . ." Chance searched for the word. "What you say?"

"Obligated?" Dutch offered.

"Yeah, yeah. *Obbligo*. I no want he should run his mouth," Chance told Frankie.

Dutch tapped his fingers on Frankie's shoulder as he talked. "What he means is let Vito think you approve of how he handled the prostitute, but that his doing so puts you in a bad position."

"What are you, a parrot? I know what he means." Frankie pulled a cigarette from a crushed pack. "We should have iced him right when it happened and been done with it."

"You no use head." Chance chewed on a toothpick as he spoke. "The Feds, they look hard at prostitution and credit card fraud. We no need publicity." He polished off his cognac. "Where's Gonzalez?"

"He lives somewhere in Little Havana." Frankie's stomach was giving him fits. He took another sip of his blackberry brandy. "He reports to Vito. I'll ask him how to get in touch with The Spic."

"Vito work for *you*, and you can't find Gonzalez?" Chance glared. "*You* no ask Vito. *You* find The Spic."

"It may take a day or two." He lit the bent cigarette.

"I tell Marin to take his time. You take maybe, two days, no more." Chance got up from the table and walked toward the door. "And don't bring me to a dump like this again."

With all the stories about Vito in the newspapers, Gonzalez had melted into the Cuban community.

Frankie caught up with Gonzalez as he came out of a Cuban coffee shop. Frankie grabbed him by the back of the neck. "Old habits die hard."

"Take your hands offa me." Gonzalez pulled away, but he did not run.

"I got an offer for you." Frankie edged a little closer. "Whad ya' say we talk?"

"No deal. I read the papers." He tossed the top from his to-go paper cup into a trash container. "So how come Vito's still in jail?"

"He's not exactly locked up. He's being detained while they ask him a few questions about The Squirrel," Frankie lied. "You're the only one who can fill in the blanks. So I thought I'd drop by and give you a heads up."

"Since when do you give a shit what happens to me?" Gonzalez eyed him suspiciously.

"Sam Marin's meeting a bail bondsman as we speak." Frankie lit a cigarette and walked in the direction of his car. "Who do you think'll be the first guy Vito goes after?"

Gonzalez trailed a couple of steps behind. "Vito knows I watch his back. He trusts me."

They turned the corner, and the morning sun glared in their eyes.

Redesigning the Mob

"He trusted The Squirrel, too." Frankie pulled dark glasses from his shirt pocket.

Gonzalez squinted. "Stanley didn't know what day it was. The idiot was a full-blown junkie."

"He knew how to set fire to Donovan's Meat Market and kill those two dogs."

"You don't know who did that job." Gonzalez took another sip of his coffee. "Stanley couldn't find his way from Miami to Fort Lauderdale. He was brain-dead."

"So now he's dead all over." Frankie dropped his cigarette and squashed it with the brightly polished toe of his Ferragama shoe. "Vito's attorney says you and your father swore you took Vito to the Bahamas on your old man's boat, and that the three of you spent the whole week fishing while The Squirrel was takin' it in the head." Frankie laughed. "Hell, I'll bet you ain't ever been to the Bahamas."

"Have too," Gonzalez sputtered.

"Vito's running scared and he ain't about to leave anyone around that can finger him. If he decides to get rid of you, he might knock off your old man, too." Frankie opened his car door. "You think about it. I'll be at the Northside Grill tonight—eight o'clock. I won't be hanging around long."

A week later, Frankie pulled into an alley behind a row of Cuban shops. Gonzalez waited in a doorway. He slid into the front seat of Frankie's Lincoln Continental.

"I talked to Vito," Frankie said as he eased into traffic. "He tells me you have a couple of Cubans you want to add to the hijack crew, and you want him to check them out."

"That's the story I gave him," Gonzalez said.

"Take a look at the fancy clothes." Frankie pushed a paper bag toward Gonzalez.

Gonzalez glanced inside the sack and turned up his nose.

"You said you didn't have clothes," Frankie said and shook the bag. "Now you're not happy with what I brought?"

"Why am I the only one who's got his ass on the line? You get what you want and I end up in the slammer. I don't like the plan."

"Don't go chickenshit on me." Frankie kept the car below the speed limit as he drove. "I don't wanna do this. Vito might blow me away." Gonzalez's voice quivered. "You said so yourself."

"Vito's out on bail. If he got picked up with a rod, he'd be looking at hard time for sure." A light turned red, and Frankie brought the Lincoln to a slow stop. "I'll be bringing him here myself, and I damn well guarantee he'll be clean."

Gonzalez stuck his newspaper under his arm and grasped the paper bag.

Frankie gave him the name of the motel and handed him the key to room 123. "It's charged on a phony Visa to a guy from Chicago for a week. Show up there on the thirtieth at noon. It's this coming Monday. People will be celebrating Memorial Day."

"What's the sucker's name?"

"You don't need to know." Frankie pulled across the intersection and stopped at the curb. "There'll be a lot of noise and commotion. Don't be late." He passed ten one-hundred dollar bills to Gonzalez.

"Ten C's?" Gonzalez's mouth tightened. "The job's worth a lot more than a grand."

"This ain't no job. This is to protect your own ass." Frankie raced the motor impatiently.

Gonzalez rammed the wad of money in his pants pocket, got out of the car and disappeared into the crowd.

Frankie cursed the Miami traffic, took an off-ramp, and stopped at one of Miami's first- class hotels. After getting a drink at the bar, he carried his glass to a hallway off the lobby and made a call. "It's going down on the thirtieth," he said.

Chance coughed on the other end of the line. "It's about time."

CHAPTER THIRTY-FOUR

Nina opened her front door. Ginger stood on the porch with a bouquet of carnations she had purchased from a street corner vendor. She held them out to Nina.

Nina reached for the flowers. "Thank you." She held them close to her nose. "Um, they smell like cloves." She held the door open for Ginger. "I'm so glad you're here. I need to talk to you about something."

Ginger kicked off her shoes. "What's up?"

Nina placed the flowers in her favorite blue vase and set them in the middle of the table. It's about Michael." Nina motioned for Ginger to sit at the kitchen table where she had prepared roast beef sandwiches and potato salad for lunch. "The seniors get out of high school the twenty-fifth of May, and just last night Michael told me he changed his mind about FSU."

"Changed his mind?" Ginger's mouth fell open. "I thought he scored high on his S.A.T.'s. Remember how excited he was?"

"That exhilaration's been channeled to the Navy. He plans on enlisting for six years."

"Whoa! That's a long time. He should join for a short stint, until he sees what it's like."

"According to Michael, he got a better deal for volunteering for six. He'll be in training most of the time, provided he stays in the top ten percent of his class. He acts like he has it all figured out."

"Maybe he does. He's got a good head on his shoulders." Ginger dug into a big scoop of potato salad. "Some kids aren't interested in college."

"He's just a kid." Nina pushed the food around her plate. "He doesn't know what he's getting into. I tried to talk him out of it, but he's got a mind of his own."

"At least it's peacetime. You won't have to worry about him being on a ship in the middle of a war. I think he'll be okay."

"I hope you're right." Nina sipped her iced tea. "How are the girls doing?"

Ginger told Nina about their dance classes, ball games, and skating rink parties.

"The older they get, the more their stuff costs," Ginger said.

"I know what you mean. Wait until they get as old as my boys." Nina scooted the potato salad bowl closer to Ginger. "Have some more."

"No thanks. It's delicious, but I refuse to gain that weight back. Anyway, I didn't come to eat. I came to see the baby's room."

"Actually, I didn't give up my office after all," Nina said as she placed the leftovers in the refrigerator.

Ginger carried their dirty dishes to the sink. "So, what are you gonna do?"

"I don't know what Anthony and Catherine have in mind. Some days they talk about leaving the baby with me when they go back to school, and other days Catherine says she might not go to college at all."

Ginger frowned. "What about the baby furniture you bought?"

Nina's face brightened. "Let me show you." Nina led the way. "Anthony's room is almost as big as mine."

A diaper bag filled with a stack of soft absorbent cloths hung on the back of the door.

"I moved the big bed to the other side of the room and set the crib up along the wall."

Ginger touched the teddy bear carousel. "Aw, this is precious." It tinkled a few short notes.

"What do you think?" Nina beamed. "The maple chest just fits next to the baby bed. It'll be good to have her things close."

"It's great. I couldn't have done it better myself." Ginger slid the drapes aside. Sunshine poured into the room. "I like the rocking chair in front of the window."

"I want Catherine to be able to see the river while she rocks Krysta." Nina ran her hand along the back of the chair as she glanced out at the flowing water. "The baby sleeps in a cradle now. The crib is a surprise. I hope Catherine likes it."

"If I didn't have a baby bed, I think I'd like whatever you bought."

Nina shrugged. "They can take the baby's furniture with them when Anthony goes back to school. Catherine says the apartment only has the bare necessities."

"Let's sit and relax awhile," Nina said as they returned to the hallway. "I'm in the mood to let my hair down." She danced around in a circle. "Would you like a blackberry wine cooler?"

"Now you're talking my language." Ginger snuggled into the recliner. "Have you heard any more about Vito?"

"Only what I read in the papers." She handed Ginger a cool glass of the bubbling wine and set her own on the end table. "Chance told me Vito's making more money now than when he was in the protection business. It's his loss of power that he can't handle."

"Did it ever occur to you that someday his ego will forget it's human, and you might end up dead or disfigured?"

"I thought about that after I read the paper." Nina fluffed a big pillow on the couch and nestled against it.

"I talked to Eunice. She said the lawyer got Vito out on bond. He's staying with her and Frankie while they decide what to do about the hooker." Ginger rolled the delicate stem of her wine glass between her fingers.

"Hooker? The paper said girlfriend."

"Eunice said she was a prostitute, but what does she know?"

Nina was hurt when Vito moved in with Maria, and crushed even more deeply to learn that he had turned to a prostitute to satisfy his sexual desires.

"Was she one of the girls who worked for Frankie?" Nina asked.

Ginger hesitated. "I think she worked for Vito."

Nina tried not to show any emotion. She had never even thought about the possibility of Vito making a living off of a woman. *I should have known. Nothing is beneath him.*

"I'm sorry, Nina. I didn't mean to convey bad news."

"Don't worry," Nina waved the thought away. "He doesn't mean anything to me anymore." Nina sipped her wine. "The newscaster called her Dahlia. Do you think she made up that name?"

Ginger burst out laughing and nearly choked on the wine. "You're so naïve." She checked her watch. "I can't stay much longer."

"Speaking of leaving, Mickey goes home every summer, and this year he plans on driving; Joey likes the idea. He wants to see other states besides Florida and Pennsylvania."

"I can understand that." Ginger finished the last of her wine. "You don't see much flying" Ginger paused. "I gotta go. I try to give Mom a break on Sundays."

Nina walked Ginger to her car. "I'm glad you came over. It's been too long."

"Yeah," Ginger agreed. "And thanks for not asking about Danny. I'm trying to put that behind me."

Anthony phoned a week later to say he had passed his finals and that they would be home on Memorial Day.

A delighted Nina said, "I didn't expect you so soon. Be careful driving. Traffic will be heavy on the holiday."

"Have you heard anything about Dad?"

"Nothing new," she said. "He's all right. He's out on bail."

"Yeah, but I got this bad feeling, and—"

Nina waited for him to finish, or say something else, but the line was quiet.

"Are you still there?" she asked.

"Yeah, I was thinking."

"About what?"

"Oh, nothing." Anthony's voice faltered for a moment. "I almost forgot. The management office said they'd rent us the apartment for the same price next semester if you'd send a deposit."

"I'll call them and see what kind of arrangements I can make. If it's reasonable, I'll send the money."

"Thanks. We really like this place and it's convenient."

All Nina could think about was having a new baby in the house. "I can't wait to see Krysta. It's hard to believe she's almost four months old."

Anthony didn't respond, and for a moment Nina thought she had opened an old wound.

"I love you," she said.

He surprised her by saying, "Love you, too, but don't forget we're telling Catherine's mother she's only two months old."

On Memorial Day, Michael and Joey decorated the house with pink crepe paper streamers and a Welcome Home sign.

About noon, a horn blew, and everyone ran outside. Anthony carried Krysta and met Nina in the middle of the yard. The baby squinched her eyes.

"Ooh! Let me hold her." Nina tucked the little bundle into her arms and shaded her granddaughter's face from the sun.

Little Krysta opened her eyes and smiled.

"Look. She knows me already." Nina cried with joy.

Anthony grinned. "She laughs all the time." He put his arm around Catherine. "Doesn't she, Honey?"

Catherine stretched. "It's good to get out of the car. Krysta stayed awake the whole way."

Bertha was standing on the steps. "Come here and let me get a look at that child." She wiped her hands on a bright green apron. "Go on in. Lunch is on the table."

Everyone sat down at the kitchen table except Nina. She was not about to give up her granddaughter. She waltzed into the bedroom and showed Krysta her crib and rocking chair. "See the pretty river?" Nina turned her granddaughter toward the window. "You'll see it every morning when you wake up."

She did not care that four-month-old Krysta Leigh had no idea what her grandmother was talking about. All the problems in the world were gone right now. She could not get over Krysta's beautiful black hair, and her dark brown eyes were so big and bright that they lit up her whole face.

Nina gentled her on the mattress in the crib, changed her diaper, and put on a new pair of pink plastic pants. "This is a wonderful day," she whispered in the baby's ear.

Catherine came in from the kitchen.

"Did you have enough to eat?" Nina asked.

"Sure did. I was starved. Anthony didn't give me time to have breakfast. All I had was a glass of juice. He was in such a hurry to get home."

Nina played with the baby's fingers and Krysta cooed.

"I have to take her to see Mama. She can probably see our car from the porch. Do you think she looks little enough to pass for a two-month-old?"

Nina looked at the baby reaching for the carousal that tinkled above her. "She does. She really does. She's so petite. I'd believe you. I'd just think she was an exceptionally bright child." "Good. That's what I needed to hear. You know Mama will want me to stay there for a while, but I'll be back by dinnertime. We're going to be here all summer, so you'll have plenty of time with your granddaughter."

"I know." Nina plucked Krysta from the bed, kissed her and handed her to Catherine. "Are you happy?"

"Yes. We both are." Catherine took her baby daughter to the kitchen. "Are you coming with me?" she asked Anthony.

"No, you go ahead. Tell them I'm emptying the car or something. I'll be over later. I want to spend some time here first. They probably don't want to see me anyhow."

"That's not true." Catherine grabbed a cookie from the plate on her way out the door.

CHAPTER THIRTY-FIVE

On Memorial Day, Frankie turned his car off the highway not far from the Miami airport. "What room did you say you were meeting Gonzalez in?" he asked Vito who was sitting beside him.

"Gonzalez and the new men he hired are supposed to be in 123. They better be on time." Vito glanced out the window. "Those ignorant Cubans don't know what a watch is for. If it wasn't for Gonzalez, I'd dump the whole crew."

Frankie pulled in front of the motel. "You think we got the right place?"

"Yeah, this is it." Vito stretched his neck. "Looks like the kind of ratty-ass place a Cuban would chose."

"I'll gas up next door and come back and wait for you right here."

Vito got out of the car and strutted inside the motel.

Frankie pulled the yellow rented sedan behind the service station. He stuck a magnetic black and white taxi dome on the top of the car and clamped a fake license plate on top of the real one. Before pulling back in front of the motel, he slapped two taxi logos on the car doors and pulled a dark golfer's cap low over his brow.

When Vito tapped on the door to room 123, no one answered. The door was ajar, so he cautiously stepped inside the room. On the opposite side of the bed a dark woman with long, bleached blond hair stood with her back to him.

"Oh! Excuse me," Vito said keeping his voice low. "I guess I got the wrong room." He backed toward the door.

The woman slowly turned halfway toward him and smiled.

"Gonzalez?" Vito whispered. "Is that you?" His eyes sqinched.

Gonzalez was silent. His smile turned into a smirk and his nose twitched like he had caught a whiff of something bad.

"What the hell you doin' in that get up?" Vito snarled.

Gonzalez's right hand quivered on the gun that was hidden in the folds of his short skirt

"Where's the men you wanted me to hire?" Vito said as he made a move to come around the bed.

Gonzalez's face tensed into a hardened mask.

"What-a-ya trying to prove here?" Vito barked. "You stupid Spic."

The slur had just slipped out. Vito had never called Gonzalez a Spic to his face, but he had told the Cuban that he had no use for most of the Miami immigrants, or for blacks either for that matter.

Gonzalez raised the gun and aimed it at Vito.

"Wait!" Vito lurched toward the Cuban, who now held the gun with both hands. Fire flashed from the barrel, and the bullet exploded in Vito's head, driving him against the wall. He landed in a clump on the orange and brown rug.

Gonzalez teetered on the high heels. He knew he was supposed to make sure that Vito was dead. But blood, brains, and tissue were scattered all over the floor and stuck to the walls and ceiling. Blood was still oozing onto the floor and soaking into Vito's light gray, silk suit. Gonzalez gagged and stepped backward. He dropped the gun in his purse and used a rag to open the door. His knees were weak, and his stomach lurched. He swallowed the sour taste in his mouth as he forced one foot in front of the other along the hallway and out the side door. Just fifty feet away the phoney cab sat with the motor running.

The streets buzzed with traffic, and from somewhere far off the faint sound of marching music filtered through the air. Small American flags were stuck in the ground along the walkway leading away from the building. Several people strolled past him without so much as a sideways glance. A black man in a suit hurried along the path and nearly knocked him over.

The red mini-skirt and the shimmring silver top accented Gonzalez dark skin. His boobs were now lopsided and his sunglasses sat askew on his nose. His toes dug into the inner sole of the high heels to keep them from falling off. The Cubans skinny legs ached, and sweat ran from his hairline, dredging tiny rivers through the makeup on his face. Just as he thought he could go no further, his hand grasped the car door handle. He sank into the back seat, and swung the door shut. The job was done.

Frankie stifled a laugh. He put the car in gear and edged casually into traffic. He had only gone three blocks when he stopped at an abandoned do-it-yourself car wash. He pulled the taxi signs and the black and white dome from the car and unclamped the fake license plate.

By then, Gonzalez had taken off the hooker outfit and put on his own clothes. He used the rag from the motel to wipe off the makeup. Frankie threw all the evidence into a brown plastic bag, put it in the trunk and pulled onto the highway. Only then did they speak.

"How'd it go?" Frankie wanted to know. "Did you make sure he was dead?"

"Did you ever kill a man?" Gonzalez asked.

"Sure, so what?" Frankie pulled into the slow lane.

"Holy Jesus. It was awful."

"What! You got religion now?" Frankie said as he lit a cigarette. "Listen, I gotta know, was there any noise?"

"Only a thud with the silencer. Vito's got a hole in his head as big as a grapefruit."

"Anyone see you come out of the room?"

Gonzalez shook his head.

"You sure he's dead?" Frankie asked running his fingers through his hair.

"I told ya—he's dead all right. What ya expect from a four-fifty-seven at ten feet? I damn near put him through the wall."

Frankie turned toward Little Havana. "You didn't touch anything, did you?"

"Only the door handle and I used a rag."

"You did good." He handed Gonzalez a brown bag. "Here's another ten grand. Where do you want me to drop you off?"

"Stop at the next corner. I know people in the bar." Gonzalez said. "I'll slip in the back and come out of the john. They'll think I've been there a while. What about the gun and stuff in the trunk?"

Frankie shook his head. "Fuhgeddaboudit, I want ya to lay low, no hijacking, and don't be flashing a big wad. Go home and stay with your old man. I'll get in touch when the time's right."

"Pull over right here," Gonzalez said.

Frankie grinned. "You'll have to tell me sometime how you got your legs shaved so nice and smooth."

"Fuck you," Gonzalez said as he slipped from the Lincoln and disappeared behind Enrico's Bar.

Frankie chuckled and dropped in a Tony Bennett cassette and took the highway north. It was a nice day for a drive.

He came to a spot where people drove their cars down narrow dirt roads to fish on the mangrove side of the Intracoastal. He found one of the many places where fishermen had made a circle of stones to cook a few fish while they spent the night catching next week's dinner.

To the strains of "I Left My Heart in San Francisco" Frankie burned the paper signs and all the hooker clothes. After using the fake license plate to scoop out the remaining ashes, he hauled back and threw the plate and dome light as far out into the Intracoastal as he could.

Frankie dropped the gun into a plastic bag, being careful not to smudge Gonzalez's fingerprints. He drove to Port Everglades in Fort Lauderdale and stashed the weapon in a long-term locker. He ran the yellow sedan through two different car washes, wiped the leather interior with alcohol, and ditched the rental car at the Fort Lauderdale Airport. He climbed into his own car and took a deep breath.

CHAPTER THIRTY-SIX

After lunch, Michael and Joey carried luggage into the house, then gathered in the living room to hear about Anthony's first year of college. He had passed all his courses and although he failed to make first string, he had gotten plenty of time on the field during regular games due to the untimely injuries of several upper classmen.

He was ready to tell them about all the pretty girls on campus when the newscaster declared, "Suspected racketeer found dead in Miami motel."

Anthony's mouth hung slack as he turned up the volume.

"Witnesses reported seeing a thin, blond woman, thought to be a prostitute, leaving the motel in a yellow cab only minutes before the body was discovered. The middle-aged white male was found by a cleaning woman employed by the establishment. No name has been released pending notification of next of kin."

Anthony looked at his mother. "Do you think?"

"No," Nina said. "Not if you're thinking it might have been your father. Someone's killed in Miami every day. Besides, your dad rarely goes to Miami, and when he does, he doesn't go to that part of the city," Nina said with conviction.

A short time later, a white sedan pulled into the driveway, and a strange man in a dark suit walked toward the house. Nina went to the door with the boys close behind. The man came up the steps with his shoulders straight and his head slightly bent. He looked as if he had made this walk many times before.

The newscast flashed through her mind. Somehow, she knew before she opened the door that Vito was dead, just as she always knew when Vito was about to explode. Only now the boys were grown, and there was no way to rush them into their bedrooms to keep them out of harms way. *Dear God, please don't let this be happening to us.*

The man flashed his badge and had hardly gotten the message out of his mouth when Anthony pushed past his mother. He pounced on the man shouting obscenities at the top of his lungs. "You pigs drive people to their deaths!" he screamed.

The soft-spoken man did not fight back. He smothered the boy in his arms until Anthony collapsed on the ground. "Can I do something to help?" the man asked Nina.

She shook her head. She was already sitting down beside Anthony, cradling him in her arms as he cried.

"I understand you're divorced, but we need someone to identify the body. His family is out of state, and it doesn't look like your son should be the one."

Nina was dumbfounded. "How could you ask me to do that?"

"It would be helpful, but it's up to you."

She began to rock Anthony to soothe his pain. Without looking up at the man, she said, "I'm sure his brother will fly from Pennsylvania on the next available plane."

"He nodded. "Thank you for your time." The man left.

Nina didn't see her two younger sons, standing, watching, and waiting for some kind of explanation. When she finally noticed them, she could think of nothing to say.

Bertha, who had now become more of a friend than a housekeeper, had heard the same news report and came over to help. She herded the two boys into the house and returned to help bring Anthony inside. Nina led him to his room and sat by his bed for the rest of the day.

He dozed and talked in his sleep, but mostly he cried.

Nina reached into the past for compassion for the man she had once loved, but found little. *Pitiful as he was, the mob used him just like they're using me. No doubt they called the hit.* She couldn't help but think that her own fate might be sealed in the same manner. Tears for her son rolled down her cheeks. She steeled herself to protect her family and get through the inevitable funeral.

Catherine tiptoed into the bedroom. Krysta was asleep and Catherine placed the baby in the crib. "I'm so sorry, Mom."

They stood close and hugged each other.

"Come on." Catherine coaxed Nina from the room. "I called Ginger. She's on her way, and Bertha's making you tea. I'll stay with Anthony."

Nina quietly came into the kitchen. Bertha had straightened the house and was putting away the clean dishes.

"Larry stopped by," Bertha said. "I told him this wasn't a good time. He wants you to call him whenever you're ready or if you need anything."

"Where did Joey and Michael go?" Nina sipped her tea.

"Joey wanted to go with Larry, and I said it was all right. Larry said if you wanted Joey home, to call, and he'd bring him right back."

"And Michael?"

"He's in his room and doesn't want to see anyone. Not even you, he said."

"Nonsense." Nina got up from the chair and walked down the hallway. She tapped lightly on Michael's bedroom door. "Michael."

"Go away."

Nina turned the handle, but the door was locked. "Michael, please let me come in. I want to talk to you."

"Leave me alone."

She waited, but the room was silent. She slowly made her way back to the kitchen.

"What do I do now?" Nina clutched her arms close around her body.

"Nothing much you *can* do." Bertha continued to tidy the kitchen.

"Vito's death took us all by surprise. I expected a reaction from Anthony, but I didn't think Michael would behave this way. It's not like him."

"He'll come around when he's ready," Bertha said, as she reheated Nina's tea. "I suspect your oldest son feels he's lost his chance to please his father."

Nina's chin jutted out in defiance. "Anthony doesn't care what Vito thinks."

"All young men want their fathers to look on them favorably," Bertha said. "Even Michael, who hides in his books, has decided to join the Navy to prove something."

"You're reading too much into this. Michael is different—he's more sensitive than the others."

Bertha sighed. "You're probably right. He might just want to see the world."

Nina ran her hand along the placemat. "At least Joey can move on with his life."

"He's too young to know what he wants." Bertha hung the tea towel over the handle of the oven to dry. "He'll probably continue to pretend his father's too busy to have time for him."

"Even after his death, Vito still controls our family." Nina shook her head. Despair began to cloud her mind. "Will it ever end?"

"Of course it will." Bertha patted Nina's shoulder. "It's just a bumpy road you're on now."

"He always thought the law or the Mafia would kill him, but instead, it was a prostitute. How ironic is that?"

"God works in mysterious ways." Bertha placed a slice of raisin toast beside Nina's tea.

Nina pushed it away. "I don't think God had anything to do with this."

"You better pray He does." Bertha returned the toast to Nina's plate. "Eat. You'll need your energy. Catherine didn't want to upset you anymore than you already are, but she told me her parents want her to get a divorce."

Nina jumped up from the table. "Divorce!"

"That's what she said. They've called an attorney and plan to go to court. They want to take the baby away from Anthony. They're against having their grandchild raised by a Mafia family."

"Oh my God." Nina plopped onto the nearest chair. "Haven't we been through enough?" She began to sob. This news was worse than Vito's death. And Anthony would not get over it, she was sure of that.

Ginger came to the house and stayed the night, and for this, Nina was thankful. She needed someone to share her pain, and even though Ginger often spoke without thinking, she meant well and truly cared.

The next morning, Nina got up early. She knew that preparations for the funeral would be a fiasco. Out of respect for the years spent married to Vito, and because he was the father of her children, she felt she should do whatever she could to give him a proper burial.

She called Vito's brother, Rudy, in Pittsburgh to offer her condolences.

"Whata *you* want?" he asked when he came on the line.

"I wanted to tell the family how badly I felt, and wanted to let you know that I'd be glad to help in any way I can," Nina replied, ignoring his anger.

"Mind your own damn business," Rudy said.

It was not exactly unexpected when he hung up on her.

Bertha, Ginger, and Nina were still sitting at the kitchen table when Anthony finally emerged from the bedroom.

He slumped onto a chair.

"You're up early." Nina waited for some kind of a sign that indicated the shock was waning.

He pushed his silky hair from his face.

Bertha poured him a cup of coffee. "Would you like breakfast? I've got a hot skillet ready to fix whatever you'd like."

He shook his head. "So, what do we do now?"

"Wait," Nina murmured.

"Wait for what?" Anthony reached for the sugar.

"Frankie called. He's stopping by this morning." Nina smoothed the fringe on the hand towel she held in her lap. "He said the police are holding your father's body pending investigation. It could take a while."

Anthony cradled his cup with both hands and stared at the coffee like it was some unknown potion. "Do you know if Dad bought a cemetery plot?"

She had not expected the question. "I guess we never got around to that." Nina glanced at Ginger.

"I want my dad to have a nice wake." Anthony said. "I'll go with you to the funeral home."

Nina swallowed hard. "I won't be going there." She reached for his hand.

Anthony pulled away. "Why not?"

"Frankie said your Uncle Rudy is flying in today. He's going to go to the morgue to identify the body."

"They aren't sure? Does that mean maybe my dad's alive?"

"No. They're sure, but they always get the next of kin to identify the body."

"Why didn't they call me?"

"Probably your Uncle Rudy thought you might not want to see your father that way. Besides the DiGregettis want to bury your dad in Pittsburgh with the rest of his family."

"Not if I have anything to say about it." Anthony stirred his coffee.

"I don't know if you do." Nina looked toward Ginger for help.

"Chance is flying in today," Ginger said. "He'll know how to handle this."

Catherine came into the kitchen. She held the baby in one arm and the diaper bag on the other. "I need to go home and talk to my parents. I don't want them to cause any more trouble."

Anthony got up from the table. "You're not taking the baby over there." He reached for Krysta.

Catherine handed the baby to him. "It might help if I took her with me. She's our baby. We're raising her, not your mother. They can't take the baby from us on account of your father's business dealings, and they can't stop us from seeing your mother." She turned tear-filled eyes to Nina. "They're just upset."

"Upset!" Anthony snuggled Krysta in his arms. "Telling you to get a divorce and saying they're going to court to take my daughter from me. They're crazy."

"It's the news media. Their friends are shocked. They think my parents didn't know about your dad, and they're too embarrassed to admit they did. They'll get over it. I need to show them that everything's all right. Keeping their grandchild from them will only make it worse."

"If you take her over there, I'm going with you. If they don't want me to come in, then the baby's not going in."

Bertha had made barley cereal for the baby and handed the bowl to Catherine. Anthony handed Krysta back to his wife and stomped off to the living room with his coffee.

Catherine gave the baby a spoonful of cereal, wiped off her chin and gave her another

"Things may not be okay for a few days," Nina said softly as she moved over to the chair next to her daughter-in-law.

"I heard what was said. Anthony's going to put up a fight." Catherine looked in the direction of the living room. "He told me he's taking charge of his dad's funeral."

"His father's family will make that difficult," Ginger whispered.

"Anthony's already called three different funeral homes for prices," Catherine said as she shifted Krysta from one arm to the other.

"What did they tell him?" Nina asked.

"I don't know. I think they asked him about a cemetery plot." Catherine laid a tea towel across Krysta's canary colored dress. "This is all so awful." She finished feeding the baby and used a warm wet cloth to clean Krysta's face.

"Here, let me hold her." Ginger placed the baby against her shoulder and patted Krysta's back until she burped.

"You wanna give her the apple juice?" Catherine handed the bottle to Ginger.

Shortly after Catherine and Anthony left to see her parents, the guard called Nina to say she had a visitor. She told him it was okay to let him in. A few minutes later, Frankie's car stopped in front of the house. Nina went to the door and Ginger followed.

"How are you?" He hugged Nina and handed Ginger a white box from the bakery.

"I'll be all right." Nina motioned him toward the living room. "It's Anthony I'm worried about. He plans to take care of his father's funeral arrangements."

"I'll make coffee." Ginger said and carried the pastries to the kitchen.

Frankie sat on the couch. "I'll ask Chance to talk to Vito's brother, but I don't think it'll do much good. It'll be better for everyone if we convince Anthony that Vito should be with his family."

"Anthony can be stubborn." Nina sat at the other end of the couch and folded her hands in her lap.

Frankie picked up the cup of coffee Ginger had set on the coffee table along with a small cannoli. "Like his father."

"No, he's not like his father!" Nina glared at Frankie. "Anthony understands his responsibilities."

"Take it easy, Nina. I didn't mean anything."

"I know." She twisted the belt of her robe.

"How are my sons going to get through the next few days? Vito's family hates me, and I don't want them to take it out on the boys."

"They won't. They'll want the boys to be part of their family." Frankie shifted in his chair. "But I don't think it would be wise for you to show up at the wake or the service if they have one here."

Nina nodded.

"The casket will be closed. There's no way—" He stopped mid-sentence. "I'm sorry, I didn't mean to—" He returned the cup to the table. "If they bury him in Pittsburgh, it would be a good idea if you called your parents and told them not to pay their respects. There are a lot of hard feelings there."

"You don't have to worry about my family. They don't want anything to do with Vito. They never did."

"So then it's settled. We let the DiGregettis take care of the burial." Frankie pulled out a pack of cigarettes.

"Please, don't smoke in the house," Nina said.

Frankie raised his eyebrows.

"The baby." Nina shrugged. "I don't want any part of the funeral, but it's not settled. It's Anthony you have to deal with."

"Let Chance take care of Anthony. He'll convince him that this is all for the best." Frankie crammed the pack of Marlboros into his shirt pocket. "Don't worry about the boys. Chance and I plan to stay with them from the time they leave here until we bring them back from the funeral."

"I appreciate what you're doing, but Anthony's of age now. This has to be his decision."

"How are Michael and Joey?"

"They're ignoring everything. I don't know how they'll be when they're faced with attending the service."

Frankie finished his coffee and one of the pastries. "I have to go now, but I'll call Anthony and make plans to take him and his brothers out to dinner tomorrow night."

When he left, Ginger came in with fresh coffee. "So, what kind of promises did he make that you know he doesn't intend to keep?"

"He didn't promise anything, other than saying he and Chance would stay close to the boys at the funeral."

"That's good." Ginger sank into the couch. "Now that no one's around, tell me how you really feel with Vito gone for good."

"I don't feel anything. I'm numb." Nina got up and walked to the window. She stared at the river. "I certainly didn't wish for him to die, but I've been divorced for two years now. A lot has happened." She turned to Ginger. "I see things different now. I've made a lot of mistakes, and I can't do anything about them, but I *can* change the future."

"Does the future include Larry?"

"Maybe, if he can forgive me for my past. Michael and Joey seem to like him, and I think he cares about them. I don't know about Anthony."

"Larry seems like good husband material." Ginger sipped her coffee.

"I'm getting out of the business." Nina stared straight ahead. "I'm going to tell Larry what I've been doing."

Ginger gulped. "When you gonna do that?"

"I don't know. I have to make sure I can get a job and educate my sons. I also have Krysta to consider, and I don't know what kind of trouble Catherine's parents will make. It may take me a while to make the change, but that's the direction I'm headed. I don't want to end up with my head blown off in a run-down motel."

Nina got up. Her robe dragged across her bare feet.

Ginger put her arm around her as they walked to the kitchen.

"You're talking stupid. You're nothing like Vito." Ginger rinsed the cups and set them on the counter to drain.

"I hope not." Nina sat at the table. "What happened to Bertha?"

"She went home. She said to call if you needed her."

"Why don't you run on, too? Your girls need you more than I do. I was awake all night. It's quiet here now and nothing's going to happen today. I want to talk to Michael, and then I'm going to bed."

"Michael's not here. I forgot to tell you. He left while you were talking to Frankie. He went to the beach. He said he'd be back in time for dinner."

Nina's eyebrows rose. "Did he say anything else?"

"Only that he wanted to be by himself, that he didn't want to listen to everyone talking about his dad." Ginger gave Nina a hug. "Get some rest. I'll call you later."

When Nina reached the bedroom, the phone rang.

"Are you doing okay?" Nana Cocolucci asked.

Nina hesitated, not knowing how much her mother knew.

"It's okay Nina, Mickey called me. He called Dominic, too. We all feel bad."

"I'm all right, Ma. It's the boys I'm worried about."

"I want to come down," her mother said. "You shouldn't be alone. There will be things that need to be done. Anthony is too young to handle this himself."

"Anthony's not going to do anything. Rudy's taking over."

"The DiGregettis. That's not a surprise. They're like vultures."

"It will be better if they handle the funeral," Nina said. "I don't think I'm up to helping Anthony get through all of this."

"I told your father you needed help, but he doesn't want to come." Her mother sighed.

"I'll be okay. Take care of Papa. He needs you more than I do."

"If you're sure," her mother said.

"I'm sure. I love you." Nina whispered.

"I love you, too. Get some rest."

Nina took a long nap and woke up late in the day. Michael, Joey and Anthony were in the living room. Bertha had stopped by with a pan of lasagna and left it on the counter in the kitchen. A large portion was missing, and dirty dishes were piled in the sink.

"I see you boys ate," Nina said.

Anthony and Michael nodded.

"It was good." Joey paged through a *Sports Illustrated*.

Nina sat next to Anthony. "Frankie said he'd like to take all of you to dinner tomorrow night, if you want to go."

"Sounds like a guilty conscience if you ask me." Anthony moved over to give her more room. "He never takes us out to dinner any other time."

"That's not true. We used to go all the time with Ginger, Danny, and Frankie. Don't you remember?"

"That was before the divorce. After that, they forgot us."

"They didn't forget. We were all going through a difficult time."

"Oh, so when people go through bad times, they're not supposed to get together with their friends?"

Nina put her arm across Anthony's shoulder. "You're upset and over-reacting."

"Yeah, and you don't care how our dad gets buried." Anthony pushed her arm away.

Nina sighed. He was right.

CHAPTER THIRTY-SEVEN

The boys were dressed and waiting when Frankie arrived.

"You've grown." Frankie cuffed Anthony on the shoulder. "And so have your brothers."

Anthony shrugged.

"Where we gonna eat?" Joey asked. "I'm hungry."

"I thought we'd go to Hollywood. Remember Joe's on the Intracoastal? They have good Italian food, and it's quiet. You've been there before." Frankie started for the door.

"A long time ago," Michael said.

"Well, then it's time we went back." Frankie glanced at Nina. "I'll bring them home early."

Anthony sat up front with Frankie, and Michael and Joey climbed into the back seat.

"Have you seen my grandparents?" Anthony asked as soon as they pulled away from the house.

"As a matter of fact, I spoke to them a little while ago. They wanted to know how soon they could take your dad's body to Pennsylvania."

"They're not taking him anywhere."

Frankie waited his turn at a four-way stop. "I told them you wanted your dad buried in Florida."

"So?"

"You gotta understand, Anthony. He's your father, but he's their son. They love him, too."

"They never cared what happened to him. The first time they came to Florida was when I got married. Before that we had to go to Pittsburgh to see them."

"Your mother's parents didn't come to Florida, either. They only came for the wedding."

Anthony did not say anything.

"Isn't that right?" Frankie asked.

The car was quiet. Michael and Joey stared out the windows.

"Well?" Frankie asked again.

"I guess so." Anthony huffed. "But we talk to Nana Cocolucci on the phone, she sends us stuff, and we stay with her in the summer. Ever since our parents got divorced, Grandma DiGregetti quit calling. We never hear from her."

"Maybe she thinks your mom doesn't want her to call."

"Mom never told her that," Anthony fired back at Frankie.

Nothing more was said until Frankie parked the car. "Chance and your Uncle Rudy are inside. They want to talk to all three of you."

"They're not changing my mind," Anthony said.

For the first time, Michael voiced his opinion. "That's right. We want our dad buried in Florida."

Anthony turned to Michael. Their gaze met and solidified the brothers' bond.

Chance and Rudy sat at a round table in the far corner of the room. They both stood up and shook the boys' hands.

"Sit down." Chance patted the seat next to him for Anthony.

Anthony noticed he had been conveniently ushered between Rudy and Chance. He glared at Frankie, who sat directly across from him. Michael sat between Chance and Frankie, and Joey sat in the only chair left between Frankie and Rudy. A waiter arrived to take their order, and Chance ordered a large antipasto for the table while they looked over the menu. When the waiter returned with hot bread, they were ready to order.

During dinner, Chance asked each of the boys how they were doing in school, and Anthony took out pictures of the baby and passed them around. There was casual mention of their father and all the good times they had when they were young and playing on Little League teams.

After dinner, Chance changed the subject to Vito's funeral.

Anthony stiffened. "My dad's gonna be buried in Florida. This is where he would want to be."

"I understand," Rudy said. "If he was my father, I'd feel the same way." He looked directly at Anthony. "But you know there are some unusual circumstances. Your father didn't just die. He was shot. So, maybe we need to talk."

"I can't see what difference that makes." Anthony pushed his half-eaten spumoni aside.

"There's a lot of animosity. If we bury your dad here, there's a good chance his enemies will—" He paused. "Desecrate his grave. Do you want that to happen?"

"Well, no," Anthony stuttered, "but I want my dad to be close to us."

"A father should be close to his sons." Rudy laid his hand on the table next to Anthony's. "My brother spoke about all three of you. He told me that he missed coming home to his family."

Anthony noticed the interest Rudy had aroused in Michael and Joey, and he did not want to disillusion his brothers by arguing the point. Their bedroom had always been on the opposite side of the house from their parent's bedroom. They had not seen the things Anthony had seen. Their ears had never pressed against a bedroom wall and listened to their mother beg his dad to stop hitting her. They had never heard the crack of his father's hand or their mother's sobs.

Rudy took a hefty swig of wine. "With you in school and Michael in the Navy, that only leaves Joey. Who's gonna look after your father's grave? Who'll cut the grass, pull the weeds, and place the flowers while you're gone?"

Anthony was glad he had called the local funeral homes. *My uncle thinks we're brainless, and my brothers are too young to see this.* "I checked several funeral homes. They all said that we can pay the cemetery to take care of the grave."

Chance spoke directly to Rudy. "Anthony has good point. Vito was my friend, and I wish for him to rest easy. Think about this favor you ask."

It appeared to Anthony that his persuasion had produced a cohort.

Chance coughed, waving a hand in front of his face. "Too much smoke, I can't breathe." He pushed his chair backward. "Come, Anthony. We get air."

Outside, they walked to the cement retaining wall and watched the dark water of the Intracoastal rush by.

"This Rudy, he pushy, yes?" Chance breathed deeply.

"Well, he better think again if he thinks he can shove *me* around."

"I no blame you. *You* are your father's son, and you have rights."

They stood quietly while Chance stretched the stiffness from his back. "Life hard without father."

Anthony nodded. Not that he shared Chance's opinion.

"Your mother has three sons to educate. You, oldest son, must take responsibility. Not always easy."

"I know my mother depends a great deal on you," Anthony said.

"I'm old and sick. I not be here to see you in your prime." Chance coughed again. "Find it in your heart to make peace with uncle. He strong willed, but not violent. You may need his support, his allegiance. This good thing for you and your brothers."

Chance turned toward the restaurant door. "We go in now."

Frankie had ordered another bottle of Chianti, and the waiter poured six glasses.

"You feel better?" Frankie said to Chance when he returned.

"Ah, *moltissimo*." Chance tapped his chest.

"So where do you plan to bury your father?" Rudy asked Anthony.

"Here in Florida." Anthony's gaze met Michael's.

"You need a crypt, or else you gotta worry about water that's only a few feet below the land. I can help you some, but they're expensive. Can you afford this?" Rudy asked.

"I don't know." Anthony answered as he fumbled with his napkin. "I'm not sure if there's any insurance."

"We checked. There's none." Rudy finished the last of his wine. "Maybe you and me could pick out the casket together?"

"We can do that." Anthony caught the satisfied expressions that passed across the faces of the men, but he was thinking, if his uncle helped pick it out, he might also help pay for it.

"Then it's settled," Rudy said. We'll have the wake here in Florida, just as you wish. You tell the funeral director exactly how you want everything, and I'll pay the expenses. When we select the casket, we can talk more about this. Maybe by then you'll have changed your mind about where the casket will be buried."

Anthony looked at his brothers. Michael nodded, and Joey followed suit.

Rudy looked at each of the boys. "You're always welcome at our home, and if you ever need help, you know you can always come to our family."

"We appreciate that," Anthony said, but the stern look he gave his brothers assured them that nothing was going to change.

"I want you to know that if the three of you decide to let me take my brother's body back to Pennsylvania, you'll not be sorry. His body will be interred in the wooded hills he grew up in. We have a nice Catholic cemetery close to Mama DiGregetti. Your grandma will pick fresh flowers and walk there on Sundays to pray the rosary for your father."

Anthony looked down at the table. "We don't want our father to think we didn't even care enough to bury him."

"He no think that," Chance said. He looked toward Anthony. "You and Rudy make plans for wake. Then you think about your uncle's offer."

Rudy passed the wine bottle around the table for each one to refill their glass.

Joey gulped. He'd barely taken a sip of the dry red wine, but when the bottle came to him, he poured in a few more drops.

They all held the glasses high in the air.

"Salute," Rudy said.

Each of them took their turn repeating the toast.

When Anthony's turn came, he said. "Here's to my father, my brothers, my uncle, and to my father's friends. Salute."

While the men tilted their heads back and emptied their glasses, Frankie downed Joey's wine and placed the glass back in Joey's hand. In a few seconds, Frankie polished off his own wine.

Joey smiled as he placed his empty glass in the center of the table with the others.

"I'll come to the hotel tomorrow around nine." Anthony stood and pushed his chair away from the table.

"I'll be ready." Rudy got up and put his arm around Anthony. "You're not too big to hug." He gave him a gentle cuff on the chin, and privately handed each of the boys a one-hunded dollar bill.

"Thanks, Uncle Rudy. I'll see you tomorrow," Anthony said.

A short time later, Frankie dropped them off at home.

On the day of the funeral, Michael stood in the back of St. Mary's Catholic Church holding a hymnal. His art pencil skimmed across the pages of his small notepad, hidden inside the song book. He focused on the prominent facial features of many of the Italian guests, sometimes leaving the sketched persons without hair or a neck, but there was no denying who the drawings portrayed.

Mafia soldiers at every entrance prevented cameras, microphones and recorders from being slipped into the church, causing the men with press badges to jockey for the best position to see and hear. There were many Italians, but men of every nationality were sprinkled throughout the congregation. Michael sketched faces of those he knew and those he did not know, burning their features into the paper and into his memory.

At the last possible moment, Michael came down the aisle and slipped in between Anthony and Joey. Vito's sons appeared to be the keystone of the assemblage as they sat in the center section of the church. They were flanked on one side by Frankie and on the other by Chance. Their father's closed casket, barely ten feet away, gave a formidable testimony to the life of the man inside.

Father Mendezino appeared at the alter and began to perform the funeral Mass, as he had done so many times before.

Anthony stared at the altar during the requiem ceremony, moving only when the ritual demanded he kneel or touch his heart. He did not pray the rosary and his lips never moved in response to the priest's remarks. If it was sorrow he felt, one could not tell, for his dark Sicilian eyes revealed nothing.

When the priest spoke, Joey looked impassively around the church, and several times he seemed totally distracted, until Frankie touched his arm, reminding the boy of his duty as a son to be attentive. Joey forgot the prayers, and only knelt when Frankie prompted him to do so. At the mention of his father's name a single tear slid down his cheek.

Michael, out of arm's reach, sometimes turned to take a second look at a mourner before spreading a few more slashes across the page. Chance and Frankie sent him several disapproving glances, but he paid no attention. Here and there, he scratched a word or two as he continued to sketch throughout the Mass.

Vito's family sat on the right side of the church. Mrs. DiGregetti lamented during the entire service, flailing her arms, as if trying to will Vito back from the dead. "Vito, Vito, my *figilo*, my son," she wailed. Her droning of the Hail Mary sometimes obliterated the priest's Latin.

After Vito's funeral service had begun, Nina had passed through the church entrance without a sound, genuflected beside the last row, and slid into the pew. Under the cover of a long black dress and a sheer black scarf, she had lowered the kneeler, gotton on her knees, and bowed her head. Before leaving, she pulled a black silk shawl around her shoulders and handed her promise ring to Sister Bernadette. She had phoned Father Mendezino, and he had promised to have it placed inside the casket with Vito.

Nina took the pathway that lead to the rectory and passed through the building that housed the Dominican Sisters. When she exited through their kitchen door, she saw two Mafiosi in black suits stationed by the back gate. They turned to look her way, and one strode off at a fast pace through a group of large banyan trees. She thought the man looked like Larry.

The other guard recognized her. "May I drive you home, Mrs. DiGregetti?"

"Ms. Cocolucci," she corrected. "No, thank you. I prefer to drive myself." She took a step then turned around. "Who was that man standing here with you?"

"I don't know, ma'am. He's from New York. Someone sent by the family to provide privacy for Mr. DiGregetti."

"Did he mention his first name?" she asked.

"No ma'am." He gave no further explanation.

This is crazy. All the times I've been at Larry's house I've never even seen a black suit, and the last person the mob would want guarding the gate is a cop. She crossed the street, got in her car, and drove home.

When the church service was over, Vito's family said good-bye to the boys. Chance and Anthony walked to Frankie's car.

"You made good choice," Chance said to Anthony. "Your father will rest in peace in Pennsylvania. Good to maintain family ties. Your uncle looks on you with favorable eyes."

Anthony glared at Chance. "Don't make the mistake of thinking I'm *stupido*. I kept the peace with my uncle in return for my mother's safety. I know my father's enemies."

CHAPTER THIRTY-EIGHT

The next morning, Bertha poured Nina a cup of coffee and one for herself. "I can see you didn't sleep again."

"I tossed and turned." Nina's hair hung in tangles.

"Catherine said Anthony was awake most of the night and wanted to sleep this morning, so she took the baby and went to her mother's." Bertha placed hot blueberry muffins on the table.

"Thanks, Bertha. You're such a blessing." Nina buttered a muffin, picked up the morning paper, and opened it to the front page.

A large tractor-trailer had crushed several cars when it overturned on I-95 during the night. Three people were dead and five others were in serious condition. The story took up most of the first page. Vito's funeral and the continuing search for his assassin had been relegated to the Metro section of the paper. Nina desperately wished Vito's news coverage would stop.

Accounts of Vito's murder by an alleged prostitute occupied several columns. She glanced at the first column, but her eyes shifted to the composite drawing of the suspected murderer shown next to an outdated mug shot of Vito. *What could he have seen in her?*

The press also printed a picture of Nina that must have been taken by a telescopic lens as she left the church. Other figures were in the background, but there was no sign of the phantom Mafia soldier in a black suit.

Joey came to the kitchen. "Can I have an omelet?" he asked Bertha.

"Bertha isn't here to work. She came to visit and have coffee with us." Nina scolded as she folded the newspaper and put it on the corner of the table. "Have one of the blueberry muffins Bertha was nice enough to bring."

Joey looked at the muffins and squinched his nose.

"Get some cereal," Nina said softly.

"Can I call Brian and see if he wants to go to the beach? I only have a few days before Uncle Mickey and I go to Nana's."

"Sure." Nina took a bite of muffin. She had been troubled over how Joey would react to his father's sudden death, but now she decided her concern was unnecessary.

Neither Michael nor Anthony got up early, but when they did, they took their breakfasts outside to the patio table. They sat barefoot and shirtless in ragged cut-offs.

Anthony spread the paper on the table. "Can you believe the shit they print?"

Michael ignored the *Fort Lauderdale News* and dug into his ham and eggs.

"They call him a 'big-time racketeer.' If he was all that bad, they should've said something before he died instead of waiting until he couldn't defend himself." Anthony said in a voice filled with contempt.

"I want to get a darker tan." Michael moved to the lounge chair and stretched out. "I hear San Diego has terrific looking chicks."

Anthony frowned at his eighteen-year-old brother. "Are you listening to me? I'm talking about our dad. The damn reporters won't even let him die in peace." Anthony tossed the paper to Michael. "Look! They printed a drawing of what they think the killer looks like right next to the picture of our own flesh and blood."

Michael opened the paper.

"How can you sit there and think about a tan?" Anthony asked. "Besides, how many girls do you think you'll meet in boot camp?"

Michael scanned the story about his father and looked at the pictures. "No wonder the cops didn't arrest him. They didn't even know what he looked like." Michael folded the paper so that Vito's picture was on top. "This doesn't even look like him."

Anthony shook his head. "You don't understand. They didn't arrest Dad for racketeering because the police are in on the deal. They're on the mob's payroll. When he made money, so did they, but they don't have to worry about the law. They *are* the law."

"Hm." Michael laid the newpaper picture of the police drawing in front of Anthony. "I have a feeling I've seen this woman before."

"In your dreams." Anthony stared at the picture. He did not want to believe the part about his father and a prostitute. "Maybe in your nightmares."

"Are you thinking the same thing I am?" Michael asked.

"She's one hell of an ugly woman?" Anthony said.

Michael laid his hand on his brother's shoulder. "You got that right."

"Dad wouldn't step foot in a room with a woman that homely." Anthony turned the picture face down.

Michael grinned. "Me neither." The look withered. "I want you to promise me something." He sat down next to Anthony.

"And what would that be?" Anthony asked.

"I'm leaving tomorrow, and I won't be here to watch your back. Catherine and the baby depend on you. Don't let this thing keep you here." Michael hesitated. "Go back to school, get your degree, and don't look for revenge."

"You worry too much. Working for Uncle Louie's nothing." Anthony cocked his head. "I make repairs and count change. Uncle Louie doesn't tell me anything, and I don't ask."

"You think I didn't know what was going on at dinner with Chance and uncle Rudy? I let you handle it because you're the oldest, but I heard you talking to Chance after the funeral." Michael gripped Anthony's shoulder. "That kinda talk'll get you killed. I don't want to lose my brother."

"Uncle Rudy treated me like a kid. I got upset and had to get it off my chest. Forget about it." Anthony pushed his unfinished breakfast aside. "It's over. I'm going back to school in the fall."

"That's good. I'll rest a lot easier if you do that."

"You go ahead and join the Navy. See if I care." Anthony looked away. "Sometimes I wish I was going with you, but—"

"But you got horny." Michael finished for him.

"Maybe *you* should look around for a girlfriend. You need someone who'll write to you when you're out to sea for months at a time. You know, all the guys on those ships carry a picture of their girlfriend."

"I got a picture."

"You still carry Jennifer's high school picture?"

"No. It's the one that came in my wallet. I signed it Love, Margie."

Anthony faked a fall off of the bench and rolled on the deck, laughing. "Hey, guy. It's your last night at home. I could take you out tonight and help you find a girl."

"I don't think that's a good idea." Michael gathered up the dirty dishes.

"Why not?" Anthony asked. "You could say, hi, my name's Michael, and my gangster father was buried yesterday, and I'm leaving tomorrow for six years in the Navy. Would you like to have sex with me?"

"Of course I would," Michael said in a falsetto voice. "I'd love to take you to my bedroom." He swung his hips like a girl as he carried the dishes back into the house.

Anthony hopped up from the deck and grabbed the newspaper. He caught up with his brother and put his arm around Michael's shoulder. "Then how about dinner with the family at Sausalito's?"

"That sounds better." Michael laughed.

The next morning, Anthony woke up first. He made coffee and put two English muffin's in the toaster. He had not thought much about it before, but now that he and Michael had finally gotten close, he hated to see his brother leave.

Michael said his good-byes at home. "I don't want any tears in front of the other recruits," he told his mother.

Anthony drove his brother to the naval station in Miami. After Michael checked in, he stood outside with Anthony until it was time to get on the bus.

"Well, this is it," Michael said. "Mom says I'm leaving a boy and coming back a man. "Does she think I'm gonna knock up some girl?"

"Nah, she probably just wants you to start paying your own car insurance." Anthony laughed and poked Michael.

"Mom said she's gonna put the Mustang in Joey's name as soon as he turns sixteen." Michael reached to the ground and picked up his overnight bag. "It's all right by me. Joey can pay for the insurance, and I'll borrow the car when I'm on leave." He started to walk away. "I almost forgot. I want you to hang onto this for me." He handed Anthony his small notepad.

"What's this?"

"Sketches I made at the church on the day of the funeral. We know so little about our dad. I figured whoever came to the funeral was either a friend or an enemy. Might be interesting some day to know who was who."

"Take care," Anthony said and bit his lower lip.

Michael gave Anthony a thumbs-up before disappearing inside the bus with the other recruits.

Anthony flipped through the notebook. Then without another thought, closed it and headed for his car. He was already late for work.

Vito's Uncle Louie allowed Anthony to work as many hours as he wanted. After a month in the game room, Louie promoted Anthony to manager, which meant he now checked on each of Louie's establishments and tracked the daily receipts and the employees' hours.

When Anthony arrived at work, a man in a dark suit and white shirt sat across the desk from Louie. Anthony stopped outside the door and listened.

"I axt him to count receipts, that's all," Louie told the mob's pencil pusher.

"Are you nuts?" the accountant asked. "The kid could talk to anyone. What if the IRS drops in and asks questions?"

"He won't talk—not that kid."

"How do you know?"

"I just know." Louie insisted.

"You know, because you talked to him? You told him not to tell?"

"I didn't talk to him. I just know."

"Hey, Uncle Louie," Anthony said stepping inside the office. "Sorry I'm late. I had to take Michael to the recruiting office. He's flying to San Diego this morning."

"C'mon in," Louie said. "I want you should meet someone."

CHAPTER THIRTY-NINE

Anthony took his family back to Tallahassee in late August. Catherine got her old job back and put Krysta in daycare. Again, Nina was paying their rent and sending extra money to help them with the bills. Nina missed the baby and phoned every few days. Catherine always seemed happy to hear from her, but Anthony usually was not there or did not want to talk.

When Nina came home early one day and placed a call to Catherine, she was surprised to hear Anthony answer the phone.

"I didn't expect *you*," she said jokingly.

"Mom," he said, "You gotta stop calling here all the time. Catherine has a lot to do and I'm busy with my studies. Now that I've made the first string, I practice every day."

"You don't have practice every night. I've called at midnight and you're not at home."

"I don't wanna talk about it," Anthony replied brusquely. "Just don't wake Catherine anymore."

"What's going on?" Nina asked.

Anthony remained cold and irritated. "Helping me get through college doesn't mean you can tell me how to live."

"I wasn't trying to run your life, but I don't like what I'm hearing."

"Staying out late doesn't mean I'm neglecting my family, or that I'm failing. You don't need to call so often."

Nina bit her tongue. She knew he had drifted away from her long before this phone call.

Soon after the rift with Anthony, Michael came home on a one-week leave before heading to a naval training school in Vallejo, California. Nina noticed he appeared to be more outgoing and happy in his structured military lifestyle. For this she was happy. The boys were maturing and she was no longer the center of their lives. After Michael returned to California, Nina wrote a few short letters, but he did not answer them and soon their communication dwindled to a monthly phone call.

Nina still owned her advertising company, and she continued to provide service to both her mob accounts and the private accounts, which provided her with a somewhat adequate while not impressive living. Although she and Larry still dated infrequently, most of the time their schedules conflicted. One particular evening, Larry had surprised her when he called to say his meeting had been postponed.

"Would you like to see *The Towering Inferno?* This is the last night it's playing."

"Sure, I'd love to go."

Larry was in good spirits when they left the movie theater, until he found a piece of paper on his windshield. He snatched it off, gave it a quick look, and shoved it into his pocket.

Nina grinned. "Who's leaving you notes?" She thought it might be an old girlfriend.

"It's just advertisement."

He had parked directly under a bright light, and she had seen the scribbled penmanship.

"Someone's hand writing a sales pitch?" Nina asked curiously.

"By the look of the name it's some Cuban looking for work cleaning houses."

"Did they say how much they charge?"

"No." He started the engine, pulled out of the lot and into traffic. All the way home, Larry was quiet.

"Are you coming in?" Nina asked when he pulled into her driveway.

"Not tonight. I have to get up early." Larry walked her to the door and gave her a quick kiss. "I'll call you."

As soon as Larry pulled away from the house, she realized she had left her umbrella in his truck. She waited ten minutes and phoned him at home. He did not answer. Nina hung up. She waited another five minutes and called once more. Again, he did not answer.

Nina lay in bed reading until the pages became a blur. She wondered if something had happened after he left her house. He had no reason to lie to her. He could have said he had somewhere to go. Now that she thought about it, Larry looked much too worried for that piece of paper on his windshield to have been as frivolous as a person looking for work. She closed the book and turned off the light.

The next morning, Nina and Joey ate breakfast together. He had turned sixteen the week before and started driving the aging Mustang. Now a junior and several inches taller, he played first string center on the basketball team. Even though he and Brian did not have steady girlfriends, Nina knew it would not be long before going to the movies with a group of friends would be over, and Joey would leave home just like her other sons.

After Joey left for school, Nina made a pot of coffee and phoned Larry again. When he still did not answer, she braved the rain, got wet and worked late. When she arrived home, she found a note from Joey saying that he had gone to the roller skating rink with friends, so Nina made herself a salad and ate alone. She tried one more time to reach Larry without any luck.

In desperation, Nina called the police station. "May I speak to Officer Macklin?"

"Officer Macklin no longer works for the city," the dispatcher said.

"When did this happen?" she asked.

"I don't have that information. If this is an emergency, I can transfer you to the captain."

"No, thanks," Nina said and hung up.

The following day, Joey had a basketball game after school, so Nina made herself a ham and cheese sandwich and took it and the evening paper to the patio. One story caught her attention. "Local Law Enforcement Beds Down With Mob."

A tri-countywide crackdown had uncovered multiple cases of police officers connected to Mafia underworld bosses. Some of the men had been suspended pending investigation, and a few had left their positions voluntarily. Nina scanned the column that listed the police departments and the cops that the city was investigating.

Her fingernail came to rest on Larry's name. She pushed the sandwich aside, read the article from start to finish. In a state of shook she mulled the article over in her mind.

The phone rang and Nina ran into the house. "Hello," she panted.

"Mom," Joey said, "I'm going for pizza with the team after the game. I'll be a little late."

"Is Brian with you?" she asked, her heart pounding.

"No. He hasn't been to school for a couple of days. Coach said he had the flu."

"Be careful driving home."

"I will."

Nina stared at the phone and dialed Larry's number again. She thought about her own situation. She had not been able to tell him about her connection to the mob. She let the phone ring ten times before hanging up.

She searched her mind for any clues that the article in the paper might be true. He had admitted to watching her house after his captain told him to stop, and he did hide the stolen Camaro papers. *That should have told me something.*

Her thoughts traveled back to Vito's funeral and the man in the black suit. With no real evidence, Nina convinced herself it had been Larry.

She paced from room to room, crying and yelling at the same time. Slowly her outrage subsided. Nina took a shower, feeling confident that her lover had been hand-picked by Chance to keep tabs on her. Anger, hurt and humiliation continued to ping-pong through her head.

The next day, Ginger called and said she wanted to get together for lunch. "I have something important to tell you."

"I'm not busy," Nina said. "Tell me now."

"I don't want to talk about it on the phone. It can wait until noon."

Nina had been working from home that morning, but after the phone call she set her work aside. Ginger could not keep gossip for ten minutes, let alone a couple of hours. It had to be something bad.

At noon, Nina parked in front of a small country style restaurant and waited for Ginger. When she arrived, the two women walked in together.

"The food's mediocre, but they're not busy, and we can talk without being rushed." Ginger requested a booth in the back and did not appear to be in any hurry to convey the portentious news.

Nina scanned the menu and acted nonchalant.

When the waitress came to the table, they ordered the roast beef special and iced teas.

As soon as their server disappeared through a pair of swinging doors, Nina said. "Did you read the story in the paper about cops being connected to the mob?"

Ginger nodded. "That's what I wanted to talk about."

"Can you believe it?" Nina sighed. "I thought Larry was my ticket out of mob life, and he's in as deep as I am."

"I don't like jumping to conclusions," Ginger said, "but it doesn't look good." She brushed a few crumbs from the table. "All the paper said was that he's under investigation."

"He's not working there anymore. I called the police station and checked." Nina wiped the silverware with her napkin. "If he's only under investigation, why isn't he just suspended?" The knife slipped from her hand and hit the table with a bang. "He's gone. Quit, fired, or something. I don't know which, and personally, I don't care."

"I think you *do*," Ginger said. "Right now you're just upset. You can deceive everyone else with that big-strong-Nina act, but you can't fool me. You're in love with him, and you're afraid to admit how you feel."

"It doesn't matter how I feel." Nina squeezed the lemon wedge into her iced tea. "He hasn't as much as called to deny it, or even say good-bye."

"And it hurts, right?"

"Well, it's not as though we're engaged or anything. We hardly see each other anymore."

Ginger shook her head and reached across the table to touch Nina's hand. "I don't want to be the bearer of more bad news, but I had lunch with Eunice and Frankie yesterday, and Dahlia came with them. She just got back from New York."

"Why do you associate with them?" Nina asked, visibly shaken. "You know they were the ones who caused Danny to go to Atlanta and left you to fend for yourself."

The waitress brought their food. When she left, Ginger leaned forward.

"You think you're the only one who hurts?" Ginger hissed. "Just because I told you that I turned my head when Danny cheated on me doesn't mean I didn't care."

Nina's eyes opened wide. Ginger had never said anything like this before.

"When you started taking over Vito's business, it changed a lot of things. Vito was in trouble, and Danny wasn't making enough to help his friend." Ginger paused and took a deep breath. "Then things got tight for everyone. Danny split for Atlanta, and I stayed friends with you. This is a tough business. I stopped trying to figure out who's to blame a long time ago."

Nina glared at her friend. "So *I* caused Danny to leave town, and was somehow instrumental in *Vito's* death, and no doubt it will be *my fault* if Larry is found guilty." Nina sat back in her chair.

"I wasn't blaming you." Ginger sighed. "I only think you should know what's going on."

Nina fought to hold back her tears. "Oh, I know what's going on. Larry works for Chance. I was probably just another job to him."

"There's something else you need to know," Ginger said. "Dahlia described the two guys who helped her get away from Vito. She said they were undercover cops in street clothes. One was a black man, but the other was an exact description of Larry."

"All those times Larry said he had to work on his day off, he was out hustling for the mob," Nina snapped. She poked at her plate with a fork. Her appetite was gone.

"And I remember something else." Ginger looked down at the table.

Nina's gaze was fixed on her frined.

"It came to me where I first saw Larry. It was at The Willows. I'd gone there with Danny." Ginger laid her fork on the edge of her plate. "We met Frankie and this pretty redhead. He made an excuse to leave the table and went into the bar. From where I was sitting, I could see the back of Frankie. The man he spoke to was facing me. He had blond hair that spilled over his forehead, and that cute grin." Ginger shifted on the wooden bench. "Most men don't smile when Frankie talks," she whispered. "I'm positive it was Larry. He wore a black shirt and pants that night, too."

Ginger's meager identification was the last straw. Nina was sure she was going to be sick.

"Excuse me." Nina hurried to the ladies' room and splashed cold water on her face. When she regained her composure, she returned to the table.

"You gonna be okay?" Ginger asked.

Nina nodded. All she wanted to do was go home. "That Dahlia woman had better be careful if she's thinking of going back to work for Frankie." Nina picked up her fork. "Chance said that ever since Frankie was indicted for fixing that horse race, the Feds watch him with the eyes of an eagle."

Ginger continued to eat.

Nina pushed her food around the plate. "I can't believe he's operating a prostitution ring and running credit cards right under their noses. He might go to jail, and Dahlia could get arrested right along with him."

Ginger shook her head. "Nah, the hotels, cops, even the judges are all on the take. No one's gonna rat him out when they're making that kind of money." Ginger chomped on the last bite of her roast beef.

"Let's not talk about this anymore. It makes me sick." Nina sipped her tea.

"I do have one good piece of news," Ginger said with a smile. "I think Danny's coming home."

"What makes you say that?"

"He sent money. Not much, but it helped, and he promised to send more." Ginger's voice filled with exuberance. "Things are turning around for him. He wants me to move to Atlanta as soon as he can afford it. Of course, I'll need to get a job up there, but I don't mind. The girls miss their father."

"What happens after you sell your place here?" Nina looked away while she tapped her nails on the table.

"I'm not sure. Maybe buy a place in Atlanta or rent an apartment."

Nina was incredulous. "You're going to rent an apartment for the seven of you? Do you realize what that would cost? It's taken you all this time to get your ducks in a row, and now you're willing to throw it away, not knowing if Danny's going to jail or not."

"You think your life's any better?"

"No. But I don't want you to lose everything you've worked so hard for, and put yourself back in the same position you were in before."

"I was happy with Danny. Now I'm lonely." Ginger stood her ground.

"What'll you do if he starts to run around again?"

"The same thing I always did. Look the other way. At least I'll have a husband and the girls will have a father. Besides, I've lost those extra pounds. I'm what Danny wants now."

"He cheated on you before you gained the weight. Danny wants to be around his girls. He'll use you to cook and clean."

"What's the difference? Him using me, or the mob using you?"

Nina took a bite of salad. It hung in her throat and settled into a lump before it reached her stomach. She pushed the plate aside. "You're right. There's no difference." She did not want to argue with the only friend she had.

When they finished lunch, the two said good-bye in the parking lot and Nina rushed home. She wanted Joey to call Brian. She would not be satisfied until she heard the truth about Larry.

Heavy rain began to fall, as Nina arrived home. The newspaper lay on the step, at the front door, and she scooped it up on her way into the house. Nina carried it into her bedroom and tossed it on the bed. After changing into a long cotton shirt, she spread out on the bed to read the paper and wait for Joey.

Jodi Ceraldi

Thunder rolled through the neighborhood, and slanted rain beat against the window panes. When lightning streaked through the late afternoon sky, Nina pulled the light bedspread around her and opened the newspaper.

The headline read: "Second Mob Killing."

Nina grabbed her glasses and skimmed the paragraphs. "Officer Lawrence Macklin—body washed up—long time—coroner—two bullet holes.

The paper scattered across the bed. "No, No, Noooo." Nina's screams echoed off the walls. She reached for the telephone and knocked the lamp over. There was another flash of lightening, and an ear-splitting crash of thunder. The room spiraled and darkness surrounded her

CHAPTER FORTY

1983

One last packing box sat open on the kitchen table. Nina stood alone, clutching a photograph of Larry. It had taken months before she could look at the picture without crying, but now, almost ten years later, it was just a memory. Chance had sworn that Larry's death had no connection to the mob, but Nina knew better. She still had nightmares about her own demise.

When he was first murdered, Nina had even tried to call Larry's ex-wife, but the telephone number was disconnected. Brian had never come back to school, but Joey had received a postcard from Illinois saying Brian and his mother were moving to California. There was no return address. She laid the picture in the box next to Anthony's MVP trophy and sealed the flaps with tape.

Mickey's car stopped in the driveway, and Michael jumped out. He looked handsome in his dress uniform. He swung his Navy duffel bag over his shoulder and walked toward the house.

He had come to see his mother and Anthony while the ship was docked in Jacksonville. He was due to leave for a short three-month cruise in the Mediterranean.

Nina ran to him. "It's so good to see you." She gave him a big hug. "What did you and Anthony do all day?"

"Same old stuff. He showed me around the marina, we went out for a few beers, and yesterday Catherine cooked dinner while we watched the ballgame."

"Thanks for bringing Michael over." Nina said to her brother. "Anthony is so busy," she said to Mickey.

"I can't stay. I'm working the early shift today." He gave his sister a kiss on the cheek. "You take care of your mom today," he told Michael.

"I'll do that." He shook Mickey's hand.

"I'll see you both at Christmas in Bentleyville." Mickey hugged Nina again. "Take care of yourself." Then he left.

Michael held the door open for his mother. "You look great. I was afraid you'd be sorry about your decision to move."

"No reason for me to stay now that my family is all grown and gone, but I'm glad you're here. I need to go to the office and take care of some changes that came up unexpectedly." Nina sighed. "I'm afraid this is going to take a while."

"What do you have left to do?" Michael leaned his duffel bag against the wall.

"Not much. I sent a lot of stuff ahead. All I have to do is put these boxes in the trunk."

"Okay, Mom, you go ahead to the office and I'll pack the car when you get back. I'd like to make one last sketch of the house and river. This is the only place we lived that felt like home." Michael's voice filled with sadness. He walked down the hallway and glanced into the rooms. "What happened to all the furniture?"

"I sold it. I haven't any use for it now." Nina looked around the empty living room. A lump swelled up in her throat. "Call me at the office if you need me."

The morning traffic was gone, and Nina took her time driving into town. She thought about the last five years. They had been an ordeal. First she had been hassled by the State Organized Crime Commission and the FBI. Both found nothing. When they finished, the IRS had audited her tax returns, but they did not detect her now defunct account in the New York bank. She knew they would not. The account had been merged with thousands of others into investments representing millions of dollars and held under fictitious names. Securities buried so deep in private trusts that only a select few even knew of their existence—funds that had allowed her to raise her sons and pay for Anthony and Joey's college education.

I'm glad it's over. Nina had paid a high price for the past thirteen years spent working for the Mafia. She felt old before her time. Her dark hair, peppered with gray and cut short, surrounded her once flawless face. Crow's feet crept around her large dark eyes, and a few new pounds clung to her delicate bones.

Nina had signed over the ownership of Elite Advertising to a Mafia-held corporation for the grand price of ten dollars. They immediately terminated all nine of her employees.

Nina parked her car and went into the building. Rocco, the man who made the transfer, sat at her desk.

"C'mon in," he said.

Nina laid her things on a chair and sat across from him.

"I want you to go through these. Make sure the contractual obligations are all up to date." He placed a stack of folders in front of her. "You'll need to sign each one over to the new ownership." He got up from his chair. "Let me know when you finish, I'll have someone carry your personal things to your car."

"I thought our sales agreement covered all the contracts." She glanced at the teetering pile of manila. "This is going to take a lot of time."

Rocco smirked. "Then I suggest you get busy." He strutted to the doorway. "Nick cleaned out your desk. I had him put all your personal stuff here." He motioned to a small table that sat just outside her office. "Nicky," he called out. "Find an empty box for the princess."

By lunch time, Nina had finished signing all the contracts. Most of the old Mafia protection racket contracts had either been closed or were operationg on a month to month basis. Only a small portion of her legitimate businesses remained under contract. She had gone against the mob and worked with handshake agreements.

Redesigning the Mob

When she finished signing all the papers, Nina said. "I'm done." She tossed his pen on the desk, picked up her briefcase, and turned to leave.

The front door opened and the mob lawyer stepped inside. He nodded to the new head honcho and walked toward Nina.

"I heard you were moving back to Pennsylvania and I wanted to say good-bye."

He was not the sentimental type, and she wondered why he was here. It could not be for money. After Vito's death, Sam had again sent a bill for her divorce, and she had paid it in full.

She walked to the small table and placed a photograph of the front of Rosa's Italian Market into the box. The spot where it used to hang above the small table showed a brighter shade of paint than the rest of the room.

"I'm sorry to see you leave, but Rocco, I mean Mr. Rotella, believes there's no need for you to stay any longer."

"I know. He told me." She wrapped a picture of her family in tissue paper before adding it to the box. "Did they call you to escort me out the door?"

"Mr. Rotella thought you might not understand. He claims you think this is a hostile takeover."

"Takeover?" Nina taunted. Her laughter filled the room. "You know better than that. It was my idea to leave." She glanced around into what had been her office and noticed Rocco was paging through the Accounts Receivable file.

"I believe he was referring to your proceeds of the sale." Marin turned his back to Rocco. "It's probably just a misunderstanding."

"The price didn't surprise me," Nina said. "Chance warned me they'd send a guy from Jersey to take it over." She laughed again and spoke loudly. "Mr. Rotella is paranoid because I told him I was amazed that he'd been chosen to run the business—that he didn't know a damn thing about advertising." *And thank God he can't read a legal contract.* She placed a gold pen set, a present from Larry, in the box. "Mr. Rotella doesn't think a woman is entitled to a vocal cord."

Sam Marin grinned.

Nina closed the box, tucking one flap under the other, and took one last look. The small business protection racket had gone by the wayside just as Chance had predicted. Now her legitimate company, a business she had scraped together herself, would become a front to launder money while the mob raped the business until it withered away to nothing.

"Things change," Marin said.

"They certainly do." She agreed.

After paying a large percentage of her advertising profits to the mob, there was not much left. Nina had earned a lot of money for the mob, but had little in the way of material things to show for it. The mob kept track of all the money she made, and she felt certain that Marin knew far more than he let on.

Marin lowered his voice. "I spoke to Dutch a couple days ago. Chance has been moved to intensive care."

"I know, his secretary called me." Nina had mixed emotions about Chance. He had been true to his word. He had closed the deal that released her from the advertising agency and the Mafia. However, like many others that the Crime Commission tried to connect to extortion when the small business protection racket folded, she had been subpoenaed before a grand jury. Nina weathered the storm by taking the fifth and keeping her mouth shut. For this favor, she was now being allowed to find a simple, unconnected job and spend her last years alone, in social disgrace, and broke. She thanked God her father was too senile to learn the truth about her past.

"Well, you take care," Sam said and picked up his briefcase.

Nina offered no response.

"I'll carry that for you," a young man in his middle twenties said as he lifted the box from the table.

He carried the box to her car and put it in the trunk. "Nice car."

She smiled. The new green Chevrolet had been a gift from Chance. It rather reminded her of the old green Pontiac she had started out with. At first Nina had not wanted it, but at fifty-four, with a dissolved New York bank account and no job, the last thing she needed to worry about was reliable transportation.

Nina drove back to the house on the river. Never permitted to buy the place, she had paid a high rent to a conglomerate that, for all intents and purposes, belonged to the Mafia.

Redesigning the Mob

As she pulled into the driveway, Michael came out the front door and down the steps. "I meant to tell you before you left. I like your new car," he said.

He walked with her to the house. Inside he asked, "Are you going to be all right?"

"Sure." She walked from one empty room to another.

"Do you have enough money to live on?"

"Yes, I put a nice nest egg away. I'll be fine," she lied. *The last thing I want is to be a burden on my children.*

Nina walked though the house, out the back door and along the path to the dock. Despite all the problems, the place had been a pleasant home. It held a mixed bag of memories that Nina treasured.

Michael finished packing the car and came to the dock to get his mother. "So what did you think of Joey's fiancée?"

Nina stood to lean over the railing and gazed at the reflection of the large trees. Her chin jutted out. "She's the boss's granddaughter. Joey's dear little Teresa thinks she's sophisticated, but she's really a snob. I thought she'd appreciate a good home-cooked meal, but she acted like I was too cheap to take them out for dinner."

Michael laughed. "Joey wrote and told me she upset you."

"She didn't. I just hated to see her bossing him around."

"Joey's a big boy. He can take care of himself."

"You're right." She sighed. "I need to let go."

"It's a shame you have to leave this place. The scenery is beautiful." Michael looked across the river. "You could sit out here in the late afternoon and paint."

"I'll be busy taking care of Nana, meeting new people and seeing old friends. I don't need a big house anymore just for myself."

"What about when the family comes home?"

"My family's always happy with a homemade Italian dinner. All I need is a stove and a table to entertain them." She patted his hand. "Besides, now that Anthony bought that big marina, he doesn't have much time to visit, and his kids are busy with school." She smiled. "Poor, Joey. Now that he has a girlfriend, he has to work night and day to please her grandfather." She reached up and touched Michael's cheek. "And now you're going away. It's

"That's what sailors do, Mom."

A tear threatened to escape the corner of her eye, but she blinked, and forced it to retreat. "While you're doing what sailors do, I'll be out having a good time."

Michael laughed. But pangs of loneliness filled Nina.

He pulled back his cuff and looked at his watch. "It's time to go. I'll lock up."

Nina lingered by the river, taking in its beauty. She thought about the mobsters who still ran prostitution stables, illegal gambling, hijacking operations, loansharking, pornography, and financed large shipments of narcotics, but the protection racket as it was once known was now a dying faction. She smiled to herself. *At least I was able to change the protection racket enough to save a few businesses and maybe a few lives.*

Michael called from the driveway.

Nina took her time walking. "You drive," she said. "I want to relax."

Michael's train pulled into the station, and people began to board.

"I have to go, Mom." He gave her a hug and picked up his duffel bag.

"I love you." Her voice cracked.

"I love you, too." He kissed her on the cheek, swung his bag onto the platform, and ascended the steps. He waved from the landing and disappeared inside the passenger car.

Nina looked from pane to pane, but each window was filled with a different face. *He must be on the other side of the coach.* When the commuter train left the station, Nina waved just in case he could see her.

She was getting a late start to Pennsylvania, but she planned to stop at a motel for one night anyway. The car radio was tuned to an oldie's station, and Jerry Vale sang *Inamorata*. She turned the volume off. Her hands shook, and for a split second, she saw blood—Vito's blood. Nina pulled to the side of the road. This was not the nightmare she had finally stopped having. She was wide awake. This was real. How could a mere song blast this violent memory through her brain? After Nina stopped shaking, she continued on her journey, but did not turn the radio on again. Eight hours later, Nina pulled into a Days Inn and spent the night.

Late the next evening, Nina parked in front of her mother's home.

"I was waiting for you. I knew you'd be tired." Nina's sister-in-law, Ruth, took her bag. "Your dinner's ready. I'll put it on the table, and while you're eating, I'll unload the car."

"You're a blessing, Ruth." Nina sank onto the couch. "I might be too tired to eat."

"Try to eat a little; it'll help you sleep longer. I'll come back tomorrow and tell you all about Ma. She fell asleep waiting for you."

Nina rubbed the back of her neck.

"She's anxious to see you," Ruth said. "Her right side is useless, but she manages quite well. She can't really talk yet, but lately she's started to make a few sounds." Ruth laughed. "Don't worry—she knows how to get what she wants. Most stroke patients don't do half as well as she's doing."

"You think I should look in on her? Let her know I'm here."

"She won't wake up until morning. If I were you, I'd get a good night's sleep. She'll keep you busy all day."

A cup of tea whet her appetite, and Nina ate a full plate of homemade *gnocchi*. She put fresh butter on the garlic toast and added black olives to the salad. The furnace was on, and the house was cozy. She wished she had never run away from this place.

"That's the last." Ruth sat Nina's box of art supplies down on the floor. "I see you have plans to start drawing again."

"Maybe. I thought I might get a job I can do here at the house."

"You can if you like, but you don't have to." Ruth hesitated. "I think Dom wanted to give you the news, but I'm sure he won't mind if I tell you."

"Tell me what?"

"Dom and Mickey are going to pay you for taking care of your mother. They would rather pay you than a stranger, and they're happy you've agreed to stay with her. They don't think it's fair for you to give up part of your life without at least being compensated."

"I don't expect to be paid for taking care of my own mother." Nina carried her empty plate to the kitchen sink and rinsed it off.

"Don't be foolish." Ruth put her arm around Nina. "You deserve it, and they can afford it." Tears filled Ruth's eyes. "I'm happy you're here, too. Sometimes I need another woman to confide in. I never had a sister. I'm sorry it took us so long to get close. It wasn't because I didn't want to be."

"We're going to get a long just fine," Nina said as she sat down on the sofa.

"Dom put an ad in the paper for a woman to work part time to help. He doesn't want you to be tied down all the time." She grinned. "You'll still have time to go out and find a new husband."

Nina was taken aback by Ruth's candor. "I'm not so sure I want to look for one. I haven't done so great in the past."

"You'll do fine. I have to run now. I'll see you in the morning."

"Thanks for everything."

The front door closed behind Ruth.

Nina looked at the stack of boxes. *Tomorrow's another day.* She tiptoed down the hallway to her bedroom and was pleasantly surprised.

Fragrant potpourri was heaped in a bowl on the dresser. The drapes that hung in the room for years were gone. Ruth had replaced them with sheer white priscillas crisscrossing the large double windows. All of the drawers had been emptied and lined with sweet smelling paper, and a new reading lamp sat by the chair in the corner of the room. *It's a lovely room. The room I grew up in.*

Nina turned down the fresh clean sheets. Her eyes closed the minute she crawled under the warm blanket.

CHAPTER FORTY-ONE

Ruth arrived early the next morning to take Nina to the nursing home to see her father. It occurred to Nina how little she knew about her brother and his family. She was even more amazed when Ruth told her that she did volunteer work at the hospital.

"How do you manage?" Nina asked. "Dominic says you're always having people in for dinner. Every time we talk, he brags about your cooking."

"Your mother taught me to cook, so it's easy to please him." Ruth turned onto the highway leading to the nursing home.

Nina and Ruth entered the main building and signed in at the desk.

"Dad's on the second floor," Ruth said.

They took the elevator and walked into the main room where many of the patients were watching TV. Nina's father was nowhere in sight.

A male attendant in a white uniform came to meet them. "Hello, Ruth."

Ruth smiled at the young man. "This is Nina, Mr. Cocolucci's daughter. She's from Florida."

He held out his hand to Nina.

Nina barely acknowledged the introduction. "Where's my father?"

"He's in his room having lunch."

Ruth led the way. Nina's father sat in his room with his hands tied to the arms of the wheelchair. His face grimaced as he strained to free his arms.

"What's going on here?" Nina rushed toward her father.

"We tie his hands every day while we feed him," the nurse's aide sitting next to Nina's father said. "If you don't, he smacks you and throws his dish across the room."

"My father wouldn't do that unless he had a damn good reason. Maybe the food's not good. Untie his hands immediately."

Ruth stood a short distance away. "Why don't we let him eat first?" she said to Nina. "Afterward you can talk to him and find out what the problem is."

Nina walked toward her father. "I can't stand here and let them do this to him. It's inhumane."

The girl stood and handed the plate to Nina. She took the napkin that hung from the opening in his shirt, wiped his mouth, and untied his hands. Nina sat in the chair beside her father. She sniffed the food and then took a little taste.

"It's meatloaf and mashed potatoes. It's good." Nina smiled at Ruth and filled the spoon. "C'mon, Dad." She moved the utensil close to his mouth. "I'll bet you're surprised to see me?"

In a split second he knocked the spoon away, grabbed the plate, and flung it across the floor. Nina looked at the doorway. The young aide turned and walked away.

Ruth took a handful of paper towels from the dispenser and wiped the food from the floor. "I tried to tell you, but I knew it would be better if you could see for yourself." She set the empty plate on the cart in the hallway.

Mr. Cocolucci stared out the window as if nothing had happened.

Ruth went over to her distraught sister-in-law and put her arm around her shoulder. "Nina, Honey, he doesn't even know you. He doesn't know me or Dominic or anyone."

Nina sat speechless.

"He can't walk and won't do anything anyone tells him." Ruth urged Nina from the chair and held her hand as they left the room. "He's been like this for months. Your mom came every day to take care of him. She did all she could, but he would scream at her and sometimes he hit her. We know he can't help it. It's just the way it is."

On the way home, as Ruth drove, Nina stared at the highway. There was nothing she could do for her father. She could not even tell him she loved him. He would not know what she meant.

Two days later, Anthony flew to Pittsburgh. He waved as soon as he saw Joey. He was the one person Anthony could always count on. Joey had driven across the Pennsylvania Turnpike from Harrisburg to meet his brother at the airport.

"Mom can't wait to see you." He gave Anthony a hug. "She's making homemade pizza."

Anthony swung his black alligator briefcase as he walked. "We're gonna see uncle Dom first. He's expecting us."

"So is Mom," Joey said.

"He's taking us to see Uncle Rudy. There's something I have to take care of right away." Anthony put his arm around Joey's shoulder. "Where's your car?"

Joey turned toward the parking lot. "Over here." He stopped at a 1979 White Mercedes.

"Hey! This is cool." Anthony ran his hand along the slick fender. Let me try it out."

"I can't. The roadster belongs to my girlfriend. She wouldn't like it if she knew I let you drive."

"You better start training her now, or she'll be telling you what to do for the rest of your life."

Joey laughed. "I don't treat her the way you treat Catherine."

"Whad ya mean by that?"

"Michael says you're never home, and that you don't take her anyplace. He says you're just like our dad."

"What was wrong with Dad?" Anthony said defiantly. "When he and Mom were married we had a nice house, and he took us out to dinner at expensive places. We never did without."

Joey looked at the ground.

"C'mon. What does Michael know about women? He's not married. He doesn't even have a girlfriend. And what girl would want a guy who leaves her home while he sails around the world?" Anthony climbed into the passenger seat. "I told Uncle Dom we would meet him at his office."

A few minutes later they pulled into the back parking lot of the medical building. Dominic was waiting in his car.

"We'll take my car," he said.

Joey shook his head. "I'm not leaving Teresa's car here." Joey stood next to the Mercedes. "Besides, I promised Mom I'd be right back, and I don't wanna see Uncle Rudy."

"No one said you had to go. I just thought you might like to." Anthony clapped Joey on the shoulder. Your girl knows how to pick her cars and her men." Anthony got out of the car. "Don't mention Uncle Rudy. It'll upset Mom. Tell her I had some business to take care of, and I'll see her in the morning.

"Sure," Joey said.

"Thanks for picking me up. I'll make it up to you tomorrow." Anthony climbed into Dominic's car.

Joey waved as his uncle and brother drove off.

Dominic glanced at Anthony. "Maybe you shouldn't have told your brother where you were going."

Anthony shrugged. "Joey's okay, he won't say anything. That's what makes him a good lawyer. He knows when to keep his mouth shut."

CHAPTER FORTY-TWO

Anthony and his uncle drove into Pittsburgh. While they waited for a red light, Anthony handed Dom a photograph.

"This is Frankie. He takes orders from a guy in New York. Frankie has a little clout, but not much. He runs a stable of hookers, and he's still fighting the courts over a thirteen year-old indictment for fixing a horse race. He lives with a girl named Eunice. With all those great looking prostitutes around him, I don't understand what he sees in her. She's a plain Jane with an IQ of ten."

"How were you able to find out who killed your father?" The light turned green and Dominic followed the curving road through Schenley Park and over to Forbes Avenue.

"When you're in business, you meet a lot people. After you called and said uncle Rudy had come to see you, I asked around."

At the next red light, Anthony pointed to a picture taken by a telescopic lens. "This here's Egbert van Dermeullen, The mob calls him Dutch. The likeness isn't real clear, but he was Chance's right hand man. Chance is the guy Mom used to work for."

"Yeah, I know," Dom said.

Anthony wondered just how much his uncle did know. "Now, Dutch works for the guy who took over Chance's position at the bank.

He has a suite at a Holiday Inn in Tampa, but he makes regular visits to the east coast and he's a killer with a capital K."

Anthony handed his uncle another snapshot that had been blown-up to a five by seven. "This last guy is the one who pulled the trigger that killed my dad. His name is Estrada Gonzalez. Dad called him The Spic."

Dom's car crept slowly through the heavy traffic. He looked over at Anthony.

"How did you come to this conclusion? What I mean to say, is how do you know that?"

Anthony let out a low chuckle. "Turns out Michael used to be a closet artist. He made sketches of most of the men who came to our dad's funeral. Michael's sketch was my first clue. Then I made it my business to talk to a junkie named Skylar who worked for Uncle Louie around the same time I did." Back then, he had a friend named Stanley who got into trouble and was found in the Everglades with a bullet in his head. The guys I talked to said it was a bad drug deal." Anthony gathered up the pictures. "The FBI tried to blame it on my dad, but he wasn't even in the country when it happened."

"Who told you that?" Dominic passed a slow-moving truck.

"Thesy. He's the guy who owns the Greek restaurant and he was one of my dad's best friends. Dad took me to Thesy's place a few times after he and Mom got divorced. So I stopped in one evening and had a long talk with him." Anthony glanced at his watch. "The Greek said Stanley had to bury his drugs to keep the Cubans and the blacks from stealing from him." Anthony laughed. "He said that's why they called Stanley, The Squirrel. I remember Skylar mooching from Stanley when he was sixteen. After talking to a few more people I thought maybe Skylar might know a little bit more about Gonzalez."

Dom blew his horn when the car in front of him stopped for a green light. "Crazy drivers!"

"You should try driving in Miami," Anthony said.

"So, how did you get this Skylar to tell you about Gonzalez?"

"Uncle Louie said Skylar usually stopped by on Saturdays so I hung around until he came in. I had things pretty well figured out, so I acted like I already knew all about Gonzalez. Skylar's still pumping drugs, so we sat down to reminisce about the days we worked together in the game rooms. While we were talking he mentioned that he overheard my dad tell Uncle Louie that he had an appointment on Memorial Day with Gonzalez at the Tropical Gardens Motel to shore up the hijacking crew."

"Having a meeting and killing someone are two different things," Dominic said and slowed the car.

"When you get a good look at Michael's sketch of Gonzalez and compare it to the newspaper composite of the hooker, you'll see it's no coincidence," Anthony said with total assurance.

Dom finally pulled his car onto Penn Avenue. The street was lined with saloons and produce houses where a lot of construction seemed to be going on. Large trucks were parked along the curb, and Dominic maneuvered his Chrysler in between two of the big rigs. He shut off the ignition and looked at his nephew.

"Let's get this straight before we give Rudy any information," Dom said. "He has to promise he won't do anything that could get you or your mother involved."

"Don't worry, I got it covered." Anthony tucked the pictures inside Michael's sketchbook.

"She'd never forgive me if she knew I was making a deal with Rudy," Dom said. She went through a lot to keep you boys out of the Mafia."

"That's not a problem," Anthony insisted. "I agree with you."

They got out of the car, went through a door, and descended a flight of stairs. A small black jazz band played on a raised platform. A spotlight hovered over the bridge of the lead guitar.

They made their way through the dark room. Dominic touched the back of the chairs to keep his balance as he snaked between the drinking patrons. He let out a sigh of relief when they reached Rudy's table.

Rudy smiled at Anthony and ordered wine. "You're looking good, Tony." He motioned across the table. "This here's Crocker. He's uh friend uh mine." He turned to Crocker, "This here's my nephew, Tony. He owns a big marina in south Florida. He's one smart kid, worked for Louie, went to college."

Crocker looked Anthony up and down.

Dominic gave Anthony a sideways glance, but Anthony smiled. He liked it when his uncle called him Tony. After he had started college most of his friends called him Tony, and once he opened the marina the name Tony had stuck.

"You remember Doc?" Rudy said to Crocker. "You met him at the hospital coffee shop the day we took Johnny D in to get his hand stitched up."

Crocker nodded to Dominic.

The waiter brought a bottle of Chianti, and Dominic reached for his wallet.

"I got it," Rudy said and poured the wine.

"So, what did you bring me?" Rudy asked Anthony.

Anthony laid the photographs on the table.

"Shine the light, Crocker. I want a good look."

Crocker pulled a small penlight from his pocket and centered the light over the pictures.

Rudy cocked his head at the photos. "I know these people. They all worked for the bastard bean counter, Chandler Barozzini." Rudy shook his finger. "Chance wasn't his father's son."

Anthony pushed the notebook of sketches toward Rudy and opened the page to Gonzalez. He laid the police drawing of the hooker beside it. Rudy rocked back in his chair at the resemblance and Dominic craned his neck to get a better look.

"For Chrissakes. I dint think the The Spic had it in 'em." Crocker's husky voice traveled to a few nearby tables.

Anthony turned toward Rudy. "What's with your friend?" Anthony motioned to Crocker. "He finds this business funny?"

"Nah, nah. He doesn't mean anything." Rudy stammered.

Anthony leaned forward. Dominic put his hand on Anthony's shoulder. Time stood as still as a snake sunning on a rock.

The band took a break, and Anthony waited until the applause subsided. "I agreed to meet with you because *you* are family." He glanced at Crocker. The man had the lifeless eyes of a killer.

Rudy motioned to Crocker. "Take a walk."

Anthony waited until Crocker left the table. "You come to Uncle Dominic with questions, and because you're my father's brother, I bring you the answers." Anthony's words were slow and deliberate. "I respect your desire to extract satisfaction for his death. I, too, wish to see my father's killer pay for his crime, but I'm a businessman, and I've got a family to think of."

"I have great admiration for all my brother's sons," Rudy said, staring at Anthony.

"Even though Dom and I want no part of your arrangement, we share your guilt because we bring you this information."

Rudy slowly nodded. "I understand."

"If this plan of yours should fail, or in any way cause me or my mother to be inconvenienced, I will personally consider it your responsibility. The fast boats in Florida will come to a dead stop, and New York will want to know why."

"Nothing will go wrong. You have my word of honor." Rudy held the palms of his hands up to Anthony. "No strife will touch you or your mother's door."

Crocker had returned and was standing in the doorway. Rudy waved for him to come back to the table.

Anthony reached for the notebook. "This belongs to Michael and I promised to keep it for him."

"You see?" Rudy shook his index finger in Crocker's direction. "My brother's son is a man of his word." Rudy handed the book to Anthony. "When you have time, come to Pittsburgh to visit us. Your grandmother DiGregetti would like that."

After toasting the occasion with wine, Dominic and Anthony left downtown Pittsburgh.

On the way home, Dominic asked Anthony, "What's this about 'fast boats'?"

"Nothing." Anthony shrugged.

"Are you running drugs?"

"Hell, no, but Rudy doesn't know that." Anthony touched the cross that Ginger had given him on his birthday many years ago. "Sometimes the union guys or other men with money come to Miami. They wanna party. I have one of the salesmen take them to the islands for a few days. It's strictly legit. I just don't advertise who's in town. It's none of my business who charters the boats as long as they pay."

Dom gave Anthony a skeptical glance. "You don't think that's risky?"

"No, I dock at the port, and the guests have to go through customs before they come back on board. I tell the Coast Guard they can search my boats any day of the week. I'm clean."

The next morning Nina awoke to the smell of fresh perked coffee. She dressed in a pair of warm slacks and a wool sweater that Ruth had loaned her. Joey and Anthony were already sitting at the kitchen table.

"I'll be there in a few minutes," Nina called from the hallway.

"Did Mom ask you where I went?" Anthony asked Joey.

"No." Joey sipped his coffee. "So, what did I miss?"

"Nothing much. We met Uncle Rudy at this bar in town and had a drink. He said he's not mad at Mom and wants to be friends."

"I don't think Mom feels the same way." Joey dunked biscotti into his coffee.

"I know, but Nana Di Gregetti would like us to visit sometime and meet our cousins."

"You gonna do that?"

"I guess so, but not soon. I want to talk to Mom first. I don't think she'll mind, but I won't go without her knowing." Anthony took a cream puff from the bakery box.

Joey studied his brother for a moment. "I thought you hated Uncle Rudy."

"I used to, but we're grown now. Things are different. He's still family."

"You think Mom's happy here?" Joey asked.

"I hope so. She didn't have much of a life in Florida."

After two days with her sons, Nina hated to see them leave. Joey took Anthony to the airport, and then drove home to Harrisburg. On that same day the mailman left a familiar cream-colored envelope shining through the cuts in the scrolled iron mailbox mounted outside Nina's mother's front door.

A letter from Michael.

Nina excitedly slid her nail along the thin paper envelope and settled on the porch swing.

"Dear Mom. It's been a while since I had time to write, but I wanted you to know how much I missed you."

Nina stopped reading for a moment. She thought about Michael, sailing around the world, doing his patriotic duty. She was so proud of him. What more could she ask for in a son? He served his country, brought beauty to the world in his drawings, and loved his family.

Relishing each word, Nina read on.

"During this tour I have seen most of northern Italy. I also took a train to visit France and the beautiful city of Nice. I spent a day at the Museum of Modern and Contemporary Art, and saw Klein's *Mur du Feu*."

Nina envied her son's world as she continued to read on.

"My bride and I will be home for two weeks during the Christmas holiday."

Nina stopped reading. *What bride?* She read the line again. *A wife? I wasn't even aware of a special relationship.*

Although Michael said he was happy, Nina couldn't imagine how he met and married in such a short time. He had been on a Mediterranean cruise, so she assumed his wife was a beautiful Italian girl.

"Mom, you're going to love my wife. We met in Greece, and her name is Jayshree Patel."

Nina tried to comprehend the startling news. *The name isn't Italian, and it doesn't sound Greek.* Her hands trembled as she searched the envelope for a picture, but there was none.

"Oh, dear. What has Michael done?" she whispered.

CHAPTER FORTY-THREE

Two months later, Nina's mother was able to stand on her right leg. This meant Nina could help her into the wheelchair. The visiting nurse came every other day to bathe her, and the therapist came three times a week. Her mother had little use of her left side, but she was able to make herself comfortable.

Things were going well, and Nina was contented. She was baking an apple pie, and her mother was sitting by the kitchen window.

"Joey's coming to see us today," she told her mother, who nodded happily.

But Joey didn't come. Instead, Dominic and Ruth arrived unexpectedly, and Ruth wheeled her mother-in-law back into the bedroom, closing the door behind her.

Dominic said. "Sit down, Nina. I have something to tell you."

"What's happened to Joey?" The color drained from Nina's face.

"Nothing's happened to Joey. Relax. I want to talk to you."

"Spit it out," Nina said, perturbed by his hesitation.

"Joey didn't come here today because he flew down to Florida. He's worried about his brother."

"Oh my God," Nina said. "What's wrong with Anthony?"

"Nothing. A guy named Estrada Gonzalez and his father were fishing in Biscayne Bay this morning and their boat blew up." Dominic took a deep breath. "A tourist caught the whole thing on video, and the Associated Press picked up the story. It's been on all the major news channels."

"So?" Nina leaned forward.

"The Coast Guard put the fire out, but not before the men were burned so severely that they couldn't be saved. They were pronounced dead on arrival at the hospital."

"What does this have to do with Anthony? Were they in one of his rental boats?"

"No, they were in their own boat, but according to someone in the Latin community, Anthony had asked a bunch of questions about the Gonzalezs' a few months ago."

Nina's hand flew to her mouth. She remembered Ginger once saying a man named Gonzalez worked for Vito. "You're telling me that the police assume if someone asks about a person, they're planning to kill them?"

"No, but they took Anthony in for questioning. Naturally, since Anthony's last name is DiGregetti, the local news media jumped all over the story." Dominic shifted his weight. "I talked to Joey. He's with Anthony, and right now there's nothing to worry about. He said he'd keep in touch with me. If I hear anything, I'll let you know."

Nina jumped up from the table. "I'm going to Florida. Anthony will need me."

Dominic tugged on her arm. "He doesn't need you. He specifically asked me to keep you here and said to tell you not to call. His phone might be tapped."

Nina was on the verge of tears. Her brother tried to placate her. "It's just an inconvenience Nina, but Joey's going to stay and work with Anthony's attorney to make sure it stays that way."

"Who did Anthony question?"

"One of them was called Skylar. They didn't give a last name, and I don't know if that's his real name or a nickname."

"That's a kid Anthony worked with at one of Louie's game rooms when he was going to college. Anthony said the boy did a lot of drugs." Nina sighed. "I never wanted him to work for Louie."

"Nina, please don't do or say anything that could make things worse for Anthony. All this notoriety might be bad for his business."

"It's bad for Anthony and good for the mob. I know these guys. They'll try to move in on him by making him feel like they're his only friends. All the while, they'll be setting him up. I need to warn him."

"He's not a kid. He doesn't need to be warned. He's a businessman, and he's lived in South Florida all his life." Dominic paused. "He knows the ropes. There's no way Anthony will get sucked into the mob. Do you think he grew up blind?"

Nina glared at her brother. "No. I think *you* grew up blind. You don't understand the Mafia like I do."

"You might be right, but you're not going to Florida unless Joey and Anthony say you can. I gave them my word."

He tried to console her, but she pushed him away.

"Nina, listen to me. All of this will pass."

"You think it passed for Vito? You think it passed for me?" She shook her head. "It never passes. It follows you to your grave. You've never understood what I did, or why I did it, and you never will."

"Maybe so. But you're out of it now, and you're staying out."

Nina laughed derisively, "What are you going to do, put me under twenty-four hour surveillance?"

"No, but I want you to promise me that you won't call or fly to Florida."

Nina listened, but didn't hear what her brother was saying. Her mind was back in Florida, looking at Guiseppi's bloody face, watching the blazing meat market on TV.

Three days later, Dominic called Nina to say Joey was home. He claimed the South Florida media was trying to portray the Gonzalez's deaths as a revenge killing for his father's murder, but that the police told him they had no suspects. Joey said Anthony was attending a city zoning committee meeting when the boat blew up.

That's ridiculous, Nina thought. It's been over ten years since Vito's death.

CHAPTER FORTY-FOUR

Christmas 1984

The angel on top of the tree brushed against the ceiling. Hundreds of tiny white lights blinked as a cascade of silver icicles shimmered on the branches. Anthony's sons, nine year-old Angelo, and seven year-old Salvatore, ran around the tree chasing each other, and a sprinkling of tinsel fell on the carpet.

Michael reached out to his nephews as they ran by his chair. "That's enough, Angelo." Michael snatched Salvatore into his arms. "Gotcha!"

Salvatore squirmed.

"You're making too much noise. Come on, I'll play cards with you." Michael said, herding the boys away from the adults.

"Let the kids alone." Anthony tied a white napkin around the demitasse pot. "Come have coffee, Michael."

Nina sat at the head of her mother's dining room table. She had helped Anthony's twelve year-old daughter, Krysta, put together a beaded bracelet that she received in a kit for Christmas. Anthony's wife, Catherine, was clearing the rose-patterned dishes from the table.

"Just stack them on the counter," Nina said. "We can wash them later."

Anthony poured his Nana a cup of Italian coffee. When he placed the cup on the tray of her wheelchair, she fondled his gold cross. He kissed her cheek.

Nina smiled.

Anthony returned the pot to the table. "Catherine, bring the pastries."

Catherine set the large box of pastries on the table, gathered the last of the dinner dishes, and started for the kitchen.

"Not in the box." Anthony shoved them toward his wife and they almost fell to the floor. "Put them on a tray, and bring little dishes with clean forks."

Nina pushed her chair from the table. "I'll be right back," she told Krysta.

Anthony put his hand on his mother's arm. "Catherine can handle it."

"Maybe you can give Catherine a hand," Joey said to his fiancée, Teresa.

Teresa didn't say anything, but neither did she get up to help.

"So, when's the big day?" Anthony asked Joey.

"February fourteenth," Teresa answered. "Valentine's Day. Everything will be red and white. My mother's sending out the invitations next week."

"That sounds nice." Nina twisted the napkin in her lap as she looked toward the kitchen. More than any of the others, she worried about Catherine.

Catherine came back with a platter arranged with pastries. Michael's East Indian wife, Jayshree, followed with small plates and forks.

"How's the Navy getting along while you take a vacation?" Anthony asked Michael.

"I suppose they'll manage. I'll be taking some new classes when I get back. Everything's computerized now." Michael sat next to Anthony, across from Teresa. "Communications, fire power, you name it."

"That's a fact," Anthony said. "I had to buy computerized equipment to check out the engines they're installing in boats now."

"How about you, Joey?" Michael asked. "Are attorneys using technology to try cases?"

"Computers have made the work load easier to handle, but forensic science is the tool that's changing how an attorney tries a case. You'll be amazed at what the next ten years will bring. There will be more convictions than you ever dreamed of."

Jayshree sat down beside Michael. He reached over to hold her hand.

Anthony rolled his eyes. "All this talk about the future—what about today? We need to sing some Christmas carols and spend time thinking about the family and how thankful we all are to be together."

The doorbell rang and Mickey and Dominic came in. Ruth followed with their two boys and two girls carrying a stack of presents. Mickey placed the gifts under the tree.

"Merry Christmas," Dom shouted.

After a flurry of hugs and kisses, they gathered in the living room to open gifts.

"So, this is Teresa," Mickey held out his hand. "Welcome to the family."

"I've heard so much about you." She smiled and tilted her head demurely.

Joey gave his uncle Mickey a high five. "I'm glad you guys finally got here. I wanted Teresa to meet everyone. Her parents are expecting us back tonight." Joey picked up his fianceé's coat. "I'm afraid we have to leave."

"You have to go so soon?" Dom said.

"It's a four-hour drive." Joey helped his fiancée put on her coat.

Nina hugged Joey and turned to Teresa. "Come visit us again." She reached to give her a hug.

Teresa turned away, pulled on her gloves and started toward the front door. "We'll see you all at the wedding."

While Michael was giving Joey a hug, Teresa gave him a sly smile.

"Men look so handsome in uniform." She fluttered her fingers. "See you in February, Michael."

"Joey, wait. I'll walk out with you." Anthony followed the couple, closing the door behind him.

Redesigning the Mob

Nina shook her head and began to clear the table. "All that fake sweetness."

"Pay no attention." Mickey said. "She's young. Maybe she's not used to so much hugging and kissing."

Nina's mother reached over, touched Nina, and pointed toward the bedroom.

"You want to go to bed?"

She nodded.

"It's early," Nina said.

Mrs. Cocolucci covered an ear with her good hand.

"You think it's too noisy in here?"

Her mother nodded again.

"I'll help." Ruth pushed the wheelchair into the bedroom, and the great-grandchildren ran to kiss Nana Cocolucci.

Nina and Ruth settled the old woman in her room while the rest of the family was in the process of chatting, washing dishes, and stuffing torn Christmas wrappings into a big garbage bag. Anthony's children were getting tired and went to play Monopoly in Nina's bedroom. Mickey built a fire in the stone fireplace. Michael turned on the TV and searched the stations until he found a musical Christmas special. Anthony came back in the house and poured himself another cup of coffee.

It was dusk when the doorbell rang. Catherine opened the door and invited the guests in. Nina came to an abrupt stop in the middle of the living room. Vito's brother, Rudy, and his wife, Jenny, stood in the entranceway.

"I told you Rudy and his wife might stop by," Dominic whispered to Nina.

"Yes, but Dom—"

"They know you didn't expect them to stop by tonight. You can fix something special the next time they visit." Dominic smiled. "Isn't that right, Rudy?"

Rudy nodded, and he and his wife stepped forward.

Not knowing what else to do, Nina smiled. "Please, take off your coats. Come have pastries. We just made fresh demitasse."

Rudy and his wife sat next to Jayshree at the dining room table, where Anthony reacquainted them with the growing family.

Dominic took over the conversation, and soon everyone appeared to relax. Nina was skeptical about Vito's brother coming to her home, but she decided since it was Christmas, she should at least be polite.

"Tell me, Jayshree, do you miss your home?" Rudy asked Michael's wife.

"I've had no time to miss my home. My studies take many hours, and my husband and I are just getting to know one another."

Michael smiled. "We're considering moving to India. Jayshree would like to practice medicine in her homeland."

"Are you studying to be a nurse?" Rudy inquired.

"No, Jayshree is a doctor." Michael said proudly. "She'll be interning here in the States."

"A smart lady," Rudy said to his wife.

"Yes, she is." Michael agreed.

After coffee, Rudy said that they had to leave, and Anthony again walked outside to say good-bye to his aunt and uncle. It had begun to snow.

"What's going on with Michael? He married the dark girl?" Rudy asked.

Anthony shrugged. "Yes, but Michael travels a lot. I'm sure it won't last. The military's not in favor of such things, and he has hopes of becoming a non-commissioned officer." Anthony turned up his collar against the cold.

Jenny headed to the car and got in.

Rudy lit a cigar. "About this firm Joey works for. You said he'll move up quickly after the wedding?"

"You're asking me to predict the future?" Anthony shivered and zipped his jacket.

"My construction company is building a big complex for Teresa's grandfather." Rudy tugged at Anthony's sleeve. "We're strong in Philly. This union is what we need to make us strong in Harrisburg. You understand."

"I *capise*," Anthony said with a nod. "All I can tell you is that the groundwork has been laid. Joey's young. When the time's right, Joey will be appointed a circuit court judge in Pennsylvania. Now we wait and see."

Anthony walked toward the end of the driveway. "There's a problem with your friend, this Crocker."

Rudy followed a few steps behind. "This thing in Florida, I didn't expect to cause you these headaches. We hadn't planned on the boat being delayed before they put out to sea. When the friggin' boat blew up in the bay—so close to your marina—I knew we had fuckin' troubles."

"Forget it," Anthony said. "The Cuban community made such a stink that the police had to put on a good show. There's nothing to worry about. Everything's under control."

"It was a simple mistake, Anthony. You can trust Crocker."

Anthony held up his palm, cautioning his uncle to say no more. "Because of you, he knows too much about my business. New York says he's not worth the risk, and I agree."

"He's not what you think." Rudy edged closer to Anthony. "I want you to talk to New York."

"There's nothing to talk about. You brought him in, and it's up to you to take him out. Don't call or visit me in Florida. We'll meet when I come to see my mother. In the meantime, I expect to read about Crocker in the newspaper." Anthony turned toward the house.

"Wait a minute," Rudy called after him. "What about Joey? I have big bucks sunk in his future."

Anthony stopped and turned around. He stood with his legs apart. "Don't make the mistake of thinking I'm the same young boy you once took advantage of. I have to go in now. My mother worries." He left his uncle standing in the snow.

"What were you doing outside so long?" Nina asked when Anthony came into the house and shook off the snow that clung to his jacket.

"I was saying good-bye to my aunt and uncle. It'll probably be a long time before we see them again." Anthony stood in front of the fire to take off the chill.

"I certainly hope so," Nina said.

Dominic and Ruth gathered their family together and said their good-byes. Mickey left to stay the night with them, while Catherine and Jayshree disappeared into the kitchen to put the food away.

Nina, Michael and Anthony sat in the living room. Only the lights from the Christmas tree were burning.

"This has been a wonderful Christmas," Nina said, looking at her sons.

"Yes, it has," Anthony agreed. "I hate to leave, but you know how hard it is to get the boys to sleep in a hotel." He rocked on his heels and chuckled. "They wanna play with the ice machine, run up and down the halls, and we have an early plane to catch."

He gave his mother a hug. "Get the kids, Catherine," Anthony ordered.

Nina wished he would treat Catherine with a little more respect and kindness, not that Catherine ever complained, but then neither had Nina.

After Anthony and his family left, Nina straightened up the house and put things back into their proper places.

The house grew quiet and Nina sat down in the living room. When she buttoned her sweater, Michael went out to the porch to get a few more logs for the fire.

Nina thought about all the years she had spent in denial, both with Vito, and working for the Mafia. Chance had told her she was the first women to hold a position in the protection racket. She did not know if it was true or not, but since her initiation, he said several other women now held similar jobs in the mob.

Nina wondered if like her, some unfortunate fate had led them to that point or if they had deliberately chosen the path. She wondered how they felt about it now. Michael came inside, his arms laden with logs, and she brushed aside her troubled thoughts.

"I've been blessed with a wonderful family," Nina said. "Look at you, career Navy, doing a fantastic job, and now bringing home a wife."

"She has a name, Mom. Don't keep calling her 'my wife.' Get to know her. See her for what she is inside, not what you see outside."

"I am, Michael. It's just new to me. Give me a little time."

"Take your time. We'll be here for a few more days." He handed his mother a small afghan. "None of us ever guessed that Joey would forget all about basketball, let alone get married. Now look at him, he's a successful attorney."

Nina placed the afghan over her legs. "Teresa may not be what I expected, but she loves Joey, and that's good enough for me."

Michael returned to his spot on the couch.

Nina smiled proudly. "All of my sons are prosperous." Nina patted Michael's knee. "The best thing is that you've all done well without getting mixed up in the Mafia."

Michael noticed his mother deep in thought. "What are you thinking about?" he asked. Nina shook her head. "Not thinking," she lied. "Just praying."

After Anthony and his family left, she had made up her bedroom for Michael and Jayshree, placed her pillow and quilt beside the couch, and put her pajamas in the bathroom.

Michael had not wanted her to sleep on the couch, but she assured him that she often fell asleep watching television and had stayed there the whole night. She would have gladly slept on the couch forever, if it meant having any of her sons close to her. For when all was said and done, it was her family that mattered most to her. They always did and they always would.

About the Author

Jodi Ceraldi capturers the essence of Mafia life not just from the mob prospective but from reality of the everyday life that American Mafia families endure. During the 1970's, Jodi lived in Hollywood, Florida. She attended Nova University and the University of Florida. She now lives in the Applalacian foot hills, in northern Georgia. This is her first novel.